interloper

interloper

Kim Erin Cowley

Dandelion Digital

First published in Great Britain in 2017 by
Dandelion Digital, London

Copyright © Kim Erin Cowley 2017
1 3 5 7 9 10 8 6 4 2

A CIP catalogue record for this book is available from
the British Library

ISBNs
Paperback: 978-1-908706-30-0
ePub: 978-1-908706-31-7
Kindle: 978-1-908706-32-4

Production by **Dandelion Digital**
www.dandeliondigital.co.uk
katyloffman@dandeliondigital.co.uk

For everyone – but especially those who don't belong.

Contents

february 1982
genies don't fit back in their bottles

· ·

She lived in her head. It was quieter there. Safer. She knew who she was in her head. But she also knew that life would need to be lived beyond, if it were to be lived at all. Lee Habens' very existence would be divided by this moment. There would be life before entering the room and there would be life after. But once the divide had been breached, she would not be the same. And the life in her head would never again, be entirely her own.

She watched almost vacantly as a hand reached out to the polished brass handle. A twist, a step through space and it was done. Her eyes stayed with the glossily painted four-panel door as she closed it softly behind her. She lingered on every detail of the wood grain before taking a breath and turning to the room's only other presence. Dr Jones' familiar thick grey curls were bowed over some papers, doubtless the notes of the previous patient – most likely someone fortunate enough to have presented the doctor with something trivial.

"Be with you in just a mo" the doctor said with a slight lift of the chin, "take a seat".

Lee was already seated. She watched the doctor's hand skate across a file page, recording information at a fierce speed. Then a flutter of white paper into a manila envelope and all of the distractions were done.

Lee was momentarily reassured by the calm, smiling moon face of a woman she'd known for over a decade. Shelagh Jones at least appeared to be in her late forties. She was known to smoke a pack a day (provided she could find the time), was at least two stones overweight and had an open fondness for single malts and fried breakfasts. These qualities made her a poor advocate of healthy living, but an excellent people person. In predominantly working class towns like Sittingbourne in North Kent, this made her the kind of doctor people liked, if not needed.

"Well now young man, what can I do for you?"

Lee winced – more inwardly than out, but enough for an experienced observer of people to catch it. Dr Jones appeared to sidestep, "You know, I was only thinking about you just the other day. How *are* you doing?"

"Not bad. Pretty good, really" Lee replied, feeling her way back after the early bump. She didn't like the sound of her own voice in a quiet room. Too soft – and entirely too low.

"You're sleeping well now?"

"Yes, yes. I'm fine with that now"

"Work okay?"

"Sure" she replied with a flat smile, "'Okay' about covers it."

Dr Jones was smiling patiently, declining her next line of dialogue.

This was really it: No segue, no easing in. Just as she'd promised herself – because promises needed to be absolute. You make them, you keep them. It was that simple. It felt good to rely upon such conviction just moments before taking one's life plan and tearing it all to shreds.

Lee's mouth took a sudden lead, "I believe fervently" the orifice ventured, "that I should be referred for treatment for gender dysphoria".

There. She had at least used the words that had been painstakingly chosen and rehearsed. She took in a shaky breath as she processed her own sense of shock.

Dr Jones was clearly working through the sentence herself. Ordinarily unflappable, she seemed for a moment not to have any kind of reply in her repertoire. Her vacant expression slowly became a nod before at last, a word was returned. The word was, "O-kay".

Lee tried to breathe some life back into the conversation, "I... have a plan – a proper one. I've done my research and I understand that I have to start with my GP".

Hesitance still, but then the beginning of something, "Well, uh you might perhaps…how is it that you think – *feel* – that this is uh, for *you*".

Lee could have responded with hours of evidential anecdotes and some considered, existential philosophy – she really could. But her breath had now shortened behind a burning face. She suddenly longed to be back out in the winter cool of the street, recovering some normality. "I suppose I just know. I've *always* known. And now I've researched things and I've learned about what's possible, about how things can be…put right".

"To make you…a female."

"To make me, *me*."

Silent seconds loitered, refusing to pass. Lee's mouth took up the task again, "Look, I know it'll be hard and I'm ready to do whatever I need to, but I just want to…start things. I need to start the plan".

The doctor returned, "Lee, you don't feel that this is in some way a reaction to…"

"To Dad, you mean?"

"To…grief."

Lee felt her hands grip each other tightly, wringing tension as she struggled for focus. "No. This isn't about that. It's not about loss. This is just about honesty and wanting to live life the way I need to." She recognised a building tremble, but hoped it wasn't too obvious, "It took a lot to come here today, to say what I needed to say. I'm not mistaken and I'm not confused. I'm right about this – and I really do need your help."

Dr Jones' eyes crinkled at the corners with a familiar empathetic smile. "I do want to help you Lee – and I'll do what I can – once I understand what precisely that is. After all, transsexuality isn't exactly an everyday occurrence – at least not for…here."

Lee blanched a little at hearing the 'T-word' spoken out loud. "You've not had someone come to you with this before then?"

"I'll be honest, I don't even know of a colleague who's seen a case – though of course, I am aware the condition itself".

"Through the newspapers, that sort of thing?" Lee smiled knowingly. She could hardly blame a market town doctor for lacking in such experience. The subject remained the exclusive preserve of wild tabloid stories and mocking urban myths – where else after all, would most people even have access to the proper information?

"That and a documentary I once watched" admitted the GP.

"*George to Julia?*" Lee offered reflexively. "I saw that too. I guess I do feel a *bit* like that". As soon as she'd uttered the words Lee worried that she may just have stapled herself to a story that wasn't her own. In the film there had been extensive wrangling over the subject George Roberts', diagnosis and even with improvements in care over the intervening three years, she didn't want to risk a similar struggle. She needed to clarify, "I mean I'm like that in the sense that I have *some* of the same issues, but I'm also…different". She hoped again that she'd said enough.

Dr. Jones shuffled some papers unnecessarily, found a full breath and looked directly at her patient, "How old are you again?"

"I'm twenty-two in a few weeks – which I think is old enough to know my own mind". The extra remark was barbed with purpose and determination.

"Well, it rather looks as though you've given *me* a little homework." She smiled with a practised ease, "It shouldn't be a problem to find out more. Let me look into the next steps and then I think we should speak again. How does that sound?"

It sounded to Lee like an agonising delay. She knew enough through her own reading to offer her GP a step-by-step guide from here, but she also knew that today's short conversation had gone as far as it could. "When? I mean, how soon can we …?"

"Oh, let's say Friday? See reception for an appointment in the afternoon". Dr Jones must have noted a trace of disappointment in Lee's expression because she quickly added, "If reception says we're full, you tell them you can take that day's 'six o' clock special'." She shrugged, explaining with a grin, "I always keep one in reserve".

The rain was sweeping into town along the A2 corridor from the west. It peppered Lee's face as she headed back along the London Road. She wasn't inclined to shelter from it. Her mind rode the top deck of a body that knew its own way home. Reflections battled in her mind to become a single, settled view. She felt pride at having expressed herself; of having survived the ordeal of honesty – and yet regret at her poor performance under the first official scrutiny. Hers had been a less than elegant progression. At least, she reasoned, the effect had been as desired. She was now the subject of a doctor's consideration. There would be official correspondence of some kind somewhere.

'Genies don't fit back in their bottles', Dad used to say. Lee's own genie was out there now, living life beyond her lips – and it had immediately enslaved her.

It was precisely one year and one day since Dad had passed. She hadn't intended at first for the interval to be quite so significant. Twelve months of stinging, burning and aching had curdled to become a taste she could now manage through habit. She told herself sometimes that Dad might actually understand what she was doing now. He would have learned just as she had over the past year, that there were no more choices. Only a single course remained.

She pictured him as she walked, a vision coming to her as instantly as a breath. She realised of course, that even as his mortal presence had faded, she had created another version of the man. He had become an ideal, enlightened by his own passing and now wise beyond the ways of his former life. His essence had evolved from everyday purpose, practicality and wry scepticism to become reason and compassion. He had in a way, led her to this point. Two decades in his presence had imbued her with the drive to seek her own wholeness.

It had been unsurprising that Dad's departure had left the wider world with more or less an even balance; the wake in the waters behind him having settled easily back to stillness. His existence at all, had only ever been known to a few and yet, he had been all that he possibly could be – and to her, he had been a giant.

They'd become a great team, Dad and Lee. There was never any confusion about who was in charge, but still they'd supported each other and had through the years, found a rhythm that worked for them both. Dad she believed, had always been the more interested parent. Lee even owed her name to him. In full, she laboured under the moniker of Lee Marvin Habens. The name of Dad's favourite actor had been worn as a strangling garland during childhood. She would resist even writing it on a form unless she absolutely had to. Discovering Lee Remick had at least been a later consolation.

A man bringing up a child alone in the late sixties and seventies was less than common. But the duty had been Robert Habens' proud priority and Lee had never felt less than cherished. In his last months before the cancer had done its worst, Dad's perspective on life had softened, impending mortality having delivered true reflection. Those last lessons in wisdom featured one phrase more than others: "Never have regrets. Never leave things undone. Get out there. Live your dreams while they still *can* be lived". Sometimes he'd make such remarks with a smile; other times with weary, tear-filled eyes. She'd asked him on a couple of occasions if he had been hinting at unfulfilled ambitions of his own, but he would never elaborate. Lee would wonder if it was Mum he had been thinking of at those times but, as ever, it was impossible to discuss someone who had no real presence. Lee's curiosity about her mother had spiked a number of times through the years, but speaking of her always seemed to physically pain Dad, and that was infinitely worse than living without answers to pointless questions.

She could still recall her mother – after a fashion. Sophia Habens had been tall, graceful and elegant. She had long dark tresses that danced around her as she moved. Her looks were very un-English and in a way, the exotic image added to the remoteness of her memory. She was never really of this place. Dad had once, in a moment of candour or perhaps a need to share, told Lee that Sophia had headed far away when she'd left their home. There was no chance therefore of her returning, or of them bumping into her one day in Woolworths. Lee had, ever since, imagined Sophia living out some solitary penitence on a windswept, barren island. On a generous day, Lee hoped that wherever she was, she had found peace, if not quite happiness. The pain caused to her Dad would not be forgiven.

Sometimes in her imaginings Lee could almost picture a face from a misty childhood memory, but she couldn't reliably sketch in anything more than perfect arched brows over soft dark brown eyes. She gave the memory a smile, even though she had no reason to believe that there had ever truly been happiness. The echo of her mother's vocal tone was always soothing. That can't have been true either, but it was an easier way to file the feeling.

Lee had been occasionally asked about it over the years, but really what was there to be said? If your mother leaves when you're six years old, displaying symptoms that in more enlightened times might be seen as those of a deep depression, you don't have much to speak *of*. There was simply neither sufficient memory nor reason to fuel the wondering. The lives that were left behind were the only ones that really mattered.

The grieving process over Dad had at least in one way, been enlightening. It had been the first time she had felt worse about something other than her own body. Something in the absolute darkness of death had sharpened her own plan for life. Nobody would follow her, she realised. Nobody would miss her the way she missed him. Legacy would not trouble her. She would matter only for as long as she breathed. If there had been only one year and a day to spare for grief and honour, there could she reasoned, be no time at all for fear. Missing Dad had now become a portable kind of pain. It went everywhere with her, carried like a stone in the stomach of a voracious dog. She could walk, talk and function with the ache nestled stubbornly in place. She'd come a long way from the early days of screaming into pillows and crying into and out of sleep. She'd run short of tears after those first weeks and had moved on to long stares into space, searching for the bliss of nothingness. The shock of being alone had threatened her very sanity and yet she could not manage the company of others.

The climb back to a semblance of life had come slowly and with the ever-present threat of falling back away from the world. But the fall never came. The strength she earned, stayed. She strung together small tasks to create routines. Days formed under her, allowing her to edge onwards and reach for another. She began to venture out, beyond her home, following a schedule that demanded she be in certain places at certain times. After about five months, she had been able to actually switch on the TV – and that had been a good thing. TV was a soothing anaesthetic. Anything factual was best. Keeping life cold sustained her through the longest winter she'd ever know.

Home was still the same modest two-bedroom council bungalow in Priest Close that she'd always known but where once there were parents who completed a family, now only the brooding child remained. Rounding the corner, she could see No. 7. She'd been careful to maintain the standards Dad valued. The small front lawn was kept neat, if rather featureless. The driveway was kept clear of leaves and detritus. Upon it stood Dad's most precious possession, a three-year-old Honda Prelude in deep red. He'd been so proud the day he'd brought it home. It had been just over a year old at the time and was by some margin, the newest car he'd ever owned.

The entrance to the little semi was reached from the driveway which ran along the side of the building. Closing the door behind her, Lee stopped and leaned back against the porch wall. She met the silence head on. 'And then there was one' she whispered from somewhere behind her eyes.

She took in the familiar welcoming scent of home. One of the changes she had brought to the house was a new kind of air. A combination of frequently opened windows (especially in the living room where she smoked) and bowls of homemade potpourri into which she dripped vanilla scented oils. Lee had grown up in a home dominated by smells of her father – the foods he liked and most of all, the skinny cheroot cigars he had smoked. Lee had for the sake of her own future, needed to make the house her own. She'd take the monumental decision to move into the larger bedroom. Dad's room. It meant completely redecorating of course, using skills that she'd largely picked up from Dad himself. She replaced his striped wallpaper with plain white walls and introduced touches of red as a sort of running theme throughout, co-ordinating her bedspread with the re-covering of upholstery on the stool seat at her dressing table. She had at first thought to be careful to avoid an overtly feminine look, but after a time she realised that it really didn't matter. No one would ever come. No one would judge.

She had been able to afford a new sofa for the living room, though Dad's dark brown leather armchair remained. Letting go of things for which she could find no use had been manageable, but not the chair – at least not yet. She rarely sat in it herself, preferring to stretch out on the sofa, from where she could look across at the old wingback, the way she'd always done – whether Dad had been in it or not. Lee had worried occasionally that perhaps she'd been a little over zealous in her pursuit of change. Dad's presence in the house had been materially reduced to that of a car, a chair, an old cowboy hat and a tin box of official papers, pictures and memories.

Priest Close was a quiet and much coveted enclave – all the more so, now that so many of the tenants were exercising their 'right to buy' options. Margaret Thatcher might not have won too many votes locally when she'd come to power, but plenty seemed to want to take advantage of at least that one policy. The next door neighbours had moved fast once it became pretty clear that Britain's first woman prime minister was likely a novelty to last no longer than a single term. Lee had thought momentarily about trying to buy No 7 herself, but meeting even the specially reduced terms for a mortgage would have meant devoting almost her entire income to the cause and in any case, the investment would have tied her to the house for more years than she could now spare.

Lee moved through the rooms inviting life back into the place. In the kitchen, she flipped on the electric kettle; in the living room, the standard lamp and finally in her bedroom, the radio. OMD's *Maid of Orleans* followed her back out through the open door to the hallway. She paused in brief debate before committing herself to the idea of a bath. She had of course taken her routine shower that morning, but felt the need for deep thought under warm water. She opened up the bath taps and returned to her bedroom to undress. There was a particular reason for the strict order. She knew that the water could run at the set pressure for about seven minutes before achieving the correct depth. This allowed only a brief opportunity for her to stand in front of a mirror and hate herself.

Self-loathing, she understood, did also include a degree of morbid fascination – rather like peeling back a bandage to inspect a healing wound. And so, with her boots, jeans and sweater removed and the latter neatly folded, Lee turned to face her three quarter-length mirror. Lee Habens stood just about shy enough of six feet to get away with a denial of breaching that particular measure. Mercies were indeed tiny.

She started at the top, because she always had done – and of course, because she could then save the worst until last. Her hair was becoming unmanageable now. Where once a reasonably neat wedge-style had been maintained, now there were shaggy, uneven layers that edged past the acceptable professional barriers of ears and collar. She re-affirmed her commitment to 'growing through' this awkward stage – there simply was no other way – and it would get worse before it got better.

Her eyes had always been in her own opinion, her least offensive feature – if only because they were the most gender-neutral element of her appearance. They were an ice-blue in colour. Perhaps she sometimes wondered, a shade too pale? She liked to believe that she had inherited her mother's arched brows. But such faith in the absence of true recall could be fleeting. And frankly, acceptable eyes faced little rivalry for approval. She would never love that nose. It was too long, too thin and entirely too prominent, it would be best ignored altogether – if only that were possible. High cheekbones yes, but an awfully long way from her jawline. The borderline gaunt features were only the first hint of her skinny build. Her shoulders had always been hopeless. If covered, they seemed to protrude past seams and padding. If left exposed, they made her look simply undernourished. Her chest was tragically featureless – unless one counted marooned nipples the size of shirt buttons. Her ribs could be defined individually from the front – and almost painfully at her back. She knew that she'd lost more weight since Dad and she maintained an intention to deal with the issue at some point. It wasn't really a concern for now. Taking up less space was anyway she felt, the very least a favour her body could do.

Down past the concave stomach was the place she most hated to look and so naturally, she would be sure to dwell there just long enough to illicit the deepest possible disgust. The pubic hair was thick and very dark. There seemed to be ever more of it, too. It looked like splashed dirt against her paleness. And through it of course, protruded the very worst of her. The part that simply wasn't her at all. The thing never looked familiar. She rationalised that any other feature – a knee, a toe, a birthmark, would be recognisable every time it was seen. You'd know your own feet before you saw them. But this – this could not be anticipated. No mental picture of it could be more offensive than the reality. This afternoon, in a combination of dim light through thick velvet curtains and the weak radiating glow of a bedside lamp, the thing seemed particularly small and sneering and ridiculous. It was hooded and slightly curled over. It looked especially vulnerable, in fact. For perhaps the thousandth time in her life, she idly wondered at how easy it would be to just remove it herself. The kitchen was just a few steps away – and it offered blades surely sharp enough for the task. But this day above all others, there was actually a good reason not to explore the idea further. Case psychiatrists she knew, took a pretty dim view of what they regarded as self-mutilation. She had also read in her research, that the surgeons would need the parts for something (she didn't properly understand what). The thing's days were surely numbered though. Today she had sown the seeds of the ultimate betrayal. Maybe now the enmity between person and penis had venom on *both* sides. She wondered idly, if it really did hate her back. Perhaps it might plot to rid itself of her first.

The water level in the bath would be dangerously high soon. She headed out into the hallway. The late winter evening settled through the so-far unheated house with a chill. She ignored it. Her naked body had never deserved comfort. She'd be under the water soon and that would help in all ways. She picked up the hallway telephone, feeding out the long extension so that it would reach all the way through to the bath itself. Closing the door, she switched on a small radio she kept perched on the window sill. A tinnier version of the bedroom's richer Radio 1 cut through the rising steam. Kid Jensen would hand over to Annie Nightingale soon.

Dani had arrived within an hour of Lee's call. Now draped across Dad's armchair, she blew a rogue dark curl away from her right eye and looked up from a smoked glass coffee mug. Delicate pixie-like features wrinkled under pale blue eyes, "So that was it? That was her reaction? She'll do some research and get back to you?" Danielle Lewis was Lee's closest and perhaps only real friend. For Lee, the relationship was a blend of three parts blessing and a quarter curse. Dani was clever, insightful and was responsible for quite the most – perhaps now the *only* – positive influence in Lee's life. She was also the living embodiment of everything Lee daily failed to be. She bore a fearless confidence and determination to breathe the best from each day. Maybe it just looked that way from where Lee stood. It was pretty hard to see the top of the pedestal from a ditch.

However steep the gradient between their respective lots, once the two friends were alone, the bond between them was as equal as it was strong. They would talk for hours, only to re-run an almost identical conversation days later. Both had a need to express and unburden and yet would patiently weigh the other's insight.

Sometimes, when Dani would be in the throes of yet another short-lived affair, their meetings would wane in number. But there was always the phone. Dad used to say that they should have simply bought shares in the GPO, but in truth he never begrudged the pair their telephonic chatterings. He'd always seemed to recognise that Dani was a good influence on Lee – even if it wasn't quite the kind of influence he might have hoped for. There had never been even the merest hint of a romance between them. Rather, Lee imagined their relationship to be sororal. She couldn't prove it of course, neither being nor having a sister herself, but she imagined it might feel this way.

They'd first been classmates in primary school – Dani as the new arrival, placed at the neighbouring desk to Lee's on a cold winter morning in 1970. Dani had been the girl nobody knew; Lee the kid most found hard to know. They had connected almost immediately and could thereafter barely imagine not being each other's first place to turn. They had briefly moved on to the same secondary school but then been inevitably divided by the gender line. Dani had scraped in to the girls' grammer while Lee had been offered a place at the boys' – or 'the place for the smart guys', as Dad used to call it, inexplicably invoking the voice and facial tic of Humphrey Bogart.

The separation had left Lee lost again for a while. At first, the demands of higher academic performance had offered enough of a distraction, driving her to invest in her classroom performance. By the third of four years however, she had disappeared into the lower half of the mediocre mainstream, polling c and b minus grades from disinterested masters. She left with five 'O' levels and an almost complete absence of direction.

Dani by contrast, had blossomed at the higher study level and had accrued a circle of excitable and passionate girlfriends. Lee regularly declined all but the occasional invitation to gatherings, but would instead listen later to breathless recitations of who was seeing whom and why so-and-so didn't really get on with you-know-who. Tales about and from, a faraway land.

Work had once more reshuffled their lives and dealt them out into a wider world: Dani after a two-year college course that equipped her with the skills to serve as a PA, with Lee bounding through a succession of bland clerical roles before her most recent and longest-lasting engagement. The more options they had as people, the more Lee and Dani seemed to want to return to each other. Maybe it would always be so.

"Yup" Lee recalled from her meeting with Doctor Jones, "Research and back again. When you think about it, there really wasn't much more she *could* say. She's never dealt with this before and well, y'know – neither have I. It'll be important for at least one of us to properly understand what to do next."

Dani drew up a knee, folding her other leg beneath her. She looked even tinier than usual sitting that way. She cradled her coffee mug in both hands, clearly savouring the warmth. "Yeah, but you *do* know what happens next? First the shrink and then the hospital, right?"

They'd both come to adopt the term 'shrink' for a psychiatrist. Neither of them had ever actually met one and the mocking term made the prospect seem rather less intimidating.

"Yes, but I still don't know what *kind* of shrink or where I'll have to go" explained Lee, taking a sip from her own mug. "I looked them up in the yellow pages and there are only a few of them around here. I don't even know if I'll be able to go to any of those, anyway. This is the kind of thing I need the doctor to book for me".

"So what time is your appointment on Friday?"

"I have the 'six-o-clock special'"

"You what?"

"Never mind"

Annie Nightingale was playing Soft Cell's *Say Hello, Wave Goodbye* and Dani grinned mischievously, "Your Dad would have loved this one, wouldn't he."

A sigh exited Lee's chest through a wistful smile, "Oh yeah". Dad had a special place in mind for any of the 'Dodgy types' he'd hear wailing from a bedroom radio or mincing through another edition of Top Of The Pops – a place somewhere shady and far away. The musical rivalry at number 7, Priest Close had always been good natured – if unyielding. Dad was a Country and Western die-hard and was never going to be persuaded that a bunch of 'floppy fairies in make-up' could make a worthwhile contribution to culture. He had clearly enjoyed teasing Lee for how seriously she took her love of music. Lee had quietly embraced the dark revolution of punk in the later 70's – if only because people in most market towns, didn't welcome it at all. But it was the arrival of 'New Wave' music that had really turned her on. By the time Bowie gave her *Ashes To Ashes*, she had a soundtrack to sing in her head and a look to dream of. Alas, the latter remained something she could only paint onto her private face – the real one for practical purposes, needing to make it to and from the High Street as unmolested as possible.

Dani flipped open a fresh pack of John Player Blue and offered them to Lee who returned a mock scowl as she reached for her own faithful Marlboro's. They both took lights from a formerly tall dining candle. Drawing deeply, Dani studied her friend, "You are glad though, aren't you? Glad you did it?"

Lee smiled and pursed a steady soft beam of white-blue smoke, "I still can't believe I *did*". She could feel her heart race again just from the thrill of sensing that a momentum – however tiny – existed somewhere out in the world without her. The loss of a little control had a heady effect in one so tightly bound.

Lee and Dani would talk long into that night, but no more about the meeting with Doctor Jones. For Lee, company itself was enough.

It was after half past eight by the time Lee left home on a grimly-lit Tuesday morning. Dani had headed home an hour and a half before, needing a quick change before catching the train to her PA's job in Canterbury. Ahead for Lee lay another day's toil on the third floor of the headquarters of IGF Insurance Group Française was the UK baby of a French parent and occupied a relatively new office building toward the west of town. It took twenty-five minutes for Lee to walk the distance between home and work – almost two years of the same routine had taught her that. She would try to arrive within seconds of nine o' clock, slicing time as thinly as possible. It wasn't that she hated her job – she couldn't actually find enough passion within, to feel that strongly. Instead her day was coloured by a grinding ambivalence. Twenty-one years old and already so jaundiced in her career ambitions that she would wish the week away. Of course, she knew she was fortunate to actually have a job at all. Unemployment had crested three million back in January and there wasn't much sign of a likely change. Having a woman prime minister was proving harder and scarier than anything the 'old boys club' had previously delivered.

College Road had been freshly dampened that morning. Even though it wasn't too cold, she was glad of the comfort of her winter overcoat. As well as offering another layer of shapeless anonymity, the pockets of her heavy wool and cashmere shell gave her hands something to do. Walking right mattered to Lee. She wanted to move with an acceptable grace. Her height and narrow-shouldered build always left her at risk of loping. Her stride was quite long, but importantly she felt, remained very straight. She may not walk as a woman, but she was damned if she'd carry a traditional male gait, either.

She moved seriously with her head dipped as always, eyes locked onto the rhythm of a remote pair of feet passing beneath her. White socks flashed atop black loafers as the flapping fins of her trouser legs kept pace. Today's blue suit, white shirt and narrow yellow tie felt less appropriate than ever. At least she hadn't needed to suffer the soreness and indignity of shaving this morning – once every other day remained enough for her light growth.

Lee had no particular love of fashion. What would have been the point? A lifetime of being pointed toward the wrong stores, full of the wrong clothes and aspirations had numbed her to any interest. Caring about her appearance had been to invite only disappointment. As long as nobody else had anything to say about the way she looked, she could almost avoid thinking about it at all. She did worry sometimes about the rather fantastical prospect of being set adrift in a sea of female standards, suddenly having to learn so much of what had been kept from her. She knew what she liked about the way women looked, but the prospect of mapping it onto her own awfulness was only very rarely palatable. Lee's method of coping had become a clinical kind of assimilation. Her daily objective was to present a clean and crisp figure – current unruly hair, excepted. She found that a certain kind of neatness in appearance would at least separate her from most of her male 'peers'. Of course, an immaculate presentation suggested to some, a dubiously-inclined sexuality – but that Lee reflected, was just an unintended bonus.

She clocked in to IGF's smoked glass reception area seventy seconds before she was due and still had time to pick up a coffee from the third floor machine on the way to her desk. The water in the machine was especially hot and she needed three plastic cups to insulate her fingers. The long narrow open-plan office was already pretty full, though not yet actually productive. There were still too many of the forty or so visible personnel on their feet for this to be a fully functioning environment. Her own desk formed an island with a facing twin, one of twelve such bases in a sea of blue carpet tiles. Buggs was already there of course, his semi-permanent smile having widened on sight of his 'compadre'.

Barry Suggs had such a prominent overbite, that Lee could never quite see past it to register other things, such as the colour of his eyes. He was a year older than her and had served two more at IGF. He had hair the colour and constituency of a pan cleaner. She had wondered how often (or indeed how at all) it was ever washed. Buggs was like Lee, rake thin – though a little shorter. Once when they had been trying to move their desks into a better alignment, the entire office had been reduced to giggles at the sight of two of the most lightweight physical talents applying themselves in vain to such a simple task. In the end, two of the motor insurance guys had stepped in – as much to express their own virility to the watchers in the nearby typing pool. The vanquished stood by awkwardly, each privately burning at the humiliation.

Buggs wore one of an ever-rotating set of brown three-piece suits – today with a broad striped coffee and cream tie. He generally offered the appearance of an underinvested wedding photographer. She had faced Buggs across the plain of grey vinyl desktops for more than nine months and had learned to appreciate the positives – such as her partner's familiarity with IGF procedures and politics. He was very, very smart and had extraordinary powers of concentration. As one of two senior fire clerks, Buggs was trusted by middle management – not least to keep an eye on underlings like Lee. What Buggs really liked to do most however, was to make Lee laugh. At this he succeeded both consistently and at great length using a combination of acute observations and stock staff impressions. For Lee, the relationship offered a haven of sorts. Buggs certainly expected nothing of her in traditional masculine terms and that allowed her to relax a little into their shared space.

'Ooh, he's up for one early' Buggs nodded, indicating that their section manager, Mr Bernard Lack had lifted his shiny bald pate above the line of his cubicle's panelled wall. Buggs had created an image of their boss as a large and lazy walrus, most of the time wallowing out of sight but with a need at intervals to surface, take in air and observe the surroundings. Lee was grateful not to be seated facing Lack's pen. There existed between them an incurable dislike. They both knew that she turned up each day short of a passion for fire insurance – although this mattered differently to each of them. Unfortunately, Lee needed the income and security – this past year more than ever. As so often seemed the way, she found herself ill equipped for the life she lived.

"How did it go yesterday?" Buggs asked.

"Mmm?" Lee replied, not looking up from her opened satchel. She'd forgotten that she had actually told Buggs there had been a doctor's appointment at all. Flirting with the truth was an odd kind of thrill. Just having people know *where* she had been going had given yesterday a sense of risk, while having them not know her appointment's purpose, allowed a semblance of control. "Oh, it was nothing" she added.

"Good, good" Buggs accepted the news with casual indifference, no doubt just relieved to know that his 'partner-in-grind' wouldn't be missing any coming days through illness. He leaned across his desk, resting a hand on his trusty Rubik's Cube and whispered, "Something shitty is definitely going on".

Lee mirrored Buggs move and whispered back, "What do you mean?"

"Naismith was down twice yesterday afternoon and now Lack's got his jacket on and he's heading for the stairs – *again*".

The fourth floor was occupied by upper management, most notably UK Managing Director, George Naismith. Naismith liked to tour the building at least once a week – usually on a Friday afternoon. They were used to seeing him waft along the aisles between desks. Once in a while, he might actually ask an employee what they were doing – and sometimes would even listen to the reply. What he most definitely did not do was appear on the third floor twice at the beginning of a week.

"What do you think?"

Buggs breathed out through his nose, while his protruding teeth made a rare disappearance. He shook his head "I don't like it" he replied, adding "It's definitely something shitty".

Much of the rest of Lee's morning was spent working through last week's 'returns'; long sheets of green and white lined computer printouts which summarised the terms of insurance policies sold by brokers around the country. Last week these same policies had arrived on Lee's desk as documents filled out by actual human beings. It had been her job to turn these forms into pure data by ticking various boxes on computer input forms. Incorrectly filled out forms would return rejected, the following week. The number of 'returns' was a fair indication of one's level of concentration and care. Buggs had a couple of pages to work through while Lee was handed a ream of paper that could serve as a footstool. It was just too depressing.

At precisely 11:15 am, the tea trolley arrived. The two-tier stainless steel vehicle bore twin urns – one containing tea, the other smaller vessel, coffee (for in the Home Counties of England, coffee would never truly know equality). The practice was to remain at one's desk while Marj, IGF's long-serving urn guardian, toured with the trolley. Once upon a time, staff were actually allowed to get up and queue. It had been an opportunity to chat and lark around a bit. But fifteen minute breaks would of course invariably turn into half hour lulls and so Lack put a stop to it. It was as Lee received her plastic cup of tea along with the exotic promise of a bourbon from the trolley, that she finally heard herself say it out loud to no-one in particular, "I have to leave this place".

The rest of the morning simply ached along. The work Buggs had once claimed could be performed by "a gibbon of below average intelligence" was now beyond Lee's threshold of commitment. She began to devote her thoughts instead to plotting possible ways out of the building. Her best strategy would be some kind of faked illness. Yesterday's appointment at the doctors would stand her in excellent stead for that. Hell, she'd be almost crazy *not* to use it, she told herself. She'd decide over lunch.

Declining the usual invitation to gather at *The Crown*, Lee took a walk into town and sat alone in a coffee bar refining her strategy. She could be suffering from some kind of head pain, maybe? Nobody ever seemed to know what that might mean. It could be plausible enough, surely. Maybe saying as little as possible would be best. Too much detail leaves a liar open to inquisition. What a contrast – yesterday she'd agonised over the most important medical issue she would ever know and now she was working up a complete lie. She simply couldn't bear the thought of another afternoon in that building. All she really wanted to do was reflect upon Friday's appointment with Dr Jones and a future beyond.

It would take about eight minutes to walk back to the office. Lee left herself five and then dragged her heels somewhat as she made her way along the London Road. When she eventually arrived back at the third floor, it was not a place she recognised. It should have been humming with early afternoon bustle. Everyone bar her, should be in place at their desks. Lack should be corralled in his little partition-walled box. Right now she should be offering her 'head pain' excuse for which she'd be sent home for the afternoon. But there was nobody in sight. Not a single desk was occupied. She was momentarily stupefied. Robotically, she headed for her own desk. On it was a sheet of A4 upon which a single word had been scrawled in Buggs' unmistakable capitals, 'MEZZ!'

The mezzanine floor of IGF's Sittingbourne headquarters had once been intended to serve as a cafeteria. The cost was deemed unsupportable and so it had become the venue for presentations and departmental meetings. Now, it seemed to be hosting the entire company. Lee squeezed through the double doors and into a wall of standing humanity.

At the opposite end of the room on a small raised platform, George Naismith was in mid-address. Lee strained to hear.

"… in difficult times. Although as a corporation we are well positioned to weather the downturn, Lyon have decided that there must be some essential and immediate cost savings."

There was a movement to Lee's right and suddenly Buggs was at her elbow.

"Nice of you to join us" he whispered.

"What the hell is this?"

"This is the something shitty I detected earlier".

They turned their attentions back to Naismith, "…The Birmingham and Reading offices will both face cutbacks and we here cannot expect to be immune. Therefore, with regret, I am charged with delivering a reduction in staff of around twenty per-cent." There was an audible murmur from the masses and a few gasps. The MD took a moment before continuing, "In consulta-tion with departmental managers, a strategy has been developed that will allow us to make the kind of changes that will best allow us to maintain our levels of performance. So, although this *will* mean bidding farewell to some members of staff – and I'm very, very sad about that – IGF will go on." The murmur level now featured grunts and sniffs. "We'll be leaner and we'll find things a little more challenging, but we must support each other in these difficult times."

From somewhere over to the left, there was a fully-fledged "Ohhh fuck this!"

Naismith straightened but did not look in the direction of the outburst, "Your managers have all been briefed and they will relay plans to you this afternoon. That's all for now. Your hard work and commitment to the cause is genuinely valued and I will be looking to all of you to give of your best in the coming weeks and months". He glared over in the direction of the earlier barb and dared another. Met with a sufficiently respectful silence he stepped down from the platform.

The moment Naismith's head disappeared below crowd level of course, the rebel contributor piped in with a rasping but clearly heard, 'Bastard!'

Minutes later, back on the third, a cocktail of stunned silence, betrayal and not just a little fear had been mixed and served widely. Lee looked across at an ashen Buggs. "You'll be all right. They're not going to let you go".

"I don't know..." The glasses were off and he was massaging the bridge of his nose. He looked especially vulnerable without his spectacles.

"I think I'm pretty screwed though, aren't I?"

Buggs replaced his glasses and pushed them back into place. His eyes were still reddened. He just shook his head very slowly and said nothing.

During the following half hour, furtive calls home to relatives were made by most IGF employees. Even Buggs had to call his Mum. Lee had no such call to make of course. She passed the time by watching her workmates more closely than she perhaps ever had. There wasn't usually the opportunity to openly gaze around the room. But here now, it was frankly hard for her to do much else. She certainly wasn't going to be investing any more of her time in policy corrections this afternoon. The expressions of concern she saw around her were perfectly understandable, but she couldn't find the mood to wear such a face herself. She was strangely calm – perhaps even a little excited. After yesterday, she almost welcomed the chance to perpetuate a sense of event.

Some of the older women seemed near tears, while at the same time Lee noticed one of the typing pool girls actually yawn. Just as anticipation was about to turn to frustration, Lack appeared from the main staircase. He clutched a fistful of white envelopes. One by one, he visited section heads, handing them the envelopes addressed to each of their respective groups. Last of all, were the Fire Department. Lack seemed to be drawing a thrill from the attention now – and not just a little smug satisfaction at the power he held. He already knew of course what IGF staffers were finding out one by one with the rhythmic ripping of cheap paper. Lee scrutinised the expressions of various recipients. The losers were pretty easy to recognise. There was a kind of phlegmatic acceptance in their faces. A kind of 'I-knew-it' look. Others just seemed to read their notes over and over again, as if they didn't dare display any sense of relief. When Buggs' and Lee's letters arrived on their desks, they looked blankly down at them and then at each other.

Finally, Lee smiled at Buggs, "Go on" she said.

Buggs took a deep breath and in one movement picked up and ripped through his envelope. He read intensely but quickly, lens-enlarged eyes flicking back and forth across the text. And then he read it again.

"Told you" Lee said quietly without dropping her smile for an instant. "I never doubted you'd be okay. I'm afraid you really do belong here."

"Thanks mate." Buggs replied, his shoulders relaxing. "Come on then, your turn".

Lee stared at the crisp white envelope. It was addressed to 'Mr L Habens'. She already felt contempt for it. She exhaled rather than drew breath. It wasn't only Buggs' news she was sure of. She took a single blade from a pair of scissors and sliced along the fold of the envelope's flap. Withdrawing the single thin page of A4, she could already gauge the brevity of its text.

Dear Mr Habens,

Insurance Group Française is, like many other companies, experiencing difficult market conditions. Increased costs and the pressures of maintaining our high standards have required us to take some difficult decisions. As you will by now have been informed, cuts in staff levels must be made in order that IGF progress. With regret, your position has been removed from the structure of your department, with effect from today. Appropriate financial obligations will be met by the company.

IGF thanks you for your service and wishes you well in your future endeavours.

The letter was signed simply, 'Insurance Group Française'. No single person could be held responsible.

"Well" she said cheerfully, looking up at Buggs, "I'm all done here, I think".

"I'm so sorry, mate. Is there anything I can do? I could try talking to Lack."

"I think we both know how pointless that would be."

Buggs offered a small, rueful grin.

Lee sent him back a full-faced smile, "Oh come on. I'll find something else out there." She nodded toward the smoked windows as she uttered the words, already feeling unemployment's blank chill beyond.

"I know you will" Buggs conceded, "but how am *I* going to cope? I'm not cool enough to talk to anyone else around here."

It only took about 30 minutes to leave the building for the final time. The handshake with Buggs was about as emotional as it got. He promised to keep in touch – she knew they'd never see each other again. There was nobody else to really speak with on the way down to personnel. Lee didn't keep very much of her own property at the office. Everything went into a single IGF-branded carrier bag. She had thought of saying something as she'd passed Lack's office. In the event, they just caught each other's eye in mutual momentary contempt. It was all their relationship merited. She had to sign a couple of forms and confirm her address and bank details. They said they'd send on her P45 form and final salary payment – pittance though that would be. At least it would be tax free.

It felt oddly early as she exited the unmanned reception area. Outside, the combination of breeze and traffic noise heralded her first steps as one of the massed ranks of jobless. 1982 she mused, wasn't going to be much kinder to her than the last year. She immediately cursed herself for such a thought. Being bounced by IGF didn't for a moment compare to the loss she had suffered a year ago. She settled for just feeling cross at the month of March – at least she wouldn't have to suffer another of those for a while.

Lee wasn't really sure of where to go next. She began walking toward home. Passing a telephone box, she thought of calling Dani. Perhaps they could meet at the station. She thought better of it, preferring to deal with the day inwardly. She had accepted enough consolation in recent times. There was nothing to be said out loud for now, and nobody to whom she would want to say it.

march 1982
twenty-one seasons

··

Argentina had invaded that morning. Not that you'd notice. Apparently there was a rock somewhere far away that should have been theirs to begin with, only it had lived under a different flag by mistake. Lee had some sympathy with South Georgia. Perhaps it really was an Argentinian Island trapped in a British body.

Lee had barely left the plot of No.7 all week. When she wasn't in the house she'd spent her time tidying the garden. Lee was always sorry that the last season in which Dad saw it, was winter.

She'd at least managed to get to the library. She had wanted to find out more about anti-androgen drugs and what they might do to her should they be prescribed. She could only find the odd mention in some medical text books and the terminology was too clinical for her to really grasp. Why couldn't there be something that explained the process in simple language? Just something like, 'Oestrogens are female hormones and Androgens are male hormones. By blocking one and introducing large doses of the other, changes will take place. She was beginning to get the impression that there was little incentive for medicine or any other strand of life to further the cause of the sex change.

Still, now at least, it was finally Friday. She'd watched the hour approach through a morning's chores and duties. Now she was out and on the way to meet her moment. She strode along College Road once more. Her pace was even with minutes to spare. Her mind had space to reflect upon the contrast with her first consultation. This time she was comparatively positive of spirit. There was an agenda now – a gender agenda! Today, she wouldn't be the only one bringing news. Dr Jones would have been working on this too – and so now there would be progress and energy from both sides.

After checking in with the receptionist, Lee selected a magazine from the main desk – something she'd been too nervous to do the first time around. Taking a women's magazine might Lee knew, tempt disapproval. She settled on a six-month old copy of *Reader's Digest*. Entering the waiting room, she took another moment to decide on a seat, eventually choosing a brown leather-backed, upright number in the corner. She reached it just as the doctor's buzzer sounded. "Mr Habens, the doctor is ready for you now". There it was: 'Mister'. Lee scowled visibly at the term, but nevertheless responded to the call. What she wondered, would Pavlov have made of that?

Dr. Jones was poised in thought, mid–note on a previous matter when Lee entered the consulting room. She motioned to Lee to sit and then completed the action of applying thought to paper. Lee suddenly began to tremble a little.

The familiarity of the question did nothing to calm her nerves, "So, how have you been?"

"Oh fine – absolutely". And there in a heartbeat, Lee had opted to withhold and therefore control the flow of, information. Her redundancy would in any other week have merited an early conversational headline. Instead she had chosen to bury the matter deep under her doctor's desk.

"Well all right then." Dr Jones opened a file and began to sort through a couple of pages of notes. "I've had a good look into things and I must say, it's been quite...illuminating".

"Okay" Lee replied, just wanting to know everything instantly.

"If this really is something you intend to proceed with, there is a long and very difficult road in front of you."

"I know". Of course it was going to be difficult – it already bloody well *was*!

"The first step really is for me to refer you to a specialist psychiatrist. They will properly assess you and co-ordinate any further treatment."

'*Any* treatment'? Lee thought to herself, '*Any*'? Of course there would be treatment. Why wouldn't there be?

Dr Jones calm and methodical approach had been seen by Lee before. It didn't seem to matter whether the issue was trivial or terminal, she always seemed to work from a steady foundation. "So now, before I refer you, I will need to understand a little more about your history in this regard so that I can properly brief the psychiatrist. For example, how long have you felt this way?"

Oh shit! This was going to be a complication Lee didn't need. She just wanted to know to where she was being referred and a time and date she should be there. She didn't expect to have to answer questions today. "God, I don't know. I mean I've always felt this way, I just couldn't…say anything to anyone about it".

"And what changed that?"

It was a stark question when Lee thought about it. For all the reasoning and the inching toward commitment over the past year, just a single bare fact had made the difference in the end. "Well, losing Dad" she said, nodding. She felt her eyes brim as panic took the first flight of steps inside of her. This was going a little wrong – and much too soon.

"Let me put something to you that might be a little difficult to hear. We touched on this before: Is it possible in any way, that you are responding very directly to that loss? Could you be perhaps, instinctively trying to protect yourself by diverting some of the pain?"

"No". Lee replied quietly but firmly. "No. This won't protect me. This is the *opposite* of protection." She gathered herself, "Look all I've ever wanted do was to get to the bottom of who I am". I tried to be what I felt I had to be. I've always tried really, really hard to do that – all my life." Her right eye was too full to contain the single large tear now weaving a slalom path down her cheek. She quickly wiped it away. This was terrible. She needed to get a grip. She reached for a tissue from the desk in front of her. She hated that she'd become accustomed to crying. All those simple tearless years, then along comes 1981 and suddenly she's a cracked vessel. The doctor would surely think her a complete flake if she lost it now. A deep breath, "I couldn't bear to disappoint Dad with all this. I just couldn't do it. He'd lost Mum, he'd given so much for me. I couldn't...let him down – can you see that?"

The doctor said nothing. Her expression suggested compassion, but Lee saw nothing useful in that. She needed something more positive, more encouraging.

"Now it's just me. There's nobody left to upset now and all I want is to make a future I can actually live in." She was quietly pleased with the sentence. It helped halt another tear.

Dr Jones smiled and nodded. Then she asked another question for which Lee was unprepared, "Do you think of your mother often?"

At least there was no risk of tears here. "Not really, no."

"It's just interesting that you have grown up without a female presence in your life".

"That's not exactly true though, is it?."

"Oh?"

"It is in *me*" Lee pressed a hand to her to her chest, a little irritated having to state the bleeding obvious. "That's the point. It's *always* been in me".

Dr Jones had paused again. Had Lee said something wrong? A long intake of breath preceded the return of the familiar smile to the doctor's face. "Well, that takes me about as far as my own psychiatric training can manage – and that wasn't very far at all really, was it?"

Lee shrugged with a pensive grin. She watched as the GP read more notes and ticked off a couple of points on a form.

"Now, what else can I ask you? Oh yes, do you cross-dress?"

Lee wasn't sure she'd heard correctly. How on earth should she answer that? Was there a wrong kind of answer to the question? She'd never thought of herself as 'cross-dressing'. She did have some female clothes in her wardrobe of course. Dani had helped her to buy a few things. Lee would try them on in private once or twice, feel disappointed and just push them to the back of the rail. She supposed the answer was a 'yes' – of a sort. She nodded in confirmation, blushing with discomfort.

"Uh-huh" Dr Jones made a further notation. Lee hadn't wanted to know what it said.

"Bloody hell!" Dani was laughing involuntarily through her hand. "Sorry – sorry" she reassured, "I'm just – I mean, where do you go after that?"

The two friends sat facing each other along the dark brown velour banquette seating just inside the main door of *The Cow*, opposite the curved mahogany bar.

Lee collected her thoughts, "Well, she talked a bit about how I could either go the NHS route or...not. The NHS is just really, really slow. There are only a couple of cases approved each year in all of Kent – and even then, it all just takes ages." She took a sip of her Pernod & black, "And the rules – Jesus! I mean I already knew they were strict, but unless you do things exactly the way the health service shrink dictates, they withdraw the treatment and leave you where you are. She didn't say as much, but Dr Jones was suggesting that they just don't want to approve any cases because the treatment is so expensive. They can probably do about half a dozen hip replacements for the same money, I suppose". Lee had learned to cost things in units of hip replacements after a discussion with a nurse during one of Dad's chemo sessions.

"Are these the rules that make you dress a certain way, that sort of thing?" Dani asked.

"Yeah. Dress like a 1950's housewife for all meetings with the consultant and try not to get the shit kicked out of you on the walk home". Lee shuddered at the mere thought of herself looking like something from a *Stanley Baxter Christmas Show* sketch. "It's more the lack of control that I worry about, having to do everything in the precise *order* and pace that someone else wants."

"Is that really so terrible?"

"Well yes, because the NHS seem to plan it so that you can't actually make it work in the real world. I mean how do you hold down a job if you have to turn up to work looking like – I don't know..." Lee searched for a suitable vision and settled on, "Danny

La Rue? Who's going to employ you then? How can you do any-thing if you have to live life like that?"

"All right, so then what's the alternative?" asked Dani offering a JP Blue which Lee accepted without really thinking. Dani lit them both while Lee lined up the explanation for Plan B. She drew extra hard on the cigarette (as was always necessary with anything non-Marlboro) and swallowed deeply.

"Like I always thought, I have to go private" Lee said firmly, underlining her statement with an arrow-straight stream of smoke.

"And what will that mean exactly?"

Lee recalled Dr Jones' expression earlier as she'd advised, 'You need to start saving. Save everything you can, because this is going to cost...a lot'. At the time, Lee had responded by earnestly relay-ing understanding. In truth she'd only a rudimentary idea of the finances involved. None of the articles she'd read had been terribly detailed about that that part – and it didn't really seem to matter just now. Whatever it was, it could be no more unreal than the process itself. "It means I'm going to have to find an awful lot of money".

"How much money"

"Between fifteen and twenty thousand – maybe more, for everything, over time"

"Jesus, you could nearly buy a house for that" Dani replied, exhaling smoke thoughtfully. "It probably doesn't help that you just lost your job then".

"Probably not. But what I do have is time. My plan takes five years."

"Five years?"

Lee nodded in confirmation as she took another sip, "Put another way, I think I can make it in twenty-one seasons".

"There are four seasons in a year. Why twenty-one?"

"This one and then twenty more from when something actu-ally starts happening".

Dani took a sip of her dry white and thought for a moment, "You really have got this worked out, haven't you".

"Oh it's pretty worked out, all right. All I have to do is find a new career, raise more money than I've ever seen and while I'm doing that, change sex without anyone noticing".

Lee had tried especially hard recently to not overthink the pub toilet experience. Her habit was to hold on for as long as possible before giving in to the need to go at all, but she'd had a rather large coffee earlier and three hours had passed since she'd last been. Leaving *The Cow*'s saloon area, she took the short passage out to the toilet doors. She prepared for the ordeal by trying to place her mind into a neutral state. All she really needed to do after all, was function at a basic level. No need to attach any more importance to the experience than that. Soon she'd be back out with Dani and the problem would be gone – at least until the next time. The doors to the toilets bore Victorian silhouettes to illustrate the gender divide: a gentleman with walking cane and top hat on one and the figure of a lady in crinoline skirts on the other – symbols made all the more incongruous by the pub's clientele being largely aged under 25. Opting for the symbol which most matched her body felt like a betrayal. She hated it – every single time. The world beyond the door to 'the gents' was even less appealing. It was very cold. White tiled from floor to ceiling with one wall underlined by a long trough urinal. The single stall today featured a taped 'Out Of Order' note. Lee's shoulders dropped another half inch. She reluctantly took the one step to the urinal just as the door behind her opened. A large man in a denim jacket stepped up next to her. She'd noticed him earlier at the bar with two other guys. They all looked as though they'd been in the pub for some time. The large man didn't look across but simply muttered "All right?" – except that, as was traditional in a mid-Kent town, the two words were pronounced as a single syllable. Lee knew the etiquette, she had to say it back without turning her head and she did so in as low a tone as she could muster. At the same time, she fumbled to find the loathsome thing through which she needed to pee. She wrestled it into the open and held it between two fingers – if only to stop it from spraying randomly like a garden hose left on a lawn. She stood joined in solemn, forced fraternity – her and a man with whom she could not possibly have less in common. Denim Jacket finished first, zipped up and walked straight back out into the bar. Like most guys, he didn't bother washing his hands. He'd probably be digging into the free peanuts on the bar though, Lee mused. She finally finished herself and had to shake the thing before tucking it away. For Lee, washing hands following a toilet experience was absolutely compulsory – for all sorts of reasons. It had been this way all her life, just noticeably worse over the last ten years – and certainly so since puberty.

Dani was being chatted to by one of Denim Jacket's friends as Lee arrived back. As Lee waited for an opportunity to slide back into her place on the seat, Denim Jacket strode across, took his friend's arm and led him back to the bar, pausing just to wink at Lee and mouth a, "Sorry mate". Lee smiled ruefully back reasoning that any other expression might have been interpreted as provocative. Dani herself didn't even mention the brief encounter with the stranger, it just wasn't that unusual.

Lee's JP Blue had pretty much burned out in the ashtray so she reached for a Marlboro. Japan's *Ghosts* started up on the jukebox as she put match to cigarette. She smiled a little to herself knowing that nobody else in the pub would have selected it. Worth 15p of anyone's money, she reflected. She savoured the toasted tobacco and took the smoke down deeply.

"So" Dani broke in, "What happens next".

"The doctor has found a specialist psychiatrist in London. She's going to try to get me an appointment with him".

"Try?"

"Apparently, he doesn't see everyone who's referred to him, he only takes certain cases".

"So, when will you know if you can see him?"

Lee exhaled and raised both eyebrows as she composed her answer, "That's the thing. Dr Jones has never dealt with him before so she isn't sure. I just have to wait".

"It's funny" Dani was smiling "After all this time, something's really happening and yet you don't seem all that...y'know – excited".

Lee flashed back to a night four years before, when she'd first trusted Dani with her secret. She'd left a trail of clues; remarks about the nature of their boy/girl relationship and hypothesising over how life would have been had Lee been born female. ('Would we still have become friends?'). Eventually, she had to put the pieces together more deliberately in a conversation that began about Renée Richards, the transsexual tennis player in America. Dani hadn't struggled with it for a moment. Never even seemed surprised. She'd said since, that it just made a sort of obvious sense. Perhaps in a way, she had always known.

"I *am* excited" Lee countered, "but I'm also nervous. It's all so...delicate just now. I just feel like it can all just close up on me again. All this time, there's been an answer somewhere off in the distance – a door I've always thought I would eventually pass through, but what happens now if I'm told that I *can't* go through? What happens if they just turn me down?"

Dani placed a hand on Lee's arm, "Nobody's going to turn you down. Once you're talking to experts, they'll take care of you" Dani punctuated her support with another sip of wine, "That's why they're experts. Anyway, all you have to do is sit there and tell them the truth. Just trust in that".

Lee took a long look at her friend. "Don't you ever get tired of talking about my crappy life?"

Dani laughed from the throat, "It hasn't always been this crappy".

Lee snorted smoke and nodded.

Dani suddenly let her tone drop, "And I didn't mean to upset you by mentioning your job. I mean you did hate it there, didn't you?"

Lee shrugged, "Oh no it's not a problem. Well it is, but it isn't – if you know what I mean. IGF was never going to be able to get me through this anyway. They sacked some guy last month for wearing an earring. They'd have probably had me lynched". She shook her head, "Truth is, I'm still not sure what kind of job I *can* get. All I do know is that it's not likely to be anything around here."

"So-ooo..?"

"So it has to be London".

april 1982
wrong half of the room

··

The call had come ten days after the second meeting with Dr Jones. At the time, she'd been trying to unblock the kitchen sink and was cursing once more, her lack of knowledge of all things practical. Dad had been so good at fixing things that she really hadn't had to try. She had still been wearing a Marigold on her left hand when she'd picked up the phone in the hallway. In retrospect, she knew that she'd answered a little tetchily, "Yes? Hello?"

A softly spoken male voice had replied, "Is that Lee Habens?"

"Ah...yes – it is." This had sounded official – and officialdom always made Lee nervous.

"My name is Doctor Adrian Garner and I work at *The London Centre*. Your GP has written to me about you". He'd left a long silence which Lee was too shocked to fill. "Hello?" the caller had enquired again, uncertainly.

"Yes." Lee had stumbled, "I – I was fixing the sink..." she'd begun to explain, waving her rubber gloved hand in the direction of the kitchen. "...except that I don't really know what I'm doing. With the sink, that is" she'd clarified, suddenly mindful that she was speaking for the first time with an actual psychiatrist. "I know what I'm doing in every other...sense" she'd cringed, allowing her words to tail off and die.

"I see. Well I'm simply calling to let you know that I *would* be prepared to see you". There was an accent there, but Lee couldn't place it.

"Thank you, yes. I would like to come...along...also" she'd winced again at her own awkwardness.

"All right then. I will now transfer you to my secretary and you can arrange an appointment. Some literature will be sent out to you explaining how to get here, fees, that sort of thing. Just stay on the line, won't you?"

"Oh, yes" Lee had replied, immediately aware that the doctor had gone and she was holding nothing but silence.

A female voice took over, "Hello there. You need to arrange an appointment with Dr Garner?"

"Yes, I do". Lee had been relieved to be speaking to a 'normal' person. As yet, she'd had just the one short conversation with a psychiatrist – and had emerged a complete imbecile. She could only hope for better in person.

"Which days do you have free?"

"Um, all of them – at the moment."

A few days later, a large manila envelope had fallen through the letter box of No. 7. In it, Lee had found a letter confirming the appointment, a map showing where in Fulham *The London Centre* could be found – and a list of fees. The expense was going to start straight away. The first appointment would cost £ 90 with follow-up sessions costing £ 50. Lee's savings amounted to about £ 2,400. She still had some of her last salary payment from IGF. She'd been making just over £ 180 each month there and now she was trying to cope on supplementary and housing benefit. The practical changes to Lee's life were going to have to start sooner rather than later.

Bromley South was ten minutes behind. The train would pull in to Victoria in no time. She'd made this journey on the Chatham Main Line so many times. Most people from Sittingbourne had. The town was only an hour and a quarter away from the London terminus. Time spent in 'The Smoke', was inevitable.

Suburban south-east London was only a single glass pane away. Lee let the rows of gardens and allotments blur as she reflected upon the hours ahead. There were only really two possible outcomes from her all-important first session with the shrink, it was telling that her mind had developed only one of these as a potential future.

The greater plan would rely upon some more practical milestones. She must quickly secure a job in London. It wouldn't be easy, but certainly more likely than back in Sittingbourne. After all she reasoned, a city of millions made new opportunities every day. She could commute at first, but she knew leaving Priest Close would be inevitable. For perhaps the thousandth time, she reminded herself that determined people make their own miracles. She'd known of plenty of former schoolmates who'd managed to cross the Medway to new lives in the capital.

Dr Garner's support would also be hugely important. He was now the single most important man in her world – and she hadn't even met him yet. Without him Lee felt, her life would cease momentum entirely and be crushed under the weight of its own disappointment. She needed this man to believe in her; to gift her the chance to progress – even if only as far as the next appointment. Dad always said you didn't have to plan all your tomorrows, today.

A short tunnel interrupted Lee's view of the world beyond the carriage pane. She caught her own reflection. She knew that darkened glass was generally kind to the viewer but she preferred – just for today – to believe that she actually did look as her image suggested.

It had been quite a challenge getting ready this morning. How should one look for a first meeting at which one wants to be considered for sex-change treatment? She hadn't for a moment considered presenting herself as female. Right now, she was if anything, more uncomfortable with the idea of being seen in women's clothes than in men's. Being beaten up for lacking in masculinity was at least some kind of badge of honour for Lee. Suffering public derision in failing to pass as a woman was on the other hand, too awful a prospect to bear.

For now, she felt she should simply try as much as possible to mute her body's overt maleness while finding some way to exist between the genders.

She had taken extra time with her hair this morning, moussing enough volume into it to at least demonstrate some effort.

She'd used quite a lot of hairspray too – just to keep her fringe in some sort of order. Her hair wasn't yet likely to described by anyone as 'long' – but there was definitely too much of it to be considered masculine in style. She'd temporarily taken inspiration from The Cure's Robert Smith. She had applied a thin level of base foundation which mostly evened out her complexion, while a modest amount of mascara at least gave her eyes the chance to lead. Sittingbourne she knew, most definitely disapproved of this kind of look and she'd felt obliged to use the car to get to the station that morning. Once in London however, she knew she'd be safe. In the city, she could be pretty much anyone she wanted to be. Even heading westbound on a train toward the capital was safer than heading east back into Kent. It was as though the draw of the metropolis already broadened passengers' minds. Not that she was about to make eye contact with anyone in the carriage. She wanted to believe that nobody had noticed her for the entire journey, but she knew they probably had – especially the two giggling teenagers who sat across the aisle between Rainham and Chatham.

She had bought a copy of the *Telegraph* at Sittingbourne station. It was pretty much all that was left and she'd thought it might keep her occupied. It was full of 'Falklands Crisis' analyses and she couldn't really muster any enthusiasm for what still seemed like too remote an event. Countries like Britain didn't do war anymore. There were more civilised ways to settle things and she had faith in diplomacy. Meetings and talks could sort out most things, she felt sure.

She stared down at her knees which were characteristically pressed together. She'd always hated the way men sat and never quite understood it. Sure, it was uncomfortable sometimes to sit neatly with a lapful of genitalia, but it could be done. Her most important ally for the day was a long black trench coat. She had wanted one since she first saw Ultravox's video for *Vienna*. She felt safe inside her cover-all sheath of blackness. She had no plans to take it off either, save for the time she would spend at her destination. Beneath, she had opted for a pair of grey, straight stretch cords – not the best look for someone with such skinny legs, but she really wasn't spoiled for options. She wore a pair of black cowboys. She longed for some pixie boots like Dani's, but there was no chance of finding those in a size 9. The most difficult choice had been over which top to select. In the end, she'd settled on a deep blue woollen sweater with a cowl neck. Dani had helped her buy it on a recent shopping trip to Canterbury. She felt just about confident enough in her appearance. It offered she felt, an appropriate blend of sincerity and aspiration. It was who she felt herself to be – on a really good day. She hoped for the courage to dress this way more openly and more often – musing that pretty soon, she might just have to.

She had her faithful satchel with her of course. It was just a soft leather briefcase on a long shoulder strap – but for now would be the closest she would dare venture to a handbag. Inside, was an A to Z street guide to London, her wallet, keys, some tissues, a mirror, hairbrush and hairspray, a small washbag containing her make-up essentials, a pack of Marlboro and some matches. Rather more importantly, it also contained two pages of A4 upon which she'd neatly written the main points she wanted to communicate to Dr Garner. If she could get these across, she was confident of making a compelling enough case for further treatment.

Arriving at Victoria was a relief – if only to unlock her knees and walk again. She enjoyed strolling across the station concourse. She was headed for Fulham Broadway; a straightforward half dozen stops on the District Line. She knew exactly where to find the staircase that would lead her down to the right platform. She enjoyed the feeling of knowing where she was going. It made her feel a little like a Londoner – as though she belonged. How long she wondered, until this would be an everyday experience? Arriving on the westbound bank of the line, she took out and lit a cigarette. She'd chosen a No Smoking carriage from Sittingbourne, not wanting to smell of tobacco. She didn't much like walking with a lit cigarette, but she took the opportunity while she could.

By the time she exited the station in Fulham, her early cool had been mostly burned back. The closer she moved to the beacon of *The London Centre* the less hopeful she became – like a moth who knew too much.

The walk from the station took about nine minutes. She hadn't quite finished her second cigarette by the time she'd counted down the door numbers and arrived at the three-storey corner building. Her journey's end was red-brick Victorian and rather unassuming. Large full hedges flanked a black lacquered door. An engraved brass plaque to one side marked the spot.

She walked past the entrance three times. Lee Habens was about to be judged. The man inside that building, knew trans-sexuals. Actual, *real* transsexuals, people who had made it to the other side of the crossing. He would know so much more than her about what it would take. If there were imperfections in her case, wrinkles in the fabric of her story, he would find them. He could stop her life dead, in less than an hour – and still charge her for the privilege.

She would have taken a deep breath if she had thought to. Instead, a single stride seemed to have taken her to the entrance and then before she even had the time to procrastinate about knocking or ringing, the door was opened. The sheen from the silky paintwork flashed as it picked up light from within. A figure swept past. She wasn't sure if it had been male or female. In here, perhaps nobody could be sure.

The figure slipped from view. Lee stepped into a hallway and walked a few paces along polished boards. There was another door open to her left. A main reception area was softly lit, a warm golden hue emanating from at least four lamps placed around the room. The receptionist sat with her back to twin aspect windows which looked back out toward the street. Lee had been seen.

"Hello". The receptionist was small and delicate. She had a short Diana cut with a heavy fringe over wide eyes. Her smile at least seemed welcoming and honest. Lee was never sure about smiles. She had mistaken mockery for affection before. Yet she *should* feel safe here of all places. She decided to trust the room. "Hi" she replied. "L. Habens? I'm seeing Dr Garner?"

The receptionist consulted a large appointment book into which names had been pencilled, rather like a hairdresser's diary. She took a moment and then another. Lee filled the seconds by worrying about the ridiculous. Maybe her name had been accidentally rubbed out by a busy sleeve. Having made it this far, she now couldn't bear the prospect of heading home without having made any progress at all. She desperately didn't want to be asked to come back another day.

"Oh yes. Do take a seat – he's running a little late". The receptionist was still smiling when she added, "Do help yourself to coffee". At the other end of a deceivingly long room Lee saw some wall mounted cupboard units, a cooker and a fridge. It was as though someone had guillotined a full-sized kitchen and placed one half into the reception area. A pair of sofas faced each other across a low coffee table while two non-matching armchairs took up much of the remaining space. Waiting room and kitchen made for an oddly comfortable environment.

Lee declined the coffee, too nervous to be around crockery. She asked instead to "borrow the loo". The bathroom even more intriguingly, was exactly that – complete with panelled bath and matching suite in peach. Lee consulted a large mirror warily. To her relief, she appeared to have weathered the journey reasonably well. She decided to brush her hair through and spray her fringe again. It was also an opportunity to finally remove her coat. Before returning to the waiting area, she took one last look at her finished reflection. This needed to be the best she could look – and all things considered, it was. She let out a sigh and pulled at the hem of her sweater so that her crotch area was covered.

Returning to the waiting room, she selected the armchair facing the reception desk. She wanted to know the very moment she should go in. She was keen not to be called twice, just in case the 'Mr Habens' moniker was used.

One other patient had set up camp on the right hand sofa. Lee chanced a look. She really couldn't be sure. Skin was very clear looking, no sign of a beard. Shortish dark hair, no makeup, wearing jeans and a dark sweater – clearly the uniform of choice today – and with a pair of trainers. The shoes were pretty small looking. She couldn't get a good look at the hands, though. Was this a boy heading toward female reassignment or a girl going the other way? It occurred to her that 'The Centre' might also deal with issues other than transsexuality. Perhaps she shouldn't be wondering about the identities of others at all.

'Michael?' the receptionist called softly. 'You can go in now'. The mystery patient rose and headed back out to the hallway, his footsteps continuing along the corridor. Of course that was a guy, Lee assured herself. Slowly she began to settle. As her heartbeat evened, she was able to recognise classical music being piped into the room. She didn't really listen to classical music. It was pleasant enough though and it did bring a certain sobriety to the occasion. She thought about picking up one of the magazines on the table. She could see the tell-tale red banner of a copy of *The Face*. She would already have it at home of course, but a scan would help fill the time and perhaps make her feel a little easier. She would have surely reached for it, had the receptionist not just lanced the calm, "Lee?" she called softly with another calm smile "Dr Garner will see you now, just along the corridor, second door to your right".

Lee gathered herself and stood. Her legs didn't feel at all reliable. She tried to acknowledge the receptionist, but when she attempted speech, there was no sound. She had to mime the word 'Thanks'. The short corridor allowed her the time only to inhale and swallow. She hoped that this would be sufficient to prepare her for what was ahead. She reached the second door – plain and wooden – and knocked.

The room into which she stepped was light, airy and not remotely clinical. She guessed she'd arrived at a rear corner of the building. Large double-aspect, sash cord windows wore frosted panes, assuring privacy while allowing daylight to spill in. This felt like more of a study than any kind of medical facility – a room indeed, designed to put the visitor at their ease. The man sitting facing the windows and therefore with his back to her, was suited in grey and had hair to match. He broke from reading the contents of a file and in one fluid easy movement, turned and rose to greet her. He was slim and athletic, perhaps an inch shorter than Lee. She put his age at late forties. He was not unattractive. She worried a little that this may affect her concentration.

Dr Garner extended a hand, "You're Lee?"

She hesitated, wondering if this was some kind of psychiatrist's trick. Wasn't shaking hands a male thing? She hadn't previously given the act that much thought. She certainly didn't want to be rude however and so reciprocated, careful not to hold the doctor's hand too firmly. She could only hope not to have sinned so early.

"Do please take a seat" her host added, motioning to a dark green leather, button-back chair placed strategically to the right of his desk. She sat down, intensely conscious of her body language. She wanted to cross her legs, but her jeans resisted. Placing her satchel and coat on the floor to her side, she settled for her familiar, knees-together repose. She looked down at her long nails. She had given them a coat of clear lacquer that morning and they shone healthily. At least she could feel proud of the very fingertips by which she held on to her nerve.

Dr Garner led the conversational way, "Well it's very nice to meet you. I do hope that this visit will be helpful." His tone was very, very calm. His leather office chair was on a swivel and so he was able to address both his desk and clients in a sequence of noiseless, easy swings. He collected a yellow file and sat face-on to Lee, scanning the top page. "So I have been contacted by your GP, a Dr Shelagh Jones. And her letter refers to your belief that you should be considered for gender reassignment. What is it that makes you feel that this course of treatment would be right for you?"

Shit! Lee had only been in the room for twenty seconds and he'd just asked her the most difficult question she had ever had to field. She tried to quell the rising panic – hoping her voice would this time be available to her and hadn't been frightened so far back down her throat that she'd need to write in later with her answers. "Um, I guess I have thought of little else for a few years now.

I have tried to find a way to live with the feelings I have inside, but I – my body, I don't think, will let me". She couldn't be sure precisely where on a scale of stupid, the doctor might score that explanation, but she had it somewhere around a six. She wanted a fresh start – after less than a minute.

"And when you say that that you have thought of this for a few years, when would you say that these thoughts first presented themselves to you?"

Lee clawed for some mental traction. How was it that feelings and instincts whole and clear within, could be so poorly served by the spoken word? She needed to concentrate, "I, well I couldn't give you a particular moment or occasion. There wasn't a time when this first occurred to me, it's just always been there". God, that was actually true. Did he believe it was true? Maybe everybody said that sort of thing.

"I see. And how would you say that these feelings manifested themselves in you?"

"I, uh..." she was searching through a vast open plain of memory for features that might offer her a route to describe. She also needed a vocabulary with which to speak of nothing more tangible than pure instinct. God, this was hard! She felt as though she were in some sort of trouble. 'Just trust in the truth', Dani had said – and in an instant, she abandoned herself to that fate, "I suppose I just had a sense of not being quite...real. It's really once you start mixing with other kids, isn't it?" she met Dr Garner's gaze properly for the first time, "That's when everything starts getting...divided up. That's when I started getting sent to the wrong half of rooms".

The doctor said nothing, but smiled in an interested and encouraging way.

Lee decided she would throw in one of the key points of her personal philosophy, one of her absolute truths. It was a huge gamble to play so early, but it was essential to her reasoning. "I've read as many case histories as I can find – in the press, at the library and in a couple of books I've bought. I keep coming across this phrase, 'Being born in the wrong body'. And I just...I don't feel that. I don't understand that. I mean, I *know* that this is my body. And I *know* that I really don't like it in here" (now, that really was an understatement), "But I'm not here asking for someone to deliver some other body to me. I know I have to make the best of this one. In a way, what I want to change is the how the rest of the world reacts to it – to *me.*" Somewhere at the back of her head, a dedicated audience of one applauded.

Dr Garner began to write in his folder, making Lee suddenly Lee felt a little less sure of herself. Had she said something wrong?

"It matters very much to you what other people think?"

"Well, not in the sense that I need their approval" Lee scrambled, backtracking uncertainly. She called again internally for focus, "It's just that I can't…I don't feel that I can honestly touch anyone – or *be* touched – not all the while they think I'm a…male."

More notes were made. Lee began to worry she might be dictating her own suicide note.

"When you were as you put it, sent to the 'wrong half of rooms' as a child, how did this make you feel?"

Lee smiled and recalled in a flash, endless playground games and bathroom signs and teacher's instructions. She remembered all of the 'girls against boys' team games and the uniforms and things coloured blue. "I just felt a bit lost." She looked up again smiling as she continued to recall the innocence of beginnings. "You just do what you're told. You go where you're told. Something isn't right, but it's just…bigger than you. You trust people around you when you're small, don't you? You believe that they know best." She thought of Dad and suddenly, desperately didn't want to blame him for anything. "You just want to *do* your best. Not let them down".

"Do you feel that you have let anyone down?"

"No" she said softly. "No, I've been very careful about that".

They spoke for some time about childhood. They talked about who Lee's friends had been and the role models she admired. (Apart from Dad, she named a couple of female teachers. Again, it was the truth, but she also guessed that it might be helpful). They made stops at all stages of her schooling and even discussed how she saw a working life for herself. She chose at this point to avoid mention of being unemployed. Oddly, Lee wasn't asked very much more about her parents and nothing at all about her Mother. She'd always heard that shrinks were obsessed with mothers. Instead for the most part, she was encouraged to recall events rather than feelings; anecdotes rather than summarised speculation. She was feeling increasingly comfortable and confident when Dr Garner suddenly pivoted from her past to the present.

"Your appearance is quite soft, quite androgynous. Have you always identified this way?"

Lee raised her eyebrows in reflection, suddenly catching sight of the skinny knees. They were still bolted together. "I suppose so. I mean I suppose my look is more about how I *don't* want to appear, if anything. I try to remove the things I definitely can't bear and then I just sort of put up with what's left over".

"Tell me more about that" the doctor replied, making a written note of Lee's line.

"God, I don't know" Lee bit her lip in thought, "I just want to find some way of being true to myself, without looking...wrong". She smiled at her own summary. Dr Garner returned the expression, but Lee wasn't sure he'd understood. She decided to offer something a little more graphic, a phrase that she'd often thought and once tried out on Dani, "Thing is, I'm just not going to slip into a floral print dress and sashay down to the shops". (She loved the word 'sashay'. It said so much about what she was desperate to avoid). "I don't want to try to be something I can't manage". She stalled and held her breath for a moment. Suddenly there were tiny alarm bells going off inside of her. She needed to do better than that. "What I'm trying to say is that I'm just not a clichéd type of person. I'm not looking to exchange one simplistic gender image for another. The way I'm dressed today is the way I'll probably dress in ten years – twenty even". Did that do it? Did that work?

Dr Garner was nodding. "So Lee, your reading and research will no doubt have informed you that the process of gender transition is very difficult, very challenging – and of course if outside the NHS system, really rather expensive. How do you see this process working for you?"

Lee felt on safer ground. She had no fear of telling it just the way she saw it. She had well defined bullet-points for this in her notes and she knew she could speak with conviction, "I think that the pacing of things is very important. I don't want to take any steps I'm not ready for, or that I can't make work with the rest of my life."

"And how long do you envisage this process taking?"

"I think, five years" Lee stated with a calm certainty. That gives me the time to gradually move through the changes while keeping my life together – and paying for it".

Dr Garner smiled. It looked to Lee like it might even be an off-duty kind of smile.

"I'm really glad to hear you say that" he said. Many people have sat here before you, wanting instant change. Your approach sounds very sensible".

Lee was thrilled. She was being taken seriously by someone serious.

"Also, when you say, 'keeping your life together', do you have a partner at present?"

"Erm, no." Lee expected of course, that this line of questioning would arise, but she was always instinctively guarded about the issue. "Not for some time".

"I see" Dr Garner noted – literally. He pressed further, "When there is someone in your life, how would you describe your orientation?"

It was an odd combination to consider – the request for emotional reflection but with clinical terminology. Of all the areas for discussion, this was the issue upon which she felt most vulnerable and yet about which she was determined to be honest. "Would it be terrible to answer that I really don't know?" she ventured.

Dr Garner answered, "There really aren't any right or wrong answers to that question, it's largely incidental to the central issue – although it is a key part of one's own sense of self".

Lee took a breath and then let it back out through loosened lips. "It's just difficult. Like I said earlier, I don't know what it's like to get properly close to people. I mean I have all of the usual worries I suppose, but I just don't see how anyone can see the real me – not as long as I'm like this."

By the age of 22, Lee Habens had been to bed with three people – and had found each experience perplexing. Maybe discussing it in a room from which embarrassment was banished, might teach her something. "I've been sexual with two women".

"Right".

"But each time when it happened, I wasn't really thinking about it. I mean, I sort of wasn't really there".

"Mmm" Dr Garner considered. "So where were you during these experiences?"

"I was wondering about what they must be feeling" Lee smiled and shrugged. "I don't know, I guess it was the only way in that I could find. I just thought that even if I wasn't going to enjoy it, I might see if I could make somebody else...sort of, happy. I suppose at the time I thought maybe that's what sex was really about. But it was more than sex in a way. For me it was a chance to at least *feel* femaleness, to be really close – even if it wasn't my own."

"And have there been any sexual experiences with men?"

"One" Lee nodded, thinking back to the summer and a meeting with a middle-aged barman in a local hotel. She had first discovered the bar when meeting colleagues from IGF – the place opened later than any of the pubs. That day however, she had been alone. It had been a Sunday, just a few months after Dad had gone. The pain had such a strong hold over her then. She'd been trying to walk off some tears and wondered if a drink might help – it always seemed to in films. His name was Ian and he spoke softly with what she came to know as a Rhodesian accent. She hadn't been especially attracted to him, but had been drawn to his gentle manner and the way he made her feel cherished that afternoon in his room, two floors above the place they met.

"I don't regret it, but he wasn't someone I wanted to feel anything lasting for, exactly" she heard herself say out loud.

A last ripple in time lapped at her. A vision of the sun's fading luminescence, warmed to gold through soft blown nets. She could almost feel again the tender caresses along her thighs. Her mind had still been hostage to grief that afternoon, but her body had been beautifully consoled.

"Do you see your sexuality as perhaps encompassing relationships with *both* genders?"

Lee smiled thoughtfully and said something with which she would later be very pleased, "I think I see my sexuality as something to look forward to".

Dr Garner made a few more notes. As he did so, Lee took the time to look around the room. It was hard to tell where a study ended and an old-fashioned drawing room began. There was a red sofa against the wall to her left. This was served by a low coffee table while the no-man's-land centre of the room was occupied by an oriental rug. It was red with white and gold detailing – and entirely too lovely to walk on.

It was Dr Garner's turn to take a deep breath. "That" he said, "is our time up". He smiled, "I would like to see you again – monthly, for a further three sessions. How does that sound to you?"

Lee was astonished that the time had passed so quickly. She was sorry it was over – though in truth, she was also pretty exhausted. "I think that sounds...good" she replied, cringing inside at her choice of words.

Dr Garner stood and offered his hand once more.

Lee was slow again to react, though at least this time she was less inclined to feel that the act might betray her. "Thank you" she said smiling and looking directly into Dr Garner's eyes, then adding – she thought bravely, "This has been really helpful to me".

She had to pay on her way out. She scheduled all three further sessions, each at four-week intervals.

In a moment, Lee was back out on a Fulham back street. It was colder, the sky had darkened and a murky drizzle had descended across the south-west of the metropolis. She felt utterly elated. In the space of the last hour, her self-image had migrated from one of downbeat, low esteem, laced with a desperate desire for identity, to a new status as a person of foundation. She felt acknowledged, validated. The arrangement of three further appointments clearly indicated that she had been judged by an expert to be a worthy case. For most people, she guessed this would be considered appalling news. Nobody ever *wanted* to be transsexual after all – but there and then, the label gave Lee Habens a greater sense of self than she could ever remember.

On the tube ride back across to Victoria, Lee almost dared her fellow passengers to scrutinise her. It didn't matter anymore. If someone were to stare at her as though she were some kind of curiosity – well, that would be fine – because now, she was *officially* outside the norm. All 'weirdness' ever needed was a little focus.

Nobody did stare. Perhaps Lee's new-found confidence was enough to satisfy the world around her, too. In the end, society perhaps asks nothing more than that everyone find their place – like some huge game of musical chairs. Today was not her turn to miss out on a seat.

Just off the main concourse at Victoria was a bank of payphones. It was pretty noisy and not especially private, but Lee was desperate to call Dani. She needed to connect with the one person who could share her happiness. Dani's Dad answered the phone but quickly handed it over as soon as he recognised Lee's voice. Lee had long been aware of the discomfort she caused him but she had no time today to feel offended.

Dani's voice chimed, "Hang on, I'm just going into my room".

Lee could picture her friend dragging the long telephone cord up the stairs from the hallway to her bedroom, "Are you there yet?" she asked impatiently as the station PA offered another incoherent British Rail apology. She had to cover her other ear to hear Dani.

"Yep, just about. So – how was it?"

Lee wondered whether her friend could sense her smile 70 miles down the North Kent Line, "It was brilliant – I think" she said almost laughing aloud. "I think it really was, really good. I mean I think I got myself across to him. I think he understood what I was saying". Lee recalled Dr Garner's smiling eyes – especially the big smile when she'd told him how she judged the timing of her transition.

"So, he was nice?" Dani asked, sharing in the exuberance.

"He was, you know – he really was. I don't know, he just took me seriously. He made me feel...I don't know..."

"What?"

"I suppose he made me feel real. I'm hardly ever real – except maybe when I'm talking to you. The rest of the time I'm not real at all. I'm just what people can see – and there's nothing much real about that, is there?"

The sense of euphoria from the meeting with Dr Garner grew within Lee as the train clattered east. There was a point during the journey where she became so heady with elation that she actually considered starting a conversation with a complete stranger with the aim of somehow skewing the agenda toward the subject of gender politics. She could maybe then segue to the matter of those challenged by issues of sexual identity and from there vent her swelling delight. Fortunately for all, there had been no likely candidates within earshot during the 75-minute journey and soon enough, the cold early evening breeze slicing along platform 2 of Sittingbourne Station, sobered the natural high right out of her.

Even though Lee didn't have a week off work from which to recover, this Saturday night did feel precious. She and Dani would head to Gillingham for a celebratory night of dance, laughs and more dance. It would be like the old days – only for Lee, a little more real.

Getting ready already presented a new challenge. Lee wanted to move her appearance along a little. She felt that she could – and even that she should. She was now after all, under the care of an expert, a man who had recognised her status as a proper person. Now wasn't a time to hide in the shadows, it was the moment to take the first dignified and deserved tiptoes into the light. She felt in fact, almost obliged to present a more daring outward appearance. Even as she'd been struggling with mousse and a wheezing hair dryer in a bid for maximum volume, Lee vowed that evenings such as these would be less compromising. Instead of looking sufficiently male to hide in the herd, she now needed to begin the act of gender secession. Tonight, she hadn't backtracked on the foundation by dabbing with a tissue to tone down the evenness. She hadn't worried about there being too much mascara and taken a cotton bud to her lashes to make them a little less full. She had even for the first time, applied a hint of eyeliner to her lower lid. She saw her reflection smile in mutual amusement. This wasn't a face she saw often – and it most certainly wasn't a face she had previously taken outside.

She had been getting ready to her '*Saturday Nite*' tape (the American spelling always seemed more appropriate). George Benson's *Never Give Up On A Good Thing* had followed D-Train's *You're The One For Me*. She was loosening up with some extravagant hipsway as she moved around her bedroom. Ordinarily, this wouldn't be her first choice of music, but 'Saturday Nites' were different. Besides, this would be typical of the pulsing soundtrack at *Rosanna's* later and so she may as well get herself into the groove. Dressing would be another challenge. She stared at the top drawer of the pine chest and knew that she was going to have to resolve the great underwear issue. She had found it increasingly difficult to wear male underpants. She didn't like buying them and she definitely didn't like what it said about her when she put them on. Keeping her inner identity demons at bay was all the more challenging when she wore something that was definitively male. On a Saturday night, she would usually make an extra effort to wear clothing that might – at least in a theory stretched wafer thin – be worn by either sex. This could hardly apply to male underwear. She would talk to Dani again about perhaps buying something more appropriate. Nothing too girly or overly feminine, just something plain so she wouldn't burn at a sense of self-betrayal. But for tonight? She came to an odd conclusion: As she would be wearing a black pair of triple pleated trousers, loose around the top and thigh, she would wear nothing at all underneath. She'd be like a politician abstaining on an important vote. It might feel a little weird, but it would free her up – morally and otherwise. She wore a black shirt. It was cotton, but had a sort of sheen to it. If it had been silk, she'd have still worn it out tonight – so devout was her self-belief. She teamed black loafers with white socks. Sometimes she thought the shoes looked a little court-like, but you had to really want them to look that way to see it. At least they were good for dancing.

She had collected Dani at about nine o' clock. It would have been nice to have been able to get ready together, but Dani had been busy with other plans and anyway, preparing together often led to the kind of overindulgence in dance and drinking that could put paid to going out at all.

Dani had slipped into the passenger seat of the Honda wearing a dark red pencil skirt, patent heels and black top with a slashed neckline. She looked gorgeous. She always did when they went out together. It had the effect of making Lee want to hide under a rock. She wondered if women generally felt this way about their better-looking friends. It was wonderful to see Dani shine, but it was cold in her shadow and Lee's own efforts to make herself palatable, felt somehow drawn into an even sharper contrast.

"You look great!" Dani said with enthusiasm – as she always did.

Lee smiled, perhaps a bit thinly. Then she kissed her friend's soft cheek, sat back and replied, "And you look too good for anyone out there tonight".

Lee's tape had come along for the ride – and as usual, the music had been turned up louder with the intro to each track. ABC's *Poison Arrow* heralded their arrival at their usual parking spot just around the corner from the club. Lee felt her nerves tingle as she turned off the engine and silenced the soundtrack. Now it was just the two of them and the night ahead. She looked across at Dani, who was touching up her lipstick in the passenger mirror. Checking her own look, Lee suddenly became acutely aware that she really had let ambition take the lead. In the half light, the foundation made her complexion look flawless. Her eyebrows had more of a daringly defined arc than usual. She found that when she dipped her head a little, her fringe broke up the line. This and other defensive techniques may be required over the coming hours. With one more rueful look across at Dani, Lee took a breath and reached for the door handle, "Ready?"

"Always."

They walked hand in hand, Dani's heels echoing back from the brick terraces. One of the quirks of the club was its location, right in the middle of a densely-housed area. Rounding the corner into the main street, Lee was relieved to see the shortest of queues. The evening's dampness was threatening to flatten her high hair and the lighting outside the door was uncomfortably cruel. Within a minute though, they were up the three steps, inside and at the pay booth. Dani funded their entry as usual – a trade for the cost of the return trip. Already still a double door and a corridor away, the music was coursing through Lee's system. Her heartbeat began to synchronise with the bass. They stepped through the outer border and into the cloakroom area. Neither of them had coats to deposit, but Dani would need her customary bathroom visit. Lee was left to wait in the deep-blue walled, blue carpeted, low lit, outer hall. Even some of the sparse spotlights were cobalt. The only source of bright white light was the cigarette machine. Lee purchased a pack of 20 just for something to do. She'd have to ask Dani to put them in her handbag when she returned. Lee hated keeping anything in her trouser pockets. She kept only flat banknotes in there. Even coins had to be deposited elsewhere. The sound of jingling change always made Lee think of Dad – and only a Dad she felt, should sound that way.

Dani returned looking if it were possible, even more immaculate. A shared smile, linking of hands and they moved together around a corner and into the main body of the club. The wall of noise beckoned them inward to join with collective pulse.

Rosanna's like most provincial venues, was a place for being seen – for flirting, meeting and beginning journeys almost certainly destined to end in regret. But it was also a place to dance. The sprung wooden floor was full as always and the carpeted areas around, heaved similarly under relentless overhead bass speakers. The central dancefloor was a single step down from islands of soft banquette seating. Walkways between the two worlds weaved a border all the way to the exposed DJ podium. Overlooking the scene, was a galleried first floor that included a small kitchen serving things-in-a-basket to those willing to squander good dance time.

Dani was the first to speak – actually *shout* "It's busy. Where do you want to go?"

"Usual?"

There was a spot at one of the back corners which both knew to have the benefit of a sill upon which they could lean and place drinks. With one of the four bars also in easy reach, Lee headed to draw a first round while Dani made her way through the throng to their rendezvous point. The crowd of thirsty buyers was two deep and it took a little while to be served. The staff were fast though – as if they were being paid according to customer consumption. Lee was served after only two records – medium white for Dani and a coke for herself. The guy who served her didn't make eye contact but instead tilted an ear toward her to catch the order. He was completely immersed in his task, his focus seemingly sharpened by the driving rhythms. He moved with the assurance of an insider, operating on a level of cool Lee couldn't hope to know. She re-joined Dani and they sipped and swayed for a while. Standing with a woman in a club like *Rosanna's* Lee knew, meant that people would just assume your status as a pair. Coupledom offered a state of safety and yet at the same time Lee was troubled by the lie. She tried not to dwell upon it, instead watching two young women formation-stepping something they'd clearly choreographed beforehand. Not the most graceful of moves, but kind of charming in a way. Lee liked the kind of friendships that still innocently included planning dance steps before a night out. She looked to see if Dani had caught the pair's act and saw from the returned grin that she had. An exchanged look pretty much had to say it all in such an environment. There was little point in trying to have a conversation with the person next to whom you stood. With music at this volume, you could pick up no more than a couple of words of a sentence and even those would need to be of no more than two syllables.

The DJ spun Candi Staton and Lee knew immediately that the only possible response lay out on those perfect dark wooden boards. They smiled and nodded knowingly to each other before taking the single step down and into the beat. Dani still had her glass in hand and she swayed, smiling as Lee fell into a very familiar shuffle under a sky of white scanners and rolling blue, yellow and red suns.

Lee really could dance. She wasn't showy about it, but had a locked-in rhythmic sense of moving that always seemed to work. Even in a tight space, she could drift up and out of a body that would never miss a note. Kid Creole and Tom Browne followed, loosening the last of Lee's earthly bonds. The Crusaders took her the rest of the way, reminding her of how if she trusted the rhythm, she could melt into it, becoming nothing more than movement and energy and hope, twisting through an intro, catching and matching a melody and surging on into a chorus.

As on previous occasions, Lee attracted a number of dance partners without ever exchanging words. Most of the time she hadn't noticed the company at all, but even when she had, communication was kept to a nothing more than a smile, allowing nothing to break the groove.

Dani drifted away in body a few times, either to have a cigarette or to chat to a familiar face (Lee never got to know any of them), but she would reappear for a track or two every so often.

It was the practice at *Rosanna's* to schedule two slow-dance breaks. One would occur just after 12:30 and the other at 1:45. The first of these arrived suddenly when Teddy Pendergrass oozed a ballad out onto the floor, extinguishing Roberta Flack and Peabo Bryson's *Back Together*. The dance crowds surrendered tenure, as couples ghosted on from the shadows to replace the revellers. Bad boys who didn't boogie would walk out with their good girls, standing still, entwined under the spinning rays of a centrally spun mirrorball. Wistful young women would look on as they were checked out from the semi-darkness by guys who played the numbers, picking off those they deemed more attractive before the third and last song of the break. Romance at *Rosanna's* may not have been entirely dead, but by the middle chorus it was pretty much on life support.

Lee's arms fell to her sides and she stepped up from the main floor to find her drink. She was feeling pretty exhausted – but also exhilarated. The music had been good tonight. The DJ was switching back and forth through the decades, picking up Funkadellic and Evelyn 'Champagne' King from the 70's and bleeding them into newer songs from the likes of Vandross and Shalamar.

Lee knew she would have to endure a toilet visit. She hoped it would be fairly quiet in there – it usually was around slow-dance time. Very few guys would want to be away from the market for the next nine minutes or so.

Dani had accepted a dance invitation from a tall blond guy in a dark suit. She peeked over and met eyes with Lee who sent back a wry look while miming the word 'Loo' and pointing in the general direction of the club entrance. Dani waved and disappeared behind the orbit of a broad shoulder.

There were 8,000 miles between North Kent and The Falkland Islands. And yet you could trace the pumped-up nationalism all the way back to this particular nightclub toilet. Things had been noticeably more intense around Medway ever since the Argentines had taken up their residence in a place hardly anyone had ever heard of. Free-flowing testosterone crackled in the air wherever there were larger gatherings of young men and with Chatham's Royal Navy dockyards just a couple of miles away, there would doubtless be sailors in the club tonight. Straight in, straight out, Lee assured herself as she passed through the matt black door to the men's room. Inside, white-tiled walls mercilessly powered back the overhead white strip lighting. The bare concrete floor hosted a large open area with a mirror at one end, three stalls on one side and a urinal trough to the left. This was not a place to dwell. Lee almost always found a way to avoid the urinal if she could. On this occasion, one of the cubicles was closed, another occupied and the third flooded out. She decided to wait a moment and glanced back toward quite possibly the most ignored mirror in the western world. The guys at *Rosanna's* didn't need mirrors. They looked all right when they left home and that's all that mattered. Mirrors were for girls and poofs. All the more galling for

Lee then, to notice how catastrophic the night's perspiration had been for her mascara and eyeliner. She was smudged under both eyes. She quickly drew a tissue from her pocket and tried to tidy herself up a bit. She was too slow on the draw.

"Fuuu-ckin' 'ell!" came a voice from her side. A large guy with dark cropped hair and a pint glass still in hand had already spotted her. "What 'ave we got 'ere?"

Lee tried to ignore him and looked back desperately toward the stall doors. Nothing free – and the big scary commentator now stood between her and the way back out.

"Are we wearin' makeup now? Eh?" The inquisitor reached out for Lee's chin and feeling the smoothness of foundation over skin withdrew his hand as if it had been stung. He wiped his fingers on his chest and then noticed a creamy smear against his blue cotton, "Ahhh, you fuckin'..."

Lee never knew exactly what kind of 'fuckin'' she had been declared. The blow when it came, was barely even seen. If she had known it was coming, she may have been able to duck, or lean one way or the other, but she'd been too keen to avoid eye contact with the owner of the fist that cracked into her right temple. Lee went over in a wide arc, the left side of her head catching the sink counter as she fell. The two successive blows put out her lights entirely for a short time. When consciousness returned, she was alone. The floor was cool and slightly damp at her cheek – and not in any kind of good way. Lee drew herself up on all fours. She vomited copiously into the corner – though somewhat neatly under the sink counter. She reasoned loosely that the deposit wouldn't make too much difference under there. At least she hadn't ruined a carpet. Mercifully, she didn't feel any actual pain at all. She raised herself up to a shaky standing position. Her reflection sent back a somewhat ghostly-looking visage with a reddened brow on one side and a crimson panel down the other. She was bleeding quite a lot from the latter and watched fascinated as the drops spattered the white porcelain sink beneath her. The bright red droplets congregated at the sink's plughole, leaving thin orangey wakes. It was a bit like a diagram she'd once seen of sperm heading for an egg in a race to make life. She sensed that she still needed a pee and so made for the now empty first stall. While standing in the cubicle, she unrolled some tracing paper-like tissue and dabbed at her right temple, unaware that the blood was coming from the opposite side of her head. Emerging, she headed back to the mirror for a more comprehensive clean up.

"Fuckin' 'ell" she heard again. Same words, different voice, this time followed by a couple of amused guffaws.

"S'okay" she waved back calmly. She ran some water into the bloody sink and wet the tissue. Her mind was beginning to catch up. She just felt pretty sad now, mopping this time at the correct temple. The bleeding wasn't for stopping. Each time she thought she had stemmed the flow, a tell-tale trickle would begin again. She needed more tissue and headed off a guy who was about to take the stall, "Whoah there!" she said holding up a bloody palm, "My need is greater than thine". Cod Shakespeare, she reflected – why the hell not? What was *he* going to do about it? She grabbed about ten sheets and formed them into a flat pad before heading back out into the club. Her clothes were pretty soaked, but she was fairly sure nobody would notice under the low lights. She would have to go home now of course, she figured. She hoped Dani wouldn't be too pissed off with her. The slow session was still grinding as she stepped gingerly around the dance floor. She was trying to identify the song while vaguely aware that she may at any moment pass an attacker whose face she couldn't recall. She was grateful for the regular rendezvous point – it at least gave her a fixed destination. Dani was still in the vicinity right enough, albeit chatting to Tall Dancer. Lee decided to wait before interrupting and so she reached around to find her glass of coke. She probably wasn't being as discreet as she'd imagined.

"JEEESUS LEE!!!" Dani screamed, causing much of the entire corner to take an interest, "What's the hell happened?"

Lee was more conscious of Tall Dancer's company than Dani, "Oh, you know – nothing good" she grinned sheepishly. She strained to shout, "I'm probably going to have to go now, though. I just wanted a little drink and to say goodnight."

Dani picked up her bag and took Lee's arm. She turned and planted a peck kiss on the cheek of her erstwhile suitor. "Sorry" she mimed and they were off.

The gum-chewing bouncer who saw them coming wasn't about to ask any questions. Bleeding patrons who leave of their own accord were to be given all possible encouragement. He opened the door for them as they approached. Lee noticed Dani shoot the big penguin a blameful glare as they passed under his arm. She knew deep down that she wouldn't be returning to *Rosanna's*. If she ever had belonged there, she certainly didn't now.

Medway General had a busy A&E department most Saturday nights and with half a dozen late opening nightclubs in their catchment area, faces like Lee's weren't entirely an unusual sight. The two friends had been calmly waved through for assessment by the admissions nurse who cleaned up the wound and replaced the ineffective tissue with a gauze and cotton pad. As they waited for the doctor on a corridor bench, Dani asked for perhaps the fourth time, "Are you sure you don't remember what happened?"

Having previously shrugged at the question, Lee ventured, "Well, I'm pretty sure somebody hit me."

"Yes, I can see that. But who? Why?"

"I don't *think* I did anything. I was dancing and it was really... good. Did you realise that they played The Ohio Players tonight?"

"Lee!"

"Oh, I don't know! There was a fist...just here" Lee motioned to her right temple. "I still can't figure out how I got hit both sides. Maybe he was really fast or something."

"Oh, Baby" Dani stretched her arm around her friend and tried to share the pain.

They sat in a sorrowful silence for a minute and then Lee sniffed, "I'm pretty sure I smell of wee."

Dani sniggered and then Lee responded in kind. They giggled and laughed and the shoulder shakes helped disguise the sobs and tears that followed.

may 1982
work, shrink, move

....

The receptionist had remembered her – or at least seemed to. The perfect smile and delicate sing-song voice had greeted Lee with a 'Hello again. How are you?' Lee had been a little taken aback and had managed only a "Fine" in reply. Perhaps, she considered now from the safety of the kitchen/ waiting room sofa, she might have reciprocated more warmly. Was the receptionist being genuinely friendly, or did she just notice from the entry in the appointment book, that Lee was a returning patient? Probably best not to completely believe in the people this side of the clinic doors any more than those outside, Lee concluded.

Despite the recent increase in the threat – indeed *acts* – of persecution, Lee had made a similar commitment in her presentation to that of her first appointment. She was fairly confident that she had found 'a look' for her meetings with Dr Garner. Slim black jeans, cowboys, a long white shirt which she wore smock-like, outside her jeans and a black suede waistcoat she had picked up at Sittingbourne market two weeks previously. The outfit had been carefully concealed once more under her protective raincoat – at least until she'd left the train at Victoria.

Lee's appearance had been further enhanced by the introduction of earrings. Dani had provided support during the trip to a local hairdressing salon, where the piercing had been given by a former school friend. Lee's lobes were still pretty sore, but it was worth it. There had been some eyebrow-raising when Lee told the part-time beautician that she wished to have a hole made in each ear. 'Oh, okay' she had said, clearly surprised. Guys 'usually only had their left ear done', Lee had been told – as if she hadn't known that already. For now, and for the next few weeks, she would wear the same gold studs as had been first introduced, but she had plans.

The good doctor was apparently 'running a bit late' again today. Lee was beginning to understand this to be the norm. She was leafing through her second copy of *Country Life* magazine, studying pictures of an impossibly beautiful house for sale somewhere in Oxfordshire when two more people arrived in the reception area. It was a woman and a man – you could tell that much from behind – even though both figures were dressed as women. After a hushed exchange of greetings at the desk, the pair headed toward the seating area. Lee quickly returned her gaze self-consciously to the magazine. From the way they spoke to each other, Lee quickly gathered that they were a couple. In fact, from the conversation alone, you wouldn't suspect anything was out of place. The male voice from the partner enquiring as to coffee or tea preference was as natural and uncompromised as it would always have been. In the meantime, the female half of the partnership (in natal terms at least), settled onto the sofa opposite Lee and sighed theatrically. Lee dared to look up and exchanged weak smiles with the woman on the other side of the coffee table. She was quite heavy in build with a round face and blonde curls. "Just got here before the rain arrived" she said, friendly eyes sparkling. Lee smiled more assuredly in return. She wanted to catch a glimpse of the other partner, but didn't dare – until the privilege of choice was removed.

"Are you okay for a drink there?" enquired the husky voice.

Lee looked up and was met by a perfectly made up face – otherwise utterly male in appearance. Perched above the paradoxical combination of features, was a dark wig, shoulder length and styled with a straight fringe. The figure was tall and broad – in other words, just about as unfortunate a physical combination as a person aspiring to femininity might hope to inherit.

Lee was taken by how relaxed and comfortable her co-habitant seemed to be, "Oh, I'm fine, thanks" she replied, suddenly aware of how comparatively soft her own voice sounded. She hoped not to have given the impression of having made a deliberate effort.

Coffee was served at the table and the new guest took a seat. In a way, the pairing made the larger figure appear all the more masculine. Lee realised that she had never actually seen a man dressed as a woman in real life and she was surprised at how the sight discomforted her. Was this how she would look to others? Was this what the guy in *Rosanna's* had seen in her and why he'd chosen to so brutally erase her from the scene. Lee of course hadn't been wearing an aquamarine cotton dress and dark blue cardigan that night – she remained a long way from such adventures. She knew instinctively that she would have neither the courage, nor defiance required to appear that way in public. It must be hell to walk down the street in those shoes, she thought to herself – not even thinking directly of the pointed navy sling-backs in size gazillion.

As the couple resumed their smalltalk, Lee continued to wrestle with her inner reflections. Did she admire her fellow patient's honesty and daring? Wasn't she in fact, envious of another's confidence and dignity in stepping out to take on a hostile world, come what may? Or was she instead just fearful of her own future? A life sentence of incongruity handed down to her by fate, or genes or bad luck, or whatever lay behind her instincts. Maybe she held a little of all of those feelings.

Relief from further reflection came in the form of a fourth figure who entered the reception. This one was unmistakably male, bearded and wearing an oversized sheepskin jacket. He was youngish, maybe late twenties. He removed a woolly hat to reveal an extremely short haircut, receding somewhat at the temples. He was slim – slight even – and not terribly tall.

The receptionist recognised him and brightened immediately, "Hi Davey, how are you?"

"All right Donna. How're you doin'?" he replied in an accent that was almost certainly American.

"I'm well, thank you. You here to see Sue?"

"Yuh"

"Well, we're running a little late today. Why don't you take a seat" she gestured toward the kitchen with one hand while ticking off 'Davey's' name in her book with the other.

The newest arrival seemed shy and clutched his hat tightly with both hands as he approached. He took the seat next to Lee and nodded to those already seated. There were raindrops on the shoulders of his jacket and he removed it to reveal a red plaid lumberjack shirt. He laid the jacket on his lap. His hands now revealed, were small and the fingers delicate. Lee had read that female-to-males could be incredibly convincing and that the hormone treatment in particular, had very dramatic effects. If 'Davey' *had* ever been female Lee thought, he'd pretty much eliminated any discernible trace. She was fascinated and would dearly love to have spoken with him.

"Lee?" came the call from the newly-identified Donna. "Dr Garner is ready for you now".

There was no need to knock this time. Dr Garner met Lee at the door of his office and once again extended a hand in greeting. Lee took it in good faith.

She sat once again in the green leather, button-back chair, placing her coat and this time, a holdall to one side of her. In another change to her first visit, she also crossed her legs – the black jeans being a little more accommodating. Dr Garner was as calming in his tone as ever. He wore a grey sports jacket with charcoal trousers. Perhaps because of the company she had just left, the sight of a man so clearly at home in his own skin, was somehow comforting. Lee felt an easier relationship with the room.

"So Lee, how have you been since we last met?"

"Oh, I've been fine" Lee answered, then supplementing "Actually I've been...better than just fine."

"Oh really? What makes you say that?"

Lee had a mentally pre-prepared opening line, "It's just really since our first session. I guess just finally reaching this point has been such a welcome relief – cathartic, even" she added, still new to a word that so perfectly framed her feeling. "I know that I'm just at the very beginning of a very long process here, but for my whole life before now, this conversation has been something I really needed. When I left here last time, I was really...relieved."

Dr Garner nodded, encouraging Lee to elaborate. She was a little disappointed that he hadn't made a note of her use of the word 'cathartic'. She went on, "It just felt good to be able to talk to someone who knew more about transsexuality than me." The 'T' word; another she wasn't yet used to saying aloud.

"In what way exactly?"

"Well I mean, apart from my best friend, I've never been able to talk about this with anyone. Sometimes it's not until you hear yourself actually say these things that they sort of...crystallise".

"Mmm" Dr Garner took a note of *that* phrase. "So you feel that you also learned something about yourself from our first meeting?"

"Not exactly *learned*. It was more that I felt I had things... reaffirmed."

"Mmm." More notes.

"I mean, I already knew who I was and what I was when I came here, but I left feeling more secure about things."

"And specifically, the commitment to your transsexuality?"

"Yes." Another key phrase came to Lee, one that she wanted to communicate as early as possible, "Since I first went to see my GP..."

"That's Dr Jones?"

"Yes. Ever since my first conversation with her and then coming here, I knew that I didn't want to take back a single step I would make down this road. I just don't want to go back." Then just for good measure Lee added, "I really *couldn't* go back."

Dr Garner nodded and smiled and for a moment neither of them spoke. Lee suspected that this was a common practice among psychiatrists; leave a gap and see how the patient fills it. Lee decided to play chicken, offering an inscrutable smile herself and waiting for the next move.

"Let's talk a bit about the kind of life you see for yourself in the future."

"Sure."

Another gap. Lee took the initiative this time – her confidence settling, "I suppose I see myself with a life that would be... normal?"

"Okay, well then tell me how you see 'normal'."

Lee took a breath as she lined up the right words "I suppose, I don't know – a *normal* kind of job, around *normal* sort of people." She laughed at her own repetition of the term. "That really is it – I just want to be...normal."

"Mmm. And you're absolutely confident that 'normal' cannot be attained as the person you are today?"

Lee's face straightened to reflect the determination of her tone, "The *person* I am, *is* normal" she stated evenly, "The relationship with the body I live in, isn't".

It was okay. Dr Garner seemed to accept the message in the manner intended. "Does this 'normal' life you foresee, include a partner at all?"

They'd been here before of course – and Lee knew the doctor would have her previous remarks in his notes. Was he looking for consistency? "I would like to think so, yes."

"And when you picture this life ahead, do you see your partner as male or female?"

"I don't know. Like I tried to say before, I'm kind of open to whatever happens. I – I guess I am more *comfortable* around women. Men are a little harder to cope with..." A fist flashed toward Lee's right temple in her near memory and she feared that she may have visually winced during the split-second recollection, "...at least as I am right now." She added for clarity, "But, I don't think of women in y'know, *that* way." She decided to throw the issue back, "Am I even being realistic in thinking that someone would even *want* to be with me afterwards? I mean, does that actually happen?"

Dr Garner's brows rose as he mentally reviewed some past cases, "It happens, yes. Sometimes it's as simple as just meeting the right person, someone who falls for you because of *who* you are – though of course it's worth bearing in mind that these are the same conditions we all require. But I do know of patients who have passed through here and gone on to have full lives with relationships and good sex lives. Not by any means all of them – quite the contrary – but it certainly does happen, yes."

"Okay. Well I guess it does no harm to hope" Lee responded, rather lamely.

"And so what about now? You say you find men 'harder to cope with'" Dr Garner read back.

"Well, I come from a place that isn't as...*liberal* as London. Looking a bit different where I come from can just get you into trouble." She actually *heard* the smack of the fist this time.

"Do you encounter much difficulty in the way you look?"

Lee smiled. "It's not exactly easy" she said, preferring to leave it at that. She needed to return to a positive tone, "But I'm committed to moving to London now and so I expect there to be less of that."

"I see". More notes." And is this move imminent?"

"Pretty much, yes. I'll sort out a job before I leave the house that I have in Kent, but like I say, I'm really committed to it now."

"London can be rather more accepting of an appearance that is perhaps...ambiguous in identity" the doctor reasoned.

"Yes, that's what I'm hoping. As I said before, it's important to me to change things gradually. Sustainably."

"Mmm – and remind me why it is that you feel that way. You do cross dress?" he searched his notes.

The term remained peculiar to Lee. It didn't feel right. At the same time she also worried that the doctor might be viewing her present appearance as insufficiently androgynous. "Um, yes, I guess – sort of. I don't really think of it that way."

"Ah yes, you remarked last time about not wanting to overdo things. Not wanting to erm 'slip into a floral dress', I think you said"

Lee smiled, "Right. Sashaying and all that."

Dr Garner pursued the issue nonetheless, "You do own female attire though?"

What was this obsession doctors had with wardrobes? Lee stepped once more into the textile minefield. It was probably best not to admit that she hated her own reflection in both male *and* female garb. "I do have a few pieces, yes." Lee admitted cautiously. "I just..." Lee struggled with the words, "I'm not good with..." Finally, she just let out the flat truth, "The thing is, I really just can't bear to look...ridiculous", she said. "I see things I like and I buy them. I try them on at home, but if they don't look right – and most of the time to me, they don't – I can't wear them again. That's just, y'know...the way I am" she shrugged.

"Is it possible that you are being a little hard on yourself? A little over critical? Perhaps you need someone else's opinion. Do you have anyone you would feel comfortable getting a view from? A friend perhaps?"

Lee ran her hand nervously through her hair as she mentally played out the prospect of some ghastly bedroom fashion show. She let out a genuinely deep felt sigh, "Dani unfortunately, is always very kind."

"Danny?"

"Yes, she's my best friend"

"Oh, I see, yes. Do go on"

Lee suddenly realised how her remark may have sounded. Would it have been more helpful for the doctor to have thought of her spending time with a male friend? Lee imagined not, but frankly she wasn't certain of very much at that moment. "She's really supportive, but I'm not sure that she's actually any kind of help in that regard. Mostly, she just tells me what she thinks I'll want to hear. I know I have to get past my issues of pride at some point. I'm just so determined to do things with patience and to be able to properly carry off what I do. I don't mind androgyny – at least just for now. I mean, this is the 80's right? You don't have to look too traditionally one way or the other if you plan it right."

"You're sure you're not actually fearful of the prospect of moving on to the next stage? Androgyny can be an all-*too*-comfortable place for some."

Lee shook her head, leaning forward a little to emphasise her sincerity, "I just want to do this right. And that's not wrong – is it?"

In all, it had been an exhausting second session and Lee slept a little on the train back to Sittingbourne. Her reflections and mood were definitely different from the last return journey. The euphoria of her first encounter with Dr Garner had been replaced by something more considered, more pragmatic. She was planning – just a single step at a time – but planning nonetheless. Her next meeting with Dr Garner would be the last of those booked. By the close of that next consultation, she would hope to have to have made her case to the psychiatrist's satisfaction. Beyond, lay the promise of real treatment. Treatment with hormones.

The prospect of physical change through chemistry, excited and intimidated in almost equal measure. She had watched Dad manage a very serious cocktail of medicines, while she herself had barely ever ingested anything more potent than a sleeping pill or aspirin.

Of course, she reminded herself, there remained the risk of an entirely different outcome to these interviews. Dr Garner could still pronounce her case unjust and that would simply be an end to it. What would she do if that were to happen? How would she cope with an official condemnation of her claims to be a true transsexual? The thought was too appalling. She had considered it before, briefly – when she knew so much less about the process and of how to negotiate a clinical passage home. If she were to suffer the catastrophe of rejection, she would be left with no life to plan at all. She shuddered away the darkness and instead recalled Dr Garner's smile. He wouldn't turn her down. He *did* believe her, he *did* get it – she felt sure.

The mood on the train that evening, weighed heavily. It was like this everywhere. Wars weren't supposed to happen anymore. A school master had once told Lee and her classmates that if there ever was another one, it would be nuclear and over so quickly that the populace of south-east England would know little about it. The teacher hadn't seen The Falklands coming though – nobody had. Now half of Britain's armed forces it seemed, were either already in the South Atlantic or on their way there. And the macho posturing in the media was being led ironically, by a woman Prime

Minister. They called it 'jingoism': the over-defensive mustering of rhetoric, wrapped in a flag – and woe betide you if you spoke against it. Lee had lost count of the number of public conversations she'd overheard between men discussing the prospect of joining up to one or other of the forces – all the more so since the loss of *HMS Sheffield*. Most of the debate surrounded which route would get you to the frontline the quickest, before the main event was all over. Radio 4 had even carried a feature about the unlikely possibility of conscription. Lee's blood had run cold at the prospect. What on earth would she do? Would she be a traitor to her country or to herself? Did they even have a place for transsexuals in the forces? Probably some kind of role cleaning something with camouflage dusters, she supposed. They wouldn't make her join up though, would they? No, it was preposterous, of course. There was no point in conscription for such a limited conflict. We wouldn't be at war for long, the experts said. Once the rest of the Task Force got down there, it would all be over in a jiffy. Nevertheless, the air of a conflict joined, pervaded. Humour even seemed uncharacteristically short in supply. Laughing was almost seen as bad form. Britain was suddenly more stoic and masculine in spirit than she had ever known.

She watched a pair of beaded raindrops wriggle across the carriage window pane, racing back toward the London she'd left behind. If another important step had been taken that day in the capital, she knew it to be only one on a very long road. After leaving The London Centre earlier, she had taken the short walk to a nearby pub, just around the corner from Fulham Broadway tube station. It had looked clean and most importantly, fairly busy. Nobody had noticed her as she slipped past the toilet door. In the privacy of a cubicle, she had carefully removed her makeup using some moisturising cream and cotton wool. She'd still needed to be wary of the tender area to the side of her face where three stitches had only recently been removed. She'd put on a yellow tie that had been rolled in her coat pocket and tucked her shirt into her jeans. Her overcoat would once again cover – this time for the lack of more formal clothing.

From Victoria Station she'd had been able to count three employment agencies, and had planned to visit each of them. She'd had to run a brush through her hair, flattening it into a more conventional style. She hoped the earrings wouldn't present too much of a problem in metropolitan London.

The agencies had all taken her details. One of them offered her an interview the next week at the London Electricity Board's headquarters. It was an accounts clerk position and it paid £ 3,600 per annum. She could make that work. The second only took her details and promised to get back to her soon. At the final agency, Lee had been interviewed by a young woman in an absurdly tight blue suit. Watching her move around the office was like waiting for an almost inevitable accident to occur. Lee had thought again of her fellow transsexual patient in the aquamarine dress and wig. Which of these two she wondered, was really the more over-ambitious?

The scary suit lady had however, come up with a couple of prospects. She'd seemed genuinely keen to apply herself on Lee's behalf. First was an administration position at Rank Xerox, but it was based over in Croydon and that wouldn't make sense to Lee either as a location to live, or work. Even though the salary had been tempting, she knew that she needed to be in the heart of London. Then came the vacancy Lee intended to really try for. It was another accounts clerk role, but at a company that managed a chain of bureau de change branches around the west end. The job would be based in South Kensington, just two stops from Victoria, making the commute from Sittingbourne bearable – maybe no more than an hour and half each way. It paid £ 3,750 per annum but best of all, was the company name. They were called 'Change Central' – an omen, surely. An interview was hastily arranged for the following Tuesday.

One of the rain beads had disappeared from view, no doubt having reached the metropolis by now. The other had become stranded in the centre of the window. Lee wondered which of these might best represent her own future.

Dad stepped into her thoughts for perhaps the third or fourth time that day. He might even she mused, have been proud of the initiative she'd shown. She stared out at the heavy clouds preparing to release several billion more drops of fortune over North Kent. She drew back her focus to the window's reflection and for a moment caught her father's eyes staring through her own – and then her mother's, too.

Five days later Lee found herself back in London for her interview. This time her inquisitor would be a Douglas White, Finance Director of Change Central. Her 2:00pm ordeal was fast approaching. She had meant over the weekend, to see if she could learn much about the company or the field of currency exchange, but there really hadn't been time to get to the library. And really, what was there to know? Take one currency, exchange it for another. Marks, francs, lire: their values changing according to the relative fortunes of the countries in question (she'd jotted that phrase down on her crib sheet). She was getting used to preparing a page of notes for meetings now. If she had learned nothing else from her recent encounters by appointment, it was that you should never risk ending a meeting with issues unaddressed. In this instance, the only real questions that mattered to Lee were confirmation of the salary, a starting date and whether she would be allowed to take May 26th off for 'an appointment'.

These items aside, Lee would need merely to convince her potential employer that she really wanted to join them. This job would if won, allow Lee to commute, relocate, save money at a reasonable speed and ultimately facilitate her transition. By the end of the decade she calculated, she might even have a life.

At least she looked serious about her intentions. She wore her most formal grey suit. It had a dark pinstripe and was probably the single most grown up item of clothing she owned – male or female. She wore a blue tie and black brogues. She even removed the ear studs – though it truly felt like a step back down her evolutionary ladder. She would need to avoid her reflection as much as humanly possible while wearing this persona. How did she ever end up in a position where the only way to becoming a woman was to appear more like a man?

The journey over to South Kensington from Victoria did indeed take no more than ten minutes – and that included waiting time on the platform. It really would be perfectly manageable on a daily basis.

She'd never been to South Kensington before. The station had a Victorian elegance, with wrought iron signage and grand white pillars. She could picture the entrance peopled by women with bustles and men in tall hats – rather like the silhouettes on the toilet doors back at *The Cow*. She found the office with 25 minutes to spare. Change Central was based in an imposing house – part of a white painted terrace, just off the main Old Brompton Road. She liked the look of it, even though it evoked still-recent memories of the Iranian Embassy Siege. She'd never worked in a converted house before. Perhaps it would be homelier than the likes of IGF.

She had time to walk around the neighbourhood a little. It was a fresh day, though not too windy. She needed her hair to stay mostly where it had been put. It was beginning to grow at a pace and was proving harder and harder to control – no matter how much hairspray she used. With about 10 minutes remaining until the appointed hour, Lee decided to make her arrival. 'Be early for anything important', Dad always said.

A brass plate beside the black painted front door featured the green Change Central 'double C' logo. Three buttons read from the top, 'Management', 'Administration' and 'Reception'. Choosing the last, Lee was answered by a tinny voice, she couldn't quite understand. She just offered the name of 'Mr White' and was rewarded by an elongated buzz, as the door lock released.

The building was at least twice the size within, as out. The carpets were deep green under crisp white walls. The sound of ringing phones came from deeper in, above – and even she sensed, below. Ahead, a winding staircase led up a flight and out of sight. Reception was immediately on Lee's left. She was seen before she had even crossed the threshold.

A glamorous young woman in a white dress with long raven hair and arched brows belonging to an era at least twenty years before her time looked up, "Hello, can I help?"

Lee stepped forward. "I'm Lee Habens and I have a 2 o' clock with Mr White".

The receptionist smiled a very white toothed smile. "Take a seat, I'll let him know you're here."

Lee made for a black armchair set next to a glass table. She placed her satchel on the floor. She wasn't using the shoulder strap today. Today her bag had to masquerade as a sort of briefcase. Everything was pretending to be something else today.

The sound of two people laughing hysterically wafted down the stairs from above, followed by an echo of scuffling footsteps and some frantic 'shushing'. Lee looked around her, taking in the modern furniture and subdued lighting. Could she really imagine walking through that front door every day for months on end? Years even?

She'd always been pretty good at interviews – at least the four she'd ever had before today. She'd been offered three of those positions and really hadn't wanted the other. She wasn't especially nervous about this encounter. Ideally it would be perfect to have such a quick and convenient solution, but the employment agencies had given her confidence that there would be other prospects. The dampened sound of a telephone buzzer cut into her thoughts.

The receptionist looked up again, "Mr White will see you on the second floor. Someone will meet you at the top of the stairs."

Lee headed for the flight upwards. She took the steps slowly, not wanting to lose her breath. Looking up, she saw a young man with short, strawberry-blond hair waiting. He was dressed in a fitted pink shirt and blue jeans and smiled at Lee as she took the last flight. 'Nearly there' he said in an accent. A black woman in a light blue blouse appeared to the man's side. She smiled warmly and laughed. It was one of the laughs Lee had heard earlier.

With one step to go, the man held out his hand. "You're Lee Habens?"

"I am".

"Well I'm Grant." The words were almost asked – like a question, with a lift to the tone of the last word. Grant, Lee felt sure, was Antipodean in origin. She took the outstretched hand and looked next toward the smiling woman who appeared to be holding off another burst of laughter – but only barely.

"Ignore her" said Grant. "She's not even really here."

The remark pierced the woman's all-too-thin veneer of self-control and she cackled heartily for a moment before adding, "I'm Miriam."

Lee offered Miriam a hand too, which made her "Ooh!" and then laugh again.

"I'll take you to see Mr White" said Grant, very pointedly pronouncing the 't' in White. "Miriam, I shall see you in my office for a stern talking to". Miriam sighed with final amusement and headed off down the stairs behind Lee.

She had met outwardly gay men before – one very intimately – but Grant was the very first *really* camp gay person Lee had properly encountered. It occurred to her that any freeze-framed image of Grant would fail to relay this. His appearance was completely unremarkable, if overtly neat. It was only when he walked and talked that you found yourself oddly fascinated by him. His animated sense of identity and expression reminded Lee of just why she needed to make her move. London let you be who you were, not what was prescribed. She momentarily wondered how long Grant might have lasted at *Rosanna's*.

After a short walk along a corridor to the rear of the building, Grant knocked at a door and then immediately opened it without waiting for a response. He stepped inside and extended an arm in the direction of a shirt sleeved man who sat at a desk, "Mr White" he indicated to Lee. The object of the introduction must have been in his late forties. He had steel grey hair and silver framed glasses. He was fairly grey all over in fact – and very, very tall.

"Mr White" Grant concluded, "This is Mr Habens".

As he unfolded his slim frame, moving to a standing position, Lee estimated her interviewer's height to be around 6' 5". She liked tall men – they made her feel less tall herself. She stepped into the room and once again found herself taking a stranger's hand.

"Thank you, Grant" Mr White said, a little tetchily, Lee thought.

"Oh, thank *you*, Mr White" replied Grant, exiting curtly.

The desk opposite Mr White's was unoccupied but bore files and papers in substantial numbers, suggesting it rather urgently required a resident.

"Please, take a seat" Mr White offered, directing Lee toward a plastic chair of the sort usually to be found in school assembly halls.

Once seated, Lee noticed that the wall behind Mr White bore various certificates and paper representations of his academic and professional worth.

Mr White peered over the rims of his glasses at Lee and then to the CV document prepared by the employment agency. "You've come in from Kent?" he smiled.

"I have, yes."

"As have I" Mr White announced, still smiling

"Ah" Lee acknowledged

"Sevenoaks."

"Oh yes" Lee offered in an appropriately approving way.

Mr White's grey eyebrows bounced with pride.

The next few minutes comprised a brief overview of Lee's career so far. There weren't too many highlights and so they moved fairly swiftly to what might lie ahead. The role would chiefly concern the daily monitoring of currency balances held at the London branches. Most of the time the work would be in the main office at South Kensington but there would also be a requirement to visit the branches around Central London. Lee liked the sound of that. Being outside and able to see some London life would certainly be a change from the suffocating monotony and unyielding four walls of IGF.

Mr White next established that the interviewee's mathematical skills were adequate and that there existed an awareness of what a ledger was. He appeared pleased to learn that Lee had experienced something of computer data. Everyone at Change Central would need to know about computers in the future, apparently.

"So, the prospect of commuting into London each day doesn't daunt you?" the inquisitor asked brightly, clearly confident of the answer.

"Not at all" Lee replied, feeling impervious to this level of probing. She'd recently had two sessions with a top psychiatrist at which the essence of her very being had been up for discussion. This was childsplay. She thought she might even venture a little ego-pandering, "I'm guessing that commuting has been a part of your life for some time" she said, without a flutter of nerves.

"Oh well, yes" Mr White replied, eyebrows raised. "Must be fifteen years now. I come into Charing Cross."

"Ah" said Lee leaning forward a little and demonstrating some interest. She'd heard that commuters were a strangely tight-knit bunch – mainly she'd been assured, so that they could share the weight of the huge chip they bore on their collective shoulders, "I'd be arriving at Victoria."

"Yes, I thought as much. Well now, that's just two stops away by Circle or District."

"I'd like to think so" said Lee with no more than the appropriately-sized smile.

"You appear to be a very confident young man"

"Well, confident – if nothing else" Lee had conceded, sending a signal that would never be received.

Lee's stay in the building hadn't troubled a second hour. It was one of the quickest such meetings she had ever had – and yet she still felt confident. Mr White had told Lee that there would be a final round of interviews and she would be contacted were she to make the shortlist.

With a brief stop at the employment agency to fill them in on her considered thoughts, Lee headed straight for home before the evening rush started. The agency called Lee at about quarter to six that evening to actually offer her the position of Currency Clerk. No short list, no second interview. What must her opposition have been like? She would start on Monday, May 14th. The agency even confirmed her day off for Friday the 26th. What she wondered, would her new employers say if they knew the reason for her needing that time away from the office?

Of course, Lee shared her good news with Dani first, meeting her friend at the station after her own daily commute from Canterbury. They went straight to *The Cow* for a celebratory drink, Dani calling home from the pub to cancel her seat at that evening's family dinner.

"I can't believe how quickly things are happening" Dani said, breathing out her first taste of a freshly-lit JP Blue.

"I know" Lee paused, setting off a Marlboro of her own in sympathy. "Thing is, I'm kind of getting the taste for change. I mean one minute I'm saying out loud what I want to happen and the next, it's actually happening."

"Yeah, I don't think it's all quite that simple." Dani cautioned. "You've had to push pretty hard – and there's a lot more to come."

Lee drew intensely on the cigarette and took the smoke down deep inside, "I suppose I don't really think I *have* pushed hard yet. Maybe the difference is that when you're focused on something important, something so fundamental, it sort of…self-perpetuates."

"So, what's next?"

Lee looked into her glass of house dry white, "Work, shrink, move".

So far, two weeks into her new role, life at Change Central was proving to be interesting and – thanks largely to Grant and Miriam with whom she shared an office, pretty entertaining. She had wondered whether she might be posted to the desk opposite Mr White, where they would no doubt have spent their days discussing the criminal deterioration in the punctuality of peak time train services. But instead on her first day, Grant had directed Lee to a desk in the corner of the room he himself shared with his erstwhile partner in crime. Lee's new colleagues sat side by side – a bit like newsreaders, she reflected.

Within a couple of days Lee had learned that Grant Jolley was actually from New Zealand ('Auckland darling, City of Sails'). He was 29 – though he didn't like to dwell on the number – and had arrived in London two years earlier. He'd been recruited to Change Central by a friend of his who had worked at the Leicester Square branch. Grant had very quickly made himself almost indispensable at the head office. Lee had already witnessed her colleague's prodigious memory for figures and ability not just to analyse a problem, but commit to a solution. If you needed to know what had to be done – and how, Grant was your man. He had responsibility for co-ordinating the network of branches and reporting on their performance. He managed with apparent ease what had apparently taken two people to handle in previous years.

Encountering Grant early in the morning Lee had learned, could be quite a shock to the system. He would already be in full flow before downing the first of many cups of coffee. Whenever he was out of the office by contrast, the pace could feel almost funereal. He lived, it transpired, in a large flat in Notting Hill with four other men to whom he referred (though only in Mr White's absence) as 'The Girls'.

Most days seemed to include a debrief of Grant's previous evening; tales of bad behaviour by one, other or all of 'The Girls'. Lee had noticed that descriptions of their activities had become ever more graphic as Grant had become accustomed to the newcomer's presence. She wasn't sure if she was more fascinated or terrified by what seemed to be going on in Grant's corner of West London.

Miriam Nash was from Battersea – or as she preferred to call it, 'Lower Chelsea'. She shared a house with her long-term boyfriend Lloyd and was responsible for just as many laughs as Grant, although many of these were borne of her own infectious cackle. At 25, she was younger than Lee had first thought. In the brighter light of the office, Lee was able to admire the most perfect skin of anyone she'd ever met. Miriam was genuinely approachable and patient – qualities worth plenty, given the sheer number of questions Lee had raised during her first few days. Where Grant managed the affairs of CC trade and personnel, Miriam was responsible for the buildings themselves and as Lee had already overheard, she could be a formidable negotiator. She loved arm-twisting suppliers and would take every opportunity to save the company money. Miriam had a catchphrase (one that Grant liked to encourage). She would only deliver it a couple of times a week, but always with aplomb. Stress was the trigger, caused usually by incompetent suppliers or some item of news Lloyd had delivered during the day. She would simply bury her face in her hands and cry loudly, 'It's *too* much for a black woman!'. No other words could bring more joy to Grant's day – and Miriam knew it.

Miriam was only the second black person Lee had ever properly met. Sittingbourne had one African family and Lee had been in the same class as their son at school. London was now opening her to the world. Languages in the street, food smells in the air – and most of all, people of every shade. She could feel herself growing in so many ways and she wondered during some of her short journeys to and from Victoria, at how small her old life had been.

When Grant or Miriam were away from their desks, the other would take up the strain. They were a terrific team. In fact, Lee was genuinely anxious about how to fit herself into their established day without ruining the rhythm. In the event, it hadn't proved too difficult. She needed only to listen intently to their tales and laugh in all the right places. It was an absolute pleasure.

Mr White – and he was always to be addressed as such – oversaw them all. Not much was known about his life outside of the office. He was a man who believed in order and formality and yet something in him seemed to crave human contact. From Lee's perspective, this actually made him pretty easy to get along with. She could engage him in conversation on a very predictable short list of matters, giving him the chance to opine at length and with evident pleasure. He may offer ten words to every one of Lee's but afterwards would clearly feel that fulfilling and friendly conversation had taken place.

Grant on the other hand, seemed to regularly perplex Mr White. Perhaps it was the camp mannerisms, the constant cheekiness – or both. Grant was smart enough never to stray beyond the pale or more importantly, to let his own performance dip. Mr White had no choice but to tolerate the behaviour of perhaps the strongest performer in the company. It didn't hurt Grant's cause that he also enjoyed something of a special relationship with the true occupant of the desk facing Mr White's. Mr Lincoln was a portly, bespectacled fiftysomething, responsible for buying and selling the currencies traded at the branches. He was a former 'City Man' who started work very early in the day and left at around lunchtime. Grant would report to Mr Lincoln on any trends, excesses or shortages around the branches. He would shout late orders up the stairs, whenever unable to reach the senior man on the phone. "Miss-ter LEEN-CONN!" would go the call, followed by something like, 'Canadian Dollar into Kings Road, one thousand!'. Pronunciation of the name 'Lincoln' would take on increasingly exaggerated forms – and simply knowing how much this irritated Mr White would be sufficient to bring on one of Miriam's coughing fits.

Mr Lincoln himself, never seemed to mind. He would refer to Grant softly as 'Dear Boy' – while everyone else had to make do with grunts and barked single syllable replies to their enquiries. For Lee, it was all a delight. For several hours each day, she belonged somewhere.

Change Central's Admin Office was more hive than house – it had to be. The pace could be furious, if cyclically predictable. Provided many of the regular tasks had been covered, it had become habit for Grant to organise a longer lunch on Fridays. Such occasions would begin with departure from the office at a quarter to one. Those invited would make for one or other of the pubs within safe walking distance for Miriam's heels, returning by 2:15pm. Lee's first and thus far only such experience, had been a trip to a 17th century inn, just off the Kings Road in Chelsea. The bar was immaculate in preserve and detail, though its most interesting facet – at least from Lee's point of view – was the label of 'gay pub'. She'd heard such places existed of course, but had never actually *been* in one. For Lee, this promised to be a trip to the far side. But if she'd imagined exotica, she was to be surprised. The attending cast had varied in size, shape and dress, just like any other cross section of the populace. Still, it felt like another step forward for Lee. There was nothing to fear it seemed, behind different doors.

Mr White had been true to his word and had taken Lee along on visits to several of CC's branches including Leicester Square, Shaftesbury Avenue and Oxford Street. Grant had also served as guide for a trip to the Carnaby Street bureau. This outing had been markedly more fun. Spending time with Grant – especially when it was just the two of them, was truly enlightening. He seemed to know so much about London culture and recent history – all the more surprising, given that he'd only been in the city for a few years. His self-assurance was extraordinary – and it had an umbrella-like quality that provided shelter for Lee while she was around him. Grant was the only man she'd known since Dad, who didn't use machismo to manage his day. Although wholly different in profile, these were two people who brought faith in their own personal qualities to the fore. Each were exactly the man they needed to be. Lee couldn't exactly imagine Dad and Grant enjoying time in each other's company, but she felt sure that they'd instantly earn the other's respect.

The more time Lee spent in Grant's company, the more she felt comfortable with his outlook. Here was someone who had made huge counter-cultural decisions about his life while growing up in 60's New Zealand. He must, Lee imagined, have felt terribly isolated in his cause and yet he had remained committed. Today, Grant was a long way from his origins – and he'd earned every mile. He was Lee's second hero and he hadn't arrived in her life a moment too soon.

London wasn't easy to leave behind in the evenings. For now, Lee would end each working day back in Sittingbourne. Although she'd mostly make it through the door by 8 o' clock, she quickly ceased to bother with dinner and had taken instead to falling asleep in Dad's chair – not to be recommended as an alternative to bed.

Ahead of Lee was a perilous three-month probationary period. Her commitment must be total. If she came through the trial, she would give notice to the council on No. 7 and would begin to pack her possessions. She had already begun to keep an eye out for rented flatshares in London. The ads in the *New Standard* seemed to offer prospects that were at least so far, rather more expensive than she had hoped, but Miriam said she knew of some agencies who might offer some affordable options. Lee had wondered aloud if her tough-talking colleague might manage rent negotiations on her behalf.

Dani had previously spoken of making the move to London herself, but through all the months of preparation and planning, hadn't raised it again. Lee didn't want to push it. She asked enough already of someone who didn't need to risk a stable life.

Fulham's *Greyhound* pub, as Lee now knew it to be called, nodded to its past with a central bar and stripped wooden floors, but the rest of the place had a brand new 80's polish about it. The clientele was mostly young and the drinks menu catered to their preference with exotic cocktails and lagers. The latter were served in their bottles and usually with the 'benefit' of a slice of lime being placed in the top. It was a new practice to Lee and she still thought it looked strange. She ordered a double Courvoisier and sipped at it while sitting at her quiet corner table. She still had the piece of A4 paper she'd taken into her first meeting with Dr Garner. It was now covered with notes – mostly paraphrases of the psychiatrist's answers, some supplementary questions she still needed to ask and other odd items of research. She could by now, re-write the document from memory if needed, but going over it one more time might just make her feel a little less nervous.

So far, being a patient under a consultant psychiatrist had installed in Lee a sense of legitimacy. For the first time in her life, instead of loathing the feeling of being different, she now felt almost proud of her rarefied status. She belonged with the non-belongers.

She surprised herself with a long, jaw-straining yawn. She really ought to be too nervous to feel tired. Would Dr Garner turn her down today? Could she be judged unworthy of treatment? Perhaps she could have done more; demonstrated a willingness to turn up in a dress to prove that she dared? She would do it of course – if that's what it really would take, but surely it had to be more sensible to transition in a way that could be sustained. She'd only just begun a new job (her progressive trump card to play with Dr Garner today). If she were to keep her post, she couldn't be turning up to the office dressed like a fool and expecting no consequence. Once again, the dichotomy tore at her. Earning the right to progress with her treatment, meant appearing more female – and yet in order to earn the money to fund her treatment to become more female, she must maintain some semblance of a masculine profile.

At least for today's appointment at The London Centre, Lee had the work-free opportunity to push herself a little more with hair and makeup – and on show today was more of each. She wore blue jeans and a long white shirt, with a low hanging belt over the top. What with the black eyeliner and small hooped earrings, she probably wouldn't have looked out of place at a Siouxsie and the Banshees gig.

Another glance at Dad's watch showed her to be still fifteen minutes ahead of on-time, but her patience had worn through. She gave herself the last of the brandy in a single shot, took a deep, deep breath and headed for the future.

Today's reception cast was rather unremarkable – there was just a rather skinny young guy who looked very unwell and appeared increasingly nervous the longer he had to wait. Lee suspected that he wasn't there for the same reason as she.

Dr Garner was apparently 'running a bit late today' which, what with it being a weekday, held no surprise for Lee. She was considering a second cup of coffee (because that couldn't *possibly* do any harm after a double brandy), when her options were once more whisked away by Donna.

"Lee, Dr Garner is ready for you"

"Not sure I am" Lee whispered to herself. Skinny Nervous Guy heard and smiled weakly.

"Lee – good to see you" smiled the doctor-come-judge-come-jury. "How have you been?"

Lee decided to start strongly, "I've been well – and have been making positive steps."

"Oh really?"

"Yes, I now have a job – in South Kensington"

"Well that's excellent. Congratulations!" There was the approving smile.

Even if she were being suckered, Lee couldn't help but bask in the praise, "Yes, and I'm now planning my move up to London to live."

"That is very positive." Dr Garner agreed, leaving a little pause before adding, "I take it you are presenting yourself at work as male?"

Lee felt as though someone had taken a sparkler from her on Guy Fawkes Night and stuffed it into a bucket of sand. "I – well yes, I have to really. I mean as I said before, I can't expect…"

"It's fine – your caution is understandable. I just thought I'd check." The smile was back, and the eyes twinkled a little.

Lee breathed a little more easily as she explained the nature of her work and outlined again her plan to use her new-found income to fund the move to the capital. Once living in London, she would be saving hard and would adhere to whatever was required of her in order to earn and maintain treatment.

"How do you see your transition…physically?"

"I'm not sure I understand the question" Lee replied – and she really wasn't.

"Well, here you are today once again looking…feminised – certainly to the point of androgyny, but what kind of *identity* do you see for yourself ahead?"

Lee was a little thrown. She certainly knew what didn't work for her and felt that she had a pretty good idea of what she could 'get away with' defensively, but she hadn't planned an *actual* future image.

Dr Garner broke the silence for her, "I'd like to get a picture of how you think your *personality* will manifest itself in a physical female identity?"

Lee started slowly, processing pictures as they emerged from a fog of imagining, "Well, I guess I'm not especially *girly*, you know? I'm not flowers and flounces. I'm tall – and I don't like that, but there's just nothing I can do about it. I know – at least I *think* I know – some of my limitations. I'm slim and I'm tall. I don't suppose I've been cute for a minute of my life. I guess I'd hope to project some kind of elegance. Does that sound ridiculous? I can't bear to be ridiculous."

"Yes, I think you mentioned that before."

"If I'm really honest, I'm just someone who prefers to live quietly. I try not to stand out too much. I've spent a lot of my time inside myself, if that makes sense." She checked the doctor's expression for encouragement to continue, "I sort of hope that a life will grow around me as I'm able to live more on the outside."

"That's a perfectly reasonable position to take. Of course, you realise that this process can often make going unnoticed rather... difficult." Dr Garner seemed to leave a very deliberate pause and then altered tack somewhat, "And how do you see your plans in terms of surgery?"

Lee shook her head a little and smiled, "There is only one surgery."

"A lot of patients have gone on to demonstrate otherwise."

Lee's smile disappeared and she spoke softly, "I just want to get rid of what shouldn't be there. I want my outside to at least *resemble* my inside."

The psychiatrist nodded appreciatively. Lee was accessing words with more ease. Feelings were becoming sentences she'd never composed, never known.

"What about anything more...cosmetic."

"Do you think I badly need it? I know my face is a bit...thin. I'd like to have a smaller nose, but so would lots of people – not that I have a budget for that kind of thing, anyway" she added.

Dr Garner held up a hand. "Once again, just asking. Some patients come in here with a long list of things they plan to fix or alter. I'm always interested to get a sense of expectation."

Lee felt herself relax back into her chair, not having been aware that she'd been leaning so far forward.

"My advice is to wait to see what hormones do for you. The effects vary hugely from one person to another, but they can be

remarkable – not least in revising soft tissue and facial character-
istics – especially with younger patients."

Hormones. The mention of them suggested promise. As if
they were indeed to arrive in Lee's life sooner rather than later.

"It helps some patients to keep a journal or diary as they progress through transition. It can be an aid to perspective as so much
around you appears to change. Do you keep any kind of written
record?"

"Well, I haven't. But that does make sense." Lee had spent
much of the last 18 months almost afraid to encourage reflection,
but maybe now really was the time to stop feeling pressured by her
hopes and start embracing them.

Dr Garner gathered in a breath through his nostrils in a considered way. "Lee, I've spoken again with your GP and based
upon this and my findings from our meetings, I'm going to pro-
pose that you begin a course of hormone therapy. These will be of
a comparatively low dosage for a month after which you will see
your GP for blood pressure and other tests and you will see me to
report back your feelings. Beyond that we may increase the dosage
accordingly.

Lee could barely breathe. She was aware that her hands were
shaking, but absurdly, she couldn't think of what to do with them.
"Okay" she said quietly and she hoped, calmly – as if she were
responding to an offer of milk in her coffee.

Dr Garner was already writing a prescription. "Now I'm going
to give you this, you can get it filled at any high street chemist,
though they may have to order them for you." He handed the
piece of paper to Lee who took it gingerly as if it were made of
fine china. "I am also going to give you this little fact sheet that
which explains some of the effects that these drugs can have. Now,
I should point out that you won't see much if anything happening physically in the time between our meetings, but there may
be some changes to your regular patterns of health and those we
must look out for. They're listed on the sheet. Now, you may find
yourself feeling some *emotional* effects quite quickly. It's a cliché
perhaps, but you may sense your moods begin to swing or become

more prolonged or intense. If you have any real confusion, concerns or suffer any major discomfort, you must stop taking the tablets and contact either myself or your GP."

"Of course" Lee murmured back, knowing that only the kind of side-effect that threatened certain death, would cause her to even consider giving up her new prize.

"Am I right in recalling that you smoke?"

"Um, occasionally. A little bit, yes." Lee admitted, applying a fully 'U' shaped bend to the truth of 'little'.

"Yes, well 'occasionally' will need to turn into a never. Smoking isn't compatible with taking large doses of oestrogens. So apart from anything else, you are going to have to become a non-smoker – immediately."

"Oh, I've been thinking about giving up anyway so this will just give me the excuse I needed." This time Lee was peddling an outright lie. Giving up smoking hadn't previously entered her head. Still, there in a flash, a non-smoker she had become.

"One other thing I should point out to you, any effects these pills might have, are at this stage, entirely reversible. You are not crossing the Rubicon just yet." He smiled his confident smile and Lee suspected that was one of his favourite lines to issue to new patients.

"Thank you." Lee wanted to say something more momentous. She did her best, "I really, really appreciate your confidence. This is honestly...I do need this." Messy, but it would have to do.

Lee could of course have taken her sweet time to get the prescription filled, but any kind of delay would have been intolerable. This was not a moment to defer pleasure – and as precious a piece of paper as the prescription was, she was desperate to trade it for something more than just a written promise. Apart from South Kensington, Victoria was still the only neighbourhood she really felt safe exploring – she worried about getting lost anywhere else in the city. She found a pharmacy just off the main Vauxhall Bridge Road. It was a fairly sizeable store and they were able to supply a month's worth of the drug. The pharmacist didn't ask Lee whether she had taken the drug before, perhaps assuming she was running an errand for someone else. Had she not still been so euphoric from the meeting with Dr Garner, she might have taken the time to feel a little embarrassed while waiting. But this day at least, she felt somehow a sense of entitlement. She almost *wanted* to be challenged by officialdom – if only to prompt the announcement that she was 'a transsexual in transition'. That phrase she considered, was going to need some work.

She was on an eastbound train within 15 minutes of leaving the pharmacy, well ahead of rush hour on what was anyway, the quietest day of the commuting week. Lee had empty seats around her. A hardened veteran of nine working days of peak-time, home-bound journeying under her belt, she luxuriated in the space and privacy. She took out the envelope Dr Garner had given her and read the guide notes to the likely effects of taking oestrogen. The first two paragraphs it turned out, were copied from the advisory note inside the box of pills themselves. It began:

'This drug is one of a group known as oestrogens. These are synthetically developed oestrogens and are designed to help girls become women.'

The passage was followed by a number of more clinical descriptions and definitions, but Lee was already lost in that first phrase. These were words she supposed had never been intended for the likes of her. She had hijacked the tiny pills, diverting them from their normal course. She clutched the paper bag tightly in her lap, feeling the potency of the contents right through the cardboard boxes and blister packs – and all the way into her gut. Her locked knees trembled. It was really happening.

She'd never expected to come home with the pills. She had imagined nothing more from this day than a verdict on her qualification for treatment. Lee didn't want to be alone when she took the first pill. She wanted her friend to be present, to share the earth's shake. Dani it transpired, did have plans but they agreed that if Lee picked her up at the station, they could at least have a little time in the car.

It was raining hard when Dani pulled open the passenger door. She held her jacket over her head like a tiny tarpaulin. Her shield hadn't functioned at all well. Sinking into the low seat and catching her breath, Dani stared over at her friend through plastered black curls and for a moment they said nothing – before bursting into shared laughter.

"Look at the state of *you*!"

"Well I didn't know there was going to be a monsoon, did I!"

Lee offered her the box of tissues always to be found on the back seats. Dani gratefully took a couple and set about mopping her face and forearms. The linen skirt she wore was properly soaked.

"I'm going to have to get you straight home." Lee said, starting the engine. "You need to get out of those clothes."

"Not until I see the little pills. Where are they?"

Lee smiled and reached to the back seat again. She handed Dani the small box. Dani grinned back. They were like naughty teenagers assessing contraband in a secret hideaway. "Oh my God" she said. "Can I have a look."

"Of course" Lee agreed, with mock nonchalance.

Opening the box, Dani withdrew a blue foiled blister pack of 30 tiny round tablets. They were set out on a calendar grid to assist taking at the correct dosage. "They're just like contraceptive pills!" Dani cried.

"Well essentially, that's what they are". Lee had read through all of the enclosed literature three times now and spoke with elevated authority on the matter.

"So, what exactly will these do to you?"

Lee recited from her leaflet, "Oh, you know: breast development, redistribution of subcutaneous fats, better hair and skin, that kind of thing."

"Wow, they sound great. Can I have some?"

"Yeah, but then there's also: massive mood swings, rashes, tiredness, headaches, nausea, weight gain – oh and apparently, all of my fingernails are likely to break off." Lee sorrowfully held out her best hand which bore a full set of half-centimetre talons.

"Okay. They're yours." Dani handed the pack over. "So" she challenged, "Is it the moment of truth?"

Lee took a breath and grimaced at her friend whose eyebrows were heading for shelter high up under the forest of wet dark curls. Popping the first Friday pill from its protective bubble, she held it up on an index fingertip. With a shrug and a sheepish grin, it was sent on its way. Dani applauded excitedly and they hugged.

Dani sat back, looked out of the window and added grimly, "I'm telling you now, if you get bigger boobs than me, I'm killing you."

Lee relayed the highlights of the meeting with Dr Garner during what was left of the ride back to Dani's. As they pulled up outside, she ventured a suggestion for the following night, "So do you fancy meeting at *The Cow* tomorrow?"

Dani hesitated and looked a little strained, "I – I can't."

"Wow, more plans?"

Dani was silent.

Suddenly Lee turned to her friend and slapped a hand against her own forehead. "Oh Christ, I've been so caught up in my own stuff! So? What's his name?"

"Rob."

"Rob" Lee repeated slowly – and then again, "Rob, is it? And tell me about the 'Rrrr-ob'"

Dani laughed "I will when we have time. Anyway, I don't want to jinx it just yet."

"Well at least give me the basics then. I need something – it's not like I actually have a life of my own!"

Dani counted off some facts on her fingers, "He's really lovely, quite tall, dark hair, a bit...older, he's a surveyor, he comes into our office quite a lot – which is how we met and he lives near Ashford. How's that?"

"Not enough!" Lee really did want more. For Dani to actually give a guy more than a couple of dates was rare – and this one sounded as though he actually had something to offer her in return. Lee was almost happy enough about it to ignore the confusing cocktail of jealousy stirring in her stomach. Of whom did she feel more envious? Dani, Rob – or both of them?

"I've really got to go" Dani said, holding up some sodden locks, "I've got a lot of work to do."

Lee smiled warmly at her friend and swallowed hard, "I have every confidence."

With a quick kiss to Lee's cheek Dani was gone, back out into the rain – this time without bothering to cover her head.

october 1982
house of shards

*M*y first journal entry. Not sure how long I can keep this up, but I'm going to give it a try.

It's a sort of happy/sad occasion. Marvin is gone – forever. And nobody cares. At lunchtime I signed the papers at the solicitor's office that officially changed my name. Now I am just plain Lee Habens. I have no middle name at all. I'm all the lighter for it. It won't become official for another couple of weeks, but the deed (literally!), is done.

Every day brings something new to my life – all the more amazing, considering the speed it comes at. But I'm hanging on. Each morning I get up in my new bedroom, in a new household, in a new city and I head off on a new route to a job that still feels pretty new.

Each morning I look in the mirror for some sign of physical change. Sometimes I think I can detect something, but it's a little hard to be sure of what's real and what is imagined (at least in a physical sense). It's like the first time you sit with your friends sipping alcohol. It's not the taste that matters – you just want to get to the drunk part and so you're wide awake on edge just waiting for what you've been told are the tell-tale signs.

I need to forget about taking the pills and just get on with – taking the pills.

London is letting me live – so far. I've heard so much over the years about how scary a place it is to live. To be honest, I can't imagine being anywhere else now. I'm still not missing Sittingbourne, but I am missing home.

Sittingbourne seemed like an awfully long time ago. Parting with Number 7 had felt – at least emotionally – like tearing out an essential organ. She was genuinely shocked at the way the move had affected her. She had of course, expected to feel that she was betraying Dad's memory – especially by leaving behind his garden. Dani had inevitably been a huge support and had stayed with her in the house on the last night. Lee hadn't really cried too much since the pain of Dad's loss had become physically bearable, but those deep, heaving moans from the gut, had returned during the last week of her residency. Crying alone scared her. The sharp breaths and shaking sobs could sound as though they were being made by someone else. For a while, the echo of grief rivalled the original haunting call and on at least one night, she feared she might never know peace again.

The administrative part of handing back the house was endless. Somewhere along the line it turned out that she owed the council several hundred pounds – though she never did properly understand why. The people in the housing office were quite helpful in arranging storage provisions for her at what were (apparently) very reasonable rates. So now, Lee was paying for one home for herself and two suitcases of possessions, while a second 'residence' held the remainder of her things – including Dad's chair.

She certainly didn't miss commuting from Kent. She had grown to loathe the steaming sauna of the train on warm evenings. She had been forced to stand more times than she'd sat for the journey home. She'd also been troubled to learn that she still felt an obligation to concede a free seat to any nearby women. Her identity may be in flux, but some habits weren't going to be ushered away quietly. She knew it wasn't entirely a gesture of politeness on her part, more a recognition that she just felt somehow, second best.

Her new journey to and from work was 30 minutes long – and it only very rarely suffered delays. Even when there was a problem on the Circle or District, she could switch to a bus. The car wasn't getting used very much at all during the week. She was thinking about selling it, but frankly given the atmosphere in her new home, it continued to offer something of an emergency escape route on evenings when the walls seemed to be moving in. Once behind the wheel, she could be out into the country in half an hour – and who ever knew that would feel like such a relief?

She'd been in the house for almost seven weeks now. Sharing with Tara, Caroline and Stuart hadn't been difficult on the surface – each behaved with perfect consideration and endless politeness toward their housemates. But even if Lee liked them, it remained an uncomfortable truth that she just wasn't actually *like* them. All of them were around the same age, it was true. But the other three residents had been acquainted for some time. Caroline and Stuart were a couple and Lee learned that the house had been rather cosily arranged until Tara's boyfriend had walked out in the summer. When she had originally come to view, Lee hadn't picked up on the delicate dynamic. Good, middle-class upbringings ensured that the sitting housemates were at least cosmetically full of cheer – and she'd naively taken them at face value.

Some other clear benefits had sold the house to Lee – such as its location in Chiswick. She'd never even been to this part of London before, but now absolutely loved the place. It had trees and tasteful shops and a calming high street with restaurants that made her feel grown up just walking past them. Best of all, it had the river – and she lived only two streets from it. The house itself was late Victorian with high-ish ceilings and fireplaces in every room. Lee had the room at the top (and paid a premium rent for it), but also had the blessing of a tiny ensuite shower room. She couldn't actually stand up in the shower as the roof eaves restricted headroom, but it helped to have the extra privacy – especially since she had taken to the obsessive annihilation of all and any body hair.

The main complaint from Lee's housemates (only ever politely suggested of course), was that she was a little too introverted and private – aloof, even. She didn't go along with evenings out very often and preferred to spend her evenings in her room with her radio or black and white portable television for company. She hadn't meant to cold-shoulder anyone, but living alone for more than a year had left a need to control the space around her.

At least after the first couple of weeks, the prospect of Lee being 'match made' with Tara had been removed from the agenda. She'd become aware of moves afoot – especially when seating was being arranged at the pub ('Lee, you sit here'), but she had been careful to demonstrate polite but casual disinterest. She had continued to push at the confines of her androgyny which had the happy side-effect of stirring an overheard debate about her sexuality. She had gathered through whispers in the kitchen, of Caroline's conviction that Lee was gay. The others had been quick to concur.

Liberated by her unspoken separation from the house mainstream, there had been an amusing and yet strange moment one evening when all four of them had been watching *Top Of The Pops*. A new band was introduced. They were called Culture Club – and the singer had caused some consternation.

Caroline: "Is that?"
Tara: "Wow. I don't know, is it?"
Stuart: "Bloody Hell!"
Lee: "Yes, he's very good, isn't he?"

Lee's preference for privacy was all the more in the weeks following. A great deal of concentration was required to keep her psyche on the daily straight and narrow. She had found the recently increased hormone dosage to be extremely challenging. She was now taking two oestrogen tablets each day and her body was beginning to submit to the daily assault of alien chemistry. The noises within her made isolation of the precise changes difficult to fix. Her feelings certainly seemed to have become less predictable; less controllable. Her previously-contained sense of empathy had become noticeably extended. An unconnected thought or a news item seemed to cut through to her core with a visceral intensity she'd not previously known. As a twist however, she also recognised a lack of consistency. Why should something be so moving one day and yet not the next? Perhaps this would be where the journal might help. Reading back entries might offer a little more perspective – just as Dr Garner had suggested.

The psychiatrist himself, had expressed satisfaction with Lee's progress – and in particular, her move to London. They had met a further three times since her graduation to hormone therapy. The conversations had been very much more focused on the future rather than the past. At their last meeting, Dr Garner had given Lee a letter – just a short note, really. ("You are going to reach a point in the not too distant future where this may come in helpful. Take copies and ensure that you have one in every bag or coat pocket. It has proved something of a lifesaver for some patients"). It was no more than a paragraph and Lee had first read it with some incredulity. Printed on the official paper of The London Centre and with Dr Garner's contact details in the heading, it read:

To whom it may concern,

Lee Habens is presently receiving hormone treatment as a male to female transsexual and is under my care. Dressing in female apparel and presenting a female identity is central to this treatment. Further details are available   from this office.

Lee had looked up quizzically at the author.

"There are still existing by-laws which make it illegal to impersonate a woman in public", he'd explained.

"Really?" Lee had answered, half laughing at the term, 'impersonate'.

"Really. But it's not arrest that should be your main worry. You need to be aware that your appearance can still be an issue for some people."

Lee didn't really need a lecture on the dangers of the societal backlash, "You would hope that we lived in more enlightened times."

"And we will at some point, I'm sure."

It may have felt a bit 'donkey and carrot', but Lee had already come to learn that there was one way and one way only, to endure the process of transition – and that was to adhere to her psychiatrist-come-gatekeeper's every instruction. Of course, she was still lying about the smoking, but had cut down drastically and was always careful not to have one on the day of an appointment. Her appearance had certainly moved on, too. Her hair was now longer than she had ever previously worn it. After what had now been an entire year since her last proper cut, it was at her shoulders. She liked it. She liked the way it looked. It had waves and since the summer, some lighter brown streaks. She also liked the way it moved when she walked or when a breeze blew it back from her face. She did find it a bit of a nuisance whenever trying to do something in a confined space. She had taken to tying it back when at home, which was rather novel as an experience. She took great care of her hair treatment-wise, but was reluctant to let a hairdresser near it for fear of male styling. After an entire 1970's of men wearing their hair longer, why was Lee's miserable luck to find herself corralled by a new era of sharp-suited office masculinity? In time, she would have to invent an explanation to offer a salon stylist – someone she could trust, who might perhaps not think too hard about the sex of the person below the hairline.

Her skin had become noticeably softer. She had used moisturisers for a couple of years anyway, but treating her face presented a different challenge now. Shaving was unsurprisingly, the real challenge. She only had to do it every other day as it was and the hormones did seem to have slowed the pace of emerging stubble. Such hairs as there were however, remained dark and hateful. Lee would become obsessive about removing any trace of beard, sometimes taking 30 minutes to razor the same spot again and again, fruitlessly chasing grey shadows rooted deep beneath the skin itself. Her face simply couldn't take the bullying and endured regular grazes and cuts making the later application of moisturiser and makeup sting.

She had also gained a little weight. She knew she had – even if it wasn't terribly noticeable to others. But there was at least one marked change she could cherish. Within two months of swallowing her first tablet, the outward shape of her stomach had noticeably altered. The top was still pretty much concave, but the bottom part, her belly, had become rounded and protruded in a characteristic that was she felt, identifiably female. It was a feature only visible when she was naked – and who was ever going to see that – but she was intensely proud of it, all the same.

Lee would have liked to have discussed the changes with Dani, but meetings with her best friend had slowed to a full stop. There had been a row.

It had happened in late August during a visit to Sittingbourne. Dani had been happier than Lee had seen her in a long time – almost heady, in fact. Clearly Rob, was having a profound influence. Lee had enquired as to how Dani's family were getting along with the new man and Dani was at first evasive and then clearly economical with the truth. 'Fine' became 'They don't really see a lot of each other' which in turn became an admission of 'I haven't actually introduced them'. When asked if even she herself might merit an audience with the mystery figure, Lee was met with 'Can't I just have something for myself?' It was very apparent that something wasn't right.

The early portrait of Rob had been as a kind and attentive partner. With Dani still so passionate and yet secretive, Lee was left to put one final question, 'Dani, is he married?'. What followed were tears and an accusation that despite everything Dani had done for her, Lee couldn't just be happy for a friend who had found her own dream.

Rob it seemed, was going to be an emotional time bomb for someone. Either Dani was going to be devastated or a marriage was going to end – perhaps both. Lee had seen a deserted partner close up. Somebody somewhere, always gets damaged – and it was rarely she felt, the person actually taking the decisions.

Dani hadn't answered Lee's calls since, nor responded to any of the cards that had been posted. Lee wanted desperately to drive back down to Sittingbourne to fix things face to face, but the prospect of both Dani *and* her father not wanting Lee in the house was so far, proving enough of a deterrent. She would persist with phone and the post and the worry – for now.

At least for Lee, her work life was turning out to be better than she might have hoped. Mr White hadn't even waited for the probationary period to lapse before confirming that the job was Lee's, permanently. Not long after joining, she'd learned that she was the fourth person to sit at her desk in just over a year. The company, it seemed, didn't want to lose another. Her salary had been raised to £ 4,000 per annum and she had responded by demonstrating a genuine focus and commitment to the cause. Grant and Miriam's efficiency and support helped hugely − as had the unrelenting pace of the job. There was supposed to be a recession on, but it hadn't seemed to affect the legion of foreign tourists who swept daily through London on waves of advantageous exchange rates.

She was taking the bus into the office today − just to vary things. She could do that now. At least there was something to see from the window of a bus. The tube offered only concrete walls or brief glimpses of the upper floors of buildings, before the train would again sink below ground, ducking the difficulties of Central London. No, the bus was definitely an improvement. She looked over the shoulder of the man in front and read his digital watch. 08:21. Making good time. As usual, she had been the first to leave the house. Maybe she just wanted out of the place more than the others.

The Routemaster lost Lee along with a third of its other passengers at the corner of Old Brompton Road. Perhaps the same number of replacement bodies passed and climbed aboard, the entire waltz around the back of the bus being completed in ten beautifully choreographed seconds. The sun broke through a slice in the heavy clouds, turning the elegant terraces of South Kensington into blinding walls of white. Lee had held a pair of sunglasses on her head as a habit since the summer − mostly to hold back her hair. She shook her head a little and at the same time, raised her brow causing the shades to slip neatly down onto the bridge of her nose. She had welcomed Autumn and the opportunity to get back into her long dark raincoat. Underneath, she was adopting a regular look of black cords or jeans and baggy sweaters. She was grateful for CC's lack of a distinctive dress code. Much of the rest of the building was still quite formally attired, but the branch admin office seemed to be allowed a little more latitude. This was not least due to Grant, to whom nobody was about to dictate terms – and if Grant got away with it, so could those who nestled beneath his wing. The exceptions to wardrobe-freedom were days when planned visits to branches were arranged. It was felt that certain standards must be observed when likely to be seen behind a Change Central counter. Those were the days Lee would once again have to encase herself in a suit and tie – a look that was beginning to appear as well as feel, ever more incongruous.

Passing through reception she exchanged 'hi's' and smiles with Cheryl. She liked Cheryl a lot – everybody did. She looked as glamorous to Lee today as she had on the day of the interview. CC's first face had a thing for 1950's style and it showed, in a good way.

Lee wondered that morning, upon whom she might one day base her own look. She gave up the idea before she had reached the second flight of stairs, it was still just too remote a concept. She didn't connect with anyone she saw in the media – except maybe now that Culture Club singer.

Grant was already in full flow, head down and tapping fiercely away on his huge desk calculator. He sent data into the machine at a rate Lee couldn't match using both hands.

"Hey babe."

"Hey" Lee answered.

"So, what's your news?" Grant continued to read from a ledger and drum buttons. Talking at the same time was his way of purging excess energy. He was probably beating out a rhythm with his foot under the table, too.

"No news. No life. No matter. Coffee?"

"Yeah babe" Grant's calculator hand paused and instead held out a candy stripe mug for a refill. Like *he* needed caffeine.

Lee finished hanging up her coat and collected the cup. She headed out to the small kitchen area. It was no more than a table in the hallway really. On it was a large hot water urn and a tray with various jars of coffee, sugar and powdered milk. When she returned to the office she found her colleague looking up at her and wearing a broad and knowing smile.

"So Babe, tell me about that home life of yours again. Are they all still diggin' your thing?" he asked.

Lee placed Grant's mug on his desk and headed back to her own, smiling nervously.

"Well I'm not exactly their cup of...well, anything"

Grant's grin was approaching Cheshire Cat proportions, "Mmm. I may have a proposal for you."

Lee's curiosity was piqued. She tried to take a nonchalant sip of her still-too-hot coffee, "Uh-huh?"

"How would you like to become the newest resident of one of the most exclusive and happening apartments in all of West London?"

"What?"

"Well I'm asking you to come live with us in Notting Hill, dorky!"

Lee must have been visibly stunned.

"C'mon Roomie – y'know you want to."

The rest of the day passed rather slowly for Lee. A rising sense of excitement repeatedly stepped between her and a deskful of work. Grant had explained that one of 'the regular girls' had left the Notting Hill flat after a period of some disharmony. Grant had been sotto voce at that point and some of his words hadn't actually featured sound at all. 'Openings' he had underlined, 'were rare'.

Lee's potential new flatmate had operated at his customary high-octane level of committed if camp productivity, as if nothing unusual was afoot.

Miriam was having an altogether tougher time of it. Her fury with British Telecom was peaking, "Roll on bloody privatisation. What happens when I buy some of your stupid shares? Who's your boss then? Eh? EH?".

It made Grant's day and he offered in a calming tone, "Too much, darling?"

"What, for a black woman, you mean?"

"Mmm"

"YES IT *BLOODY* IS!"

Lee had laughed along with her colleagues, though made little other conversational contribution that afternoon. She was anxious not to appear over-familiar with Grant in Miriam's presence. She was also a little concerned about Grant's reaction should she – as was highly probable – have to decline his invitation. Should the monthly rent exceed that she currently paid, this would be a step she simply wouldn't be able to afford. Then again, could she really continue suffocating in the Chiswick house? At least the dilemma wouldn't spin for long. It had been agreed that Grant was to take Lee to view the apartment that same night.

They had travelled on the tube together a few times before, but this felt different. Most of the usual elements were still there: Grant leading the way with an occasional guiding hand to Lee's back – even though she pretty much knew where she was going these days. There was the constant chatter about people and issues at work and of course the application and commentary of his never-erring 'Gaydar'. Grant believed with utter conviction that he could tell who was and who was not, gay. He believed he could do this on sight and that nobody could hide from his sixth and keenest sense. He claimed that his 'gift' was founded on the way men would meet his direct and intimate gaze – and what irresistible baby blues Grant had. The reddish blond colour of his hair did not extend to his lashes. These instead, were suspiciously dark. Lee had never questioned him about them, but close up she found their length and separation to be quite remarkable.

The walk from the tube station took only a few minutes. It was a comfortingly elegant neighbourhood. More large, expensive-looking Victorian terraces lined impressively wide roads with names that Lee found oddly familiar. They crossed Ladbroke Road and entered an area Grant explained was actually Holland Park. She was apparently never to refer to it as such however – it simply wasn't as 'cool' as Notting Hill itself.

They rounded a corner into what Lee could make out from a road sign was Moray Crescent. Grant halted at a black wrought iron gate leading to a hedge-lined entrance way. "Here we are then" he said. The few steps to the front door of a pristine-white corner townhouse were paved in black and white tiles. Lee looked up at the two floors above. Golden lamplight promised warmth and shelter within. Grant took the lead waving aside the large black front door to reveal a cavernous lower hallway. The temperature inside was certainly welcoming – and quite possibly Lee considered, bore a scent of vanilla. A large radiator to one side was hidden by a wooden lattice cover and the mantle above bore the remnants of that day's post. Grant quickly checked for anything in his name while Lee took in the small chandelier above them and the deep blue carpeted staircase ahead. Finding only a single envelope of relevance, Grant set off up the stairs, typically taking them two at a time. Lee tried her best to keep up but arrived at the top of the penultimate flight out of breath. The cigarettes really would have to go.

"Tah – and quite frankly, darling – Dah!" announced Grant, slotting his key into the door of flat number 3.

The world on the other side of the door was inevitably walled in white. Framed black and white photographs were hung at regular intervals. These seemed almost exclusively to offer images of male beauty. One featured a boxer, paused during a training session, his smooth ebony skin glistening; every curve and ripple of his torso accented in the half light. Lee would like to have studied the picture longer, but Grant was off ahead like the proverbial White Rabbit and had already ducked left, disappearing from sight. Lee followed and was greeted by more snowy décor in a huge living room. The carpet and twin facing sofas were pristine in their purity. Lee realised that Grant had kicked off his shoes on the way in. She self-consciously removed her own. She looked up. The ceiling must have been all of twelve feet from the floor. A central rose – whitewashed of course – dangled a modest chandelier into the room. Leaning against a wall to the left was the largest mirror Lee had ever seen. It had a rather ornate, gold-painted frame, the sort of thing that one usually saw bearing a painting in a stuffy museum. It didn't look stuffy here however.

Nothing did. Lee caught her full-length reflection and turned away in reflex before the image could mock her.

The wall opposite bowed out into a huge bay window. Lee noticed that there were no curtains or blinds. The room wasn't overlooked, but to a natural hider, clear panes did carry a worrying threat of exposure.

The room was lit by a pair of tall, standard lamps, each of which wore soft golden hats and served the room its warm glow. Music played softly from a stack system which sat on the floor next to the sofa opposite. Lee recognised Talking Heads' *Psycho Killer*. Seated close enough to reach the controls was a man Lee guessed to be about thirty years old. He wore a mint green silk robe which ended at the knee. He was sitting with his long, slim legs crossed – legs that were most definitely shaved. He held to his ear the receiver of a gold trim phone. Lee noticed that he had excessively plucked eyebrows. The man winked at Lee and she realised that she was staring. She averted her gaze shyly – but toward his feet. She smiled when noticing that he held a smoking cigarette between his toes, a glass ashtray strategically positioned below.

"Mmm, don't take any notice of *her*" Grant cautioned as he opened the envelope he'd carried up from the lower hall, speed-reading the contents, "we'll deal with her in a minute".

"Right, yes". Lee wondered how to even begin to *not* take notice of things.

Grant replaced the single sheet of paper into its envelope and filed it on a small shelf in the hallway. He called back into the living room, "This way! This way!"

Lee followed Grant into the next nearest room. A trio of spotlights lit a modestly proportioned kitchen. The wall units and cupboards had been tastefully matched in beech and fitted perfectly around all three facing sides of the room – not something Lee had ever come across for real. Dani's house had mostly matching white units, but they hadn't been all the same kind of size, like these. Grant opened a cupboard to reveal the contents of what it became clear, was actually a refrigerator. Now that was definitely something new. There was a large sink at the opposite end of the kitchen and another window with a view to the street below.

"Wine?" Grant asked already pouring white into a pair of glasses he'd produced from an upper unit.

"Um, sure". She really didn't need a drink and certainly wouldn't have thought to have one at this time back in Chiswick.

The tour guide handed a glass to Lee and then clinked his own against it, "Chin, chin".

Lee smiled and sipped obediently.

"So this is, you know – the kitchen. We all take care of our own and we keep it pretty clean".

Lee had noticed that it was in fact, spotless. She had wondered if perhaps it didn't see a lot of use.

Grant scotched the theory, "It can get pretty busy in here – especially at breakfast time, but we make it work." He placed his glass back on the work top behind him and picked up his satchel. "Well, so on we go!" He led off again back out to the hall. As they moved on from the kitchen Lee noticed a large movie poster, just to one side. It was from an old western and featured a smiling Jane Russell flanked by Clark Gable and Robert Ryan, their names stacked above the title, *The Tall Men*.

There was another corridor to their left along which Lee could make out two white gloss panelled doors to one side and one more opposite. As they passed down along the passage, Grant threw a fey wave at the first, "This is where our token 'proper man' does his thing. James won't be in until later but that's where he holes up. He's closest to the smaller bathroom so he tends to use that one. It saves him queuing up behind the girls in the morning." Grant doubled back, passing awfully close in the narrow hallway as he did so. Lee got another look at those too-dark eyelashes again. Pointing at the single door, Grant dropped his voice confiding, "This is the recently *vacated* room". He grimaced theatrically and Lee returned an uncertain smile.

At the foot of an open staircase opposite the living room, Grant turned and announced grandly, "And now it's on up to the heavens above!"

Thirty or so steps led up and back on themselves before depositing Grant and Lee at the uppermost floor. Clearly this one huge apartment could become at least two separate homes. A similar hallway to that below, presented four more doors.

"Now you shouldn't let this affect your impressions, but I have to warn you that there is an Australian and a grumpy Brazilian living up here. Rikki is the hag presently spoiling the look of the living room downstairs and Luka is cruising bars and probably won't be in until the wee hours. The boy will be moving downstairs shortly." Grant headed over to the room Lee estimated must be directly above the kitchen. Opening the door and flicking on the light in a single move, "Of course *this* is the room everyone wants to get into."

Quite what Lee had expected she wasn't sure, but the reality seemed immediately to make sense. The room was mostly the same uniform white as everywhere else, though not quite of such grand proportions. The double bed in the centre was resplendent in a bright rainbow-striped bedspread. Clothing was scattered along both sides and the double doors of a huge built-in wardrobe were open wide, revealing a crammed rail within. Each door bore shirts and sweaters, hung in improbable number. Above them an enormous paper globe of a lightshade was suspended from high above. A half closed black Venetian kept the world at bay, beyond a tall sash window. A white painted dressing table was covered in bottles of aftershaves and toiletries. There were a few items of makeup there too, pencils mostly and a hair drier perched on top of a stool, topped in deep velvet.

Grant dropped his satchel on the bed. "So, this is me" he announced, waving an arm in a grand arc around his lair. Lee was still taking it in even as Grant was heading back out the door, "And you...would be around here". She quickly scrambled after her host and in a moment was standing in the bedroom next door. It was long and narrow. Just about wide enough for a double bed turned crossways. Another tall sash window at one end looked out to what Lee estimated must be the back of the house. A built-in double wardrobe with slatted doors was ahead of them. The room was pristine and fairly minimalist. A tall black framed mirror leaned against the wall to their left while a flat-topped wooden chest next to it, doubled as a dressing table.

Lee felt Grant's arm wrap around her shoulder, "Yes, someday Grasshopper, all this could be yours".

A second voice came from the other side of Lee. A devil opposite Grant's angel, "And there, as they say, goes the bloody neighbourhood". It was a soft and yet hoarse voice, one honed Lee imagined, from years of smoking, shouting and drinking to excess. The accent was unmistakably Australian. She turned to face the flatmate from the sofa. He was as tall as Lee, though maybe a stone or so heavier in frame. He held out a hand which Lee noticed was tipped by red painted fingernails. "You may call me many things, though I will respond only to compliments of beauty and to the name, Rikki".

Lee smiled and accepted with amusement, a surprisingly firm handshake. "I'm Lee. Grant was showing me the room..."

"Yes, he does that"

"Now, now. Back in your box, you old hag. We don't need the likes of you scaring off a good potential tenant."

Rikki seemed to lose about an inch in height as he relaxed into a more casual stance and smiled warmly at Lee. "You look like a nice kid. If you *are* going to live here, that'll change of course, but I'm delighted to have met you in such an unsullied and virginal state. It's a bit like being in on the 'before' part of a 'before and after' ad".

Lee wasn't sure how to respond. She decided to simply comment on the flat. "It's an amazing place. Really, really lovely."

Rikki launched an eyebrow at the comment and Lee was suddenly conscious that she was blushing.

Grant eased the burning sensation in Lee's cheeks with a change of tone, "Right then, haven't you got a show to get to? From the looks of you, you've got an awful lot more getting ready to do."

Rikki shrugged at the barb and touching Lee gently on the arm confided, "She's harsh, but she's fair. *Really, really lovely* to meet 'cha then". With another warm smile, the six foot, silk robe wearing, nail varnished Australian turned and padded back out to the landing and beyond.

Lee looked back to Grant. He too was shrugging – this time in conclusion. "Well?" he said.

She simply hadn't expected to like the flat so much. Actually, *liking* the place didn't do justice to her feelings. She really loved it. Could she see herself living there? In truth, yes – almost as soon as she had headed back out into that dark West London night. The real question was, could she see herself being anywhere else? It was a beautiful home filled with people who seemed right for all the wrong reasons. And a drag queen? Really? Back in Sittingbourne, there weren't yet three outwardly gay men in the entire town, never mind at a single address.

The world was changing so fast, Lee reflected. People and places like those she had just left seemed to be at the forefront of a new kind of revolution – one that allowed people to live free of a fear of being judged. She wanted to be a part of the change. She wanted to take her place alongside the colourful and the confident, but could she really? She had to remind herself that she had only just embarked upon a carefully designed plan. It had a direction – and a strict budget to go with it. Could she really abandon caution at the very first temptation? Surely this would simply be too expensive a move at too delicate a moment.

There was another potential complication too – though she wasn't sure how much of a problem it might become. The famous Grant 'gaydar' had, she felt sure, identified her as gay. More than that, she could almost feel herself being positioned as some kind of potential protégé. Was that his doing or was she through admiration of a man who was already her colleague and friend, subconsciously complicit?

Was it she considered, any less of an issue to be mistaken as a gay male than a straight male? Being a part of an outwardly gay household could perhaps help her with other issues of confidence. There were definitely some shared challenges and sympathies. They lived closer to their own hearts than so many in the straight world. Theirs were colours nailed to an all-too-visible mast. Moray Crescent was home to the alternative collective.

The tube ride back to Turnham Green station passed in a blur of inward reflection. Prudence and conservatism battled excitement and seductive promise. Lee knew by now that she definitely didn't belong to the straight set in Chiswick. She would still harbour dreams of finding her place in that world – but only after some major changes on both sides.

The heat from the debate in her head sustained her on the walk back to the house. Hands thrust deeply into the lining of her pockets and chin buried in a white woollen scarf, she barely noticed the biting wind.

The house she entered was warm like a womb. She closed the front door quietly behind her. Doing things quietly had become second nature. She padded softly along the hall, pausing at the living room door. Stuart and Caroline were on the sofa – she reclined and with her feet in his lap.

Tara looked up from an armchair "Have a good evening?"

"Oh, yes. Just a drink with someone from work."

Tara nodded.

Stuart peered back over the sofa, "Did you want to sit down mate? We're just watching the news"

"No, I'm fine thanks" Lee replied with a smile. They were all so nice. She couldn't wait to get the hell out of there.

november 1982
view with a room

....

*My journal is the last thing I'm packing. Only Tara is down-
stairs. I guess she's the one appointed the task of seeing
me off the premises and making sure I haven't swiped the
silver. Stuart and Caroline signed a card that was waiting for me when
I got in last night. They're still in bed right now and I don't suppose
they'll get up until I've gone.*

. . . .

"My, you do travel light" Rikki remarked as he peered over the
rim of a pair of Ray-bans and into the Honda's open door. "Is this
really everything?"

Lee had a couple of boxes and some carrier bags in the boot,
two suitcases on the back seat and some heavier items of clothing
hanging from the grab handles inside of the rear windows.

"I haven't been able to move house in a car since I was nineteen" Rikki recalled wistfully.

Grant appeared to his side and muttered through chattering
teeth "You were never nineteen, hag".

Lee's new flatmates were up early for a Saturday – especially
such a cold one. It was only half past nine. Rikki looked rather
less extraordinary than the first time he had introduced himself.
He stood on the pavement outside the entrance to the apartment
looking deceptively unspectacular in jeans, a thick black, polo-
necked sweater and woolly ski hat. A couple of days of beard
growth also made him appear older. Grant looked pretty dishev-
elled too. He was wearing a camel coloured duffel coat and was

hugging himself against the brisk wind steadily funnelling along the Moray Crescent canyon. Lee guessed they'd probably both had a late night.

"Thanks so much for getting up so early. I'm really grateful."

"Early? Shit, I thought we were still in yesterday!" Rikki stood back and looked around distastefully, his steamy breath disappearing into the bright clear day, "If this is what you people call 'morning', you can bloody keep it." He pushed his sunglasses back up onto the bridge of his nose, "And you need to do something about the lighting too – it's friggin' fierce out here".

Grant sighed and looked apologetically toward Lee, "Early start, heavy lifting. I thought, y' know, call in a drag queen – that should do it."

It took them only a couple of trips each to empty the car. The kettle was hissing to a boil by the time Lee had followed the last of her things up the stairs. It felt odd to think that this was her new home. She wasn't really sure yet where in the communal rooms to put herself and so instead continued on up to her new bedroom. She was grinning as she arrived at the top. In daylight the hallway was so much brighter. Each floor had a tall hallway window out to the rear. Winter sunshine was pouring in as Rikki emerged examining his fingernails. Seeing Lee, he removed the Ray-Bans, "Well kidder, the last of your stuff is up. We've just put everything in there in a pile for you, but you're in, sure enough. No going back now."

Lee bit her bottom lip with an excited smile, "Thanks so much again – for all your help"

Rikki held up a middle finger in what might have been a provocative gesture, were it not for the now familiar raised eyebrow and mock tone "I have sustained a chip" he remarked gravely. "There is always a casualty. Always a sacrifice" he sighed, heading off down the stairs and calling back, "Tea in the kitchen in two!"

"I'll be right there" Lee returned, feeling oddly natural in her tone. Then she looked ahead and stepped into her new sanctuary.

It was amazing how much life could be crammed into a few bags. Unpacking them took a good couple of hours, what with the interruptions. And then there was the moment that side-tracked Lee entirely – Dad's tin box of papers. It had once been red painted, though any consistency of colour had long been worn or peeled away. Made of a triple layered sheet metal and about the size of a Lee's own satchel, it felt to her like a relative she saw only rarely and didn't really understand. It lived in the bottom of drawers or the back of cupboards and only ever surfaced during a move or particularly keen search for something else. Dad hadn't kept anything terribly valuable in there, it was just supposed to be a safe harbour for documents he needed not to lose. Lee had been through it several times since Dad's passing, but on being re-acquainted, found herself inspecting and opening it again. Handling things that had been of interest to Dad was one way to keep him a part of the mortal world.

She leafed thoughtfully through some financial records, insurance documents, some old cheque book stubs held together with elastic bands, Dad's passport, Lee's birth certificate (a document that surely *deserved* to be lost) and an assortment of official letters – some of which related to his later health condition – these she thought, she may dispose of. After all, there was nothing of Dad in the pernicious awfulness that killed him. Maybe in a way, she could kill it back. She returned to the passport, running her finger along the gold embossed seal of Great Britain and Northern Ireland. As she did so, a small envelope fell out. It was made of a high quality stiff paper – the kind in which one might find a card accompanying the gift of flowers. It hadn't been sealed, only folded closed. A single piece of paper was inside. Lined note paper, not of the same quality, but more likely ripped from a pad. It featured only a neatly handwritten address:

223 Calle Nueva
Constantina
Andalusia
España

Lee stared at the words in the address for some time, trying to map out reasons for the information to have been recorded in the first place – and then kept. Dad had only ever been to Spain twice himself. Once with his wife the summer before Lee was born and then again six years later when they'd all visited as a family. Her memory held some images of constant sunshine and the side-by-side smiles of her parents, but she knew better than to trust the flickering pictures in her head.

The envelope was dust free and showed no sign of having aged. What exactly was Lee holding? Was this where her Mother had gone? Perhaps where she'd be now? Had Dad really known? And if so, why wouldn't he have shared the information with Lee? She went over the address again – and again. She went over it until she knew the shape of every handwritten character. And then she placed the piece of paper back in its envelope, the envelope back into the pages of Dad's passport and finally the passport back into its own envelope before returning them all to the bottom of the tin box. She looked around the room for her options and then finally and with care, placed the box in a back corner of her new wardrobe on the floor, covered by shoes – where she'd never see it unless she really wanted to.

Lee sat on the floor with her back to the bed for support. A fuse was fizzing toward the darker half of her mind. It was extinguished by a knock at the door.

"Um, yes?" Lee called out uncertainly, as if defending the occupation of a public convenience.

Grant's head, shoulder and arm appeared. He had brought with him a mug of tea. "We take God's nectar very seriously around here, y'know."

Lee smiled "Oh, of course."

"You didn't come down, but I'm afraid you can't hide."

"Please come in"

"It's all coming together for you?"

"Slowly. I don't have much, but it seems to be enough to create quite a mess whenever it's disturbed."

Grant slid his hands into his back pockets and looked around the room, "There'll be a right place for everything".

Lee borrowed the sentiment, "Including me?"

"Most of all, you."

"Thanks, that really means a lot."

Grant sat on the corner of the inherited double bed, "There was never any doubt in my mind that once a place opened up here, I should offer it to you. You clearly weren't happy where you were and I just reckoned you deserved something better."

Lee took a sip of too-hot tea and sighed, "I suppose you can't underestimate the value of having a place that you actually *want* to come home to."

"Everyone needs one. Whatever you're here to do, this will give you a platform to do it." Grant smiled some intensity right into Lee's eyes, "Everyone who comes to this city is looking for something – whether they know it or not. Sometimes its work, or love, or adventure – maybe even a place to hide. Whatever you're here for, you've just given yourself a better chance to find it."

"So what about you, then?" Lee probed, "What are you here for?"

Grant's serious expression softened and his voice lifted "Oh, I'm here for a little of all of the above. And tonight, that means just enough *Crush* to make a weekend."

"What?"

"*Crush* is the club Rikki works at and we're going along tonight to see him do what he does."

A greater part of Lee had just wanted to stay in that night – to consolidate her move. The day had after all, been big enough already and an exotic night out felt like too much to manage. Yet she knew that having made the move, she must embrace new rhythms. She was after all, 'one of the girls' now.

Lee first encountered her newest flatmate as she was making for the kitchen. He was about her age, slight of build and really rather beautiful. He had very short-cropped curly dark hair and large almond-shaped eyes. His skin was smooth and Latino dark. He flashed a perfect, white smile when they came face to face on the lower landing.

Lee caught the look. It was fleeting, practised, but unmistakable. Luka had checked her out – head to toe and back again. She was discomforted. She felt as though she had been both assessed and dismissed in a single moment. Had he simply judged her the way he would a young male peer and possible rival? Was she being weighed as potential prey? Whatever the sentiment, the invasive gesture had made her feel immediately and instinctively wary.

"Luka" the stranger confirmed in a thin, raspy voice.

"Oh, hi – yes, I guessed so. I'm Lee."

"Your room okay?" he asked

"Oh, yes – perfect. It's just what I was looking for".

Luka nodded, still smiling but adding no more words.

"I was just going to make some tea…" Lee began, glancing over her shoulder toward the kitchen. When she returned to face Luka, it was to see the back of his slender frame disappearing into his room.

Later, on the tube-ride into the West End, Lee quizzed Grant about him, "I met Luka this afternoon"

"Ah" Grant replied with a knowing smile, his freshly moisturised skin shining in the sepia neon of the Central Line carriage. "The Diminutive Derivative – as Rikki calls him".

Lee noticed again that Grant referred to Luka in the masculine. Gender labels seemed very portable in the gay world, according to mood and levels of affection. Luka it seemed, was apparently not 'one of the girls' – even if he was naturally more effeminate in appearance than any of them.

"That sounds like a nickname with a story" Lee offered, hopefully.

"Well, I shouldn't really say this, I mean you've just arrived and I wouldn't want you to imagine that we're a house with issues…"

"But..?"

"Okay, well it's just that Luka is a bit…he's sort of slightly – well not slightly, I mean he is completely…"

"What?"

"*Chameleon*-like".

Not entirely what Lee had expected, "Excuse me?"

Grant hesitated, and then took a breath. "Luka was brought home one night by Ange – that's Andrew, who used to have the room Luka is in now. Ange met him at a club in Chelsea, I think. Anyway, when we first saw him he was all very quiet and polite. He was a bit of an urchin to look at – like he was straight out of Dexy's, you know? He had this quite long, straggly hair. He stayed over a couple of nights and then he was gone and we thought that was that – Ange was pretty promiscuous."

"Had you known Ange long?"

"A couple of years, I guess. He was another Kiwi and we'd been introduced by…Christ, somebody or other – I don't recall. Anyway, he was always pretty outgoing and never settled into any kind of relationship for long, so nobody was surprised to see the back of Luka. But then a week or so after, and Luka is back. We were a bit surprised but we just figured Ange was maybe a bit more into this one, than usual. Well after a couple of weeks, Luka was *still* in the house. He just never left. After a while, Ange just gave him a key and that was that."

"Did he ask you before Luka moved in?"

"Not really, no. It just kind of happened. But the thing of it is; Luka started changing. First it was the super-short haircut, then the eyebrows were being shaped…" Grant traced a pair of elaborate arcs across his own brow. "He was suddenly wearing the tighter denim and T-shirts until before we knew it, he just looked like a sort of smaller version of Ange himself."

"Didn't Ange see that happening?"

"No. I swear he didn't."

"Well, so did you and Rikki say anything to him?"

Grant shook his head, his eyes clearly spooling through scenes past, "He was in love. I mean, I'd never seen him like that. They went everywhere together, like a pair of twins. We didn't see very much of them really – just caught them as they were coming or going. Then things started to go wrong. Luka was a lot more confident and he was flirting when they were out. Ange hated it. They used to have huge rows, just in the bedroom – and you know those rooms aren't really *that* big. We used to hear Luka throwing things. Rikki starting hiding the breakables, just in case. Luka moved upstairs to your room, but he really wanted the one Ange was still in. About two months ago, Ange told me he was planning to head home. His visa was pretty much up anyway and he'd had enough of Luka. That's how we ended up with the hole in our household that you've so beautifully filled. To be perfectly honest, we were really hoping that Ange would change his mind and stay and then maybe Luka would leave instead, but it hasn't worked out that way."

"Wow" Lee sighed before wondering out loud, "He does pay rent and everything though, right?"

"Yeah, he does now. Ange used to pay everything – even the rent on the separate room Luka had taken. He works in a posy clothes shop in Covent Garden and he makes more than enough. We just told him that if he was going to take Ange's room, he'd have to pay the rate."

"So, do you and Rikki have much of a relationship with him?"

"Oh look, we all get along, but we don't really know him. He does his own things at the weekends and we don't see that much of him. It was just that seeing a person *transform* like that – right in front of you, y'know? You just can't trust someone like that."

Despite being a Londoner of some months standing, this was still only the third time Lee had ventured into Soho at night – and the first occasion accompanied. It was all dark corners and bright spot lights. Coloured neon whispered promises to anyone willing to stray from better worn paths. Exotic smells escaped from kitchens and mingled to create something even more alien. Languages could be overheard, but not recognised. People came to this place from all over the world to do things Lee couldn't imagine. Instinctively, she loved it. There were no outsiders here, only people making exchanges – Money for drink or drugs and sex for money. Trades being made against a race with the morning. Tomorrow Lee knew, all of this would be gone. But until then, everyone and no-one belonged.

The club was in a basement just off Golden Square. It was surprisingly soundproof. The pumping bass didn't really hit them until they began their descent from street level. A huge bouncer barred their way at the bottom of the stairs. He wore a leather jacket with the sleeves cut off. His arms seemed to be about the same size as one of Lee's thighs. He stood to one side of the entrance, looking past the two visitors. It was as though they didn't exist to him. Perhaps he was himself, more interested in being seen than actually seeing. A heavily moustachioed young guy in black matched their names against the guest list. Rikki had been as good as his word. They checked their coats with a scarily thin girl who appeared resentful at having to park her cigarette in order to exchange apparel for a pair of yellow tickets. Lee shared Grant's amusement at her discomfort and then headed down a further short flight of stairs.

Donna Summer was wailing about fingers on triggers as they emerged into an unexpectedly spacious area – apparently decorated by agents of the Underworld. The walls were a deep red, jewelled by occasional spot lights in blue, red and white. Two long bars flanked the main room. All of this occupied a raised level, with a dance floor several steps down below. Centred on a far wall, was a stage dominated by a DJ's desk. Behind it a mohawked man in a black T-shirt bobbed, busy cueing whatever would next assault their ears. Behind him against the raw brick wall, the club's name was emblazoned in red neon, '*Crush*'.

The venue along with another in Edinburgh was owned and run by Anita Macintyre, the widow of club entrepreneur John Macintyre and the majority shareholder of the holding company, Headrush Ltd. Rikki had told a story of how Mrs Macintyre had begun her career and relationship with John while working behind the bar at the Edinburgh club. They had been married for just two years when he'd died of sudden heart failure while away in Europe. To everyone's surprise, Anita had picked up the reins of the business and over the next five years had grown it beyond even the plans of her late husband. Her humble beginnings had given her a basement view of how to run a successful club business and she'd applied herself with certainty and drive. Staff often referred to her respectfully as 'Madame'. She was one of the first club owners to operate themed nights throughout a week. Gay nights, S&M – whatever would make a draw, Crush would give it a home – even if only for one night every two weeks.

Saturday nights were accessible to everyone and it seemed to Lee that a number of nightlife's United Nations had sent along representatives. Space along the bars was already beginning to fill. A few early dancers posed below. Some of them, Lee guessed, must have had some formal training. She watched a young woman with a shaved head and vest, topspin some moves that were beyond anything she'd ever seen up close. Almost everyone else she could see so far was male. Then she corrected herself, having learned better: Almost everyone she could see at least *appeared* to be male.

Rikki suddenly emerged out of the semi-gloom. He was wearing another silk dressing gown and clenched a long cheroot between dark red lips. The make-up, including staggeringly long false lashes was really quite scary close up, though perhaps only to Lee.

Grant seemed to be completely immune. "And here's the old hag."

"Aw, you came!" Rikki cried "Or to re-phrase – Ohhh, *you* came"

"Fuck you…"

Rikki joined his flatmate to complete the sentiment in unison, "and the bed you laid in on".

They air-kissed, neither wanting to share Rikki's makeup.

"God babe, you do look a fright", Grant said cheerfully as if delivering the most polite of compliments.

"Thanks sweet, it's all because of you – this is how you make me feel inside." Rikki turned to Lee, extended a red-taloned hand and stroked her cheek maternally. "Hi darling. Lovely to see you – especially as you had to make the whole journey next to this sad old queen" he nodded toward Grant. "Was it very terrible for you? Did she make you cry on the bus?"

"You look erm, amazing" ventured Lee, not quite knowing how to compliment someone for looking ridiculous.

"You wait 'til you see me in the wig".

"Oh, have you trapped it yet?" Grant interjected. "Bloody thing keeps escaping and going off on its own."

"Mmm, at least it's not my real hair that's leaving" Rikki nodded, looking just above Grant's eyeline.

"Drink for the bitch?"

"Ooh yes! Get me a glass of red, would you"

"Lee? What are we having, honey?"

"Oh, um, I'm not sure" she answered, genuinely not knowing what to order. She wanted to stay in control of her faculties, especially in such a strange environment. From the scent she was picking up in the air, she was pretty sure that even the sober would leave the place stoned. Her senses were stressed enough just pondering what might be coming at her next and while that did have a certain exciting appeal, she might settle for just surviving her first night and making it through to a long Sunday morning lie-in. "Could I maybe just have a coke or something? I'm not really that much of a drinker at the moment"

Grant looked as though he had just been served someone's underwear on a platter. "Bloody hell! We may need to do something about that!"

Lee laughed at her friend's appalled expression, "Okay, but maybe not tonight".

Grant left for the bar, leaving Lee to stand next to the extraordinary vision that was Rikki. She noticed for the first time that the tall Australian was wearing a pair of pink fluffy bedroom slippers.

Rikki caught her stare and shrugged, "You might laugh, but after three hours on your feet, you'd understand why" she explained.

"I'm sure you know what you're doing"

Rikki raised his glass to toast the sentiment.

"What is it exactly, that you…do, do here?"

"Well tonight, I'm just DJ-ing, so nothing too strenuous. Gone are the days when I would strut the stage and do a full show for an adoring public" she smiled. "Times are changing. I still get the gear on, but these days it's just to mime to the odd Bonnie Tyler or a bit of Divine. Mostly I suppose, I'm no different to him up there" he nodded toward the nodding mohawk at the turntables.

"Well, you're certainly different to anything I've ever seen". Lee hoped her remark would be taken as a compliment.

"Oh, bless you" Rikki replied. He looked a bit wistful in the semi-darkness, "You should have seen me in the old days. I don't suppose you ever saw the inside of a real drag club?"

"I really didn't" replied Lee, who really hadn't – and frankly wouldn't have ever known where to have begun looking for one.

"Oh, some of the most beautiful boys you could imagine – and some of the dodgiest old creeps, too."

"When was this, exactly?"

"The dying days of the real Soho" Rikki explained, "mid 70's. I got to London just in time to catch the end of the party. There were four or five great clubs you could work, back then. We were like exotic birds, colouring the lives of a grey audience." The memory faded from his painted face and was replaced by a smile of resignation, "These days, half the punters are wearing more makeup than me. They bring their own colour."

"I suppose that's a good thing for them though, isn't it? These are at least, better times – you know, to be…different"

"That, they are. Oh, to be young now." He narrowed his eyes and smiled sideways at Lee, "You know, you'd have done okay at drag. You've got good skin. Do you moisturise?" He stroked Lee's cheek again and she let him without flinching. She found herself quite enjoying the intimacy of friendly human contact. She noted the comment as a compliment too.

Rikki had to head backstage shortly after the drinks arrived. Within half an hour he emerged on stage in a plume of dry ice and to the opening strains of Depeche Mode's *Just Can't Get Enough*. His familiar Aussie rasp cut through both, "Well good evening boys, girls *and* others. Well nobody said the 'D' in DJ had to stand for Disc…"

The volume had been building. By now you pretty much had to shout directly into the ear of your neighbour to be heard. Grant did just that, "If I've heard her use that line once, I've heard it a hundred times"

Lee noticed when he stepped back from her that Grant was nonetheless smiling. "It is true though, I suppose." she called back.

The music was a mixture of 70's Disco-in-Irony and New Romantic in earnest. Everything was greeted enthusiastically – a sign that the atmosphere had achieved just the right blend of heat, noise, pheromones and marijuana. The main floor was never less than full and people were pretty much dancing everywhere. Even the guys behind the bars were moving in time to the music. There were three serving on each side – and all of them had dispensed with shirts. For Lee, it was a strange celebration of masculinity. There were the same lusty chases that she knew were being played out in clubs all around the country at that very moment. What was missing she realised, was conformity. There were different 'looks' at every quarter. There was no official right or wrong way to appear, move or even watch. She couldn't recall being among so many men without any sense of threat.

Grant had been approached a couple of times by guys. Lee was pretty sure he must have known them. The greetings had a certain openness. Suddenly there was tap at her own shoulder. She turned to be met by a tall, red-shirted blond. She imagined his age to be around 30. Beyond that, she had no idea who he was or what he could possibly want. He was awfully close – though in fairness, that was the only way to make himself heard.

"Are you with anyone?"

"Um, well I'm with my friend"

"Can I get you a drink?"

"Well I do already have one" Lee replied, holding up her second coke of the evening.

Red shirt nodded intensely – and then disappeared back into the crowd.

"He was cute" somebody shouted.

Lee turned to realise that the comment had come from Grant. "Uh, he was" she replied while thinking to herself 'was he?'

"Not for you though?"

"Not for me."

It wasn't the first time Lee had woken in a strange room, confused by where she was and how she had come to be there – but this morning she was surprisingly calm about it. Perhaps the lack of panic or worry had something to do with the sheer rate of change her life was experiencing. Almost every day seemed to bring something new. Today it was the very first morning in her new bedroom. She lay on her side and let her back send out sensory feelers to check whether there might be anyone behind her. She had arrived home perfectly sober last night she now recalled, but what with every corner potentially hiding a surprise these days, it did seem reasonable to expect the unreasonable.

She'd had to make her own way back after *Crush*. Grant had paired off with a bearded American student and Rikki would be at the club until about 4:00 am, as a matter of routine. The apartment had been silent when she arrived. She hadn't heard anything as she'd passed Luka's room and so imagined him also to be out doing whatever he did. It had been almost 3 o' clock on Sunday morning when she'd turned out her new bedside lamp and now, however many hours later, there were piercing blades of light forcing their way through venetian slats. She pulled focus on the red digits of her clock radio. It was in fact, 10:17. She rolled onto her back. Her hands were under the duvet and she let them fall onto her stomach. She ran her fingers down until they arrived at her little bump of a belly. Right now, along with her longer hair, it was the only part of her body she actually valued. She slept in just a pair of briefs these days. Enough at least, to cover the unbearable. A deep breath and a two-stage stand later, Lee was greeted by her reflection in the full length mirror she had inherited. (Luka had apparently wanted to take it, but it hadn't been his to begin with – as Grant had been quick to point out). As usual upon waking, Lee needed to pee and this had had the worst possible effect on her maleness. The thing stuck out, half rigid, held to one side by the fabric of her underwear. She stared at it in disgust. Sometimes when she saw it like this, she wondered if it were actually possible to break it off. She tried to ignore it, picked up a long-toothed comb and ran it through her hair as she took a bottom to top excursion along the reflection of her full frame. Still too straight and featureless. She looked at her legs. They were a bit stubbly and the drag of strong new hairs against sheets had caused the usual red rash around her upper, inner thighs. Full leg shaves hadn't been easy in the tiny ensuite at the Chiswick house. She wondered if the process would be any more manageable here. At least she had the comfort of knowing that Rikki was probably suffering in the same way – albeit without the secrecy.

There had been no real advance in breast growth. There was certainly a hardening behind her nipples though, almost as if a pair of buds were gathering themselves to flower, but she'd had these for a while now and she was beginning to think that there might not even be a next step for them to take. She was probably just expecting too much, too soon. Dr Garner had warned against that.

She grabbed her towel and dressing gown from the back of the door and ventured out onto the landing. To hell with it, she would risk her shaved calves being seen. Maybe that would be the first habit to change under the new roof. She listened at Grant's door. There were no sounds of snoring – or anything else. She guessed he must have gone back to wherever the American lived. She padded on down the stairs, made a quick visit across the landing to the bathroom to wash and rid herself of the loathsome protrusion, and then headed for the kitchen.

As the kettle hissed into life, she took in the view from the kitchen window. A low wintry sun brightened the mixed sky and lent colour to the trees and street furniture outside. Otherwise, everything was pure, pristine, Notting-Hill-come-Holland-Park white. She stood on tiptoe trying to crane a look as far up the street as was possible, idly twirling a lock of hair as she scanned the row of parked cars for sight of her own.

The soft hallway carpet masked his approach, leaving the silence vulnerable to the rumble of a deep and dark voice, "Morning stranger."

"OH, B-JEEESUS!" Lee simultaneously spun back into the room, dropped to her heels and clutched her dressing gown to her chest. She didn't have any Irish descendancy and had never actually uttered such an exclamation before. On reflection, she concluded that it had probably been a combination of 'bloody hell' and 'Jesus', delivered through panic.

The man with one hand on the fridge door was clearly amused at her state, "Are you visitor or resident?"

Lee tried to recover her Anglo dignity. Fridge Man's looks weren't making matters any easier. "I'm new" she stumbled, cursing her own stupidity. What was this, *primary school?* "I'm Lee, the new…person" she added, further compounding her inner wince.

"James" greeted James, extending the traditional hand.

Lee took a moment and then reciprocated, trying to measure the appropriate return for his firm grip. She didn't want to be overly butch about it, but was somehow reluctant to be considered just another member of the effete set. James was perhaps six feet two in his bare feet. He had wavy brown hair, green eyes and even in faded old Levi's and a baggy rugby shirt, he cut an athletic figure. It occurred to Lee that for anyone actually *aspiring* to be male, James offered about as ideal an image as one might aim for.

"So, how was your first night here?" he asked in an accent that suggested public school.

"Um, *interesting*. I went out with Grant to see Rikki at his club"

"Oh yeah, *Crush*, isn't it? Just off Regent Street somewhere?"

"Yes, have you been?"

James smiled broadly, "No. A bit more trouble than it's worth for me. There are only so many times you can hear yourself explain 'I'm straight', before it actually does start to sound like an excuse."

"Oh, yes of course". The kettle bubbled to the boil and Lee reached for an extra tea bag, "Would you like..?"

"Coffee for me" James replied, opening a cupboard and selecting his preferred mug. After a quick pour and stir of instant, James headed back out of the kitchen before turning and asking, "Have they shown you up top yet?"

"Up top?"

She had wondered what the A-frame ladder was for. When she'd first noticed it on the landing outside her bedroom, she'd assumed it was needed for repairing something or perhaps some decorating. She hadn't imagined it to be used as a final flight upwards. James steadied the steps, climbed up and opened the hatch Lee had assumed led to an attic. It became clear that this was instead a roof access. After the quick recovery of a pair of trainers, Lee headed up to join James, the pair combining to safely transport the steaming mugs. The morning chill took the first few breaths away from Lee, but as she calmed her pulse and adapted to the slice of breeze on bare ankles, she began to fully appreciate the astonishing view around her. It must only have been another twenty feet or so of elevation above the kitchen window, but it made all the difference. The flat section of the roof was surrounded by a raised sill which edged the build-ing's border. You could see about 200 degrees around before the pitched rooftop of the adjacent house blocked the view further. Lee could make out the river to the south and Post Office Tower to the east.

"Not bad, is it?" James said raising his mug of coffee appreciably.

"Amazing" commented Lee, inadequately.

"The weather hasn't been especially accommodating for a while, but when I saw the sunshine this morning I thought I had to get up here."

Autumn continued to meddle with Lee's inappropriate attire, stirring the sore bristles on her thighs. She wasn't sure how much longer view would win over comfort.

"On summer days it can get pretty hot up here. Back in July, we had the hatch open most days."

Lee looked at her most recently discovered flatmate. "How long have you been living here?"

"Just about 18 months now"

"You like it?" Lee was curious about the dynamic of having a straight man living alongside such 'alternative' company.

"Yeah, I suppose I do. It's pretty strange sometimes, but for the most part it's got what you need. The address is great, the space is excellent and the place is always…"

"Neat and tidy?" Lee ventured, grinning.

"Yeah, absolutely" James laughed. "It may be a bit of a gay stereotype, but that doesn't stop it being true".

Lee thought she'd test her own bravery "You don't mind living with gay guys?" She was conscious that she'd at least hinted at a fraternal link between her and the others.

"I really don't, no. They do their thing and I do mine. They're good guys." He reflected for a moment and added "A bit freaky, sometimes – granted, but they've been good friends".

Lee pulled her dressing gown tighter around her legs, conscious of the gesture, "How did you come to be here?" she asked.

James shook his head as though trying to quickly shuffle the memories into order, "I suppose it was Andy I knew first – through work".

Lee noted that 'Andy' was how the straight world must have known 'Ange'. "Oh right. And what is it that you do?" Lee quickly added, wondering if she wasn't stacking the questions a little too high.

"Oh, boring really. I work for the investment arm of an oil company. It's mostly evaluating venture capital opportunities, that sort of thing."

"Oh."

"Yeah, exactly. Boring" James laughed and Lee joined him, having been hoist by her own single-syllabled reply.

"But that's where you met An..dy"

"He had the desk opposite. I'd just broken up with my girl-friend of the time and needed a place to crash – quickly. To tell you the truth, I expected to only be here for a couple of months, but then I just thought, what the hell."

There was a silence for a few moments. Lee was using it to summon up another question. She hadn't realised that James was doing the same. Their opening words emerged in the same instant: James' "You.." playing Lee's "Isn't..".

"Sorry, you first" Lee offered.

"No, I insist" James insisted.

Lee was charmed by the politeness. She liked the way it made her feel. She wasn't sure if her continued curiosity would sour things, but she pressed ahead to a place she had no business visiting, "Doesn't it make it a little difficult for you to bring anyone here? The *differences*, I mean."

James took the question in without prejudice, "Not really. I don't have much of a social life. I play a bit of rugby, I go out with some of the guys after work, that's about it."

He hadn't actually touched on the subject Lee was really interested in, but by not mentioning a partner, he sort of had. She wasn't foolish enough for a moment to imagine that anything could happen between them, but she liked the frisson of excitement that came with even the remotest of possibilities. They were just two single people standing together. It might take a nuclear wipeout for such a prospect to make any kind of sense to a beautiful straight guy like James, but those odds would do for now.

march 1983
pins and needs

*M*y hair is now past my shoulders. If I tip my head back, I can feel it fall on my back. It's the strangest feeling – and I love it. It really annoys me that I could have had this years ago. I wonder how much hair I've been forced to cut off over the years for no good reason. It is getting me into trouble at work though. Mr White makes at least one remark a week now. So far I just ignore it, but what do I do if he insists I have it cut? I can't lose my job – that would be unthinkable. But at the same time, I can't reverse my own 'feminisation' (Dr Garner's word) – that would completely defeat the whole object.

I've been using my hair to keep out unwanted attention too. If you can't see them they're not really there!

Had a really good look at my face this morning. I studied every feature really closely and I think there's a rounder shape to things – especially around the cheeks. This is probably what Dr Garner was talking about when he told me to wait and see what the hormones would do.

When I look in the mirror, close one eye and squint a bit with the other, I can almost see a future.

. . . .

She loved the sound of rain on an umbrella. She loved it almost as much as she cherished the privacy of walking with a black protective dome around her. Grant claimed that everyone looked better under an umbrella – something to do with the top light being toned down. He sounded like he knew what he was talking about.

Lee didn't ordinarily head out for walks when the rain came, but today she needed to clear her head. She wasn't sleeping properly at night or delivering as well as she might, during the day. She'd been trying all morning to learn some of Miriam's duties in advance of her colleague's forthcoming Easter holiday. She'd almost nodded off a couple of times and had to apologise profusely to her tutor. Miriam looked a little put out, but saying sorry seemed to help and Lee promised to do better after lunch. She would cross the Fulham Road and spend a couple of minutes by the river. Moving water always seemed to put things in perspective.

The money wasn't accumulating fast enough. The worry was a distraction and it was beginning to cast a shadow over everything else. Her research had told her that she would need to draw together around £7,000 to add to the savings she already had. It was a huge amount – almost double what she could make in a year. That would get her through the electrolysis, shrink bills (which ironically grew), and the main surgery. Of course, she'd already been warned that surgeons raise their prices with inflation too and so you could probably put another grand on top of that figure by the time 1987 arrived. Times like these made everything seem so remote. She had in some ways, come a long way since that first visit to Dr Jones' surgery. But then there were the moments of doubt. That she should be trying at all was never at issue – she recognised that she'd never really had a choice about that – but did she have what it would take to finish what had been started? Could she come up with the necessary resources – financial and otherwise?

The cost of day-to-day life was defeating her, pushing her back down the steep slope she was trying so hard to climb. Her room at the flat cost more than she had budgeted – and so did everything else. She kept running the numbers. How was she was only barely managing to save £150 a month? She was turning down pretty much every invitation to go out in the evenings and bringing in her own lunches from home. Only one further economy remained to be made: Soon, she would head back to Kent to recover or dispose of the things she'd left in storage – she simply couldn't afford to pay for warehousing any longer. Beyond this, it was hard to see what else she could do. She could always move to another house

in a cheaper area. But how much would she realistically save –
and what kind of environment might she inherit? Moray Crescent
gave her so much in terms of protection and a sense of confidence.
Yes, it was expensive, but its true value was beyond mere money.

If she couldn't cut costs, Lee would have to do something about
her income. Grant said he didn't see any pay rises coming at CC
this year. The papers seemed sure of an election this coming summer. Maggie was certain to be returned after the whole Falklands
thing and that meant times would stay tough for a while. Changing
jobs wasn't she felt, a realistic option. Instead, she would need to
take a second one. Passing a showroom she caught her reflection
in a glass pane. She cut a figure that at a glance, might just perhaps
be taken for female – at least from some angles. She turned from
left to right, studying her image – until eyed by a sales assistant
within, prompting her to blush and move along.

The hissing of tyres on wet tarmac grew louder as she arrived
at the Fulham Road. Once across, her mind drifted again. The first
electrolysis session was approaching. She had found a beautician
called Carol who practised from a private clinic in Earls Court.
While there, two weeks before, she'd had an initial consultation
(more money), at which the treatment was applied to a sample
area. Carol had worked on the area where a sideburn would normally be (had Lee ever actually grown one). It was explained that
there would of course be pain involved – and plenty of it. Lee
learned that every hair had three growth stages and that therefore
each follicle would need to have an electric current applied on at
least three occasions – more if they were stubborn. An average
beard was possessed of 30,000 individual hairs. Even a young face
like Lee's would likely take three years of regular attention. She
would need to visit at least once every couple of weeks and would
have to leave a small patch with some growth each time for Carol
to work on. Lee hadn't quite figured out how she would be leaving these little islands of hair on her face without attracting odd
glances. She could start with the sides she supposed, although it
had been explained to her that the most dense areas of hair growth
were around the top lip and chin and these really ought to be the

priority. By unhappy coincidence, these were also the most painful sites, as they covered areas of intense sensitivity. The rule was: the closer to the lips, the more work you need and the sharper the pain.

Lee was quieter than usual on the tube journey home with Grant that evening. Ordinarily her colleague and flatmate would have simply filled the vacuum with as many of his own words as possible.

He clearly recognised that there was a problem, "Are you going to share it?"

"Mmm?"

"The burden that is clearly weighing so heavy on your slinky shoulders"

"Oh. I don't know" Lee tried to shrug her mood away dismissively, but then accepted the offer to express. "It's just that I need to make more money – somehow."

"Well don't we all, sunshine"

"No, you don't understand. It's just, I'm saving for something and I just really need to get the money together by a certain time. It's like a target I've set myself".

"Well, targets are good" Grant acknowledged approvingly.

"Yes, but not when you see yourself falling behind. I just can't seem to make any real headway. I save what I can each month, but it doesn't seem to amount to much."

"You could always sell your body".

Lee groaned "Sure"

"Well okay – sell *my* body. I don't mind" he offered cheerfully. "I think it's called pimping. Funny word that. *Pimping*", he repeated to himself.

Lee turned to look out of the window, following the lines of piping on the tunnel walls as they rose and fell on their parallel trajectories.

Grant clearly felt obliged to do better with his suggestions, "C'mon" he urged, standing up and in the same move taking a firm grip of an overhead grab handle, just as the train braked into High Street Kensington, "You need a drink."

"I'm not sure I do."

"Well then, *I* need a drink."

Henry's was an American-styled bar just off the main High Street. Every surface – including the ceiling – was lined with road signs and other US memorabilia. The place was sparsely populated so far, the hour being early, but music took up the slack. Michael Jackson's *Billie Jean* pounded off the walls (just as it seemed to, everywhere). Grant bought Mexican lagers and they took to a pair of high stools at a centre table.

Grant served. "Miriam said you weren't yourself this morning."

Lee sighed as she stared at her bottle's label, "I know. I really must apologise again to her tomorrow morning."

"So what's going on, Babe? What's got you so distracted all of a sudden."

Lee looked rueful, "I only wish it were just today. Truth is, I'm all over the place."

Grant took a slug of cold, fizzy beer, "Then pull it back. Get some focus. Sometimes all you really have to do is to understand problems for what they are. You have to get some perspective. Once you do that the solutions are obvious."

Lee grinned sceptically, "That simple, eh?"

Grant was emphatic, "Just that simple. Maybe you're trying to start by thinking too much about the solution. I'm telling you that the solutions are the easy part. It's the problems you need to really understand."

"If you say so."

"I can prove it if you tell me what's going on."

There it was. The first time Lee had been challenged to discuss her situation with someone who wasn't part of her programme of treatment – and also wasn't Dani." Lee studied the man who faced her again. Could Grant really handle this? Of course he could – nothing would surprise him, Lee felt sure. She kissed some beer and snapped to a decision, "Do you understand the term, gender reassignment?" she asked, feeling goose bumps spread down from the crown of her scalp.

Grant smiled, inscrutably.

"I'm undergoing treatment" Lee added evenly. "I'm nearly a year into it now."

Still no words from Grant. He had conceded the floor.

"It's difficult and it's...expensive."

Grant's smile had grown an extra centimetre each way, "I knew it" he said triumphantly.

"You did?" Lee was genuinely surprised.

"Well, maybe I didn't know it was that *exactly*" Grant admitted, "But there was something interfering with the gaydar – and now I know what it was." He smiled some more and leaned across to take Lee's hand, "Well, good for you, chicken!"

The short version of Lee's tale took about half an hour. Once Lee began talking about it, she had trouble stopping. Every time she explained something, she felt obliged to add another couple of items for background. Once again, it felt good to let go of a little more control – but not too much. "I really don't want anyone else to know – not yet."

"Really? Why?" Grant looked a little disappointed.

"Because..." Lee was sifting through thoughts and emotions, trying to refine her reasoning, "Because right now, I'm just not... good enough." It was an admission as much to herself as to Grant. "I don't want the others to look at me and think that I must be kidding myself. I have to believe that I can get to the end of this, but it's going to get a lot harder before it gets better. Once I feel that I'm closer to where I'm going than to where I started, I'll be ready to explain the whole thing."

"Okay" Grant agreed, "I'm pretty good with secrets. It's all about what you know about who you know...y'know?"

"Um..."

"*I* know a lot about a lot of people. Your secret is safe in here" Grant assured, taking Lee's hand and placing it in a heartish kind of chest area.

"Thank you" she said, conscious of the publicly physical gesture, but really not minding at all.

"So you need to make more money?"

"I do."

"And just so I'm clear, you're definitely, *definitely* ruling out the pimp thing?"

They ran into James on Moray Crescent and he fell into step with them, brightening Lee's mood somewhat. In the few months she had known him, her liking for James had grown hugely. She was desperate to keep her feelings private, but how could she not enjoy him? Yes he was completely unattainable, but wasn't that part of the attraction itself? She didn't see enough of him; he worked long hours and spent a lot of weekends away. Whenever he was around however – like this evening, the apartment felt just that bit more alive to Lee. She reasoned that this might be to do with his upping the 'straight' quotient – by 100%, in fact. As much as Lee found exposure to the gay lifestyle liberating and fascinating, she'd discovered that she had a need to access the straight world too.

It was agreed that they would all have dinner together that evening – a very rare treat.

It would be pasta and vegetables with a sauce whipped up at very short notice by Luka (a positive contribution from him, for a change).

Luka had continued to be an enigma to Lee. She found him intimidating. It was also frustrating to feel that his approval should matter to her. His coolness weighed on her. Whenever they shared space, she found herself over compensating, picking up the slack he would leave. Even that night, she had offered to help him by stirring the sauce while he went to fetch something. His only response was 'If you like'. No smile, not even a little eye contact.

At least everyone else seemed to get on. They all sat in the living room with their bowls of pasta and huge salad set in the middle. There was no table of course, and only three seats on the sofa. In the event, Lee, Grant and Luka all sat on the floor while Rikki and James took the role of peculiar parents up on the furniture.

"So, young Lee, what *are* we going to do with you?" Grant offered outwardly, prodding the air with his fork.

"Oh, I don't know" Lee shrugged a little uncertainly, carefully forking some penne so that she didn't have to look at anyone directly.

"Well what needs to be done?" Rikki asked.

"Little Lee needs to make some more cash – and it ain't going to happen at CC."

Rikki began as if to suggest something.

Grant cut across him, "– And we've already done the gag about selling his body."

"Well then, he could sell mine instead. I believe they call it *Pimping*'."

Grant rolled his eyes.

"Could you not just look for something with a better salary?" James suggested as the voice of reason.

"Do you mind?" Grant interrupted. "It took us long enough to find someone to fit into our office, I'm not going to have you packing off our little workhorse for someone else's benefit".

"You could always sell your weekends" Rikki said thoughtfully.

"How do you mean?"

"I don't know, bar work maybe?"

"Do they need anyone at *Crush*?

"No, but you know we have the new place opening down Chelsea way – I don't think they've finished recruiting there yet. Madame has to vet everyone herself and she starts by seeing people recommended by the trusted few" Rikki arched an insider's eyebrow.

Lee turned to assess the prospect a little more keenly, "Would you ask for me?"

Luka got up and headed out to the kitchen, clearly uninterested in a conversation that hadn't cast him in a lead role.

Rikki ignored the departure, "Do you have any experience of bar work?"

"No"

"Are you thinking of perhaps developing a career in hospitality?"

"No"

"I see." Rikki digested the Lee's answers along with a sauce-covered mushroom. "Then we will try a different method of promoting your talents. Let me ask you these questions: Are you a heavy drinker?"

"No"

"Consumer of drugs?"

"No"

"Have you ever been convicted of stealing from an employer?"

"No!" Lee laughed

"Have you ever actually stolen from an employer and just got away without being convicted because you were so high on drink and drugs that you couldn't actually remember *committing* the offence?"

"No!"

"Well then, you're a shoe-in, from what I can tell"

"That's it then" Grant agreed.

"Good job you weren't asking those questions of Luka" James quipped, surprising everyone.

"Ow! Nobody bitches like a straight boy" Grant remarked to laughter – and general agreement.

It would be called *Oasis* and it was situated on the lower reaches of the New Kings Road, opposite Eel Brook Common. It had once been a private club of an entirely different sort and then a suite of luxury offices. Now it was intended to become a cool, but accessible nightclub. It would follow the same pattern as the other Headrush venues – specialist weeknights but a broader mainstream clientele at weekends. Unlike the other clubs however, this one would also promote itself for daytime use.

Until it was up and running, the place would be directly and intensely managed by Madame herself, Rikki had explained. Opening night was now just three weeks away. Madame it was known, liked Rikki a great deal. She enjoyed his infectious humour and his ability to pick up a dead dancefloor and spin it into a living pool of humanity. She had said of him more often than once, 'He knows when to be Rikki and when to be Rick. That's why he's never in the wrong room'.

When Rikki had proposed a good friend of his for a part-time staffer's position, his boss simply agreed to take them on his recommendation, right away. When Rikki admitted that said friend had no relevant work experience, she had moderated her offer and insisted on at least meeting the applicant. Thus Lee found herself at the entrance of a work-in-progress at five minutes to one on a Tuesday. She'd devised a plan with Grant that involved the delivery of some currency into CC's Kings Road branch and then going on to lunch. It wasn't entirely untrue of course – though the drop really didn't need to be made when it was, by whom it was.

A number of things made *Oasis* unusual. First there was the entrance – five steps down from the pavement. A dark brick atrium with darkened windows protruded from the building front. There were double doors which were for the moment, wedged open to ease the constant passage of decorators, builders and technicians. A reception desk and payment area were already in place – the latter protected by a security screen – but there were still cables hanging from the ceiling. On the wall, behind a glass pane, a huge logo, light blue on white, spelled out the club's legend in a neat lower case font. Lee gave her name to an overly stressed-looking young woman who was distracted by some small boxes, stacked just inside the doors. She waved a hand she really couldn't spare, ushering Lee on into the building. Beyond a second set of double doors a wide passageway led through to a further set of stairs, this time leading upwards. What Lee emerged into on the other side was like nothing she'd ever seen.

It was a huge space – and space was the right word. The sense of openness was incredible, especially for a building in this part of London. There were two clearly divided sections. To her left some distance from where she stood, she could make out maybe fifteen or twenty people working on what appeared to be the main club area. She could certainly identify a dance floor. There was a darkened ceiling from which elaborate black painted rigging and lighting gantries were suspended. Below, was a clearly defined wooden plateau that Lee guessed hid some lighting of its own. She could make out at least three separate bars. She would be able to take in more detail when she was nearer, but that would have to wait until she'd processed the sight immediately in front of her. She had an elevated view through huge glass panes of Oasis' flip side. Below stretched a curved, blue-tiled swimming pool at the bottom of which another '*Oasis*' logo was picked out in white. Fifty feet of water sparkled and shimmered where frankly, nothing ought to. The other three sides of the pool's border featured Roman villa-esque canopies, tiled in terracotta. Above it all, another huge sloping expanse of glass, made up the roof. Light flooded in, bouncing from the watery floor to create reflected waves of pearl and turquoise along the walls. There were actually potted palm trees down there, Lee realised – along with ferns and other exotic-looking foliage. She could even make out sun loungers under canopies, still wrapped in their delivery plastic.

Lee was rooted to the spot, not knowing quite where to head next. She was excited and intimidated in almost equal measure. She wasn't even sure she'd be allowed in as a customer, never mind be offered a staff position.

"Hello? Can I help?" The voice belonged to a coffee-skinned twentysomething man in jeans and a white T-shirt, both of which he fitted very precisely. He had spoken from behind Lee and now that she turned to face him, she could see beyond his well-defined shoulder to a further surprise; double sliding doors revealing an open plan office suite which extended back over the passageway through which she'd entered.

"Oh sure, I'm here to see Ma-Mrs Macintyre"

"And you are?"

"Not very sure" Lee muttered

"'Scuse me?"

"Lee Habens."

"Oh, thanks Rafal, I've got this". The accent was definitely Scottish – and if Lee could trust her limited knowledge of such things, softly Edinburgh in flavour. She appeared to be in her late thirties. She was glamorous in a way that suggested success and standards. She wore a dark blue pencil-skirted suit. Lee had known her less than five seconds but she already suspected that this was how Anita Macintyre dressed most days. She had shoulder length straight hair which was raven tinted and shone expensively. Her polite smile came with a dark shade of red – not the kind of colour you'd normally see in daytime. It gave her an exotic edge and hinted at a lifestyle that didn't end at the evening rush hour. Lee was facing an entirely different kind of self-made woman. This was someone who set goals she probably never, ever failed to achieve.

"Come on up" she called.

Lee took the three wooden steps up to the white office carpet and waited to be ushered to a meeting point – which turned out to be the nearest end of a very long table. Lee watched her CV being read – with no little discomfort. She felt obliged to say something, "This is an incredible place".

"Yes." Mrs Macintyre replied without looking up from the page. Clearly it would be best to wait until she was spoken to before speaking again.

Reading of the document completed, Madame fixed her gaze firmly on her visitor for several very long seconds. Lee felt as though she were being X-rayed.

"Rikki thinks rather a lot of you".

"Oh, I take him tea and toast on Saturday mornings. He'd think a lot of a monkey that could do that."

Again, a stretched second or two of silence. "I think a lot of Rikki."

Lee nodded and tried to swallow. The unblinking scrutiny was almost unbearable.

"You're quite unusual looking."

"Oh, I don't know…"

"The long hair and are those plucked eyebrows?"

Lee wanted to run – now, before things got any worse. She hated to let Rikki down.

Mrs Macintyre continued to probe, "Your look doesn't really work with what you're wearing. Where is it you're working at the moment?" she glanced again at the CV and answered the question herself before Lee could form the words, "Change Central. Are you happy there?"

"Oh, it's fine, really"

"You're young and living in London. It's the 1980's – do you really want to settle for 'fine'?"

"I...have a plan" Lee blurted out, perhaps a little defensively.

More silence before Mrs Macintyre's perfectly painted face was suddenly warmed by a smile, "Good" she remarked, "I'm glad to hear it"

Lee was relieved too, but was still hating the experience. All she wanted to do was make a bit of extra money clearing glasses or fulfilling some other kind of menial task. She needed work, not a career.

"I have a plan, too. This place is the latest part of it. I'm trying to do something a little different here, something new. I want an operation that can run at night *and* on the following morning. People will come here to be a part of something beyond their normal daily lives. Whatever is back beyond those doors out in the wider world, won't matter to those in here. Here, everyone is safe and treated as though they matter. The people I employ to deliver that service will all need to understand that. If you just want to work in a bar, then that's okay – you can work in a bar. To be part of this, you need to properly understand about the desire for more from life than just being 'fine'".

It was Lee's turn to be silent for a moment. What the hell, she had nothing to lose – maybe afterwards she really *would* just go out and find 'work in a bar'. "I understand better than most what it's like to want more, to *need* more. I'm learning all the time about determination and commitment and I've come a long, long way from where I started. I always try to give myself to whatever I'm doing – and I never, *ever* let people down."

"I see you have no experience of hospitality work"

"Neither does anyone else – until they get some" Lee shocked herself with her own challenge.

Anita Macintyre laughed out loud, "That's true enough. You would have to start at the beginning though. You'd be collecting glasses, clearing up afterwards, lending a hand to pretty much anything the management ask you to do – and that can mean anything from shifting boxes of stock to helping clear a toilet blockage. Are you up for that?"

Lee smiled, "I'm up for that."

"Rikki tells me you'd just be available at weekends"

"At first, yes. I'd only be able to work Friday and Saturday nights, but I might be able to do some weeknights as well, later on." Lee knew that last part was probably unlikely. Where would she find the energy – especially while trying to balance shifting hormone levels? Still, she was in her early twenties, it had to be possible to do nothing but sleep and work for a couple of years, didn't it?

"Rikki trusts you" Mrs Macintyre said before taking another moment. She bit her lip as she mentally concluded the inner debate and executed one of a hundred decisions that day. "*I'm gonna trust you, too*".

Lee lay on the treatment table and stared up at a poster pinned to the ceiling above. It was a sort of hippie image of mountains and streams and elf-like people born of the thoughts of an artist who'd evidently overdosed on prog rock concept albums. She wondered how many times she would see this picture in the months and years to come. She wondered how many of those times it would take before her loathing for it would become pathological.

"I change that every month or so" Carol Ward explained, as if reading Lee's thoughts. "It gives you something to look at though, doesn't it?" She was quite diminutive in height and rather generously proportioned width-ways. Her sing-song, midlands accent made almost everything she said, sound quite hopeful. Nobody this positive, could bring anything bad to an experience. Could they?

"So we'll start doing some of the area on the side and then maybe we'll just do a couple on the top lip as a sample area before you go".

The idea that there was a 'we' involved in the process sort of helped, but from the moment Lee felt the first needle-like probe enter a follicle and instantly heat it to around 50°C, she was pretty confident that she would be managing the pain part of this process all by her lonesome. The contraption delivering the charge had dials and switches on it. It looked heavy and a bit like something that belonged in a mad professor's laboratory. Carol, in her crisp white clinician's outfit, had wheeled the device in on a trolley, a sight that transported Lee instantly back to IGF and mid-morning tea breaks. She wondered how Buggs was doing these days. And then a moment later she couldn't think of anything else but how miserably painful it was to be electrocuted right in the face. The end of the probe was close to her right ear and she could hear the crackles and fizzes as the hair follicles burned with the delivery of each charge. She tried not to jump every time Carol's trigger finger sent down a pulse. She *tried*. Perhaps a little conversation might help her to relax. "So have you treated many transsexual people?" Lee asked, wincing at the latest pinprick. The small treated area was now beginning to feel like a proper burn.

"Oh, a few now" Carol replied.

"Do you think I'll be a difficult case?" Lee asked, hopeful for good news.

Carol sat back on the high stool she used to rest against during treatments. "Well, you've got a good combination. You're pale skinned and have dark straightish hair. That's what you want for this really."

"That's good. It's nice to feel that I'm actually *advantaged* in some way" Lee smiled weakly.

Carol turned Lee's face back into position "Mmm. You're young which means that there isn't too much of a mature beard, but *being* young, you never know if you're going to develop hairs in other parts of the beard area during the treatment. Are you on anti-androgens?"

"I will be soon" – Dr Garner had indicated as much.

"They'll help a lot".

"Good. I'll take all the help I can get".

Later, when Carol had 'zapped' (her term) a few of the hairs around the mouth area, Lee had learned a whole new level of pain. It had taken every ounce of her much-depleted willpower to hold still, but when Carol had noticed the tears emerging from the corner of her patient's eyes, she decided to call it a night. They'd work on another area in two weeks. She'd given Lee some lavender gel to put on the treated patches. There would be a visible swelling and redness for up to 24 hours and she was advised not to shave those parts of her face for a while if possible.

Sitting on the bus now, Lee tilted her head toward her fellow passengers, using her curtain of hair for protection. All she could think to encourage herself was that others had been this way before her. If they could manage transition and miserable experiences like these, then she would too. After all, what choice was there?

august 1983
thin on the ground

....

*A*ndrocur *is an absolute bastard! I swear, if ever I do hate a man enough to do them harm, these little pills will be my weapon – slipping them into someone's tea wouldn't be too hard. I'm prescribed one a day now – to block the male hormones still being created and released into my system. These on top of the female hormones! I'm sicker than ever, more tired than ever, my skin is spottier than ever and I can't keep a balanced mood for more than half a day. All I want to do is lie here on my bed and curl up.*

Even today though – <u>even today</u>, I don't doubt what I'm doing to be right. NOT FOR ONE SPLIT SECOND! Through all the wretched hormone sickness and the secret appointments, the financial strain and even the downright agony of having my face burned off every other week, I know that this is right. I have plenty of doubts about how I'm going to manage it all or if I have what it takes to see it through – but whether I should be trying to do it at all? No.

. . . .

The angle of the street meant that Dr Garner's reception and consulting rooms were in shade by mid-afternoon. Never had Lee been more thankful for that relief than she was now. Funny thing about summer, it makes people remove clothing. This is fine for most, but absolutely terrible if you are in the process of changing your body and your sexual physicality. Lee was nowhere near confident enough to wear clothing in public that could be definitively described as female – and yet she absolutely could not attend an appointment looking like someone clinging to a life raft of masculinity. And so, despite a temperature in excess of 30°C, she was in black jeans and boots – albeit with a wide necked long and baggy, royal blue T-shirt which hung off of one shoulder. It was the best she could do. She promised herself that she'd be in a better position by next summer.

Sitting in the cool of the waiting room, consuming her second glass of water, she was at last feeling the sweat on her forehead and upper lip dry away. She pushed her sunglasses back up further on top of her head, holding her hair away from where it might still become dampened. The worst thing of all about the heat was that it made heavier, concealing makeup almost impossible to wear. As an extra bonus, she now understood the summer conditions to encourage a more rapid growth of facial hair. This meant that she'd had to take the entire day as a holiday for no other reason than it allowed her to shave as closely as possible to the appointment time. She'd made a point of trying to get some colour into her face – after all, if makeup couldn't be used, she had to find a better way to even out any shadow patches around her top lip and chin. Sun tanning was an unsatisfactory and unreliable method, but it was all she had. She had been wearing mascara – at least when she left home. While she'd been trying to put herself back together in the bathroom a few moments ago, she found it had mostly headed off on multiple escape routes. She did the best she could to remove the melted black residue and freshen up her lashes.

The mirror in the bathroom was set at a height that only allowed viewing of the torso. She judged the T-shirt option she'd chosen, to be pretty lame on the whole. Dr Garner probably wouldn't be too impressed. What else could she do though? Again, she wondered at quite how she'd arrived at a position where she daren't actually appear to be either male *or* female.

"Hey Donna, how're you doin'?"

Where had Lee heard that before?

"Hi Davey, you here to see Sue?"

"Yuh."

'Donna' the receptionist – Lee really ought to have remembered the name herself – was greeting the figure Lee believed to be the guy-in-progress. And what excellent progress it was. Davey was also in jeans and a T-shirt. His lower half now that Lee could manage a longer look, was a little heavier than it should be compared to his slight torso. His shoulders weren't quite the width they should be compared to his hips and yet for all that, he was utterly convincing. Indeed if Lee had encountered him in a different environment, she couldn't possibly have suspected a thing.

Davey took a seat opposite Lee on the other side of the coffee table. As he was reaching for a magazine, he met her eyes. "Hey" he said, with a white-toothed smile.

"Hey" replied Lee. She got a close look at Davey's beard and wondered how long he'd been growing it. It must have come in fast she thought, recalling that her own first facial hair appeared when she was about 15 and yet even last year she wouldn't have been sure of her ability to grow anything as neat and even as Davey was sporting. She wondered as to the strength of the male hormones he would be taking. Feminising drugs seemed to drain her of energy, while she'd read that the taking of testosterone caused a surge of it.

Lee was a little surprised when Davey spoke again. She'd taken him for the strong, silent type.

"You were here last time I was, I think"

Lee nodded. "Yes, I remember you".

"How you doin'?" he asked. Lee wondered how many times he must say that in a single day.

"I'm okay. Trying to deal with the heat, you know. How about you?"

"Yeah, kinda the same. This is more like the summers back home though, y'know."

"And where is that, exactly?"

"Portland – Portland, Maine"

Lee nodded with an expression of understanding. "That's on the east coast, right?"

There was that smile again, "Yeah, right".

There was silence for a while and then Lee decided to have another of her increasingly common 'what-the-hell' moments. "Do you mind if I ask…"

"Mmm?"

"Well, what you come here for?" The question hung in the air for a moment and Lee was suddenly doubtful of her daring.

Davey's expression migrated from slightly surprised to calmly considered, "My treatment is co-ordinated through here. I'm undergoing gender reassignment."

It was so good to hear another actual human being speak those words. "You don't look to me like you need any more co-ordinating. I think you look great."

The smile was wider and whiter than ever this time. "Well thanks. I been doin' this a while now so I guess I forget how far I've come. I still have some steps to consider though, y'know."

"Not as many as me, I suspect" Lee admitted with a wan smile of her own.

"You look like you're doin' pretty good to me. I guess headed in your direction the early part is the tough part. For me it's the other way."

Lee wasn't sure what he meant and he caught her quizzical look.

"The drugs – they're incredible when you go 'f to m'. The changes…" he indicated with a wave of his hand toward his face "they're fast and they're clear. But the surgeries? Those wait for you at the end and they're really tough – depending on how far you want to go."

Lee was genuinely intrigued. Here was an opportunity to learn something. This was already the longest conversation with a transsexual she'd ever had. Not least because it was the *only* conversation with a transsexual she'd ever had. "Did you know anyone else who'd done it before you?"

Davey shook his head. "No. I just read things in magazines and stuff. You hear about a few cases through the lesbian community y'know, but I never actually met anyone. You?"

"Nope." Lee smiled. "We are a bit thin on the ground, I suppose."

"Yeah" grinned Davey, adding with a little mischief, "Imagine if we weren't though."

There wasn't time for Lee to play with the idea.

"Lee?" Donna interrupted, "Dr Garner will see you now"

Lee reached for her satchel and stood. "It was really good to meet you"

"You too"

As she headed away from the table, Lee looked back. "Great beard, by the way". The last she saw of Davey that day was another of his white smiles.

Despite the outside temperature, Dr Garner was still wearing jacket and tie. What Lee wondered, did that say about him? Did he just believe that certain standards must always be upheld? If so, what did that mean for his judgement on her appearance today?

"Good to see you Lee. You're looking well"

"Um…thank you." She hadn't expected that.

The doctor relaxed back into his seat, the folder with her notes already open on his desk. Lee headed for the button back chair, as usual.

"So how are you?"

"I'm well, I guess" she nodded. "But I'll be glad when this summer is over"

"Oh?"

"It's just that the heat makes things difficult when you have… wardrobe issues." She wasn't sure if he'd pick up the allusion.

"Tell me what you mean by that?"

She cursed inside and then considered her words. "I'm trying to be subtle with my transition. I'm trying to hold down two jobs and share a home with a group of guys. Only one other person in my daily life knows what I'm trying to achieve and the rest of the time, I'm just trying to get by while protecting this big secret. The summer doesn't help. Lots of baggy layers of clothes *do*. That's why I'm so desperate for the Autumn."

The doctor nodded in appreciation and then asked, "What do you think would happen if people around you were aware of your transition?"

Lee considered it for a moment. She tried to imagine Mr White's face wearing an appalled expression – a look that would make it appear longer than ever. Almost horse-like in fact. She broke from the image, "I think they'd sack me from my day job – obviously."

"You're sure."

Lee hesitated again. "Well I can't be *absolutely* sure. I mean it's never happened before – either to me or them. I just can't *imagine* them wanting me around. And they can just sack me, can't they?"

Dr Garner took a long considered breath in through his considerable nostrils. "I'm no legal expert but you wouldn't be in breach of contract – unless there was a clause about revealing any major medical conditions. They could accuse your condition of being compromising to the image of the company. That's not so much of a problem if you work inside the civil service of course, but you're at…" he consulted his notes.

"It's a foreign currency agency."

"Mmm. I can't really advise conclusively either way, I'm afraid"

"That's okay." Lee replied. "I'm just saying – that's the reason I can't wait to get away from hot weather."

"You said you were holding down *two* jobs?"

"Oh. Yes. I'm also working weekends at a club in Fulham. I just needed to make the extra money. I'm saving as hard as I can."

Dr Garner nodded encouragingly.

"It's tiring – and not terribly interesting. Most of the time I'm just collecting glasses. After 2 am, I'm doing ashtrays and cleaning tables – and sometimes the floor." She looked up and realised he was unsure of the duties she was describing, "People drink too much and sometimes they don't make it to the loo when they realise they've overdone it."

"Mmm, that *does* sound tough."

"Yeah. Not exactly what I thought I'd be doing with my weekends." She was conscious of wanting to appear positive and thought she should add something to dilute what might appear to be a moan, "It's an amazing place though. It's new and there are all kinds of interesting people coming in and out. It's actually easier to be a little bit different there than it is at my day job."

"That's good"

"Yes. Actually, I'll be there working tonight, being as it's a Friday".

"So you're not getting too much time to relax at the moment?"

"Not really, no – but I'm young, y'know, so..." again she felt the need to paint everything positively. Could he see through that, she wondered?

"And how are you finding the drugs?"

"Oh fine, really".

"Energy levels okay?

"Absolutely".

"I can see that there has been a slight weight gain"

Lee must have looked a bit surprised because he added, "In a good way, I mean. Your face is more rounded and there are some signs of other developments" he was nodding toward her torso.

Lee pulled self-consciously at her T-shirt, which laying heavily against her chest did suggest the outline of a pair of small bumps, "Um, a little bit, yes. Not enough though to really..." she smiled, stopping herself from adding the word 'matter'. Positive, *positive.*

Dr Garner returned the expression and repeated something he'd told her in a previous meeting, "Breast growth is generally the feature that male to females look for more than any other. Sometimes there is next to none and sometimes it can be quite remarkable. What you have to remember is that your breasts are growing from an already developed frame. Your dimensions as a male would likely be different to what might have been, had you been born physically female. As a result, anything your body now tries to develop in a female mode may be to a more modest scale than you might wish for"

Lee had already read much the same in one of the support pamphlets. "It would be nice of course. I mean having them is one of those defining aspects physically, isn't it? But I'll just wait and see what...turns up." She pulled again at her shirt.

"That's a good attitude."

Every tick of approval earned by Lee in these meetings mattered and she glowed inwardly. Sure, she was telling her psychiatrist what she guessed he wanted to hear, but she was also trying hard to believe in it herself.

"Tell me a little more about your home life."

Lee was alerted by the shift in subject matter, "What do you want to know?"

Dr Garner was looking in his notes again, "Let's see, you're now living with four young men?"

Lee smiled broadly, "When you put it like that, it sounds pretty cool."

Dr Garner stuck firmly to the line of enquiry, "And what is it like in actuality?"

"Um, well I suppose it's challenging at times, like any shared home."

"And are none of them aware of your transition?"

"One is now, the rest I'd rather didn't – at least for a while."

"How do you think they *do* see you?"

"Well, three of them are gay so that's a pretty strong flavour in our household. I guess overall, they regard me as gay, too."

"And how do you get along with the party who is straight?"

"Oh, he's lovely" Lee replied, conjuring an image of James on the rooftop where they continued to run into each other. Such encounters would generally require Lee to cover up – though in compensation, James was tending to the opposite.

"Yes, that's not really what I meant", Dr Garner smiled.

"Oh no, of course – Um, he's fine with me. He's fine with everyone. I mean living in a gay house I thought would be difficult for him, but he's really well adjusted."

"Do you ever imagine anything happening between the two of you?"

"Maybe in a fantasy, but I try not to imagine anything happening between me and anyone."

Dr Garner made a note and then the probed further – as Lee feared he might, "You are still resisting any chance of a relationship?"

"I couldn't have that kind of complication in my life. I need to get through this on my own. I need to be someone able to love before I can *be* loved." Once again she surprised herself. That was absolutely her conviction, even though she'd not given voice to it before.

"You don't feel that you would benefit from the love and support of someone close?"

"Honestly and with all sentiment aside?" Lee clarified, "I don't believe I can really miss what I've never had."

"Support of any kind from those who care about you can be very, very helpful."

Lee felt an itch in her eyebrow and scratched at it while she was thinking. She felt her nose run a bit and then a huge tear came out of nowhere. It dropped into her lap and she tried to laugh at it, slightly embarrassed. "I – I'm sure that's true" she managed. "I miss my Dad..." she began, but her voice cracked suddenly. She tried to clear her throat, to claw her way back to steadiness. She saw Dad again in her mind's eye. It had been a while. And just then she did miss him, all over again. His voice, his smell, the stupid cod-wisdom. She felt an echo of him come to her and then pass away as she realised that he wasn't there with her at all. Nobody truly could be. There was just Lee alone, trying to do what something inside told her must to be done. She was pursing her lips – hard. She absolutely mustn't cry. Not here, not now.

She did cry though – and quite a lot. It had been quite hard to stop once she'd started.

Lying in the bath and looking back now – as she had done a dozen times since, Lee thought Dr Garner was pretty good about it. He'd handed her a box of tissues and let her pull herself together slowly. She'd apologised and he had of course given the impression that it was absolutely nothing. He understood the effects of the hormone-induced, 'emotional rollercoaster' he had prescribed. She reassured herself that a psychiatrist probably appreciated seeing some raw emotion, otherwise they might suspect you really were hiding something. But in truth she was pretty sure she'd lost some points today.

Dad of course, really would have hated it. For all his compassion and sensitivity, he could be hard of heart when he felt it necessary. You couldn't blame him for it, that's how he'd made it through Mum leaving and then later, his own illness. He'd lived it and so he had a right to say "Feel sorry for whoever or whatever you like – but not yourself. *Never* yourself. There's always something more useful you can be doing with your time." She could see him again, his face set strongly and a tone of utter conviction, "You get up and you get on – or you go nowhere."

Even after a bath she'd ended up being more than half an hour early. She had heeded Dad's distant words and refused to spend any more of her day in pointless reflection.

She hadn't felt the need to eat anything. Heat at least did wonders as an appetite suppressant. The journey from home to *Oasis* could be made in forty minutes ordinarily, but even that had been quicker than usual this evening.

She thought about stopping off at a pub, but Mrs Macintyre was clear that one shouldn't do so when wearing the staff uniform. Once again, Lee found herself mentally beckoning autumn, when she could put a coat over her prescribed outfit for the evening. The uniform itself was simply black trousers or skirt (clearly it was going to have to be the former for Lee – at least for now), and a black t-shirt which bore the club logo in pale blue. Customers were to be aware of staff, but only really as background.

Elvis, one of *Oasis'* enormous body-building bouncers, was already out front. He was the right man in the right job at the right place – and was evidently contented with his lot. "All right Lee?" he said cheerfully as she stepped inside.

"Yeah, you okay?"

"All set" he confirmed. That had pretty much been the extent of their relationship since the first time they'd been introduced. Lee didn't really have much of an affiliation with her fellow staffers. She was at the bottom of the club's food chain anyway and so had little to offer.

To date, she'd only made no more than twenty entrances to the building and so was still hugely impressed by the sight of the pool area, in particular. The decorative finish with the white walls, clean lines and wooden decked floors always evoked for her, a sense of continental glamour. Like taking a tiny holiday.

She looked over her shoulder to see if there was anyone in the office. Just Rafal. If he was there at this hour it meant Mrs Macintyre was around somewhere.

She carried on past the dance floor and bars and through a corner door which led out to a corridor and the staff locker room. She had intended to simply park her satchel and head back to the bar area in search of any early duties, but instead she found Mrs Macintyre speaking with Lynne, the shift manager.

Lee felt immediately that she was imposing and so without making eye contact simply whispered, "Sorry. I'll just lock this away and be out of your way."

"Mrs Macintyre looked at her watch, "You're early, Lee."

"Oh, yeah"

"There's your answer" Mrs Macintyre said to Lynne. "Train *him* up"

"Yes, but that's not going to help us tonight really, is it?"

"We'll try to get someone across from the other rota, but in the meantime this will have to do. You've got about an hour before opening and even after, things will no doubt start fairly calmly. Lee's bright – he'll pick it up."

Lynne looked at Lee doubtfully.

"You'll do your best for me, I know you will – both of you" Those were Mrs Macintyre's parting words and it was the last they'd see of the boss that evening. What followed for Lee, was a six-hour blur.

Lynne had been quite forthcoming. The problem at Oasis stemmed directly from the arrest that afternoon of Jeff, one of the usual bar team. The police had found something under the front seat of his car that Lynne had described simply as 'illegal'. He was still being held. The failure was being taken very personally by Madame. It remained to be seen whether the offence if proven, would ever be forgiven.

Lee was to take up the slack caused by Jeff's absence – at least for that night. She had no experience of serving drinks and she was surprised at how nervous she was about her impending debut. There was only a short time for her to become familiar with the mechanics of the bar – how the cash register worked and protocols for taking money, ('when receiving a banknote always identify it out loud so that the customer hears you and then place the note on the clip at the front of the cash register while drawing change'). She was shown how to use the pumps and optics and the mixer pump, a marvel of a contraption that could deliver different soft drinks from a single nozzle. Lynne was a patient teacher, having introduced quite a number of rookies to bar duty. Lee surprised herself by picking up the instructions fairly quickly. Perhaps it was all those nights of waiting with an order at *Rosanna's*. She was placed with Becky and Elaine, two experienced staffers of whom she was encouraged to ask questions. There were plenty of those during the first hour or so of opening when there were fewer customers and ample time to serve them. Later when the pace picked up along with the volume of music and excited voices, Lee found herself taking more of a support role. Becky and Elaine were both very good at the job – or at least so it appeared. Lee enjoyed the way they danced around each other while serving. They had a knack of identifying the customers who would be buying one or two drinks at a time and they'd prod Lee forward to take care of those while they dealt with the longer orders. It was surprising Lee thought, just how well one could actually make out people's words from behind a bar – especially once you had the hang of the acoustics. There were only so many words you needed to learn to either lip-read or filter vowels. Women were easier to hear over the bass tones of the music, she found – provided they spoke up. There were some mistakes of course, twice she got a drink order wrong and once she caused Elaine to spill a pint because unlike Becky, she couldn't yet predict her colleague's moves.

She was still buzzing with excitement and energy by the time the bar closed. Becky and Elaine cashed up in their practised manner, leaving Lee for a moment with nothing to do. To the amusement of her teammates, she continued to walk floors and collect glasses – just so that she didn't have to stand or sit still. She stayed on to fulfil her usual clean-up duties and eventually left the club quite some time after 3am.

Her heart rate had begun to slow down by the time she eventually tiptoed up the stairs to her room. She flipped on her bedside lamp and looked across at Dad's chair. It worked there in the corner – even if it was being used as something of a clothes horse. She made a space and took a seat on it, replaying the better parts of her day in her mind. She thought of Davey, she thought of how busy she'd been at the club. Finally, she thought of Dad again, until she dozed off in his embrace.

By the Sunday afternoon, the ludicrous temperatures had given way to something more traditional. It was raining across West London. Lee had been in bed since getting home from a second incredibly demanding night at *Oasis*. By the end of that shift she wasn't too far from the pace at which Becky and Elaine operated and she'd already been told that she would be back on bar duty for the next weekend. Jeff's arrest had turned into charges and Mrs Macintyre's hands had taken an early wash.

Lee had showered and consumed a cup of tea and two slices of toast. Beyond this, she really wasn't sure what to do with herself. Grant apparently, had another 'encounter' with a handsome stranger last night and if past patterns were anything to go by, he wouldn't be back until late that night. Rikki and James were both away for the weekend – though pursuing very different aims. Luka as ever was doing who knew what, where – and with whom.

It was while she was sitting back in her room puffing out her cheeks at the promise of boredom that the idea first occurred. How long had it been? She couldn't remember. Strange really, because it would be more reasonable to do it now than ever – yet this was the first time since the move to London that opportunity and inclination had shared the same place and moment. She looked across at the larger suitcase which stood against the wall to the side of her wardrobe. "Girl clothes" she said out loud, to nobody.

Why not, she reasoned? Why not an afternoon of indulgence? Hadn't she done enough to deserve it? All the hours and days and months of sacrifice, wasn't it fair just to let her feel good about herself and have some fun in private for a short while?

First she had to do something with her face and hair. There wasn't much point in doing this unless it was to be done properly. She could use the whole thing as an exercise, marking her progress by how much her appearance might have improved since she'd last tried. She needed to set a studied, calming atmosphere. She introduced The Cure's *Faith* album to her bedroom and began.

She did a pretty basic makeup job, not much more than she would wear on a night out now, just perhaps with a little more work on the eyeliner and the addition of lipstick. She could still see a slight grey shade in places where the subcutaneous beard follicles lay beyond her reach. As long as those were there, she would never dare to do this in public.

She added some mousse to her hair and scrunch-dried it upside down with the dryer. When she sat back upright, she laughed out loud at her reflection. One huge do. She began to tease and spray it until she felt it had the right volume without quite crossing over into fright wig territory. What she retained of a fringe, flopped over one eye – a little seductively, she thought.

Bedrooms, she reflected – was there ever a better stage for the shallow of confidence?

So what to try on? She had a dress she'd bought and always hoped one day to wear for real. An ambition to genuinely grow into. It was made of a stretch jersey fabric, knee length (even on her) and had three quarter length sleeves. The front and back were cut with deep V's although it was otherwise straight. She dug out a pair of black courts that she'd bought on a brave day out in Maidstone a couple of years before. They were of course, a size too small and she knew that they would bite back at her after a couple of minutes of wearing.

She moved back to the mirror and began her assessment. Her immediate reaction as usual, was to look away before any deep disappointment set in, but she pushed herself to dwell more constructively on her reflection. Her calves were still pretty skinny, but that was okay. In the winter she knew she could get past some of that with black tights. She was still awfully straight in body shape. She was fatally short of a decent pair of hips. Would those come in time? It was unlikely. Dr Garner had said it generally took 18 months to 2 years to see how far hormones would take her. Time was just about up on that score. She was a little happier with her top half. Her little breast bumps were still rather ridiculous. Isolated islands of interest lost on a barren plain. She may find them protruding when wearing a flat fronted T-shirt, but in any-thing shaped for a proper neckline, she looked entirely inadequate. Still, she liked that the tiny buds did at least actually appear in the right places. In truth she wasn't as bothered about her breasts as she had thought she might be. Maybe she would have to opt for some surgery later – but in the meantime everything else would take a back seat to the priority of what she now knew to call 'SRS', or Sex Reassignment Surgery. It remained for her, the only oper-ation that mattered. The rest she reflected, would be just padding – literally.

She did concede that the changes in her face shape combined with longer hair, did do wonders. She covered the lower half of her face with a hand. What still showed, worked. Hopefully, there was nothing more than Carol Ward's electrically-induced agony between Lee and a face she could show the world. The dress did show up one other problem though. This sleeve length served to emphasise her hands. Lee didn't have big hands exactly – not like Dad's. Hers were just very long in the finger. Too long. There was no way of knowing by how much, but it was clear that visually, it would have to be either no sleeves, short sleeves or long sleeves. Anything else just made her look like she could play ping pong without a bat. Her arms had changed. Where once, tendons and veins were features clearly defined, now the cylinder of her limbs appeared more consistently round.

The shoes were beginning to hurt at the heel. Before she took them off, she wanted to remember what it was like to walk in them. Her room wasn't long enough for more than a couple of paces, but if the long mirror was lined up with the door out to the landing, she could get an idea of whether what felt okay, looked okay. She tried it out once by walking to the far bannister and then back again. She repeated it. It seemed okay. She could never quite rationalise why it was easier to walk in heels on a carpet than on hard surfaces. Logically, shouldn't it be the other way around? She used the distance to get another perspective on her proportions – where they worked and where they didn't. It was when she turned to the right that she realised Luka had been watching her. He was standing on the stairs with a hand on his hip and a very wide smile on his lips.

"Uh-huh" he said nodding slowly.

Lee was mortified. She could just run into her room, but she wasn't sure her legs would co-operate. And anyway, she wasn't doing anything wrong. She tried to bluff it out. "*Uh-huh*, what?" she tried, rather uncertainly.

Luka continued staring, his wide smile seemingly fixed, "It's okay, it's your thing." He waved a patronising hand as if to grant acceptance of her little quirk.

"I'm just…" she began, running through a menu of potential excuses she might try. But as she felt the crimson complexion of shame envelope her, no such defence could be selected. "You don't need to know about…any of this." She could hear a tremble in the rising tone of her voice and she knew Luka had heard it too.

His smile widened. He nodded again and oozed in his campiest tone, "Ohhh. You want to be girl."

"That's…It's just nothing to do with you!". Embarrassed and confused, Lee covered the remaining few steps to her bedroom – her practised walk at least, still intact.

Lee didn't emerge from her room until gone midnight – and only then because she was so desperate for a pee that the thought leaving it any longer might be damaging to more than just pride. She was up for work earlier than anyone the following morning, the sting of humiliation motivating her out into the streets at an almost indecent hour.

She took the bus and made for the seat up top – at this time of the morning she could sit pretty much anywhere she liked.

"Tough night, huh?" The voice came from over her shoulder. She sighed deeply. Grant. "Jesus! What are you doing here?"

"Welcome to my world. This is when I usually head for the office."

She turned to face her flatmate. "You don't usually take the bus."

"No, but you do."

"You followed me?"

Grant shook his head, "You really aren't a morning person, are you? You were barely aware of traffic on the walk to the bus stop."

Lee leaned back against the window and sighed again. "You know, my weekend was going quite nicely until I saw Luka".

"Yuh, and he saw you." Grant was grinning.

Lee shook her head and looked down at her knees "Ohhh God – it's just unbearable."

"Why? Why should *you* be bothered?"

"Well this is not exactly the way I had intended things to come out."

Grant laughed sympathetically, "Things that matter rarely stick to the script. They're too exciting and dangerous to be controlled that tightly."

Lee watched as a milk float disappeared up a side street – a rare sight this close to Central London. "Was Luka mean when he told everyone?"

"Not especially. He's the Poison Dwarf right? He thought the story would speak for itself scandal-wise."

"So how did the others react?"

Grant took a recollective breath, "Well let's see, James said something like 'Oh well, that'll be new'. He asked whether he'd have to start leaving the loo seat down."

Lee grinned. She knew James was relaxed, but really – *that* relaxed?

"and Rikki? Rikki said – and I quote – 'Ooh goodie, a sister!' So there you are, how's that for a messed up family unit?"

"Luka must have been pretty disappointed" Lee mused recalling the gleeful expression she'd last seen him wearing.

"Are you kidding? Luka's happier than anyone. I don't know when I last saw him so cock-a-hoop – If you pardon my entendre."

Was nobody going to be predictable? "Why is *he* so pleased?"

"Because dummy, now he's back to being the youngest, cutest gay guy in the house. You're what put his nose out of joint in the first place. Now he doesn't see you as a rival anymore."

"I was *never* a rival!" Lee pleaded.

"Yeah, well he didn't see it that way. He does now. I mean, you know he barely acknowledges the existence of anyone with a vagina anyway, so as far as he's concerned, you're headed for some kind of oblivion."

"Nice."

"Isn't it though?" Grant agreed, eyeing the suit who'd just joined their deck.

christmas 1983
party on

. . . .

*I*t feels like a long time since I've been excited about the build up
to a Christmas. Dad always used to over-compensate for Mum
not being there. We had some really great times though. All of
that shiny, sparkly excitement is back for me this year – and in the
company I keep these days, the celebrations are bordering on the
insane.

Dad and I used to think it was special to have a couple of people
over to watch TV and enjoy a beer. Now one of the craziest parties
I've ever seen, will be happening one flight down from my bedroom.

I haven't felt the loneliness I've feared – at least not yet. Last year
I couldn't see past Dad's missing presence. This year I'm surrounded
by celebration. And now I have Grant & Co. to help make sense of the
season – and beyond.

. . . .

He'd been pretty weird since the autumn, Rikki said. But
Grant was so manic in the build up to the party, that by the previous morning Aussie flatmate had to sit Kiwi flatmate down and
give him a proper telling off, "Cause he really does need to calm
the fuck down – that's what he needs to do!" Rikki quacked, wild-
eyed and waving a mascara wand.

Lee grinned, "And you really were just the man to tell him."

Rikki shook his head, the blonde beehive he was wearing, shimmering in the light of his bedroom's mini chandelier. "Well, it's
ridiculous. It's a fucking party! We do know how to have a party,
don't we? Why does he have to be all over every fucking detail?

Where's the room for a little chaos?", he sighed away some stress and tackled a self-inflicted pencil smudge.

Lee's grin was still in place, "There. Finished moaning? Feel better now?"

"Yes, thank you" Rikki replied sweetly. "Now piss off back to yours and put your frock on."

Lee got up from her seat on the corner of Rikki's bed and re-tied the belt on her dressing gown, "Oh sure, like I'm really going to do that".

"Well why not, honey? It's the perfect night for you to reveal yourself in all your twisted, bizarre glory."

"Gee thanks – but if you don't mind, I'll carry on with my low profile."

"Yeah, well I will, if you will, kidder" Rikki called, the door closing on her words.

The apartment had hosted a Christmas event a couple of years before and it had become the stuff of minor legend. Grant announced that this year more than any other, the event must return. From that moment on, he had planned obsessively. "We're going to put the fairy on the tree of *all* Christmas parties!"

Things were off to a pretty good start when it transpired that Luka was going home to Brazil for two weeks and wouldn't actually be there at all. He'd left the day before. James would attend – although he hadn't invited anyone. Presumably, none of his friends were quite broad-minded enough to witness the Moray Crescent Zoo.

Lee was only able to be there herself on the second Saturday before Christmas because she'd agreed to work at *Oasis* on both Christmas Eve itself and New Year's Eve. She was glad she'd be working, though. Good to be busy.

Grant came bustling past. He was wearing white linen trousers and a crisp white shirt – with the festive touch of a thin red belt around his waist. Lee noticed he was looking especially slim these days. He'd clearly made a new buckle hole on the belt and his trouser waistband was looking rather cinched.

"Shouldn't you be getting changed?" the host urged, looking a little more intense than he really should. Lee decided that staying out of the way of the household's senior member was the only sensible course. "Yes ma'am!" she answered, bounding up the stairs to her room. She sat down in front of her mirror. She'd finished hair and makeup before visiting Rikki so there really was only the easy part left. Getting dressed. For about the tenth time that day, she toyed again with the idea of presenting herself as definitively female. The others wouldn't mind now, she was sure. Since they'd all found out about her treatment, her flatmates had been supportive though by no means reverential – the small box of tampons anonymously introduced to the upstairs bathroom was testament to that. However, having others wise to Lee's plans, applied a different pressure. She was terrified that when they finally did see her presented as a woman, they'd be somehow less than impressed. Still, she would continue to edge her way there modestly. She smiled into the mirror and underlined her strategy, "How to change sex in front of people, without them actually noticing."

She'd been keeping up regular electrolysis appointments and had now suffered through four ceiling poster changes. She was taking pain killers just prior to appointments. This may have been working, though it was frankly hard to tell – the intensity of the pain was still quite shocking each time. The season helped. Carol could work on larger and more central areas of her face and then once Lee was back outside, the chill weather would help calm the fresh burns, while the dark nights provided some cover for the great swollen patches of redness. The others had become used to her arriving home on such nights and heading straight for her room. Eyes would be co-operatively averted.

She would have been consoled by a reduction in the number of hairs on her face, but this didn't appear to be the case. There had been perhaps a slowing of growth in certain areas, but when she ran a razor slowly over her skin, she could still hear the blade crackle with the slicing of each stiff hair shaft. She would go over the same spot again and again until there were no more sounds. By this point she would usually be blade-burned or bleeding in one or two spots, but at least she wouldn't actually be able to feel the stubble. Of course as ever, the further price to pay would be the stings and fizzes from moisturisers and makeup as they were applied to fresh wounds. For a night like tonight the regime had been a strict one, planned on a sort of countback system. Her last visit to Carol had been on the Wednesday night in order that she would have healed sufficiently to shave on the Saturday afternoon. This she would do around 5:00pm so that the soreness and any new cuts would have time to respond to antiseptic creams and she would be ready to use moisturisers and foundation in good time. Simple really – putting on a bit of slap just meant a four-day plan, that's all. Rikki had a special masking cream which somewhat covered grey beard areas. You didn't want to be wearing it under bright lights or close scrutiny he had advised, but if you combined it with regular foundation, 'stayed in the shadows and waited for guests to get shit-faced', it would work brilliantly.

She would go for a sort of female-leaning brand of androgyny tonight, she decided. She would put a pair of tight white jeans under a long black silk shirt around which she would wear a thin black belt. Shoes were going to be a problem, until Rikki had loaned her a pair of flat black ballerinas which worked surprisingly well, despite being at least a size too big. She was wearing a very pale lipstick – almost flesh coloured. It was an idea she'd had after seeing Adam Ant wear it in an interview. Her hair, which she was having to wear in a ponytail at work (much to Mr White's grinding disapproval), was longer and bigger than ever for the occasion. There was probably half a can of hairspray in it. She vowed to steer clear of smokers lighting cigarettes.

The older guests started arriving at around nine. Their priority would be to speak and be heard and so they knew that they needed to dominate the quieter hours early on.

Rikki had emerged in full drag and party mode. He looked wonderfully ridiculous in silver lame and was breaking ice at the door with the arrivals. Grant was zipping from kitchen to living room to landing to bathroom and bedroom. In short, he was everywhere – and all of the time.

Lee took to trying to support Grant – especially when it came to fixing drinks and distributing snacks. She didn't know many of the guests who'd arrived so far. In truth she probably wouldn't even later. She'd done about all the wine pouring and peanut distribution that she could politely do, when thankfully through the front door, Miriam arrived. Grant's CC-sense picked up her presence immediately.

"Oh, there she is! Queen of my heart!", he called from the kitchen doorway. He waved over and shouted a paraphrase of her office mantra "Darling, I'm telling you, it really is too much for a gay boy!"

She laughed generously, "I'm a guest so you're on your own!" she called back.

Lee stepped forward with a slightly sheepish grin, "Take your coat, Ma'am"

"Oh crikey!" Miriam was surprised but smiling. "Well look at you! Is this the effect living with Grant has had on you?"

"Er, not entirely" Lee replied

Rikki arrived at Lee's shoulder after a prolonged visit to the lower bathroom, "Do you mind, we're a very conservative household here I'll have you know. Large 'C', obviously." he added.

"Rikki! You look…"

"I know, baby – *I know*".

Miriam herself was wearing a rather tight leopard skin number. Lee was mesmerised by her curves. "God, you look amazing."

"Well thank you. Lloyd wasn't entirely comfortable with me coming out in this dress, until I told him it would be a party full of gay men."

"Where is Lloyd?" Lee asked. "I thought we would finally get to meet him."

"Like I said, I told him it was a party of gay men." Miriam grinned. "He did promise he'd come in for a drink when he picks me up. He's out with his mates right now, probably being extra-blokey and overcompensating before setting foot in here."

"We do actually *have* a straight boy here somewhere" Rikki interjected. "Has anyone *seen* the straight boy?" he called out.

Grant had momentarily finished in the kitchen and came across, "I saw him with Oliver and Simon a few moments ago"

"Bloody Hell! Snaffled by the Sisters of Chertsey? Rikki exclaimed. "Cry havoc and let slip the dogs of bore! I'd better go to his rescue."

Grant embraced Miriam. Lee watched and was taken by how long he held her. He'd closed his eyes, too. For the first time, she had the feeling that there was something going on – something not being shared with her.

"Mother of God!" Grant said under his breath as he stepped back. He was looking over Miriam's shoulder at the extraordinary sight of a huge drag queen dressed head to toe in scarlet chiffon. "Grant!" the visitor growled cheerfully, "You old cow!"

"Oh darling!" Grant replied. "Look I did say we were all going to make a bit of an effort with our appearance tonight. So why don't you just pop upstairs and let's see if we can find you something a bit more cheerful."

"Very good" scarlet replied. "All I can say is that they seemed happy enough on the bus I took to get here."

"Seriously?" Grant laughed heartily.

"What? You think I was going to deprive West London of this?"

"Oh yeah, I was going to wear that" James said quietly to Lee in passing as he headed to the kitchen.

Lee giggled and then watched James all the way to the fridge.

Rikki had made tapes using the decks at work to create a perfectly flowing soundtrack. Some of the club numbers and synth stuff were really rather cool, but no more than two tracks at a time would take themselves seriously before giving way to some clichéd Christmas or party-style nonsense. He had years of experience at knowing how much of what to put where. Bow Wow Wow were going *Wild In The Country* when Lee stopped to ponder just how much more she had drunk that night than for a very long time. It was nice to be consuming drinks rather than either serving them or trying to clean them out of a carpet. She was definitely seeing walls sway a little and she decided to take a seat on the stairs. She wanted to hold on to the buzz for as long as she could. She'd seen too many revellers at *Oasis* cross the line from happy to tragic in one drink too many. Besides, from up here, she could get a good look at the number of people crammed into their formerly spacious home. She recognised maybe a third of the faces from various pubs and clubs she'd visited either with Rikki or Grant. The network of friends they had was fiercely loyal, if perhaps rather clique-inclined. Lee suspected that there were rarely strangers in their midst. Absent friends were much discussed of course – even if they were only in the next room, likely doing the same. In all though, they were a happy crowd. She compared them to the brooding malevolence she used to witness at occasional house parties back in Sittingbourne. Emotionally repressed men, disappointed women, alcohol – it was rarely a safe cocktail. Here, there were all the usual colours that come with life: love, money, sex, heartache, recovery, jealousy – but they were debated, discussed and dramatised. Maybe the whole party was a bit like Rikki's tape – just enough silliness to keep anything from being too intense. It was a warm and wonderful mood to be around – if not entirely a part of. Lee wondered what else these people did with their lives when they weren't partying. Did they really have normal jobs?

By no means all of the attendees were exotically costumed, but where they were, it seemed to be enjoyed by everyone. How it must be, she wondered to be so liberated that your Saturday nights begin by standing in front of a wardrobe and thinking that anything is possible.

Derek the Dog stepped out from the living room. Lee had met him when he'd arrived. Moustachioed and six feet three in leather jeans, biker jacket, big boots and sunglasses that were never, ever removed, he had actually introduced *himself* to her by that name. She'd politely enquired as to whether she might take his jacket and he'd begun unzipping it before Grant had interjected, pointing out that Derek traditionally wore nothing underneath and that he should probably keep his clothing on – at least this early in proceedings.

Lee smiled as she watched the faux biker follow a slightly built young man down the corridor toward Luka's room, which the flatmates had decided would be used as the 'cloakroom' for the night.

The party was generating body heat and smoke. It occurred to Lee that if she popped the hatch upstairs, both would have somewhere to go. She set up the ladder, climbed and lifted the lid away. She paused for a moment looking at the stars and further supposed that maybe a few minutes topside might help clear her head.

She headed up into the night and walked across to the far end of the rooftop. The city really did look quite glorious like this. The West End to her left, felt to her like the heartbeat of the world these days. She'd heard plenty of stories about the swinging sixties, but really, had there ever been a cooler time to be in London than right now? Pop stars, film stars, great designers, amazing clubs – including *Oasis* of course. Britain's capital seemed to be everyone's first city right now.

"Ah, there isn't anyone else up there, is there?" James' voice called from behind her.

Lee turned to see his head sticking up from the hatch.

"No, it's all clear" Lee replied before laughing at the sight of her flatmate's face lit from below "you look like a scene from an old horror movie."

"Well thanks!" he replied.

"I meant with the lighting and…" Lee thought better of any further explanation.

James lifted a can of Budweiser out onto the roof and then followed it with the rest of himself. "I'm running out of rooms to hide in"

"Simon and Oliver?"

"Yup. They're convinced that we know each other from…I don't know – somewhere or other."

"I see you found the beer, then" she remarked, recalling that Grant, who regarded lager as rather uncouth, had hidden it earlier in the understairs cupboard.

"Oh yes. It was inevitable" he said straightening and joining her at the roof edge. He breathed out a steady, steamy stream of inner warmth. "Mmm, not too chilly really, is it?"

"It's bloody freezing" Lee laughed, folding her arms tightly. Clearing her head had also reduced some of the numbness of several hours drinking.

"Yeah, it is, isn't it?" James stuffed a hand deep into a pocket while using the other to drink.

"I love the 'Bers, though" Lee sighed.

"The what?"

"The 'Bers. Septem*ber*, Octo*ber*, Novem*ber*, Decem*ber*" Lee explained. "The '*Bers*."

"You don't prefer the summer?" James asked

"Sweaty tube? Tiny clothes? Burned skin? Nooo thanks"

"O-kay" James remarked sceptically. He took another mouthful of Bud, "So anyway, how *are* things with you now?"

She looked at him a little surprised. "Um, not bad" she replied.

"You know, I've not told you that I think you're being pretty brave doing…y'know, what you're doing."

Lee smiled widely and looked at him again, this time in the eyes. She shook her head before adding, "It's not brave"

"It isn't?"

"No. It isn't" she affirmed, coughing a little as her lungs began to purge themselves of several smoky hours in the rooms below.

"Well what would *you* call it then?"

She took a moment and then replied, "I'd use *your* term: inevitable".

James gave that a little thought and then shook his head, "No. Can't agree" he declared. "*Beer* is inevitable, your thing is brave".

"Well that's very nice of you to say." She warmed to his compliment and without thinking, she let her heavy head fall against his shoulder. He put an arm around her shoulder and they stared out at London together. It really was so beautiful.

"James?" she said softly.

He turned to her, their faces far closer together than they had ever been. She felt drawn to him, almost as if she were being physically pulled. She lifted her lips to his.

"Oh" he said, stepping back. Now his hand was on her back. "No, I'm sorry, I didn't mean..."

Lee was mortified. "Oh no, no – it's my mistake entirely" she said. She was suddenly sobering up very fast.

"You know I really am straight. You do know that?" James said gently.

"Yes of course" Lee assured him, before adding under her breath "So am *I*."

"I hope you haven't taken any offence there, I mean I – I'm just really sorry."

"No, no – seriously. *I'm* the one who's sorry."

"Oh well, now THIS is definitely NOT the time of year to be saying sorry."

Lee was confused for a moment. She hadn't seen James' lips move when he'd said that.

"If you're saying sorry at Christmas, then you're just not doing it right."

It was a slurry-spoken Grant, head through the hatch and grinning woozily as he scanned back and forth from Lee to James.

"Er, coming up, Grant?" James asked.

"Would like to".

James and Lee helped their flatmate up through the hatch. Both of them at that moment relieved to have company.

"How's it going down there" Lee asked.

"I think it's okay. Did you think it was okay? I thought it was going okay" Grant said uncertainly. Then he spotted James' can and pointed accusingly "Beer!"

"Yeah, I'm sorry, but I didn't think you'd mind if I was out of sight."

"Aw shit, I don't mind" Grant conceded. He melted and hugged James tightly. "Fuck it, whatever you straight boys get up to – as long as I don't have to see it – it's all right"

James laughed as much as his depressed chest would allow and as he did so, he smiled at Lee, helping her to feel just a little less awkward.

Grant lurched toward the roof edge, with James holding on to his arm. "Ohhh, it is lovely up here at night."

"Yup" James agreed "bloody cold, though"

"Is it?" Grant asked, looking a little confused. He took a deep breath of West London air and smiled to himself, as if about something secret.

"You worked really hard on tonight. I'm glad you've enjoyed it" Lee said placing a hand on Grant's shoulder, adding "– as has everyone else, of course."

"It was important. It was so important." Grant said softly.

There was definitely something. Lee probed a little, "Why. Why was it so important tonight?"

Grant looked up, a passing taxi's headlights playing across his features. "Because it's sort of my goodbye party."

"Goodbye to what?"

"To all this" he called out. Then gazing around, "And to that over there!" he waved theatrically at the sparkling lights of Kensington.

So there it was. "What do you mean?"

"I have to head home."

"Home where? *New Zealand* – home?"

Grant bit his lower lip and nodded earnestly.

James stepped in, "What is it mate, visa problems?"

Grant smiled again, but sadly, in a resigned sort of way, "There's a serious illness in the family and I have to get there."

"But you can come back, right?" Lee was finding this all a little difficult to follow.

"I have no plans, apart from just getting there. I've told Mr White and he's been really good."

"Well how soon?"

"Three weeks – almost"

She lay on her back, just breathing and thinking. She didn't want to do anything else with her Sunday. They'd put Grant to bed shortly after getting him down from the roof. People had been drifting away by then. The last couple of hours had been pretty gentle, with just small groups of people sitting around the place drinking tea and chatting. Lee, Rikki and James had finally shut the door on the last to leave at about three. Another hour had passed by the time some rudimentary cleaning and the process of makeup removal had taken place.

The memory of James' startled expression visited Lee's mind and she winced in embarrassment. A lot of things had changed last night. The kiss that never was, would be expensive. The price no doubt would be the easiness in James' attitude toward Lee. He would never quite be comfortable around her again, she felt sure. But that was as nothing compared to the prospect of Grant's departure. The loss would be shared by many of course, but others didn't rely upon him quite as much as she did. They didn't owe him as much. Grant had in one way or another, determined most of her days since moving to London. He had been the person who had first helped her feel safe in the city. He taught her how to feel ordinary about extraordinary people and places. He helped her to find her feet at work and brought her into the place she now called home. Grant had cared for her without needing to.

There was a soft knock at Lee's door. Only Grant ever knocked on her door. Neither James or Luka would have reason – and Rikki had a tendency to simply walk in regardless.

"Hello?" she called out

Grant's rumpled hair and bleary features peered around the door.

Lee sat up. "Come in" she said, smiling and holding out her arms, "Pleeease".

Grant was only wearing his party shirt and some boxer shorts. He looked cold. It *was* cold. Lee lifted the duvet and beckoned him in.

"Ohhh, that's so much better. It's only bloody December out there, y'know."

"I know" Lee answered, adding with a snort, "You know, I used to wonder if this would ever happen."

Grant laughed back, "Oh, you should be so lucky. I don't sleep with girls – you know that."

"Bless you."

"You know, you looked great last night. I didn't get the chance to tell you that, did I?".

"No, but that's okay. It means more to hear it today. I think Miriam was a bit freaked out though."

"Mmm, this time it really may finally have been too much for a black woman," Grant agreed. "Seriously, you should tell her the whole thing, you know. She'll be cool."

"Maybe" Lee pondered. She turned on her side and rested her chin against Grant's shoulder, looking up at the side of his face as he in turn stared at the ceiling. His hair smelled of old party. She guessed hers probably did too. "Last night was real, wasn't it? You meant it when you said you were going." She watched a small smile play across his profile, pressing tiny ripples down toward his ear.

Grant closed his eyes before speaking. Perhaps he was saving all of his concentration for the words, "Yes, honey. I have to go"

"Please don't."

The smile widened and Lee watched him breathe in through his nose as if to gather himself.

"Have to."

"I know." She moved her forehead down to rest against the same shoulder. "You've never spoken much about your home."

"Not much to tell really. It's Auckland. It's Mum and Dad and a brother. Its home."

"I guess I'd got it wrong. I just assumed you didn't get on with your folks."

"Yeah well it took me a long time to realise that they're not the enemy" Grant said softly, "they're just family".

Lee planned to have a Christmas Eve to forget. Few could have been aiming quite so low for their festive experience. All she wanted to do was work straight through it, earn some exhaustion, go home and sleep through Christmas Day. That way she didn't have to think about Dad, Grant's pending departure, James, her financial woes, or the increasing frequency of headaches and nausea attacks gifted by the prescribed cocktail of hormones and anti-androgens. For the next seven hours or so, she just needed to be a machine.

The working relationship between Lee and her bar partners, Becky and Elaine had matured. There was an equality of effort and understanding between them now. The history the other two shared no longer seemed to exclude her. She had found their rhythm and joined the dance. For the duration of a shift, she could kid herself into feeling like 'one of the girls'.

Lee was tying back her hair in the staff room when her teammates arrived.

"Your 'air is really gettin' long now, Lee." Becky commented in pure South London.

"You should get your ends done though" Elaine added. "I'll do it for you if you like."

"I don't know, It's been a long time since I was anywhere near a pair of scissors."

"Yeah, but you wanna look after it though, don't you? It's lovely 'air. Elaine used to be a hairdresser."

Elaine nodded in confirmation, "Come 'round to mine sometime and I'll trim the ends for you"

Lee didn't like the idea that her long hair didn't look as it should. She didn't want it to look accidentally long, she wanted it to look as though it had been grown by design. Neat ends would be a sign of the pride she genuinely felt. She had recently begun to enjoy occasional car horns as she walked along the street. She liked the idea that she appeared to be female to the occasional passing man – even if the pass itself was from behind at a speed of forty miles an hour. They all counted.

Becky was foraging in her bag as she looked up, "So, this'll be your first Christmas Eve behind a bar, then?" she grinned.

"Uh, yes. Usually, I've been very much on the other side."

The approaching hurricane of Christmas Eve had long been anticipated by the staff at Oasis. It was likely to test the place to its limits. It was a ticket-only event with admissions ending at 10:00pm – Headrush policy for all its venues that night.

"Once those doors close, nobody else gets in" Becky under-lined. "It'll be the same everywhere so nobody's leaving either – until they're done for the night."

Elaine was smiling and shaking her head as she removed her rings and placed them into her locker, "People are gonna hit the bars early and just keep going. They'll start fast and stay fast." She looked up at Lee's apprehensive expression. "Well, it could be worse – you could be on puke duty."

Becky cackled at the last remark. Then she dropped her tone, "Do you use anything, Lee?"

"What do you mean?"

Becky grinned again and shared a knowing look with Elaine. "Y'know..." she urged, with a single sniff.

Lee shook her head, feeling a little embarrassed. Drugs hadn't really made it to the mainstream clubs back in Kent. It was still just about booze back there. Narcotics must have been present in some small way she guessed, but she'd never seen any evidence. She knew that Luka used coke, so did Rikki and probably Grant too, but they always treated her like the kid from the sticks and so tended not to involve her or James in either buying or taking.

"You ain't gonna make it without taking somethin'" Becky said, reaching inside her bag. "Here. You can pay me back another time." She handed Lee a small piece of folded paper. For a moment, Lee thought about trying to bluff it out, but she'd prob-ably only end up making an idiot of herself. "I'm not very experi-enced, I'm afraid"

"Awww" Elaine soothed, amused at her colleague's naivety.

"It's just 'whiz'. 'Speed' – y'know?"

Lee knew enough to be aware that it at least wasn't one of the scarier drugs. She looked at the two of them a little closer, "You take it a lot?"

"Fuckin' right, on nights like this!" Becky laughed.

"Wouldn't get through without it" Elaine added.

Maybe Lee considered, this really was how it was done. Perhaps everyone was doing it and she was the only one on the outside. She held up the little piece of paper, "What do I do with it?"

She could still taste it an hour later. The girls kept laughing whenever they saw her taking a sip from a glass of coke she stashed on the back counter. Lee hadn't liked the idea of snorting the tiny pile of cream-coloured powder so they'd told her about another way. Elaine had brought in a glass of water and Lee had been instructed to tip the powder onto her tongue. It had tasted absolutely vile. The smell and initial taste had made her think of soap powder. She was urged nonetheless to swallow hard and then immediately drink the water. She'd successfully fought the instinct to gag but had gasped out loud once she had drained the glass – much to the Becky and Elaine's amusement. Lee had an overwhelming urge to shave her tongue.

"You'll be buzzin' in about half an hour" Elaine said.

And so she was. Lee was filling one order and taking another before the price of the first had been met. She was seeing customers three layers back and remembering what they'd ordered on their previous visits. She was singing along to the music while calculating change. She was totally locked into to her function. Lee's experience of intoxicants had been limited to alcohol. She was familiar with the sensation of being gradually detached her from her surroundings, but this was a different experience altogether. Speed made her feel intensely connected to what was going on around her. Maybe this was what the term 'wired' meant.

She took only one break the entire night – and even then she found herself collecting glasses on the way back from the bathroom. She really wanted a cigarette – and badly – but apart from that manageable craving, she actually felt pretty good. She noticed that on a couple of occasions, she'd caught people staring at her. Ordinarily, this would make her want to shrink, but instead she found herself looking them straight back in the eye. Instant confidence, imported in powder form.

She thanked the girls for perhaps the twentieth time outside the club as their cab was waiting. There were hugs and wishes for Merry Christmases all round. The scarcity of cars that evening had meant that four girls were sharing one vehicle. They offered to let Lee lie across them on the back seat, but she wasn't ready to be at home yet. The walk would delay her appointment with sleep, but with a bit of luck, might actually help facilitate it.

She'd never seen London quite so still. Even the incessant Fulham Road wind had been stilled. At times it was as though the entire city had frozen in a moment, leaving her alone to move through it. On the rare occasion a car did pass, she would hear the sound of its approach and fade for an age. She began to feel better about Christmas. Maybe there was some magic still left in it after all. She watched the toes of her boots moving rhythmically in front of her, one after another, her pace constant. She covered the two and a half miles in about thirty minutes and was through her front door before 4:00am.

She was beginning to wind down a little as her face tingled to the indoor warmth. She had an urge to eat something, but she didn't know what. It was strange to have the place to herself. With James visiting family, Luka still far (though perhaps not far enough) away and Grant embarking on what he had termed his 'farewell tour', spending Christmas with friends in Bath, there would only be herself and Rikki at the flat – and if form were anything to go by, Rikki was highly unlikely to appear until sometime tomorrow.

Giving up on the idea of food, she headed for her room. In the semi darkness, she could make out an A4-sized piece of paper on the staircase. It bore a message in large, scrawled handwriting, 'YOU HAVE COMPANY!' She looked around the landing and then went back to the living room. Nothing. She headed back upstairs. Reaching the top landing, she could see that the lamp in her bedroom was on. She didn't know anyone who would visit her here – let alone on a Christmas Eve. Quietly entering her room she was amazed to find a small figure wrapped in the duvet, seemingly fast asleep. She looked closer and saw the unmistakable dark curls. "Dani..?"

Dani breathed in deeply through her nose as she began the short journey back to consciousness. Lee sat down at the corner of the bed, utterly astonished. The sight of Dani waking was something she'd witnessed on a hundred other mornings. It was so familiar and yet so alien to her now. Certainly she had given up expecting ever to see it again. The deep hazel eyes squinted open and Lee watched her erstwhile best friend slowly take in the surroundings. "Oh my God, Lee?" she sat up straight into an embrace.

They clung to each other tightly and began the process of re-joining their lives.

"Where on earth have you come from?" Lee asked stroking Dani's hair.

"Oh, it's a long story"

"I have time" Lee replied, softly kissing the top of Dani's head and remembering the scent of her hair.

Dani leant back and took a longer look at Lee. "Bloody hell" she smiled, her puffy features suggesting that there had been some tears before sleep. "You're actually doing it."

"Doing it?"

"You're changing. I can see it. Your face is different. Look at you. And your hair!"

It was Lee's first 'before and after' and she hadn't really been prepared for it. Here was the person who had known the 'old Lee' better than anyone, and was now exposed to the new version – albeit a work still in progress.

She shrugged, "Well um, yes."

Dani nodded, looking Lee up and down, "Wow. Mad…"

Lee smiled self-consciously and then shook off the moment, "Cup of tea for Sleeping Beauty?"

"Oooh."

Lee lent Dani a sweater and they padded back downstairs, Lee switching on lamps as they went, bringing the apartment back to life.

"It's a really lovely place" Dani said.

"You got the address from my letters?"

"Eventually"

"How do you mean?"

"I didn't get those until two weeks ago."

They settled in the living room where Dani wrapped herself in a throw she found on the sofa. She found her handbag and pulled out her cigarettes, "Are you still not..?"

"Never can and never will" Lee confirmed, "but you can go ahead. There should be an ashtray around here somewhere."

Dani already had it – and looked to have deposited a half dozen stubs earlier that evening.

Lee headed for the kitchen and returned soon after with two mugs of tea. She should have let the pot brew longer, but couldn't wait to get back to Dani. Her mind was still racing but she could no longer tell whether she was wired by the speed or from shock.

"So?" she said slowly lowering two mugs carefully to the floor.

"God, I'm really not sure where to start."

"Well, I'm going to guess that it all *starts* with Rob" Lee ventured.

Dani smiled and stared at the steam rising from her tea. "Actually, it sort of starts with the end of Rob."

"Oh", Lee smiled sympathetically. "So how far did things get with him?"

"I got a flat in Canterbury – just a one-bedroomed place. He used to give me money towards it each month." She smiled again at the thought of it. "It's so silly isn't it? You're in a situation like that and you think it's one thing when anyone else can see it's really quite another."

Lee was shaking her head as she grasped the nature of Dani's arrangement. "So you really were sort of..."

Dani pursed and exhaled, a stream of grey white smoke preceding her confession, "Meet the 'other woman'" she declared, accenting her words with a theatrical pose.

"Wow. That sounds a bit grown up."

"If only! When you boil it down, I was living in something little more than a bedsit near an industrial estate, just sitting waiting for him to turn up every other evening – and for what? A couple of hours here, half a night there. It seemed as though however long he stayed, he was always beginning to leave, you know? I always seemed to be saying goodbye. That was the thing I'll remember most, I suppose. More goodbyes than hellos."

"He was never going to leave his wife." Lee observed. "That did look pretty clear at the start – and I always thought that you'd known that deep down, too."

Dani nodded and extended the border of the throw to cover her toes, "I suppose. But there always seemed to be enough hope. The entire time I somehow managed to tell myself that it could just be a month away from really happening. I mean, he was always going on about how bad things were at home, how little there was between them. I just kept hanging in there. You think, maybe they'll just have one big row too many..."

"What changed?"

"It was a Friday – back in October, it must have been. He was supposed to be staying all night for once. I'd been really looking forward to it, you know? The feeling of waking up with some-one on a Saturday morning? I had it all planned, breakfast in bed – everything."

"And?"

"He'd been there about two hours. We were in bed and sud-denly he tells me that he won't be staying after all. She'd be expecting him, he said – something to do with some 'social obliga-tion'." From her expression, the term was still poisonous to Dani.

"What did you do?"

"I suppose I went a bit nuts", Dani admitted. "I called him a liar. He got out of bed and started getting dressed. I was in tears. And then, as he's putting his jacket on, he pulls out this envelope with money in it. 'This month's rent' he says. He left it on the bedside table."

"Oh Jesus" Lee whispered. She reached over to Dani's shoul-der, but her friend was still steady, just rueful in expression.

"That was the moment I put it all together – at long last. There I am in a bed in a cheap bedsit. There's a guy going out the door and we've just had sex. He's left some cash beside me..."

"No. No, you know it's not the same"

"Oh, it's exactly the same. *Exactly*." Dani's eyes had definitely taken a glassy turn. She took a sip of tea. "All the time I thought I was waiting for my life to get better – and it had actually been sinking like a stone. And there I was at the bottom, with nothing. I had no friends – I didn't see anyone anymore, just in case Rob would be free and I'd miss him. They'd stopped talking to me at home the moment I'd moved out. *They* knew what was happening. *They* could see it, just like everyone else. Everyone except me."

"I'm really sorry" Lee said softly, rubbing Dani's shoulder.

"You? *You're* sorry?" Dani asked, with quiet incredulity, "You shouldn't be sorry. You saw it before anyone. And I thanked you by just…cutting you off." There were definitely tears on the near horizon now and her tone had become pretty shaky.

Lee put down her own mug and leaned across to hug Dani. She placed her chin on top of her friend's head and thought about how many times they'd done this over the years. They held the embrace, but continued the conversation.

"So did you see him again after that?"

"No, that was the last time", Dani sniffed. "Thing is, I can't even blame him. All he ever did was take advantage a bit at the start of the relationship. Without realising, I was just encouraging him."

Lee wanted to assure her friend that it could happen to anyone, but she wondered if it really could.

"I wrote him a letter. A really long one. I wrote about how I knew we would never amount to anything and that I wouldn't wait any longer. I said that I wouldn't take any calls from him so he shouldn't bother. I had the weekend to pack up. I got everything into a cab and I went to my Mum and Dad's."

"Wow. How were they about it?" Lee asked, leaning back to see Dani's expression.

She was mopping up with a tired looking tissue, "Hah! They loved it. They'd been proved right, hadn't they? Stupid little girl comes home, needing them more than ever." Dani sat back upright, blew her nose and took another sip of her tea. "Thing is, I can't criticise them for anything either, you know? They may not have been calling me after I went to Canterbury, but I hadn't called them either. And yet, when I suddenly turn up at their house with a cab full of all I had left…" she shrugged and shook her head in memory of that autumn afternoon "They never hesitated. They just took me back in. They didn't even ask me about what had happened until the next day."

"So you've been living there since?"

"If you can call it living, then yes."

"Oh dear."

"It was like being twelve again. The rules, the questions, the stern faces. It was like…it was like, I don't know, being in trouble – but permanently. It was as if I was being told off, but for two whole months. I had to give up my job, obviously. I couldn't be bumping into Rob three times a week, so there I was, at home the whole time"

"And what then?"

Dani grinned sheepishly and looked into her mug, her hands cloaked by the long sleeves of Lee's sweater, "Then – I had to write *them* a letter."

"Ah." Lee said warily.

"Oh, it's okay, this one wasn't angry. I just said that I was finding it too hard to be there. I didn't blame them for anything and I accepted that they felt they had to be pretty hard on me. I said I just needed to be away for a while. I just needed to think about my next steps. That was last weekend."

"So where have you been since then?"

Dani took a breath as she cued up her answer, "Let's see, I spent the first night at Carrie's place on her sofa – you remember Carrie"

"Oh, yeah" Lee replied. She didn't have any idea who Carrie was, but it helped the story move along.

"Then I went to Michelle's in Faversham – you don't know her, she's from my old work. We always got on really well and she was really happy to help but of course she had loads of questions and not much space and y'know, it's a bit hard to look ahead when all you're talking about is what you've left behind."

Lee smiled, "I can't imagine."

Dani laughed, appreciating the irony. "Okay, okay. That's been important actually. All the time I'm thinking about how to start my life again and I'm remembering you and how you approached it. How tough you had to be when it came time to leave your old house. I mean, how could *I* fold up and go to pieces with my challenge when you'd faced yours head on. And so…" she looked up at Lee, brighter eyed, "I thought I'd take a chance – see if you were still here."

Lee's smile grew, "You'll never know how glad I am that you took that chance."

"Even though it's Christmas?"

"*Especially* at Christmas."

Dani looked doubtfully at her friend, "So you don't have lots of festive plans?"

Lee relaxed back into the sofa and rested her head, "I have *no* plans – festive or otherwise." A question formed earlier, returned to the front of Lee's mind, "So why did you only just get my letters?"

"I don't know if she withheld them on purpose or if she just forgot, but Mum finally gave them to me a couple of weeks ago. She didn't actually have my address in Canterbury so she couldn't have sent them on anyway. She'd kept them in a carrier bag on the back of the door to the cupboard under the stairs."

"Nice."

Dani sniggered, "Well *she* didn't know!"

"So you were walking past my heartfelt words for weeks."

"I know, I do feel awful knowing that now – and they'd have really helped me at the beginning when I moved back, too. I'd have been here earlier, if I'd known where you were. It's just…the way we fell out over Rob. I wasn't sure you'd want to hear from me after it all went wrong. It was only when I read the letters that I knew you wouldn't be doing the 'I-told-you-so routine'. That's when I started thinking that I had to try to find you. I still wasn't completely sure that you'd be okay with me because I hadn't written back, but I had to try."

"I'd never turn you away. I'd never, not be here for you".

"I knew that the moment I saw you tonight."

"Added to which, I owe you so much. After Dad…"

Dani placed a hand on her friend's knee.

Lee suddenly seemed to wake to the present, "Christ, who let you in last night anyway? What time did you get here?"

"I don't know, about eight I think."

"I'd have been at *Oasis* by then" Lee had a flashback of bad-tasting speed.

"That's the club you work at?"

"Mmm."

"You have two jobs? God, how do you manage?"

"Easy. I don't have a life. I'm just a savings account now. All that matters is how much money I can squirrel away."

"It is so great to see you doing so well, though."

"I don't know about 'well'. It's harder than I ever imagined, but I guess I'm more or less sticking to the plan."

"It was Rikki who let me in."

"Oh dear"

Dani pursed her lips and then said, "Bloody hell!"

"Yes, we don't usually let him answer the door. What did he look like?"

"He was in black chiffon and he had a long dark wig on."

"Kate Bush night" Lee deduced.

"What?"

"You know he's a drag jockey – queen – whatever?"

"Well I didn't think he was a bus conductor."

"He might have been." Lee suggested, "I mean everyone needs a hobby."

"For a split second, I was a bit worried that I'd find you looking, you know…like that."

Lee nearly sprayed tea at the idea, "Oh, how proud Rikki would be if I did! No, I leave the theatrics strictly to him."

"He did seem really nice. He asked my advice on which shoes he should wear"

"He usually just goes with the kitten slingbacks"

"Yup." Dani recalled. "He was really sweet though. I must have looked a bit desperate. I can't believe he was happy to let me stay here on my own – I mean, he didn't even know me. I told him I knew you, but that's all he had."

"Well not exactly. He'll have also had about twenty stories I'd have told him about you and me over the years. All you had to do was tell him your name."

"Ah" said Dani "That makes sense. He didn't ask too many questions. He had to go not long after I arrived, so I was just left to wait for you. In the end, I just needed to be on a bed for a bit. I've had two nights of sofas and I just needed to lie down properly. I didn't really mean to fall asleep."

There was a moment of silence between them and then Lee asked, "Do you know what you want to do next?"

Dani looked doubtful, "Not really."

"That's okay. You don't have to know anything yet. You can stay with me as long as you need."

"Thank you. I can't tell you what that means."

Lee straightened, "You know, you're going to have to speak to your parents eventually though."

"I did already. I called them this afternoon. They're not thrilled – especially about me being away at Christmas. I think they were just relieved to know I was safe and not sounding too crazy. They might feel I'm messing them about a bit – and that's fair enough. But I know I can't go back there – not to live, anyway. I have to come up with a different plan."

"Not tonight you don't. All you have to do tonight – what's left of it – is sleep. And so do I."

They headed off to bed and didn't re-emerge until early afternoon.

Perhaps because of Grant's absence, there wasn't a great deal in the house for them to eat – at least not immediately. There was a frozen chicken, which was still very frozen; some carrots, peas and sweetcorn – and a fair amount of champagne left over from the party. The chicken was set to defrost, leaving them with cheese on toast for their Christmas lunch.

Rikki returned that evening and spent half an hour with them. He looked positively shattered after almost 24 hours of what he'd described as 'glorious excess'. He'd retired to his room with the words "I came, I saw, I Christmassed."

The next morning, Lee and Dani made a journey neither much relished. London's streets had remained seasonally empty, ejecting them in record time to the suburban, industrial and finally rural folds of Kent. It had been a year and a half since Lee was last in Sittingbourne. She glimpsed the red brick block of IFG's offices as they coasted into town. It was eerie. "It feels so different, even though it hasn't changed a bit."

"But *you* have" Dani had reminded her. Lee glimpssed a corner of her face in the rear view mirror. It was easy for her to forget that she no longer fitted the town's frame. The thought helped her to decide that she should wait patiently for Dani in the car rather than face a scowl from her friend's father. Dani emerged after almost an hour in the house, having made an uneasy peace with her sceptical parents. She'd squeezed her life into two suitcases and a carrier bag.

For old times' sake, they stopped for a quick drink at *The Cow*, before leaving town. Lee had attracted rather more attention than she ever used to. It hadn't been easy in London to measure her migration toward a more publicly feminine appearance, but ten minutes in a Sittingbourne saloon bar offered a real barometer of change – and not an entirely positive one. Some of the girls had stared and whispered, while the sneers from a couple of the guys at the bar held promises of real menace. She wouldn't again be using the male bathroom at this particular pub. She could hold it in – for days if necessary. In one way at least, Lee felt a little less threatened than she'd used to. She now had the security of a haven just seventy miles to the west. Soon they'd be back among strangers and outsiders, where being an alien was to be in the best of company.

Dani looked different against the backdrop, too. She didn't seem to fit anymore, either. She'd seen beyond the walls of the old town and had been coloured by her witness. There was no way back for either of them – and that shared realisation was the cue to leave glasses half full on their old favourite table.

Once back in the car behind the reassuring purr of the Honda's engine, Lee felt able to speak freely. "Well that was horrible."

"I'm really sorry" Dani agreed.

"Not your fault"

"No, but it is *our* town – or at least it was." She sounded more than a little fearful when she added some minutes later, "It's all changing, isn't it? Nothing will stay still anymore."

They headed west, Lee subtly accelerating past the turn off to Priest Close, without looking.

Life around the flat was not returning to normal. Christmas Day had fallen on a Sunday, which meant that Tuesday 27th was still a bank holiday. Lee and Dani had spent much of the morning slumped on the sofa in front of the TV, consuming the usual festive prescription of old movies. Lee was beginning to doze off on Dani's shoulder when the sound of the front door closing tugged her back to the present.

"Morning. Oh, and hello". James was clearly surprised to see a woman at the flat.

"Hi." Dani straightened, thereby completing the waking process for Lee.

"I'm James" he said, putting down a large sports bag and offering his hand.

"Dani" replied Dani, having to half stand to bridge the distance over the arm of the sofa. "I'm – er, a friend of Lee's."

"Right, yes. Well, me too" James replied, flashing a kind of smile Lee couldn't quite recall ever seeing before.

Lee suddenly decided that she may as well try out 'Proposition Dani' on the easiest-to-read member of the household. "James, Dani's going to be staying for a while. She can share my room."

"Great." He was swapping smiles with Dani again.

"I just want to check, do you think the others will be okay?" Lee asked, if only to fill air that needed filling.

James looked back at Lee and seemed to be replaying her words again at a slower speed for analysis. "I...don't see why not", before suddenly seeming to remember that he'd just arrived home after several days away. He was unshaven and rumpled – not that he couldn't pull off that particular look. "Uh, my family Christmas ended with an impromptu game of rugby in the back garden. I think I probably need a shower." He returned his gaze to Dani, "I'll see you later".

"Okay" Dani smiled back, with an expression Lee definitely had seen before.

Grant himself, appeared about an hour later. Lee was coming out of the kitchen as the front door opened. Grant closed it gently behind him. He looked slightly breathless and really tired. Christmas for Grant had been a dizzying list of visits to make. He had planned as had been his seasonal habit, to travel across the south of England to see old friends in Bath and Salisbury. It took some careful co-ordination and a thorough understanding of off-peak British Rail timetables. Lee imagined that he must have been saying some emotional goodbyes. He looked drained of colour and somewhat diminished of spirit.

Catching Lee's concerned expression, Grant straightened and grinned, "Hey sugar. How's it been?"

Maybe it was because she knew there wouldn't be too many more opportunities, but Lee responded to her instinct rather than her sense of reserve. She put down the two mugs of coffee she'd been carrying and just went directly to Grant, embracing him tightly. Grant was a little taken aback for a moment, before returning the hug. Lee felt him cough a little before he turned it into a laugh.

"So are we going to be doing this every day now?" he asked "I'm just checking because you know, it might make things awkward when I bring a date home."

Lee let the hug go, but held on to a hand. "I've just missed you, that's all".

"Good" Grant replied, "That's how I like it". He looked over Lee's shoulder and saw a hesitantly approaching Dani, "And hello – who might this be?"

"I'm Dani" she replied, stepping forward to Lee's shoulder.

Grant looked curiously at the new guest and then back to Lee, "*The* Dani?"

Lee nodded with a smile, "*The* actual one."

"Well" Grant smiled, "I've heard some tales about you. But don't worry, nothing too tawdry".

Again, Lee thought it best to be right up front about Dani's presence, she wanted to establish her friend's residency as quickly as possible. "Would it be okay if she stayed in my room for a while?"

There wasn't even a moment's hesitation from Grant, "It'll be lovely to have a genuinely pretty face around the place."

Rikki minced across the landing in a long dressing gown, his hair wrapped in a towel "Bitch! I hear every bloody word, y'know!"

january 1984
star in the descendancy

* *

I hate 1984. I can't see how this year is going to make sense. There's not much for me to do in it. No big steps ahead. Just month after month of taking pills, having my face sparked and going over the same conversation with Dr Garner:

Yes, I still feel the same way.
Yes, I am happy with my steady progress
Yes, I'm keeping to the correct hormone dosages
Yes, I'm still working
Yes, I have a good support network
Yes, I am extending and developing my female persona
No, I'm not in a sexual relationship

I'm also feeling sick of feeling really sick when I wake up in the mornings. And I'm just so tired all day long.

Mr White is going to start interviewing for Grant's job next week. God knows what we'll get.

I can't believe he's going. I can't stand it that he's going.

I WANT GRANT BACK! And he hasn't even gone yet.

. . . .

They drove in silence under a deep grey ceiling of pure January. Occasional small talk about tickets or the length of the flight punctuated otherwise private wonderings. For her part, Lee was still clinging to some desperate hope that Grant might just suddenly break his mask of stoicism, turn theatrically toward her and shout 'Fuck it! Let's blow this off and go for an early and very long lunch!' It wasn't going to happen of course. Not this time.

Even the traffic seemed to be co-operating – ridiculous for a Saturday morning. There were green lights and unclogged junctions everywhere – even through Shepherds Bush. It was like some kind of sick conspiracy. Lee chanced a quick glance over at Grant. He was looking away from her, out through the passenger side window. She wondered if he was quietly bidding farewell to each side street as they passed. She imagined that he'd have a tale for every pub and club they were passing. The whole of west London was his story. London needed him in it.

"The window sticks in summer" Grant suddenly said.

"What?"

"The window in my bedroom – It sticks when the window frame expands in the summer. You should tell Dani".

Dani was the inheritor of Grant's room, much to Luka's chagrin. It had been reasoned that it simply wouldn't have made sense for Lee to have been on a separate floor from the apartment's newest resident. Besides, Dani was earning more from her temp work than Luka could make. There were doubts that he would have been able to manage the rent at all.

They finally hit some traffic approaching Chiswick. Grant faced forward and his features seemed to relax a bit more. He let out a deep sigh, perhaps in reaction to Peter Powell's nervous chuntering on Radio 1. "At least in that way, things couldn't have worked out better."

Lee wasn't entirely sure what Grant was referring to. She wasn't sure if it was something the DJ had just said.

"Dani arriving when she did, I mean. It saved us trying to find someone else for the room – and she's just great. I am really, *really* pleased she's going to be there for you."

"She is great" Lee placed her hand on Grant's "But I'd still rather have both of you around."

Grant gave a reciprocal squeeze of Lee's fingers before allowing her hand to return to the gearstick. "You've got plenty of love around you. More than most, I reckon. You just need to stay focused and keep moving forward. I have every faith."

Lee smiled out into the traffic, "I'm glad *you* do. Sometimes I wonder what on earth I'm doing with my life. That's when I need your guidance."

"You don't mean that you have doubts?"

"No, it's nothing like that. It's just that there really isn't much going on right now. I'm just taking pills, growing hair and saving money – that's about it."

"Well, Baby wasn't built in a day!"

Grant had of course, tried to decline Lee's offer to walk him to the departure gate, but Lee would not be denied these last few moments in her friend's company. The check-in queue was fairly long, but of course that day it moved swiftly. Lee had time to buy a couple of take away coffees for the pair of them. Even that tiny shared experience was precious. She really was clinging to the last ledge now.

Finally, they walked to security. Grant turned his body to Lee as if to say 'this far and no further'.

"You do realise that I'm going to make this same trip too. And soon, if I can" Lee smiled, her eyes already beginning to glisten.

"What are you talking about you daffy bird?"

"New Zealand. I'm going to come and see you."

"No. You're not" Grant looked quite serious.

"I have savings"

"…and you're going to use them for exactly what was intended. You blow them on an air fare and you will break my bloody heart."

Grant had never been one for public demonstrations of affection. He had been known to round on a date who had dared to put an arm around him in what he described as a 'Straightsville' setting. And yet, faced with Lee's crestfallen expression, he had little choice but to offer his shoulder. He put down his bag and jacket and took Lee into his arms, "Oh, come here."

In a way, the gesture made things worse for Lee. She fought the tears and the sobs, but couldn't hold back the tiny shudders coming from her gut.

"Thank God we're at departures. They're used to seeing this kind of car crash" Grant murmured.

Lee took a half step back and rummaged in her coat pocket for a tissue, hiding her face behind a curtain of hair. She looked up at Grant again, "I have to see you again. I can't just…not *know* you."

Grant stared back at her for a while. Then he looked across to a sparsely occupied bank of blue upholstered seats. "Over here" he gestured. They sat down and Grant visibly began to compose something in his head while looking back over at the beckoning security gate. "You know, you have a bad habit of making me break rules."

"Sorry" Lee sniffed, not really sorry at all.

Grant was staring at his shoes and shaking his head. Finally, he looked up again, seemingly resigned to his course. "You don't need to know this – and you most definitely don't need to know this, *now*."

Lee hadn't heard this serious tone in Grant's voice too often. It was very much at the deeper end of his vocal range and was in truth, a little scary.

"Fuck it" Grant quietly cursed. "Look honey, the thing is this: The illness in the family is mine. I am the one who isn't well."

The thought that had recently made a home in a darkened corner of Lee's mind, took a small step toward the light. Nevertheless, she asked a question she knew Grant probably couldn't answer, "I don't understand this though. Why do you have to go to New Zealand to deal with it?"

Grant let another breath go, "Look love, my star is most definitely in the descendancy. I'm not going for treatment. There *is* no treatment for what's going on inside of me. There's just an end."

It hit Lee like a physical blow. Something in her nose sent out a wave of numbness that then extended out and around her face and down around the back of her head.

"What is it?"

Grant smiled sadly, "What it is, is too high a price."

"Why didn't you tell me? Does anyone else know?" Lee wasn't even sure why that mattered.

"I talked it over with Rikki. We've both lost people to this. We know how it goes. Nobody's safe. Nobody is immune – pardon the pun." He exhaled and in doing so, seemed to shrink a little, "Well *this* wasn't supposed to happen."

Lee's eyes were still sore from the farewell tears of moments ago. Those already felt cheap compared to what was welling up now. "Why? Why couldn't *I* know?"

"Because you lost your Dad and because that alone was too much for you to lose." Grant's hands rose over Lee's shoulders and around the back of her neck, holding her to the eye contact he'd made, "You don't want to go feeling that pain again. You don't need that and I certainly don't want it for you. All I was doing…I was just trying to be a memory *first*. It would be less… difficult that way."

"Less *difficult*?" Lee responded with quiet incredulity.

Grant was shaking his head again, this time it seemed, at himself – perhaps at everyone in general. "This is really not the parting conversation I wanted to have with you. You can't imagine how much talking I've done about this since I found out. How much thinking I've done. I've been scared and angry and sorry and then scared all over again. But you figure out pretty quickly that it's all just about time – and I just don't have enough of to sit and stare at a wall, or have endless conversations with people who want to tell me they understand. I have places to go, people to see and a whole lot of peace to make."

Lee was remembering Dad again. She was trying to remember what she'd learned. Trying not to make the same mistakes again. Grant would be her loss, but his was the loss that mattered more. She had to show that she got that, "You'll be so far away. Will they…your family?"

"They know what's coming. They're ready for me. And I'm ready for them, too. Look, If I stay here, if I wait, then this is where the end will be." Grant shook his head, smiling "Don't get me wrong, I love this city. London gave me my life – and now I suppose in a way, it's taking it back." He curved a palm around Lee's cheek. "What I'm left with now is home – and I know where that is. In the end, we all do. My time is soon, yours will be later." He grinned and added, "Plenty later."

Lee tried to collect some words she might offer, but none came to her lips.

Grant pulled up a sleeve and raised his wristwatch, touching it to Lee's ear. He leaned closer and whispered, "You hear that? That's the sound of all our lives, leaving – moment by moment. Know that. *Understand* it – and don't ever forget that it's happening. The fewer of those little ticks you waste, the more sense your life will make."

Grant picked up his shoulder bag and put his jacket over his left shoulder. He stood up slowly. Lee reached out and took hold of a hand. Squeezing hers in response, Grant leaned back down and kissed Lee on the lips. "You see this thing of yours through. You do it for you" he smiled, "and maybe you do it a little bit for me, too". His hand finally slid from her grasp and he covered the last few yards of open England to the security gate.

Lee couldn't watch. Years later, she regretted not looking up. Maybe she missed one last glance back from Grant. Maybe there was a final smile that she never got to see.

The drive back took longer. Now that she didn't need to cling to the streets like a reluctant child being carried off to bed, she was finding that getting anywhere at all was frankly a struggle. It was early afternoon when she finally parked the car and headed back up to the apartment.

Only Rikki was home. He'd clearly not long emerged from bed and was still wearing a dressing gown. A bowl of half-finished cornflakes left hopelessly by the side of the sofa. He was sitting where she had first seen him the night Grant had brought her back to see the place. He was plugged into the same stereo, piping black vinyl into a chunky-looking pair of headphones. Lee stared at a stilled figure unmoved by the frantic bass beat that leaked out into the room.

She wasn't going to say anything at all, but the movement of her half turn, alerted Rikki to her presence. He pulled the phones from his head, momentarily upping the volume. He slapped the power switch, ending the incursion entirely. Lee thought he looked as though he hadn't properly cleaned off last night's eyeliner.

"You okay, kidder?"

She stood in the doorway, wondering how to respond to the question. "He told me before he left."

Rikki nodded solemnly in consideration, "That can't have been easy."

Lee shook her head, "He was amazing. He's somewhere in the air right now and all I want to do is follow him. Help him somehow."

"Did you suggest that to him?" Rikki grinned.

"Yes" she admitted, feeling a little sheepish at her own predictability.

"I hope he kicked your arse all over the place for that one."

Lee crossed the room and sat down next to her favourite drag queen, resting her head against his shoulder as they both eased back into the sofa.

Rikki's arm snaked around Lee's shoulder. He took a deep breath and let it seep back out, loaded with reflection, "We've played our part, kidder. We've been here, right where he needed us and right *when* he needed us. Now he needs what's on the other side of the world."

"I can't help it" Lee managed hoarsely, "I just don't want him to be gone."

"Then don't think about him that way. Look, I don't need to tell you that everybody has to leave sometime. For those of us left behind, the memories have to be about the life – about the real person. Look, I don't know about you, but I doubt that my last moment will be my best – not unless I have a cardiac in the middle of giving the greatest ever Shirley Bassey, on stage at the Albert Hall."

Lee coughed up an unexpected laugh at the image.

"I'm just saying that I want people to remember my greatest hits."

Lee laughed some more – involuntarily. "*Hits?*"

It could have been the first occasion Lee would have had the bed to herself again, but Dani sensed that there should be at least one night when Grant's room remained respectfully empty and so she slipped under the duvet with Lee once more. She didn't yet know the full story. Lee would tell her the next day, once Moray Crescent had begun again.

The new week arrived with a mixture of relief and new dread. Lee was glad to be facing a day that would make demands of her other than emotional. And yet, there was an office to face which would bear a very obvious Grant-sized hole – and for the very first time, in Lee's experience.

Miriam was already at her desk and on the phone. She must have been on hold to one of the branches, because she was able to say an audible 'Hi' upon seeing her one remaining team member. Lee gave a reassuring half smile back and set about trying to recall her point of progress with the desk full of paperwork she'd left on the previous Friday.

The morning was an exercise in absurdity. Only one person may have been missing, but that still left two people to handle the work of four. Mondays were routinely a busy day, but Grant had been able to shoulder most of the burden without breaking stride. Now Miriam was regularly holding two phones at once – often with another call holding. Lee herself tried to field as many of the branch enquiries as she could. She ran messages for Miriam and tried to keep the coffee coming between trying to work her own ledgers error-free, but in double-quick time. Finally, at around half past twelve, there was a moment when neither of them had a phone to their ear.

"So" Miriam ventured, looking across the room, "how are *you* coping?"

Lee thought about just taking the easy route, but what was the point. She and Miriam knew each other better than that.

"I'm…working through it" Lee replied, trying to sound as assured as she wished she felt. "And you?"

Miriam shook her head with a sad smile, "It's just not right, is it?"

"No. No it's not."

Miriam placed her palms on the desk in front of her and straightened her back, physically committing herself to her announcement. "That is why, in my role as the senior member of staff in this room, I declare that we should depart immediately for a long lunch tribute to Mr Grant Jolley."

They'd visited the bar once before for lunch, not much more than two months ago. It was part of a hotel, but was open to non-residents and business types. Grant had been particularly keen on their swordfish and so both Miriam and Lee ordered it in his honour.

Miriam took a generous sip of her white wine, "How was he at the airport?"

Lee chose her response carefully. She still didn't know how much Grant had told the woman he'd spent most of the last years sitting next to. "He was…honest."

Miriam nodded thoughtfully. She curved purple-taloned fingers around her long-stemmed glass and took another sip. "He told you."

Lee nodded, relieved that she could speak honestly, "I think I just wore him down, in the end. What with me standing there on the one hand, and his flight being called on the other, I think he just sort of ran out of room."

Miriam smiled at the thought. "You do know why he didn't want to tell you?"

Lee's thoughts went somewhere else for a moment. "My Dad never gets any easier to miss. It really wouldn't have made any difference."

Miriam leaned across the table for two and placed a hand over Lee's, "Grant really loved you, you know. I think he really felt like a big brother."

"I know" Lee nodded solemnly, "I really have to stop losing family."

"You know, we can't ever blame Grant for the decision he made"

"No. No I'd never do that."

"And for us now, it's just change. And we can't be afraid of change, can we?"

If a week full of long days at CC called much upon Lee's emotional and mental reserves, at least the weekend nights at *Oasis* were making sense. Somehow the unearthly environment of pounding bass beats and spinning, weaving shafts of light against darkness, were serving as something of a tranquil haven. At *Oasis*, Lee knew what she should be doing and where she should be doing it. There were no great decisions to be taken or opinions to be held. She could function with cold efficiency, focusing on the tasks in hand minute-by-minute rather than reflecting upon her life and the absence from it of those she loved.

Lee's ability to lip-read was now so good that she didn't need to even bend toward the customers to learn their orders any more. Perhaps her heightened senses owed something to her a now regular consumption of speed. She was five weekends into applying it routinely to her job. Friday nights in particular, might otherwise have been beyond her. Becky was able to let Lee have a wrap for just £4. Lee would split it into two, taking one half for the first part of the night and then the other during her break. Becky could still get coke, but that was generally reserved for special occasions – rather like a good wine.

Lee had observed with amusement, the shrinkage of her genitalia under the influence of speed. She'd wondered how much you had to take in order to make things disappear entirely.

Lee excused herself the tag of junkie. Quite simply, when not at *Oasis*, she had no desire to take anything. Speed was nothing more than a tool to help her to work and generate money. Oddly, as Lee's familiarity with the drug grew, she became more aware of others doing the same. She could recognise the symptoms; the increased rate and volume of speech, the intensity of stares and yet the restless rotations of heads suggesting the consumer's need to know of everything going on, all of the time.

There was no opportunity for Lee to engage anyone in conversation during work hours. Instead she drew intimacy from the movements of those around her. But everything on these nights, belonged to the music. The sound of 1984 was smooth. From Ashford & Simpson to Midnight Star, the sophistication oozed. London had Loose Ends and now Sade. The warmth was seductive, but left her wanting more. She took to choreographing her moves around the club. If collecting glasses for example, she would plot a point between one bar and another and would try walking almost on her toes, avoiding being bumped or touched by any revellers.

Within the darkened sanctuary of the club, Lee worried less about being noticed. She didn't even attempt to disguise the now visible bumps in her t-shirt. They weren't by any means breast-shaped – just small protrusions, really. In the dark, and with the t-shirt tucked into her waistband, her shape wasn't actually compromised at all, but she knew that in regular light, changes were making themselves known. She sensed that Elaine had picked up on something the previous week in the staff room, but nothing had been said.

There was always a price to pay of course. Working on speed at night meant borrowing energy from the morning after. Across the course of a weekend, Lee would barely even see daylight. Dani would visit her room with the occasional cup of tea and would pop in when it was time for Lee to get ready for Saturday night shifts. Lee knew it must be frustrating for her friend. It would have been wonderful to have had some nights out in the West End together, but Lee had made a commitment to prioritise the raising of funds and with her schedule now in place, there could be no slowing of tempo. She had to be single-minded. Somewhere out there in the future she had to believe that all of this would finally be balanced by better days.

Life she knew, would have been significantly darker without Dani. Sittingbourne's other exile was adapting to London life rather well. She was now in the fourth week of a temp job at Bush House for BBC World Service. She'd landed a three-month contract as PA to a senior executive in finance. He was responsible for a department which handled low level procurement and expenses. Dani said she'd seen some bizarre claims – though she took the confidentiality agreement she'd signed very seriously and so disappointingly wouldn't spill any of the details. Lee was a little jealous over Dani's job. Sure, it may have been fairly mundane in itself, but she did get to carry a BBC pass.

Dani had been wonderfully supportive over Grant's departure. She'd never had the time to get to know him herself, but she knew how important he had been to Lee. In the meantime, she had made Grant's old room her own. It had her stamp of neatness and freshness on it. There were touches and cues that were quintessentially hers. Lee recognised certain themes from her friend's bedroom back in Kent: the crisp white bedspread and pale pink cushions, a straw hat with pale blue ribbon that hung on the wall and a pair of white linen curtains with tie backs that she'd bought from *Barker's* department store with her first week's paycheque. Oddly, as much as Lee liked visiting Dani next door, they pretty much always seemed to end up back in her own room. They had both readied themselves in there tonight ahead of a trip down to High Street Ken in search of pizza and some one-on-one conversation.

Being out with Dani as always, gave Lee a little more confidence. Walking with anyone at all allowed her to look up from her shoes, but remove Dani from the picture and back seemed to come the seething contempt from occasional groups of young men – or a suspicious look from a shop assistant. It was still a picnic compared to life outside of the capital and most of the time, Lee felt pretty much unnoticed by her fellow Londoners.

They settled on a place near the south entrance to Holland Park. They had no idea if it would be any good, but they both agreed that they liked the chequerboard tiled floor. Lee habitually manoeuvred her dinner partner into the seat facing out into the restaurant, leaving her to face the wall behind Dani. She did it almost unconsciously now. It wasn't about what one could see, it was about whether one could *be* seen.

Nights like these gave the friends a chance to return to simpler times in Sittingbourne. The same kind of small talk would begin – usually about people they'd seen on TV or a picture from a magazine – only now the famous weren't so far away.

Dani had been told that Nick Rhodes of Duran Duran had been witnessed getting out of a car near Baker Street that very week. "Wearing an awful lot of makeup apparently."

"Yes, but quite well" Lee pointed out with a grin. She knew of plenty of places where one could probably see a pop star or two. She was pretty sure she'd seen Adam Ant a couple of weeks before while out walking with Rikki to the delicatessen. Rikki had declined to confirm the sighting due to his own fragile ego. Proper Londoners of course didn't get overly excited about the famous and so Lee and Dani had to move on from the subject fairly quickly. Back to the real world.

"I've barely seen Rikki in the last couple of days" Dani remarked.

"He does this every so often. Just disappears. He stays over with people he knows." Lee considered the matter a little further, "Or people he's *getting* to know."

Dani ran her finger down along the stem of her wine glass, "Hasn't what's going on…changed anyone's habits?" she asked carefully. "I mean isn't promiscuity taking chances?"

"It's changed everything" Lee asserted quietly. "People are more careful and more scared, but they're not really sure what's going on. Some of them are just determined to carry on as they always have. Maybe whatever Rikki's doing is helping him to deal with missing Grant."

"I thought Grant might have written a letter or something to you all by now."

Lee smiled. "I don't think he ever intended to keep in touch. He said goodbye to London. He wouldn't want there to be an open line back to life here. It took me a while to understand that."

The pizzas arrived. They were huge. Lee and Dani giggled at the sight of them.

The waitress sprinkled parmesan and peppers for them, departing with, "Enjoy your meals, ladies."

Lee looked up at Dani in complete surprise and saw the expression mirrored in her friend's face. They giggled some more. Sure, the waitress was middle aged, wearing glasses and looking pretty disinterested in her customers, but Lee was happy to take the compliment.

"See!" remarked Dani, "that wouldn't have happened back in the old days."

Lee was blushing quite deeply, "Sometimes at *Oasis*, I just get the feeling that some of the customers think I'm…y'know."

"Maybe they do. They *probably* do. You wouldn't necessarily know what they were thinking, would you? People don't generally make a point of remarking on the sex of the person serving them." Dani chewed on an olive, grinning and then added, "It's going to happen more and more often, the closer you get. You're going to…blur."

Lee laughed out loud at the idea of 'blurring' and then silenced herself, concerned that her pitch might not be appropriate for a person already identified by the waitress as one of the 'ladies'.

Dani sighed, moving the conversation on. "I can't work out James"

"What to do you mean?"

"Well, he's definitely *not* gay, is he?"

Lee's mouth was otherwise engaged so she shook her head to confirm the negative.

"He's not even a little bit gay, is he?"

More head shaking, this time with a grin.

"So how did he come to live in the gayest flat possible?"

Lee swallowed and took a sip of wine. "It was something to do with someone he knew and just needing a place to stay at first. But he's really level-headed and just doesn't have a problem with the gay scene. He gets it – and he's not spooked by all the scare stories. I think he finds it all quite entertaining from a safe distance. Also, I think he secretly liked being the only straight one around the place – made him feel a bit special. On the outside, all you get from being straight is feeling normal."

Dani was about to ask another question when Lee put out a hand and froze the moment, "Wow, I've just realised: we're now a straight household."

"How do you mean?"

"Three to two. You, James and me are straight, while Rikki and Luka are gay. It hadn't occurred to me before." Lee gave her own observation a little more thought, "God, I hope Rikki isn't spending time away because he feels alienated."

"He wouldn't, would he?" She dismissed the thought. "No, Rikki would be Rikki no matter where he was."

Dani selected a little mushroom from her pizza topping, "Same as James, in that respect."

"I guess." Lee thought back to the party. She almost didn't mention it – but this was Dani, how could she not? "For a while before Christmas, I couldn't look James in the eye."

Dani offered the required expression of surprise.

"I made a bit of a mistake. I got kind of carried away at our party and I sort of...tried to..."

"What?"

"...kiss him" Lee admitted with a wince.

"You kissed James?" Dani responded, perhaps a little too loudly for what was still a fairly sparsely peopled restaurant.

"NOOOO!" Lee replied in a hoarse whisper. "I said I *tried* to. We didn't *actually*. He wasn't...wasn't as drunk as I was."

Dani looked up at Lee through her curls, "But you do fancy him?"

Lee hid her sheepish grin behind the bowl of her raised wine glass, "Well yes...I mean, no. Well there's no point, so it doesn't really matter, does it?"

april 1984
short ladders, long snakes

ecalmed, that's what I am. Like when a sailing boat is in the doldrums. There's just nothing really happening and nothing more I can do right now to make any further change. I took another long critical look in the mirror last night. Honestly, I feel that there really isn't that much to show for all I've gone through.

What <u>have</u> I got out of this so far? I've put on about a stone in weight, my tummy sticks out and there are small bumps behind my nipples. I watch my so-called 'boobs' every day, but I don't see much change really. They are incredibly sensitive though – and really not very comfortable. They hurt when I'm running downstairs. I'm getting pretty protective of my chest area in crowds, too. I haven't actually bumped into anyone yet, but I just have a feeling it would hurt.

I think my boy bits have shrivelled a bit, but that could just be wishful thinking. Dani also said that my bum had changed shape a bit. As usual, it's hard to know when she's just being kind, though.

Finally made the switch to wearing only female underwear – just plain M&S. I had held on to a couple of pairs of boy stuff, simply because the horrid things between my legs fit better into them. I hated wearing them though and I've just decided that I'd rather be uncomfortable in body than in mind. Chucked the last couple of pairs into a bin near the tube station!

God, I can't bear shaving anymore. It hurts so much. I'm cutting myself every single time now. I end up with sore patches all around my mouth.

To be honest, I'm not even sure the electrolysis is really working for me. Carol says this is all normal and she promises that all of a sudden, I will start to see a real difference. Thing is, what else <u>can</u> I do? I dream about just being able to peel off a whole mask of skin and *seeing it take all of the hair and the soreness with it. Underneath, I'd be smooth and unblemished. Actually, I'd quite like to do that with my entire body.*

. . . .

"I don't get it." Lee said, finally vocalising a thought she'd harboured ever since she'd first been introduced to Rikki.

Rikki himself was seated in his favourite spot on the sofa, applying a deep red nail polish to his toes. His right leg had been bent up at an improbable angle – his heel on the seat cushion with toes protruding. He didn't break concentration, "Mmm?"

"Drag – I don't get it."

Rikki looked up with a 'what-was-that?' expression.

"I don't mean that I have a problem with it or anything, it's… fine. I just…"

"…Don't get it" Rikki confirmed.

Lee shrugged. "I'm just curious, I suppose. Why would you want to dress up as a woman if you either aren't a woman or… well…don't want to *be* a woman. I'm just not sure where the motivation comes from."

Rikki smiled broadly and returned his right foot to the floor, crossing his legs in a fluid movement. He shook his head a little and sighed, "Lee, Lee, Lee – oh little Lee."

Lee grinned at the tease.

"Now then – you're seen my set at *Crush*, haven't you?"

"Several times, yes" she admitted, now smiling widely.

"And you've seen me here in all of my finery?" Rikki's arms swept wide, theatrically.

"I have."

"You have seen me at my very, very best – the ultimate in Drag Jockey expressionism", his eyes were closed as if he were blissfully drinking in the adoration of an appreciative crowd. He snapped back to the moment, "– And did you ever, before during or after these occasions, even for one tiny, teeny moment, actually consider me to *be* a woman?"

Lee took a moment and still smiling, shook her head, "I did not."

"And there my dear, you have it. Drag has nothing to do with either being, or wanting to be, female. It's just an expression – a show. Its theatre, baby." Rikki was beginning to wave his arms around for emphasis again, "People like to see an absurd version of themselves – and that's what drag queens are for. We're a combination of man *and* woman, twisted and reflected back to the audience – a beautiful tragedy. And let me tell you, this is not an act anyone can really pull off for long. You think I'll still be able to make a living like this, five years from now? – Ooooh no. We burn bright, but briefly in this game."

Lee decided to push her enquiry a little further, "So you don't do it because you...like it?"

Rikki laughed until his smoker's cough choked all the fun out of breathing. He quickly fired up a Chesterfield in a hair-of-dog bid to ease the hacking. "Honestly kidder, I do it because I can make a living at it. It was a way of getting my first gig and it's worked for me ever since. Truth is, it's a bloody curse. Getting ready takes half a day, getting back out of drag afterwards takes an hour and in between, I can't even step outside of the club. Sure, I love seeing people smile and having a good laugh. I like being provocative and a bit ridiculous, I even get a bit of a kick out of trying on the odd crazy outfit, but I swear..." he paused for effect, "I *swear,* I would give it all up tomorrow if I could find a better way of making two fifty a week." He seemed to watch Lee for a sign of understanding. "Does *any* of that help answer your question?"

It did. Lee was glad she had asked. She really liked Rikki – nobody made her laugh more – but she had sometimes worried that others might judge a parallel between Rikki's job and Lee's aspirations for life. It hadn't been a pleasing thought. Now she felt more than a little foolish, having even considered it.

"What *you're* doing on the other hand" Rikki continued unexpectedly, "is amazing to me."

"Oh? Why?" Lee asked, with more than a little trepidation.

"'Cause it's deadly fuckin' real with you, kidder. It's like you're trying to get changed in the middle of the street. I mean, I can be hilariously bad at looking female-ish, but you're going to have to be right on. You're going to need to be real – every day" he shook his head, "– that's pressure. That's fuckin' brave, is what it is."

She was getting used to hearing that view, "I wish people would stop calling it brave. It just isn't. I mean, seriously, what else *can* I do? This is my only chance at having a normal life."

Rikki laughed hoarsely again, puffing out a cloud of blue smoke, "And how's that for an irony. 'Normal' – I love it!"

Lee smiled along with Rikki's observation. "It is strange, especially right now. I feel like I've left one place, but haven't arrived at where I'm going. I'm sort of…nowhere. People are beginning to be unsure of how to take me." She brightened, recalling a recent incident buying a tube ticket, "I've been called 'miss' a few times recently. And when I was out for a pizza with Dani a little while back the waitress referred to us as 'ladies'. That felt pretty good."

Now it was Rikki's turn to smile at his friend's words. "Yeah, it is gonna happen. You have some good round features going for you, y'know. You're young and slim, you've got all that hair – these are the cues."

"What do you mean, 'cues'?"

Rikki took a deep drag on the cigarette, "It's one thing I've learned with all of the messing around I do with wigs and make-up. You don't need to be perfect to get your message across. All you need to do is to cover a few key points – the *cues*. People don't look that closely at anyone unless they're attracted to them or have to answer to them – they just don't have the time. Most people appear as wallpaper, right? They only stand out if they have a defining feature; a big nose, bright red hair. For the rest, if you get the cues right, the human eye of the beholder will just fill in the rest of the picture."

"O-kay…"

"Look, those things I referred to earlier – your hair, the shape of your face, your slim figure. You put that together with a certain walk and people who see you will just take the cues and fill in the rest of the picture. You give them girl-*like*; they'll see girl."

"Mmm" Lee considered a little less than convinced. "What was that about a walk?"

"Well look, I mean you have to figure out that stuff for yourself in order to make it really *you* of course. Shit – you try walking like I do in heels and you're going to get a whole different kind of reaction." Rikki's expression suggested he was giving his own theory a little more thought. "See, what *I* do is walk like a drag queen." He stood up and straightened his dressing gown. Up on his toes, he sashayed from one end of the living room to the other while commentating on his own moves, "And I'm crossing over the toes and I'm swaying the hips – that I don't really have. So, I'm *over*doing everything. No woman actually walks like this – and yet, the exaggeration comes from a basic truth. You just gotta think it through. Women move the way they do because of the shape that they are." He was into the lesson now and tracing lines against his silk robe with enthusiastic concentration. Women aren't straight like us... well, like men", he corrected himself. "The hips are wider and the top half of the leg comes back into line down to the knee. You know all that stuff anyway, I'm sure – but the bottom line is: guys point outwards, girls point inwards. You remember that and you won't go too far wrong."

"I guess."

Rikki sat back down, crossing his legs elegantly, "Look, don't get me wrong, I'm the last person who could teach you to behave like a woman" he dropped his voice to a baritone "– although I do know a thing or two about hiding the manhood."

"Let's hope I don't need that in the long term" Lee chuckled.

"Right." Rikki acknowledged, "Anyway, you don't need to be *like* a woman, you need to be your *own* woman." He let his words hang in the air for a moment, seemingly rather pleased at the way he'd summarised things. He drew again on his cigarette and gathered his tea cup and nail polish together, preparing to leave. "Seriously though, if I were you, I'd take some time to visit the library and have a look at some books on anatomy. I know that your body is changing, but surgery and drugs won't give you everything. You're going to have to *think* your way through this too."

Lee smiled warmly. She'd been surprised by Rikki's insight. "I wonder what kind of woman you would be" she ventured.

Rikki turned back at the living room door and grinned "Oh I'm what a woman would be like if she had no morals, no worries, a permanent hunger for sex – and a dick. Believe me, I really am right where I should be in this world."

There was an impromptu and very unofficial meeting going on in the reception area of Change Central. Reception was a crossing point in the building and a place where a lot of the natural gossip moved from one department to another. Cheryl the receptionist almost certainly held more secrets than anyone. She would keep them quiet too – unless you *wanted* her to spill the proverbial beans, in which case she could distribute a story faster than a virus on a hospital ward. Just now however, rumour was all they had.

Zoe Moreno was the focus of any number of viewpoints and almost limitless speculation. It had been three weeks since she'd arrived at CC. At first the assumption was that she was in some way, a replacement for Grant, but it became quickly apparent that Grant's role was to be taken up by Miriam in the form of additional duties. There would be no new member of the Branch Admin Department. Instead Zoe Moreno was to replace Mr White who had been moved to a 'consultancy role' wherein he would be required to spend only two days a week obsessing about train commutes. From the expression he'd worn ever since the re-shuffle, nobody had actually consulted with him about his consultancy.

Ms Moreno had spent her time moving from department to department, asking quiet questions and making thoughtful notes. She stood no more than five feet two and was probably about ten pounds heavier than she should be. Her hair was short with a deep red tint and was cut into a perfect point at the nape of her neck. Her accent was unsurprisingly Hispanic, though Lee couldn't be sure of her origins. She smiled quite a lot, although only with her dark red lips. Those deep brown eyes Lee felt, rarely seemed to fit the same picture as the rest of her face.

There were most agreed, big changes ahead.

Miriam was already looking worn out and beaten down. Her days were starting earlier and ending later. Lunch was a thing of the past and frankly even the sympathetic efforts of Lee and Mr Lincoln to relieve some of the pressure, weren't saving her from pending burnout. She and Lloyd needed the money too much for her to consider quitting. Lee had tried to argue that money wouldn't be of much value if there wasn't enough of Miriam left to make use of it.

Not much of any worth had been accomplished in the building that morning. According to widely circulated memo, there would be an announcement at midday, 'following consultation and extensive strategic reviews'. Lee Habens was twenty-four years old and already jaded by this kind of event. It was IGF all over again as far as she was concerned. She wondered however, if they could afford to cut her role, given that they'd already divided three jobs into two. If Miriam had to pick up Lee's duties as well, she would probably implode sometime around late afternoon.

Cheryl's red phone rang out a single tone. It was an internal call. She listened earnestly to a message and then gently replaced the receiver. She stood, resplendent in a late fifties blue two-piece and pearls and informed the crowd in her clearest, most official tone, "Everyone to the boardroom, right away please."

Almost fifty people crammed into a room designed to seat twelve. The lack of space was made worse by the comparative chasm of carpet between the Chairman, Managing Director, Mr White, Ms Moreno and the rest of the staff. No-one else seemed inclined to flirt with the four executives of the apocalypse.

The MD stood to make the announcement. Lee had worked in the same building as this man for almost two years. She'd probably seen him fewer than a dozen times and had never held a conversation with him. Michael Ruck was a surprisingly young man, no more than forty. He was slim, sharp suited, dark haired and with a Freddie Mercury overbite that just barely prevented him from being seriously attractive. "Morning everybody. I'm going to make this very brief. I know there has been plenty of rumour and conjecture about what's to happen. I'm here to inform – and to a degree, to reassure."

Lee looked across the room to see Miriam. She'd not been able to leave her desk until the last minute and she was caught at the back of the crowd.

The announcement continued in silence, "This morning is the culmination of a lot of consideration and fresh thinking. There are indeed going to be changes here – and for some of you, these will be significant changes. But the first news I want to impart is that there are no plans to lose any of you." He paused for a moment. "Let me underline that: there will be a place for everyone at the new Change Central." Again, a pause as he let the thought settle over whispers and murmurs. The slightest sense of relief began to relax the audience. He whipped them back to attention with a slightly louder first word, "Now" he said, his chin lifted for extra authority, "this does not mean that we won't be losing some jobs – because we will. The world of commerce is moving on and we intend to keep pace with it. Ms Moreno who comes to us from one of the city's major merchant banks has been gathering thoughts and observations and she is going to be central to our approach to modernisation. It is 1984 and we need to ensure that we look like we belong in these fast-moving and increasingly professional times." Ruck paused again and checked behind him, "I'll now invite Ms Moreno" to provide a little more detail for you."

Zoe Moreno stood, though only the front three rows of staff were able to attest to this. For the rest a disembodied voice would have to do. "Hello everybody." She spoke with an assured tone, although not terribly loudly. It meant that no-one could make a sound lest they miss her next remark, "Now, I will be visiting the departments throughout this afternoon and tomorrow to explain more about how the changes will be affecting you. In general, what you need to know is that some jobs will be disappearing because as a company we just don't need those roles anymore. For those whose jobs are removed from the structure, other positions around the branch network will be made available." A little sub-murmuring swelled. Ms Moreno waited until silence returned. We will be presenting a more modern front for the future. You will notice some re-branding in our logo and corporate colours, you will also notice the appearance of some desktop computers which will be introduced to one or two departments. Those concerned will of course be trained in how to use them. We will also be introducing various codes of practice including strict adherence to hours of business and to standards of appearance. For the ladies, this will mean no more trousers to be worn." More whispers. "And for the gentlemen, we expect suits, ties and neat haircuts."

Lee's felt her stomach fall to her feet. Ms Moreno was looking directly at her as she spoke – as were a good number of colleagues.

"The watchwords ladies and gentlemen, are 'progress' and 'professionalism'. We are going to look and feel like a company that is aiming high. We want all of you to be a part of a brighter future and we look forward to you playing a full part in the future of Change Central."

She was going through the motions, just filling in columns of figures and processing some simple arithmetic – the kind of thing she could manage easily enough with only a small part of her consciousness. Lee's heart had left the building shortly after the meeting broke up. Four hours later, what remained of her was simply marking time and awaiting a departure date. A number of co-workers had made supposedly humorous remarks about 'the chop' toward Lee. She'd smiled, but remained silent on the matter. She had granted an answer only to Miriam's enquiry. "What will you do?"

"Well, I really don't think I can be what they want me to be" she had replied.

"The world's gone mad. Completely mad", Miriam had remarked gloomily, before returning to her overwhelming duties.

A short introduction of clicking heels on the parquet flooring in the hallway eventually heralded the arrival of Change Central's very own grim reaper. Zoe Moreno stood for a moment just a single short stride inside the room. She was consulting the notes on her clipboard. She looked up smiling – at least with the lower half of her face. "Now, Miss Nash" she began.

Miriam smiled weakly, "That's me."

Ms Moreno stood directly in front of Miriam and with her back to Lee – who for the moment it seemed, was not to exist. "You are one of my good news people."

Miriam was mustering as much of a positive tone as she could – which took her to about half the level of a normal Monday morning, "I am?"

"You are, yes. You will be getting some much-needed help."

Miram's shoulders sagged with relief, "Thank God!"

"Yes, you will be one of the first people to move to using a computer. It'll be arriving…" she consulted her clipboard again, "next Wednesday."

Miriam had sagged a little further.

"The training courses will begin on Monday night up in my office."

Ms Moreno smiled again – Lee could tell even through the back of her head.

"Trust me, you won't believe you ever got along without one." She turned to Lee and covered the three paces to her desk slowly while reading another note. "And Mr Habens…"

Lee wasn't about to reply to that title.

"You will also be required to train for the computer as back-up. You will not need to attend until a week on Monday, 6:00pm in my office." She looked straight into Lee's eyes, a crisp smile fixed into place, "Now, you heard about the new formal standards of appearance. We will expect you to comply with these by Monday. That gives you time to arrange for a haircut and to make the necessary additions to your wardrobe."

Lee smiled back at her. "You're absolutely sure about this?"

"Excuse me?"

"I mean I couldn't just tie my hair back neatly? I mean I could go along with the suit thing if I had to, but…"

Ms Moreno was already shaking her head, "How many top executives have you seen wearing ponytails? The ponytail is for little girls. You are expected to behave like the grown man you are." She smiled again and tapped her pen on the corner of Lee's desk, "By Monday" she chirped, through another red slashed smile.

She turned to leave but was stalled by Lee's words, "Yeah, I'm sorry but that's…well it's just not going to happen." Lee stood up taking a brief and very rare pleasure in being a good six inches taller than Ms. Moreno.

CC's newest executive manager never missed a beat. "Your choice", she chirped.

It's the extremities that always go first, Lee found. Being drunk meant that she lost feeling in her nose, her lips and her fingertips. She couldn't find her key. It was in one of her pockets, though she wasn't sure which one. She tried her trousers, but of course she never kept anything in those anyway. She tried her raincoat again. Not there. Now she remembered. Her key was in the top pocket of her denim jacket – the same denim jacket that right now hung on the back of her bedroom door, upstairs. She rested her forehead on the cool black gloss paintwork of the front door. She was going to have to buzz. She hated buzzing, it was an admission of guilt and of incompetence. She buzzed.

It seemed an age before she heard the inimitable raspy grump of Luka over the intercom 'Yeah?'

'Oh hey, I'm really sorry, it's Lee and I've…"

The door clicked and was released from its latch. It took Lee longer than usual to climb the stairs – as though an extra flight had been installed while she'd been out. At the final turn, she could see that the door to the apartment had also been opened, presumably by Luka. A pale blue light flickered across the emulsioned ceiling and out through the two-inch gap to the hallway. He must be watching TV, she realised. She stood for a moment in the isolation of the landing, adapting to being inside the building and yet not quite home. She looked back down the shaft below her, enjoying the synchronicity of white painted banisters below. She let the hand-rail at her side, support her weight for a moment and as she did so, felt the carrier she held, swing gently against the back of her calf. Nearly two years at that office and she'd been able to pack her personal effects into a single plastic bag. Sure, Change Central had been little more than a practical solution to some medium-term problems. It had allowed her to move to London, it had introduced her to a friend, who in turn had introduced her to a home and a life. She hadn't loved the job itself or particularly cared about the work – though she felt she'd been conscientious enough. She had liked being there a lot less without Grant, and she was pretty sure that the changes being introduced by the new regime would have made her days pretty much unpalatable. Even so, this was no time to be unemployed. She had saved just under £ 3,100 so far. She was going to need at least £ 6,000. Electrolysis appointments needed to be increased in frequency – and soon. She just couldn't afford to not be earning money – and really *good* money. She raised her free hand to her forehead and then swept her fingers through her hair. Hair. She was now out of a job because of hair. Her life had come to this.

It had been impossible to adequately explain to any of the small band of colleagues who had joined her at the pub earlier that evening, just why she'd been unable to 'buckle down' and just get a CC-prescribed haircut. They seemed to think that she was either being heroically counter-cultural or simply plain stupid. Miriam's expression throughout, had been one of detached bewilderment. Lee already knew she'd miss that face terribly.

A severance cheque including outstanding salary and holiday payments would be in the post along with the dreaded P45 form, Lee had been informed. Her departure had of course, been counted as a resignation and she had been advised that this would prevent her from drawing any benefits for six weeks. A colder analysis of events might theorise that Zoe Moreno had simply identified a small threat to the plans and new look of the company and she had reasonably enough eliminated it. The decision wasn't personal – it hadn't had time to be.

Lee reflected vacantly upon the progress she'd made and of how this single setback could potentially ruin everything. Hers was a life of short ladders and long snakes. She blinked again at the flickering light of home and with a deep breath, hauled herself up the final few steps.

Lee tried to measure her drunkenness. She and Dani had recently devised a special 'Bus' scale for such conditions:

Level 1 would mean that you were too drunk to drive the bus.

Level 2 indicated that you could no longer run and reliably make it onto the rear platform of a moving bus.

Level 3 described a state of physical helplessness that would prevent moving away from the resident bus nutter, ('upstairs at the front and on the right by the spyglass thingy – every bus has one', Dani had asserted).

The fourth and final level of drunkenness meant that you were in fact, the nutter herself.

Lee was pretty confident that she was no worse than a 2. She was also wide awake which made any suggestion of rest, rather unlikely. She estimated that it wouldn't yet be 11 o' clock. Dani was an early riser and she'd probably be asleep by now. There was nothing left for it but to make for the living room. Sure enough, Luka was there – and alone, unfortunately.

She took a seat at the far end of the sofa so as not to come between Luka and whatever he was watching. He didn't acknowledge her presence. She sat in the semi darkness, reclining into Rikki's spot. The TV beamed the image of a moustachioed man, speaking into a telephone. He looked impeccably strong and masculine. She looked at the actor's short, sleek dark hair and then down at the back of Luka's head. She focused on her distant flatmate's neatness. His cropped curls offered an example of how Lee *should* look if she was serious about making a living in 1984. Her own locks now rested at the top of her chest. She wondered idly for a moment about how she might persuade a hairdresser to style her hair short, but still in a feminine way, maybe like Princess Diana or something – it had after all, worked for George Michael. She immediately dismissed the idea. Rikki had been right about 'cues'. The long hair was serving her well. Besides, it also hid her face when she needed it to – either from enquiring eyes or after a brutal session of electrolysis. It was a part of her identity now and she loved it – a distinction which, given the level of loathing she held for just about every other cell of her physical being, did count for something. In truth, it probably wasn't her view on the issue that mattered most anyway. She was pretty sure she knew what Dr Garner would make of her ascribing to a less feminine hairstyle. She had always tried to be honest with him about how publicly she displayed her female identity. The sight of her shorn, could undo a lot of progress. No, there had to be some other way to move forward without such a compromise.

Lee returned her gaze to the TV. An elderly woman had appeared in the scene now. She couldn't make out what the actress was saying. It took a moment before Lee realised that she was watching a foreign language drama. Channel 4 showed some pretty exotic stuff she knew, but this didn't have any subtitles. It was only then that she noticed the green digits of the counter on the video cassette recorder changing. This programme was on tape. Perhaps Luka brought it back from Brazil. It didn't matter, Lee was past having any interest in a plotline, she would just sit and watch the images – anything to avoid heading for bed. Within five minutes however, the screen faded to black and some credits appeared. Luka was mostly turned away from Lee, she could only see his profile at a quarter angle. A single tear ran down along the contour of his cheek. He remained still for a moment and then brushed it away, sniffing as he reached across to switch off the tape player. Lee was completely taken aback. Her flatmate looked suddenly smaller than usual – and vulnerable. Still he said nothing. He pressed the rewind button and knelt in front of the screen with his back to the room.

"You okay, Luka?" Lee heard herself say.

"Sure, why not?" he replied softly, his silhouette hard black against the fizzing screen of the TV.

"It's just…Was that a sad film?"

"Not really." The cassette's reels spun noisily as the tape was re-gathered at full speed. Luka had been holding a tissue in one hand. He used it to blow his nose.

"You seem…a bit upset."

"S'nothing."

Another moment passed. Lee wouldn't have pursued it, but as the VCR clunked to a stop, Luka offered into the silence, "I miss home."

Lee found herself in the strangest of positions. If Luka had been almost anyone else in her life, she would have reached out to him to offer consolation and support. But it was *Luka*. She looked back out toward the hallway hoping for another flatmate to happen by and break the tension. She could still just get up and walk away. Why shouldn't she? She and Luka weren't friends as such. The only thing they shared was a roof. Nevertheless, she didn't wish loneliness on anyone (except perhaps tonight, Zoe Moreno). "Was that something from home?" she enquired, already knowing the answer.

Luka slotted the tape back into its slipcase, switched off the screen and finally turned. There were signs of more than a solo tear. He sat on the carpet and looked at the cassette in his hand. "It's just a stupid TV show I like. My mother tapes it for me. I pick up tapes whenever I go home. I sit in here late and I wear out the tapes just to see home."

Lee needed to give a little more thought to her next words. "How long *have* you been in London now?"

"Nearly four years" Luka grinned sheepishly at the realisation.

"And you're still homesick?" Lee smiled back, hoping that the mood was about to lighten.

"Not every day. Just…some days."

"But you feel that London is definitely the place for you?"

Luka expression suggested that he was anything but sure. "There is nothing at home for me. There is just love. Love won't give me a future."

'A future'. Lee understood the sacrifice of now for later. "So, we're both living for tomorrow."

Luka conceded a reflective smile, "I guess."

"It's hard"

Luka nodded sadly, staring at the carpet.

"I lost my job today." It felt odd to hear herself say it aloud.

"Fuck" Luka repeated, now looking up.

"Yeah – fuck. I don't really know what I'm going to do." Another strange statement for Lee to consider. "I have to have money, you know? For my treatment?"

Luka said nothing for a moment. Then he nodded, "You gotta do whatever you gotta do." He said determinedly. "In Brazil the transgênero, they let nothing stop them. They give their lives to be who they need to be. You need money? You make money. Nothing can stop you. You can't feel sorry for yourself..." He smiled ruefully, "Not like me". He raised himself up and returned to the sofa, scooping up his cigarettes and an ashtray in the same movement. He lit one, the flame from his match illuminating both of their faces. He hesitated for a moment and then offered the pack to Lee.

She smiled in appreciation of the gesture. "I'm not allowed. The drugs..." she explained.

"I knew someone jus' like you...at home" Luka began, exhaling a thin stream of grey into the blackness. "Is how I knew the signs" he confirmed, jutting his chin toward Lee. "She went to my school when she was a boy. I saw her after she started the change."

"Really?" Lee was suddenly hungry to hear of anyone else's transition.

"She was pretty, you know? She could do it". Luka shook his head at pictures playing somewhere inside his mind.

"How did she..?"

"She could not get work." He shrugged, "*I* could not get work. There *is* no work in my town for the young." Luka took another drag, the red embers fizzing through the end of the cigarette's paper sheath. "She became hooker, just like they all do. But is dangerous, you know? Drugs, bad men."

Lee's heart rate slowed with disappointment, "How did it work out?"

Luka shook his head and tapped at the rim of the ashtray, "I don' know. I don' think she made it."

Lee nodded glumly.

"Life is too hard for them" Luka went on, "but they never stop trying to find a way. They never stop."

She wasn't feeling too bad, physically. Her mouth was a little dry and she was anything but rested, but at least there was no hangover. She drew focus on the red digits of her clock radio.

She had switched off the alarm function after slipping under the duvet last night, knowing there was no point in rising early. It was now just after eight o' clock. A familiar double knock at the door was followed immediately by a dagger-sharp shaft of hallway daylight.

"Jesus! What are you doing? Do you know what time it is?" Dani was peering into the gloom.

Lee heard herself croak, "I do now." She hated speaking before she'd had a drink in the morning. A night of sleep would relax her vocal chords making her voice eerily deep.

"Are you not well?" Dani asked, stepping into the room. She was wearing a dark blue sweater over a white frilled blouse, making her almost Sloane-like in appearance. Her face was freshly painted.

Lee always loved the way Dani looked just before she went out. "I'll talk to you tonight about it." She knew Dani would have to leave and really didn't want to get into the whole story yet.

"Tell me a little – a headline. What's going on?"

Lee groaned and pulled the duvet over her head. It was whipped back almost immediately by Dani.

"Lost my job yesterday."

"Oh *Lee*..." Dani brushed a palm across Lee's forehead. Lee caught her friend's perfume in the gesture and suddenly wished that she too was up and ready to face the day.

"Go, go – I'll be fine" Lee shoo-ed. "We can talk later. It's all going to be fine – really."

Dani kissed her fingers and touched them to Lee's brow. She stood, turned and left, closing the door quietly. Lee inhaled a parting-scented breeze and sighed to herself. Until a few moments ago, she had considered giving herself the day off to mark the end of the era that was Change Central. It was however, still early and there were plenty of things she could do with the day. She considered how much better she would feel if by the time she next spoke with Dani, she had a solution to her problem. The warm duvet would be difficult to leave, but fortunately she was pretty desperate for a pee. She lifted herself upright, swung her feet to the floor and stood. She looked down and gave the thing a disdainful sneer. Months of hormone treatment had at least put pay to any of the other types of auto-erections she suffered, but the dam reflex which signalled the essential need for a morning pee, persisted. Always good to begin the day with some loathing, Lee reflected. She put on her dressing gown, grabbed her towel from the radiator, held it in front of her groin area and headed for the bathroom.

Ordinarily, she would have to plan to the minute her visit to and residency of, the upstairs bathroom. Mornings had become a tightly drilled routine since the matching of Lee and Dani's office hours. But that was then. Now there was time to spare. Rikki was the only one left in bed now and he wouldn't emerge until after lunch. She switched on the radio to take in the last hour of Capital's Breakfast Show. She reached for the shower, but then opted for the rare decadence of a bath instead.

There was an embarrassment of riches in a bathroom frequented by Rikki. Lee had been able to select from a bewildering number of bubble bath choices. Within minutes she lay under a blanket of foam. It was supposed to bear the scent of lavender, but she could no longer detect it. Bananarama were singing about Robert De Niro in the uptempo way that morning radio playlists demanded. Lee tried to go with the positive beat. A setback she considered, is only really a setback if you let it bed in. She revisited the previous night's conversation with Luka. His description of Lee's counterparts in Brazil and their complete commitment to their cause was sobering. She had never felt part of a transsexual community – let alone a global one – but it did no harm to see the bigger picture. Right now, she imagined, there would be others just like her, beginning far more challenging days. If those people had the advantage of living in a European city with a reasonable education behind them, surely they would find a way to make it through transition? She was pretty damned sure they wouldn't give up just because of a failure to hold down a clerical role at Change Central. If as Luka suggested, they couldn't be shaken from their convictions, how possibly could she? The blow from losing her position at CC had been a bitter one – if only because she had just begun to feel her plans gaining some balance. She had been on course. Still she told herself, this was London – and London always had possibilities.

The lunch rush was ending as she took a corner table at the *Argyle Arms*. The morning had been an education. She knew now what she was up against. She had dressed 'male smart' in her blue suit and had tied back her hair – today demanded she be as ruthlessly and aesthetically practical as she could bear. She had begun with the nearest employment agency to Marble Arch and then had worked her away along Oxford Street through three more. She had form-filled and smiled her way through the opening interviews – and been offered precisely nothing for her efforts. There may have been another 3 million unemployed out there in the rest of the country, but today Lee felt like the only one. Everyone else with whom she shared the streets seemed to have a purpose. They were all on their way somewhere, to do something. After just half a day of unemployment, she was already hungry to be back racing the other rats.

The first agency had politely told her that there simply weren't too many accounts clerk-type vacancies around. The second and third both made reference to her appearance and were clear that her long hair would be held against her at any interview. The last agency recommended that she take on some new skills in typing or word processing in order to enhance her prospects.

She thought about heading down toward Victoria where she'd been lucky before, but there were lots of streets still closed off in SW1 while the Libyan Embassy siege was still going on. She could instantly conjure a picture of the smiling policewoman who had been killed the week before. Everybody could.

She was done with agencies for the rest of this day anyway, she decided. She removed her neck tie, pulled out her hairband and shook her hair loose, running her fingers through it to separate the locks. The gesture attracted a wolf whistle from the bar. She scowled in the direction of the source – two young suits with pints and cigars. She stared at the single brandy in front of her. She had intended Plan B for tomorrow, but she badly needed something from today.

Rafal caught her movement as she reached the top of the stairs. He looked up from the office telex machine. He never appeared pleased to see Lee and today's surprise visit clearly wasn't melting his heart. He scanned her, top to bottom. "Why are you here?" he asked, returning to reading the printout.

Lee was no more enamoured of the jumped-up receptionist and didn't bother being polite, "I'm here to speak with Mrs Macintyre."

"She's busy".

"I would imagine she is. I'd still like to speak with her."

Rafal appeared to be considering another line of defence, but Lee looked past him to their employer. Anita Macintyre's desk could be seen from the main floor when the rear of the office was lit.

Lee strode past the guard poodle and approached Madame directly, "Hello" she began.

Mrs Macintyre looked up from her computer. Lee eyed the machine warily and wondered if she ever would learn how to use one. Why did work have to get so complicated?

"Lee. We don't usually see you in daylight hours?"

Lee had grown to genuinely like Mrs Macintyre. She couldn't quite reconcile the undoubted business acumen with the kind of thinking that would employ the likes of Rafal, but in every other respect she held her boss in the highest possible regard. She hoped that the risk she was about to take wouldn't backfire. If life were a gaming table, she was about to bet the house on black seventeen. "Could I speak with you for a few moments?"

Mrs Macintyre glanced at her watch, "Yes, I have a few moments – take a seat. You look as though you've come straight from your day job."

Lee blushed a little, "Well actually, I've come from trying to *replace* my day job."

Mrs Macintyre raised an eyebrow.

"I lost my job yesterday – not because I'd done anything wrong. I'd had a really good two years there and I certainly hadn't planned to leave."

"And yet..?"

Lee tried to recall the term she'd decided upon during the bus ride down to Fulham, "They issued some new terms of employment. One of these was that I had to cut my hair short and well, dress more...like this."

"Their prerogative" Mrs Macintyre declared calmly.

Hearing herself explain her departure from CC out loud made her feel more than a little foolish. She began to doubt herself, but there was nothing else for it now, "I wasn't able to accept the new terms."

"So, you gave up your job?"

"Unfortunately, I had to." Lee hesitated over her next sentence, "Please forgive me, I'm not used to telling anyone what I'm about to tell you and I'm afraid I'm not terribly good at explaining it..."

Mrs Macintyre sat impassively and said nothing, allowing Lee to collect herself. Perhaps she at least thought that this might be something worth hearing.

"I – I'm presently undergoing treatment to um, change sex." Lee suddenly thought how incongruous those words sounded in the workplace. She suddenly remembered that she had intended to offer Dr Garner's official letter as proof of her seriousness. She produced an envelope from her inside pocket. "I have a document in here from my co-ordinating consultant" (she left out the word psychiatrist), "It confirms...things."

"Mmm." A thoughtful reply. "I see."

"My bosses at my day job didn't know. I'm pretty sure that they wouldn't have been able to accept it though – and that's why I couldn't go along with the new terms. My treatment is sending me a very certain direction, but doing what I was being asked by my employer would have set me back and made life impossible."

"Lee" Mrs Macintyre began, "Why are you telling me this?"

She took another deep breath, "I guess I'm hoping that there won't be the same problems working at a nightclub. I've heard of someone else like me who works over at The Hippodrome. She's further along than I am and she works as a waitress – not that I'm suggesting…I just…I wondered if I might work some extra shifts. I'm so desperate now for the money. I'll take anything you have."

Mrs Macintyre studied Lee's face. "I imagine deep-down you knew I wouldn't have a problem with it. You're a good worker and I've not had any issues with you. Provided your performance continues and our customers are not inconvenienced, I'm happy to open up the roster to you. We'll give you whatever we can, shift-wise. Flexibility is definitely helpful to the overall cause."

Lee had sensed the ground beneath her to be fairly firm, but still her relief was palpable. She managed a breathy "Thank you."

"You know that I'm pretty broad-minded about these things, but I would ask you to keep me informed. We will need to *manage* things. To…integrate them."

"Yes, of course."

"For the moment then, we just keep this between you and me."

august 1984
gone south

I think I'm losing weight. I shouldn't really be surprised. It's not good though, I know that. Dani keeps reminding me that I need to give the hormones 'something to work with'. My body doesn't really have much in the way of curves to offer as it is.

I'm a stick. I'm a stick with hair.

I had a second cut from Elaine on Sunday. She's really not bad at it. When Becky's there they can be pretty persuasive too. I let Elaine put some blonde streaks in this time. I was really worried it would all fall out, but looking at it this morning, I still really like it. Hope it goes down okay at Oasis. It won't be a problem for my shifts at Crush. The gay scene really couldn't care how the likes of me look. I still have to wear the club t-shirt, but apart from that, there's nothing to think about.

Oasis is all about disappearing into the background. (Blackground?). Black clothes and efficiency are all that is required of me. I tie my hair back and only wear a little foundation, some eyebrow pencil and mascara. Anything more might attract attention (unhelpful, while I'm still trying to prove my worth to Madame).

It's so funny that I get next to no attention from the customers at Crush and yet I've been asked out a couple of times at Oasis – both times by older men. I think they were straight and I'm pretty sure that they knew what I am, but you can't be totally sure. Not that I would risk anything with a customer.

I'm still not earning as much as I was at CC – even though I'm now working five nights a week. I'm trying to space out the sessions with Dr Garner to save some costs, but I may have to think of some other way to bring in some money.

Even on Sundays and Mondays – her only nights off – it was hard to change from her now established sleep pattern. The world, as she had once known it, had been turned upside down and back to front. She would generally get home from *Crush* around 4:00am on Wednesdays and Thursdays or 3:30am from *Oasis* on Tuesdays, Fridays and Saturdays. There were more staff at *Oasis* and so clearing up was quicker.

She would try to be in bed by 5:00am, depending upon whether Rikki would delay her. They were crossing paths regularly these days, especially on *Crush* nights when they would often journey home together on the night bus. She would rise around the middle of the day and try to catch the lunchtime news, if only so that she could feel a vague connection to the world most other people lived in.

In most other respects, adapting to life as a night person had come surprisingly easy to Lee. She had no difficulty with her diet. Breakfast had taken the place of lunch, which had moved on into dinner territory. She didn't bother with anything when she arrived home as she didn't like to sleep on a full stomach. It was the experience of coming home itself that was so substantially different. A normal day used to mean returning home to noise and conversation, watching TV or even going back out again. Getting home now meant a quick cup of tea and off to bed.

Lee did prefer the streets at night. She liked the comparative stillness. London pulsed around the clock, but the rate fell dramatically after midnight. Arteries were freed of traffic and tension and everything breathed more easily. She came to recognise drivers of night buses – and sometimes the passengers, too. Some of the office buildings near *Crush* were cleaned by tightly-drilled teams – usually women and mostly Caribbean in origin. She took to waving hello whenever she saw them working in the reception areas. The community spirit of a collective who otherwise never met.

It wasn't easy to sleep on the hot days. She would open her window and bedroom door to try to get a breeze going, but there had been a couple of July days that had been near unbearable.

This Saturday night hadn't been such a problem. Under a fine spray of rain, the West London streets had been a pleasure. Lee was refreshingly soaked by the time she made it back. The walk had relaxed her and she decided to give the customary tea a miss. Rikki wasn't going to be home that night so there was no risk of a late-night chat. After pouring a glass of water she tiptoed up to bed, careful to avoid the creaky fifth and eighth steps on the way. She couldn't have been quieter. That's probably why the naked figure emerging from Dani's room looked so shocked. "Jesus!" James whispered.

Lee said nothing.

"I – I'm just. The loo…"

Lee turned into her bedroom leaving James to do as he needed. She closed the door, sat on her bed and stared into space – for a surprisingly long time.

Morning sliced in past the bedroom door, at the shoulder of an uninvited Dani.

"Are you awake?"

Lee thought about it. She didn't want to answer. She didn't want to engage with anybody. The door began to close, "Yes" she heard herself grumble in an irritated tone.

Dani re-entered the room and perched on the bottom corner of the bed. "I just wanted to come and see you. To see if…you're all right."

Lee didn't get up. She lay in a half curl underneath a single sheet, her hair splayed out behind her across the pillows. She drew in a long breath through her nostrils, "I'm all right."

"Are you?" Dani asked, looking immaculate. She was wearing a light cotton dress that Lee hadn't seen before. She looked as if she were headed off to church. "Last night…"

Lee cut across her, "Last night was last night – and I don't want to talk about it."

"Nobody is doing anything wrong" Dani said gently. She lay a hand on the sheet which separated the intimacy of skins.

The touch burned. "I'm not saying anything's wrong."

"But you are being…weird about it."

Lee waited a moment. She really hadn't been ready to talk about it, but the talking had begun anyway. "How long?"

"What?"

"How long have the two of you..?"

"A couple of weeks" Dani answered before posing a question of her own, "Why does that matter?"

Lee sat up and pulled her knees up to her chest, careful to cover herself with the sheet. There was little to see of course – and certainly nothing of which Dani hadn't already had a hundred views, but somehow it was important to Lee that she be covered. "I don't know why it matters. It probably doesn't. It's just..."

"What?"

"It's just...I don't know. It's just that I knew you before you knew him. I knew him before he knew you – and yet somehow I'm the last person to know that anything is going on between you."

"That's not really so surprising, is it?" Dani's tone had risen a little. "I never see you anymore. How can I tell you anything? James and I have been getting closer for weeks, but you've never been here to see it. We don't talk anymore – even when you promise we will."

"Well I'm sorry that I have to work all bloody night, I really am." Lee hated the sound of her own bile and sarcasm.

Dani let a moment pass. "That's not what I meant and you know it isn't. I know you have to work. I know why I don't get to see you – I understand all of that. But that doesn't mean that *I* can't have a life. I work hard as well. I deserve to have a future too – *and* a present, come to that."

Lee leant back against the wall and felt the cool painted plaster against her skin, "It's just...James. Why did it have to be James? He was *my* friend."

Dani moved a half seat up the bed and placed her hand again on Lee's knee. "Is it because of what happened that night on the roof? You can't hold that against him. He's completely straight, you can't blame him for that."

Lee felt her temperature rising. She locked her jaw and slowly said in a half-whisper, "I'm straight too."

Dani's hand raced to her forehead, "Yes, yes, I know" she said impatiently, "God, now I've said the wrong thing."

"Brighton!"

It was a statement of fact – and delivered in a less than welcoming tone. Lee woke with her arms still folded tightly and her legs crossed just as they had been, ten minutes out of Victoria. She had dozed quite heavily without moving. It was amazing really, considering that the carriage had been fairly busy with Monday day-trippers who seemed mostly to be mothers, aunts and grandmothers-with-children. It had been a while since Lee had undertaken a train journey. She wasn't the same person who had commuted into London from Sittingbourne. Some things never changed through – she still hated the forced intimacy of faced bench seating. At least with her hair curtains at each flank, she could shut out the surroundings by simply dipping her head. She was wearing her sunglasses too – fake Wayfarers she'd bought last year from Kensington Market. It was disorientating to fall asleep in one place and wake in another. Her senses were still gathering themselves – and nowhere near quickly enough for the guard.

"You're in Brighton" he repeated, "Come on, we've got cleaners coming through".

Lee grabbed the satchel she had squeezed between herself and the train bulkhead. She rose a little unsteadily. She was clearly somewhat taller than the guard had anticipated and he backed off a half step as she rose. She reached out of the window, grabbed the handle and opened the train door, leaving it ajar behind her.

Brighton indeed. She could hear the cry of the gulls overhead, echoing along and under the station's iron-framed, glass roof. She thought she could smell the sea too. This was what she needed; time away from the familiar, time to think and to properly assess events. Rather inevitably, she headed for the beach. She wore her favourite black jeans. They were quite tight, but also quite soft. They would be conducive to the extended period of sitting she had planned. She had risked wearing her black ballet pumps, imagining that they'd be easy to slip in and out of as she moved between street and beach. Her long white t-shirt and bleached denim jacket were grudging nods to summer.

It wasn't that Lee needed especially to be by the sea. She could have gone anywhere to be away for a day. Brighton though, while a world away from the metropolis, was actually just an hour to the south. Grant and Rikki had both spoken of some good times they'd had in the town during summers past.

She had planned the trip while brooding throughout Sunday morning in the darkness of her bedroom bunker. She hadn't felt able to face Dani or James. The couple – as they must now be thought – had gone out together sometime around lunch. Only then had Lee been able to leave her confines for a much-needed bathroom visit and some breakfast. Dani had tried again to make contact when she'd returned, but by then Lee had retreated to Darkworld and had been able to pretend she were asleep. She hated not being able to speak to her closest friend, but she had neither the right words, nor mood.

She had been up excruciatingly early and had showered at 5:30am. The objective had been to beat Dani out of the apartment that morning and so to prolong the term of estrangement. It hadn't worked. She'd taken too long with her preparations and so once more she had to field a Dani visit. She'd been asked why she was up so early. Lee had been as monosyllabic as possible and hadn't even turned to face Dani. She had continued applying mascara while offering answers such as 'Reasons', 'Out' and 'Later' to enquiries about her early rising and plans she might have for the day. At least she reasoned, she wasn't actually *saying* anything cruel through her bitterness.

The walk to the beach took her little more than ten minutes. It was a few degrees cooler than it would be back in London – probably no more than seventy, she judged. The look of the architecture and bustle of the shops reminded her of South London. She supposed that Brighton had been and remained in many ways, an extension of the capital. From the look of many of the people around her, it still was. There was certainly a cosmopolitan feel to the streets. Nobody seemed remotely interested in her. Perfect. She was sorry in some ways, that she hadn't found Brighton sooner. She liked the white painted houses she glimpsed along side streets – even though they did recall South Kensington and therefore, Change Central.

The beach didn't look too busy from the elevated platform of the promenade. It was a pebble beach – she supposed that she should have known that about Brighton and yet she was still surprised to see it. She couldn't quite understand the popularity of a pebble beach. It wasn't as pretty as a sandy one and it surely wasn't likely to be as comfortable a place to sit. She hoisted her satchel further up onto her shoulder and took the nearest set of steps down. She became oddly self-conscious as she tried to find a place to settle. It seemed an unwritten rule that in a public open space, only a single attempt to select a spot was acceptable. Once one is seated, there can be no second choosing – at least not anywhere nearby. She sensed that the beach-collective was eyeing the newcomer, just as she would herself scrutinise later arrivals. Space would be her main concern. She didn't want to be so near to others as to overhear conversation. All she wanted was the sound of the lapping waves and the cry of gulls. The beach was quite steeply banked. She needed to be high enough on the incline to get a decent view and yet low enough to feel sheltered from a circulating breeze. She settled for a position just about halfway along, between the two piers. The pebbles gave easily as she lowered herself to create a surprisingly comfortable seat. She drew her knees up and looked along the surf line. Nobody was swimming, but a number of children and young men were inevitably throwing and skipping pebbles into the waves.

She looked to her left at the Palace Pier. From where she was sitting, it was still every inch the Victorian dream. There were any number of shapes along its span, not all of which she could identify. Some of the iconic structure she knew to be closed. Still, it looked positively crawling with life compared to the decrepit wreck that was the West Pier. This was completely shut and looked very uninviting. Some sections of the hulk were blackened by decay. Why had one pier thrived and been blessed by the attentions of investors and visitors, while the other was shunned and condemned to ugliness. 'Dani and me' Lee reflected, further indulging the day's predisposition for self-pity.

She lay back, resting her head on her satchel and bathing her face in a gently warming, cloud-filtered sun. She wondered what Dani would be thinking right then. She'd be upset – as much by Lee's offhand attitude this morning, as anything. Childishness was hard to own. Dad would be appalled – and Grant no doubt disappointed. They had all made her walk taller. Now without them, she was faltering and failing to control her reflexes. She tried to crystallise the instinct that had sent her into such an unpleasant tailspin. So Dani and James were seeing each other; was it surprising? Was it unreasonable? What she was feeling was deep green jealousy of course – and several layers of it. She was still a little in love with James, a little in love with Dani and totally excluded from the beautiful point at which they met.

Of course, she'd always known that nothing could realistically happen between herself and a heterosexual male, but at that moment with James on the upper floor landing, she'd been rudely forced to set light to her own fantasy – and the embers weren't done yet.

And where did that leave her with Dani? Everything about her closest friend had always been of interest to Lee. Her thoughts and views – even the sight and sound of her. The fascination hadn't dimmed through the years. Living vicariously through her Dani had once been enough. But since the process of transition and the beginnings of a life had arrived, her aspirations had grown. Now Lee could be disappointed like a normal person.

She wasn't sure how long she'd been out. With eyes closed beneath her darkened lenses, she had inevitably dropped off – probably only for a few minutes, she hoped. Her mind had been lulled by the comfortable warmth of the sun and the gentle soundtrack of children's voices over tidal rhythms. She drew herself up onto her elbows and then sat upright. She reached into her satchel for what was now a rather flattened cheese sandwich and a can of lemonade. She opened both. "Dine like a Duchess" she murmured to herself, taking a bite.

"You often talk to yourself?"

The question belonged to a male voice coming from her right and slightly behind her sightline. She turned to see a smiling man in his late twenties or early thirties. His blond hair was parted at the centre in a style not widely worn for at least five years. He had chosen to team this with a slightly darker moustache – an odd combination, Lee considered. He wore a crisp white shirt with rolled up sleeves and some brown pinstriped trousers. He'd taken off his shoes and socks, which protruded from beneath his neatly folded jacket. He looked like an office worker on a break. She hadn't heard him approach or sit down. He'd pitched himself awfully close – closer Lee felt, than a stranger ought to. She thought better of engaging him in conversation. Instead she offered a weak smile and returned to her view of the sea.

Perhaps a minute passed before the voice spoke again. "I'm Lancing, by the way. Jeremy Lancing." He was very well spoken and the pitch of the voice was deeper than was natural. It was an authoritative tone, but by design. Men who spoke that way usually craved leadership – or attention. In this man's case, she suspected it was more likely to be the latter. This was planned to be a solo day. No time had been allocated for others. She turned again to see that Jeremy Lancing's hand was extended toward her in greeting. She looked at it, still holding her flat sandwich with her own right hand. "I'm just trying to have a little lunch" she explained, as patiently as she could.

"My, and that does look appetising." Lancing shuffled forward until he was shoulder to shoulder with Lee. "I only wish I could find somewhere around here that served this kind of delicacy. Can you recommend such an emporium?"

Lee lifted her sunglasses and observed her new visitor more deliberately. He had hazel eyes and white teeth – the latter permanently displayed, courtesy of the constant smile. It was a bit like sitting next to a huge Labrador, Lee thought. She looked back at her sandwich, "Well, this one comes from a kitchen about a hundred miles away."

"Ah, a fellow visitor. Another lonely exile, far from the comforts of home."

"I'm not lonely – and I'm definitely not exiled." She re-thought her last statement for a moment, imagining how awkward it was going to be to return home to face Dani and James.

Lancing looked apologetic, "My mistake, I shall leave you to await the return of your many associates." He prepared to stand.

"What associates? I don't have associates?" Lee winced inwardly, realising that she probably shouldn't have replied.

"No, of course. Mon erreur! I meant of course, your significant other."

She definitely shouldn't respond to that, "There isn't one of those, either."

Lancing relaxed back into his seated position. One side of Lee's mind, gave the other a sharp jab with a cranial elbow.

"So this is it? You've travelled a hundred miles to sit on some pebbles by yourself and nibble at a sandwich that looks like it's been ironed?"

Lee felt the corners of her mouth smiling. Drink orders aside, she didn't often talk to strangers and they tended on the whole not to talk to her – at least not in a pleasant way, but she couldn't see the harm.

She parried, "You, on the other hand are clearly having a great day. How on earth are you managing to find the time in your no-doubt fascinating and packed schedule, to trawl the beach talking to complete strangers?" She noticed that she'd upped the level of her own annunciation in an attempt to meet Lancing's. Poshness was way down on the list of qualities to which she aspired, but it was evidently in there, somewhere.

"I *make* time. One must after all, stretch oneself" Lancing grinned again. "Anyway, you're not a stranger." He lay down, supporting his head with his hands.

"You don't know anything about me!" laughed Lee.

"I know everything about you" he announced with Zen confidence.

"Oh, I doubt that."

After a moment of reflection, he was back up on his elbows, "Let's see" he began, looking along Lee's seated figure and back again, "Early twenties, a modicum of education – though probably didn't study as hard as you should have. Living in London; dissatisfied with work. You've fallen out with someone, somewhere recently and you've headed for the coast to get away from it all."

Lee lifted her sunglasses on top of her head again, sweeping back her fringe. "Those are the kind of generalisations that would fit most single people on this beach."

Lancing's smile broadened. "I haven't finished yet."

"Go on then."

"You are generous with your affections; you have an uncontrollable desire for blond men and a secret penchant for a well-groomed moustache."

Lee laughed out loud, partly at the limp audacity but also as a reflex to an actual flirt. She wasn't imagining it; he *was* actually flirting with her. But she wondered, did he see her as boy or girl? Was he gay or straight? And even beyond those questions, was he genuine or just playing some game? Perhaps she was a bet he'd made with some hidden partner who would be watching somewhere from a safe distance. She was curious enough to try some conversational tricks of her own. At least she could try to establish what Lancing thought he was dealing with. "Okay Mr. Perceptive, what's my name?"

Lancing wrinkled his nose as he strained to work through a number of possible answers, "Aphrodite" he offered, mischievously.

Damn! Depending upon the level of irony intended, that wasn't entirely conclusive.

Lee dared to take another bite of her sandwich, even though she could feel him watching her. "Mmm. Must be my Greek profile" she said dryly, her cheek full of bread and cheese.

"Got one of those for me?" Lancing asked.

Lee looked at him in surprise. His expression remained inscrutably hopeful. She handed him the remaining half of the sandwich. He held it by one corner, inspecting it doubtfully as it drooped to one side.

"It's a bit…flaccid" he observed, prodding the limp end.

Lee snorted as she finished her last bite, "It'll perk up. You just have to hold it right."

Lancing turned the sandwich on its end, "Oh yes, I see – much happier."

Lee giggled, opened her lemonade and took a sip. "So, I assume you do this often."

"Whatever do you mean?"

"Talk to complete strangers on the beach."

"Oh absolutely not. I simply noticed you sitting here alone and thought well, here we are, two singletons in this...paradise of a resort. Striking up a conversation seemed like the civilised thing to do."

Lee looked sceptical, "I'm not the only person here on their own."

Lancing sat up straight and took in a complete sweep of the beach, "Oh, I think you'll find that you are" he said confidently.

Lee quickly panned from one side to the other and was amazed to see that Lancing was quite right. There were couples of all ages – and there were families. There were even one or two single parents with small children, but there weren't any other loners. "Oh" she conceded. "Still, it's not...normal, is it? And you don't look as though you've come dressed for the beach, either. Where should you really be right now?"

Lancing lay back again, closing his eyes. "I should be in the fourth row of a seminar on venture capital financing, up there somewhere." He pointed with a reversed thumb back toward the sea-facing hotels above the promenade.

"Won't you get into trouble with your bosses?"

"I seriously doubt it."

"How come?"

"Well, because I know and they know, that I'm bloody good at my job and an hour in a stuffy hotel meeting room really won't make one iota's difference to my performance."

"I see" Lee considered, by now unsurprised at Lancing's self-confidence. "And what exactly is it that you're so 'bloody good' at?"

"I make people's dreams come true" he answered with a wide toothed smile. "I give them money to grow their businesses and they give me even more money back."

Lee watched a small boy trying to dig a hole in the wet sand. His pit was fast being swamped by the incoming tide. "What happens if their business doesn't work?"

Lancing sat back up and stared straight into Lee's eyes. "Those would be losers. I only back winners."

"Oh really. And what makes you so sure that you always back winners?"

"Because, as I said before" he replied patiently, his white toothed, shark-like smile widening, "*I* know everything."

Another half an hour of playful conversation followed, each of them probing to find out a little more about the other. He, it turned out, was based in Cheltenham and was in Brighton for the next three days. She allowed him to know that she worked in nightclubs, though she wouldn't admit to which ones ("because you *are* a complete stranger!"). He liked sunshine, good food and wine. She offered her appreciation of late nights and city views. He admitted to a fairly comfortable upbringing and a public school education. Lee conceded that things hadn't always been easy and that she had done her best at a single sex Grammar in Kent. She left out the single sex in question.

Suddenly without warning, Lancing consulted his watch and stood up. He brushed himself down and picked up his jacket and shoes. Lee watched, more than just a little disappointed that the game was ending. "Oh" she said, "Is that it?"

"Well yes, I'm rather afraid it must be. Missing one seminar could be regarded as careless, missing two would be just plain reckless."

Lee wanted to be grown up about the encounter. "Well thank you for entertaining me" she said offering her hand to shake.

"It really has been the most delightful pleasure" Lancing returned. He bent down and took Lee's hand, kissing it lightly on the back. She felt the tickle of his moustache and then something else flutter inside of her.

Lancing straightened, took a look out to sea and then another back down at a still seated Lee. "Six o' clock all right for you?" he checked, as if arranging an item on a regular schedule. Those white teeth were showing out again.

"For what?" Lee responded, removing her sunglasses altogether.
"Well, for dinner of course."

Lee laughed from her stomach, the elevated angle of her head
inviting the generosity of emotion. "I can't have dinner with you",
she asserted.

"Six it is. We'll meet outside *The Grand*" he turned and began
to head back to the promenade.

"I can't have dinner with you" she called again.

Lancing waved without looking back and then pointed over to
his right, "*The Grand* – it's over there, you can't miss it."

Lee heard herself laugh again. She was wearing the same
smile the whole time she watched him walk back across the pebbles. Finally, as he reached the staircase back up to the promenade, Lancing turned back and caught her staring. She could see
those white teeth in the shadow below that dark blond moustache.
"Shit!" she cursed.

Lee Habens was familiar enough with strange, isolated adventures of the heart. She knew better than to take them seriously. After
all, the conviction she held, that in her present form she simply could
not be loved, was absolute. What after all, would be the point? She
was a work in progress. Any relationship begun now would be out-
manoeuvred by her own future. She still held out the slimmest hope
that she might one day be a person worth loving, but she certainly
wasn't about to seriously count on it. Whatever his plans, Jeremy
Lancing wasn't likely to figure largely in any version of tomorrow.
He was nothing more than a dusk-dwelling firefly – and there would
be a whole lot of empty nights to follow his fleeting presence.

It was the need to pee that eventually brought her up from the
beach. She asked in a pub whether she might use their facilites
if she made a donation to their charity box. The ladies and gents
were side by side. She had the option. Perhaps it was because she
was away from home and feeling quite brave, perhaps it was the
confidence she earned from flirting with a stranger, but she opted
for the ladies. Nobody raised any objection when she passed back
by the bar on her way out.

She really wasn't sure what to do with her afternoon. The shops looked interesting. She walked slowly, enjoying life at a different speed to those around her. This was after all, officially her day off – a time to be planless. She saw a phone box and momentarily thought about calling Dani at work. It might at least take some of the tension out of the present situation. Something inside prevented her. She hadn't totally rinsed the poison of resentment from her gut. She still felt pain when she thought of Dani and James' happiness. She sighed and blew out her cheeks as she stared at the red box. She hoped that she might mature to fully fledged adulthood by the end of the afternoon.

She had followed Church Road, increasingly charmed by the accompanying Victoriana. She particularly liked the occasional ornate iron balconies on the first floors of some of the houses. She tried to imagine how it might be to emerge from bed on a summer's morning and step out to take in the morning air. She could still catch sight of the sea every so often to her left as she looked down along crossing roads. As long as she could glimpse dark shimmering blue, she remained secure in her geography. The temperature had risen as the cloud had been burned back from the coast. Lee now found herself choosing to walk on the shady side of the street. She wasn't wearing very much make-up – and nor could she in the summer heat – but still, she didn't like to sweat.

Her interest had been drawn by the stone clad building ahead. She liked the porthole windows on the upper floor. It looked old, but almost certainly beyond its actual years. She was nearly upon the entrance by the time she realised it was a library. Rikki's advice came back to her almost immediately. She wondered if they might have anything useful on human anatomy. She took a look back along the street in the direction from which she'd walked. Half an hour in the cool of a reference section wouldn't hurt.

The department was overseen by a typically studious-looking young man who wore a small, limp pony tail. Clearly Zoe Moreno had never passed this way. Finding the medical aisle was straightforward enough, but Lee probably worked through the indices of a dozen books before she was able to garner anything useful.

The academic writing style made the language challenging, but the occasional diagram helped. She took a particular interest in skeletal differentiation. Certain obvious differences between the male and female figure were common knowledge. The pelvis was the main one, the female being generally wider and more shallow, to facilitate gestation. There were mentions of something Rikki had alluded to in the workings of the limbs. As the song went, the bones were all connected. Slimmer shoulders affected the arms and the differences in the pelvis set-up directed the way the legs were structured and thereby dictated their movements.

What fascinated Lee most, was a study she read about hands. The male index finger apparently, could be shorter than the ring finger. In females, this could be reversed. It wasn't a universally consistent indicator, but it was recognised as a sex difference. Lee of course, immediately assessed her own hands. Index finger and ring finger were of identical length. Typical. Oh, those hands. The fingers were slender, but so long. She held them in front of her for a while, studying them from different angles. She noticed that a hand looked larger when the fingers were apart or bent. She saw that she could reduce the impression of the width of a hand by tucking her thumb under and keeping it straight, pressed against her palm – a trick that might prove helpful. She didn't really want to rely on illusions to get by in life but she mused that in a way, everyone did.

An hour later, Lee found herself staring at the Brighton Pavilion. She was a little unsettled by it. It was of course, utterly incongruous. It belonged to a place she suspected had never actually existed – unless you counted 50's Hollywood's version of India. She wasn't sure she liked what she saw. She could admire the daring in creating such a thing at all, but she found herself unhappy that it hadn't tried to fit in with the Regency elegance around it.

The clock was ticking – literally. It was almost five o' clock and she really had to make a decision about where she would head next. She knew that she was pretty much equidistant from the station and *The Grand Hotel*. Home, without question made the most sense. It may take more than two hours to get back. She really should speak to Dani face-to-face that evening, to damp down any retaliatory resentment from this morning's exchange. She reflexively drew up her hand to support her chin. She could feel the first tell-tale needle-like hairs poking through the skin along her jawline. That really had to seal it. She should just quit with this morning's compliments while she was ahead. Why waste time having dinner with some stranger she was never going to see again when she should really be elsewhere? Was she honestly going to be suckered in by a few kind words and some well-spoken charm? Surely her ego wasn't that weak?

Oddly, he came from the same direction as she had, moments earlier. She had been five minutes late and having not seen him outside *The Grand*, had instantly assumed that he wasn't coming; that it had all just been a stupid ruse.

"I'm so terribly sorry" Lancing spluttered, breathlessly, reminding her for an instant of Alice's White Rabbit.

She grinned at him. This was ridiculous, she thought. "This is ridiculous", she echoed out loud.

Lancing glanced at his watch, "I'm only a couple of minutes…"

"No, I mean the whole idea. I've still only known you for what – less than an hour?"

"Quality time though, you must admit" he countered.

It was then that she noticed he was carrying a small bunch of yellow roses, perhaps half a dozen of them.

He held them up to her. "These, are for you."

She was more than surprised. Did this answer the question of how he saw her? "Um, thank you" she said. "They're lovely." How many times had she heard women say that when receiving flowers? Surely a human reflex – this was the first time it had ever happened to her and yet she'd immediately reached for the clichéd response.

"I take it you know the significance of the colour?"

"Oh yes" she replied confidently. Then she thought for a moment. What if yellow was a bad thing? "…Or more accurately, no."

"Ah, well yellow roses are for joy and for friendship."

"Well, okay" Lee responded, now further confused by Lancing's motive. Still, at least it wasn't too scary so far. "So" she sighed, hoping to draw a line under the moment, "Where are we going?"

Lancing looked up at the glazed porch entrance to the town's premiere hotel. "Well we're not going in there, for a start. Nothing ever actually happens at *The Grand*."

They walked along the seafront for a while. Lee was relieved to have the sunlight at her back. She was worried that her skin might still show a graze or two from her hurried attempts at shaving in a hotel toilet, forty minutes before. She had bought a razor, foam and some moisturiser from a pharmacy and had taken her chances strolling through the fairly busy foyer of one of the larger hotels. Grant always used to say that if you looked like you belonged, nobody would think otherwise. That approach got her all the way to a deserted ladies bathroom. There she'd had to tie back her hair and quickly wash her face before moving to the privacy of a cubicle. Using the razor's dismantled plastic packaging as a tiny sink to hold a few thimblefuls of water, she'd carefully scraped her way through a rudimentary shave. She had tried to breathe slowly to slow her heart and had stroked the razor in small, careful movements across her skin. It had hurt like hell of course. Her skin had been made extra sensitive by the effects of that day's sunshine. She had moaned audibly by the time she applied moisturiser. She'd needed a break for one or two tears before re-applying makeup. All the while, other visitors had come and gone, using cubicles either side of hers'. She had of course, been intensely envious of them all.

She had emerged after perhaps twenty minutes. A hasty inspection in the mirror had shown a slightly reddened jaw line, but nothing more serious. She'd hoped the early evening breeze might cool the throbbing. She may have attracted a curious glance from the reception desk on her way out – she wasn't sure. She'd walked purposely and straight toward the door. 'Like you belong', she'd heard Grant urge again.

Lancing had selected an Italian restaurant just a block and a half back from the promenade. There had been plenty of available tables at that time of the evening. Lee had been offered a choice of which seat to take and she gratefully selected the one with her back to the evening sunlight. She really didn't want to be thinking too much about the way her face might appear.

Lancing eased into the seat opposite. He smiled warmly, "If we were actually in Italy, we'd most likely be eating outside on the pavement. All of their restaurants are like that. Can you imagine that here?"

Lee smiled back, "Mmm. Chill breezes and car exhaust fumes with your salad? I don't know…" she pondered.

They ordered quite quickly. Lancing joked about a number of potential choices – in particular, steering Lee away from fish options. Had she not seen the state of some of the people paddling in the sea earlier that day? Lee didn't feel she could manage a starter and Lancing, politely she suspected, joined her in opting for just a main course of pasta.

Lancing had asked for a bottle of the house red and white to be brought to the table. He offered both to Lee for her consideration. It was to her, an extraordinary gesture. Lancing's self-confidence was alienating and compelling at the same time. Lee could never issue instructions the way he did. She would worry that the staff might take offence at such assertiveness or that other customers might stare. Lancing clearly believed that it was his absolute right to be in complete control of a moment. What was it about him that had led Lee to turn toward their meeting rather than withdraw to the safety of home? Did she really like him? She certainly didn't have much in common with him? Could it be as simple as just needing to feel attractive to someone? Anyone?

Lee couldn't decide on a wine option to select. Lancing chose red on her behalf. Lee almost immediately wished she'd chosen white, but didn't feel she could correct the order. When the wine did arrive, Lancing insisted that she be the one to sample it. It was another first for Lee. She had always watched and waited as others would assume the role of taster. She was used to being the person at the table who knew least about wine – even when the only other diner was Dani. She sipped at the splash of dark redness that had pooled in her glass. She probably would have shown approval of anything – but actually, she really did like what she'd sampled. Even now, she was picking up a sense of berries in the aftertaste. The filled vessels Lee suspected, would empty easily.

Lancing raised his glass and offered it to Lee, "To strangers on shores" he proposed.

Lee laughed and clinked her glass against his, "The stranger the better" she added, not really sure what she'd meant. They tipped their stems in unison. Lee decided that the wine tasted even better than she'd first thought. She looked closely at Lancing's dark blond moustache, idly wondering if the wine would stain it. "So, what's with the moustache then?" she heard herself ask.

"What's *with* it?" Lancing queried, stroking it either side of his mouth, using his thumb and forefinger.

"Mmm. How long have you had it?"

He shook his head as he swallowed another taste of house red. "Born with it" he asserted, "straight out of the womb".

Lee giggled at the thought, "Your Mum must have been a bit surprised."

"No, no. We don't have growing up in our clan – too bloody boring. We generally skip childhood and adolescence and go straight to chequebook-owning adulthood."

Lee smiled, "Your Mother isn't Margaret Thatcher, by any chance?"

"Wouldn't that be something" Lancing wondered aloud, genuinely appearing to favour the idea. He toyed again with his furry facial feature, "No, I don't know. I suppose I just thought that once I could grow a decent one, I should. It did make me feel sort of grown up. I actually had it before I finished school and I can tell you, it does get you taken more seriously at the bar when you're still seventeen."

"I imagine" Lee nodded, imagining.

"After that, it just sort of belonged on my face. Can't really imagine it not being there."

Lee smiled and tilted her head in thought, "You're pretty comfortable with who you are, aren't you?" She asked, genuinely wondering what that must be like.

"Of course. I mean I can't take much credit for being healthy and such, but the rest of what makes me who I am, has pretty much gone to plan. It's the same for everyone, isn't it? We can all be what we want to be if we put in the work"

"That what you really believe?"

"Don't you?

"*I* believe" Lee began carefully, "that we can *reach* for almost anything. But life isn't that fair. If I've learned anything, it's that we don't necessarily get what we deserve."

"That would suggest you've had a disappointment or two along the way."

"Everyone has setbacks" Lee conceded, staring into her glass.

"Yup" Lancing jabbed, clearly seeking to cut short the dip in tone, "Trick is, to keep moving forward. Keep your eye on your prize – whatever that might happen to be."

Lee felt her expression lighten as she met Lancing's smile with one of her own.

The pasta came and was as easily consumed as the conversation. Lee enquired after Lancing's afternoon seminar and listened with amusement as he described his fascination with the main speaker's extraordinary hairstyle. It had apparently been a masterpiece of hairspray and hope. The lecturer had been rather bald but had drawn up hair from each side of his head to meet across the middle in a sort of suspended arch. He'd been backlit during his speech and this had created a 'halo' effect. Lancing admitted that he couldn't actually recall much of the speech's content.

Lee gave an edited account of her own afternoon; the walk, the shops, even the library – minus an explanation of her choice of book.

"And you say this is your first visit to Brighton?" Lancing asked as he filled Lee's glass from a second bottle of wine.

"Yes. I never really had the time before. There's still so much to see and do in London and I haven't really wanted to get away like this before."

"A likely story. No, I thought as much." Lancing asserted, tapping the table in triumph, "You're on the lam! What is it? A run-in with the fuzz?" He offered some guesses "I know; you robbed London's worst sandwich shop and headed to the coast with your ill-gotten gains"

Lee almost lost the wine she'd just sipped, barely holding it in with a pursed smile and shake of her head.

"Clubbed a Chelsea Pensioner for being old on a week day? A bit harsh, but fair enough really – they've been warned."

"Nope"

"You've been expelled for driving something other than a GTi."

Lee laughed generously. The wine really was very good.

Lancing clearly enjoyed the outward demonstrations of his companion's pleasure. "And so here you are in this...*sinful* town" he summarised, waving a hand in the direction of the streets outside, "and what kind of person we wonder, will London receive back?"

Time blurred. There were moments – certainly in the early part of the evening – when Lee would check its progress by glancing at the clock high up, behind the restaurant's tiny bar. She would hastily calculate how long she had left before needing to make her way to the station. She slipped through the train schedule from later train, to penultimate train, to last train, mentally adding a 'there probably *is* another one after that'. They were the last to leave the restaurant. Lancing had been utterly charming to the last and had insisted on settling the bill.

The air outside was still warm from the day and it bore smells from other neighbouring restaurants. Lee's senses could barely take in anything more. She was already heady with wine, flattery and flirtation. The streets were quiet now. Brighton was closing. Lee was taken by surprise when after no more than ten steps, Lancing slipped an arm around her waist and pulled her to him. The kiss felt so easy. She just relaxed into it. She felt the tickle of that moustache again and was surprised at how soft it seemed against her own cheek.

"I really do hate to leave" Lee heard herself say.

"Leave? How are you going to do that?" Lancing smiled, closer to Lee's face than ever. He seemed so assured, as if he already knew the answer to every question he asked. Perhaps he wasn't Alice's White Rabbit; perhaps he was really the Cheshire Cat.

"Well I thought I'd use the return part of my train ticket."

"Mmm."

Lee enjoyed the sensual tonal vibration from his chest as it worked through the cotton of her t-shirt and entered her own.

"You do know the time?" he added.

"Late?"

Lancing glanced at his watch, an old-fashioned face on a simple brown leather strap, "I make it ten to Tuesday. Monday's schedule has I believe, been completed."

"Oh." Lee did know this of course. She just didn't care. She was intoxicated – and in more ways than one. Time didn't matter. London didn't matter. All there was for her was the way she felt at that moment. She just wanted everything to stay just the way it was. Nothing needed to close completely. No more lights needed to be turned out and Tuesday itself could quite frankly stay away. Couldn't they just wander the streets of Brighton for the rest of the night, occasionally wrapping themselves in a velvet shadow? Maybe they could lie on the beach and stare up at the stars, while the pebbles warmed beneath them.

"There's always my digs?" Lancing offered.

Lee had been in hotel rooms before of course. There had been the holiday in Spain with her parents and then a package with Dani when they were little more than eighteen. There had also been the afternoon with the Rhodesian barman back in Sittingbourne. None of those rooms had been quite in this league however. The hotel was front-facing and Lancing's room had a view. It was four flights up, she recalled from the lift lights. It wasn't especially large, but the chrome and dark leather furnishings were right up to the minute. There was a smoked glass table in one corner surrounded by four black chairs. Lee chose the one closest to the rest of the room and turned it around so that she was facing inwards.

Lancing hung his jacket and produced from one of its pockets, another bottle of the restaurant's house red. "I felt we needed one as they say, for the road."

The room had its own bathroom, from which Lancing appeared with a pair of glass tumblers, "Elegant, eh?"

Lee smiled. A reality was dawning in a far-flung corner of her consciousness. She'd been swept along by the evening, but sooner or later she would have to have *the* conversation with this man. As he handed her a filled glass, she decided it would be sooner. "We haven't talked about…partners."

"Mmm?" Lancing imbibed at least a quarter of his glass before taking a seat on the bed facing Lee.

"Is there a girlfriend somewhere?"

Lancing looked doubtfully toward his guest, "You really want to get into that now?"

"I'm curious" Lee explained, having broken the ice and now genuinely more curious than ever.

Lancing breathed in deeply and then released the tension in his chest. "There's someone. It's not serious." He added, "It's just me. I don't do serious."

Lee pressed on for clarification, "But there is a girl?"

Lancing's eyes narrowed and his smile returned. "Yes" he said guardedly.

Lee smiled back and took a sip of her wine. It still tasted good, but she'd had enough. Perhaps more than enough. "So then, why am *I* here?"

Lancing opened his arms widely. His span seemed to take up much of the room. "You're asking *me*?"

"I just. I'm not sure what you…want with me."

Lancing scratched his head and furrowed his brow. "God, I don't know. We met, we got on, we met again, we fancied each other, we kissed, now we're in a hotel room late at night. It's not *that* complicated." His smile remained, but with just a little more strain behind it, "It's just being grown up, isn't it?"

Lee looked back at him and then down at her ballet pumps. "Actually, it might be complicated."

"Really?"

"I'm not…I'm…Look, the thing is…"

"Yes…yes…come on, you can do it" Lancing urged, the Cheshire Cat smile fixed in determinedly now.

"I'm transsexual."

Lancing waited a moment and then let out a generous laugh in his rich, deep tone.

At least he wasn't furious, Lee reflected.

Lancing held up both palms, one of them still holding a now empty glass. His laugh fell slowly in tone and bled into measured words, "Look, Lee…I'm sure that probably is important to you, but I don't have those hang ups. Like I say, it really isn't that complicated."

Lee wanted to press further. "What did you think I was? Did you know?"

Lancing grinned as he poured another glassful. "I don't know. Thought you were a girl at first, on the beach. Then after a few minutes I thought you were probably a boy – a sweet one, mind" he added hastily. "It didn't matter to me. I mean, we clicked didn't we? We had a laugh. I just – I went with it. It's who I am. It's what I do."

"So, you…you kind of go both ways, is that it?"

Lancing was beginning to look just a little irritated, "Go both ways?" he mimicked. "God, look I go any way there is. Life is to be explored. I just enjoy the ride. I mean it's all just a big…gamble, isn't it? You put in, you take out. So, you're a transsexual – well okay, I've not been *there* before. So let's see what happens. Hell, a shag's a shag, y'know?"

The last light in Brighton suddenly went out. Lee put her glass down on the table. It made an uncomfortable clang as it landed. "I'm sorry, I really don't think I can do this." She stood up and grabbed up her satchel.

Lancing stood at the same time. He was between her and the door. "Hey, heeey" he soothed. "There's no need for this. Trust me, you just need to relax."

He moved toward Lee, taking hold of her upper arms firmly. Lee didn't feel terribly threatened. Not yet. She'd been on the receiving end of bully boys since school days and she'd grown immune to the fear of harm itself. She just wanted to follow romance out of the room and off down the corridor to the lift, but a part of her was also oddly curious to see what really might happen next. If this man had genuinely not been so bothered, wouldn't he have been quite happy to see her go? Why was he trying to persuade her to stay? Why did he care? *How* exactly did he care?

"Let's just try each other out. C'mon. All we've done all day is help each other to enjoy our time. Why should it end with nothing?"

Lee's eyes were close to Lancing's. His pupils were huge, barely fringed by hazel in the room's dim lights. "I just, I just hoped you saw me as..."

"A female?" Lancing proposed, using a rather more clinical term than Lee would have preferred. He shrugged, "I just saw you as attractive. Can't that be enough? I mean, it was for me. Seriously now, you do just need to relax." Lancing sat back down on the edge of the bed, this time taking Lee with him. "Seriously, how often do you find yourself in a position like this? You should try a little spontaneity in your life. Be a bit more impulsive perhaps. Wouldn't you rather be killed by curiosity than boredom?"

Lee felt her jacket being drawn from one shoulder. She made removal from the other arm easier. Lancing began to kiss her, quite tenderly. She felt a hand run through her hair, his fingertips tracing around to the back of her head and on down her neck. Her t-shirt was drawn up and over her head. It was discarded somewhere. She dispensed with eyesight and drew on only her remaining senses. She felt him lean her back. At first her stomach muscles resisted, holding her stubbornly upright. There was a tipping point, she wasn't sure when. It was probably when his hand touched her bare shoulder. She buckled slightly and then gave. She could hear both of them breathing. There were kisses, too. Was she kissing back? She briefly opened her eyes again and saw him looking along her torso. He traced her areola with a finger, one to the other. Her eyes closed again. Lying back reminded her of how much wine flowed through her bloodstream. She felt dizzy, even in her own blackness. Her body's sensitivity came and went. Feelings from her nerve centre at once acute and then almost completely detached. She sensed her jeans leave her and heard the sound of them passing down along her legs, replaced by the cool wave of the bedspread beneath her. Had she arched herself just slightly to help? The kisses continued to travel along her. Every so often, she would hear his beautifully proper tones encouraging her, assuring her that this was the right thing to do. She should 'relax', 'let go' and 'give in to the moment'. She felt exposed and yet uninvolved, a strange conspiracy of sensations she hadn't the focus to puzzle through. Her stomach muscles tightened again and he traced them at first with those fingertips and then with his lips and tongue.

She heard more rustling of clothing. Knowing she had none left to lose, she guessed Lancing himself was undressing. She rolled to one side and half-opened her eyes. The curtains were not drawn. She could see out past the bunched yellow roses she'd placed on the table. Coloured lightbulbs cabled along the promenade below, swung soundlessly out in a breeze she couldn't hear. She felt a long way from home – wherever that was.

She felt a warmth at her back and the bed deepen. He was pressed against her, top to bottom. An arm of his, wrapped over one of hers. It seemed to be almost twice the girth of her own. She realised that his penis was at the base of her spine. She felt its heat and power. She wondered if she should reach back. Should she be reciprocating? Was it right that this should all be happening *to* her rather than with her? How could she have lived her years and yet be so new to a moment like this? He was kissing the back of her neck and tracing the line of her body from shoulder to buttock. He pulled at her underwear and she felt her right hip exposed. She tried again to make sense of it. Her last layer of protection was being peeled away. Did she want this? She wanted to be wanted, but by a man who didn't care *what* she was, never mind who? Liberating it may be – but so much so, that perhaps the experience wouldn't count for anything at all. Her underwear was being pulled away from her. It was too late now. Was it too late though? Did she really want this? The questions wouldn't stop. The speed of her thoughts was increasing, racing the pace of events. But there were no answers; no conclusions. She felt his penis being pushed between her legs from behind. It pressed against her underneath. It was so much more real than the thing attached to her. It felt unstoppable. He was probing her with his fingers, pushing up inside her. She guessed he was preparing her. It made what was happening feel suddenly to her, as though it were a gay act. Not wrong, but not right for her − not anymore. What would this make her now? She wished there were more time. She needed time. There was no more time.

"No. I can't..." she heard herself say.

"Shhh" he ushered pressing at her, increasing his weight until she rolled.

She grabbed the corner of a pillow and flung it away to the side. There was nothing to be done. "Really Jeremy, I don't want to. I'm not..."

"So, I can want it for both of us" he whispered.

She was entered. It wasn't violent, but it was a surge that pushed the breath right out of her. Her mouth was wide open with the stress of it. She could feel the crisp hotel linen against her lips. There was pain. She couldn't accommodate him − and yet she had. He moved within her and she felt him anchor her with a hand beneath her stomach. He was breathing heavily above her, clearly as detached from his normal persona as Lee had felt from hers. Now neither of them was in control. The moment owned them both. His movements were rhythmic. She felt his hips press into her, seemingly further each time. She felt him deeper in her. There was no room within her or around her. She felt herself stretch beyond the possible. She wanted to vanish out from underneath him, to appear somewhere else unscathed and untouched. He would finish. He had to finish. She knew it. Nothing could prevent him now, she understood that. She felt damaged inside, but she couldn't know how much until it would be over. She tried to relax, trying all too late to draw her mental self to the fore and to cut the last ties to her physicality. It didn't matter, she told herself. It's just a body. It's just the wrong, worthless body.

She felt the tell-tale pulsing behind her, within her. She felt herself drenched inside. She wanted to vomit. His weight increased as his muscles loosen. He fell away from her and to onto his back, breathing hard. Her back felt cold as the damp of his sweat dried on her skin. She turned her head away from him, but abandoned the rest of her body where it lay.

She heard Lancing's mellow voice return to the room. It was the same voice she'd heard from behind her that morning on the beach, just a little less than a lifetime ago.

"For what it's worth, *I* think you're really rather beautiful." He got up from the bed and headed for the bathroom.

She heard the door close. She sent instructions to her limbs, but they denied her sovereignty. She re-took herself from the fingers down, raising first her arms and then peeling her chest from the crumpled bed below her. Her lower back felt broken. She cracked it back into shape and rose onto her knees. She was trembling from her core. She didn't feel that she could sit and so instead reversed off the bed. 'Away!', she ordered herself. Reflexively more than anything, she took a corner of the white bedspread and dabbed it against her underside. There was blood. She'd expected it. Perhaps not so much as to suggest a flowing wound, she considered. She could still make it out of the room and then figure out her next move. She had to find her clothes. Her jeans were at the foot of the bed and her jacket close beside it. She couldn't see her t-shirt or her underwear. Her mind was planning ahead now, accelerating through the present. Dress in what you can find – anything else after that, you can carry. She eased into her jeans and drew them up slowly. If anything, they were tighter than at the beginning of the day. She was particularly careful drawing them up around her rear. She slipped her jacket on. The metal buttons were cold against her chest, but she fastened them anyway – all of them. She saw a shoe poking out from under the bed and found the other next to it. She picked them up rather than sit to put them on. As she straightened, she heard the voice again. The smiling Cheshire Cat voice.

"I'm sorry" Lancing said softly, standing in the doorway to the bathroom. "I guess I've hurt you, I didn't mean to do that. I was just lost in the passion, I suppose."

She looked down at the towel he was holding. It had smears of her blood on it from where he had wiped himself down.

"You're leaving."

"I just. Yes…" Lee was staring at the floor now. She didn't want to look anywhere else.

"I was going to ask you to join me in the shower". He was almost jolly, "We can get you cleaned up."

"No. Thank you" she said quietly.

Lancing sighed and ran a hand through his hair, his arm and torso expressing the full-bodied physicality of a simple act. "Look, I'm not a bad guy. You just need to loosen up. You've got to stop taking sex so seriously."

She didn't reply.

"Oh hey, if you want to go, then go – I'm not going to stop you."

She had one hand on her satchel strap and the other on the door before he'd finished his next line.

"God, you're certainly uptight enough to be a girl."

He probably added to those words after she'd closed the door behind her. She didn't care. None of them belonged with her.

She didn't want to wait for the lift. Her gut was fearful that Lancing might change his mind. She opted for the stairs. The concrete was cold on the soles of her bare feet, but she was two floors down before she dared take a moment to put on her shoes. She moved through the deserted reception at pace, ignoring the front desk entirely. Sorry Grant, she couldn't look like she belonged – not right now.

The temperature had dropped considerably and a breeze was rising. Her pace picked up as she headed back along the promenade in the direction of the town centre. Her stride was shorter than normal. It didn't hurt so much to move that way. She was completely disorientated. She had emerged from Lancing's hotel an altered being. Her point of contact with the world had been relocated somehow. She couldn't quite grasp how or by how much. Out here, while she was being altered, things had also moved on – but how far? She couldn't be sure of the time. How long was she really in there? It had happened fast in some places and agonisingly slowly in others. She wondered how long it would be before the trains began again. Would there be buses to London before then? She brushed some hair out of her eyes. She must look an awful state. She imagined her mascara wouldn't be too tidy. Maybe she should do something about it. She couldn't stop her legs from walking. She couldn't stop thinking of questions. Lee Habens didn't seem able to stop anything.

She was reduced to short staccato breaths by the time she reached the pier. Most of the empty structure was in darkness. She made her way along the boardwalk a little, but saw that meshed gates had been closed, about fifty yards along. The tide was high and waves were rolling in beneath her. She walked as far as the gates and tested them. They resisted her effortlessly. She moved to one end where a sharp-edged shadow sliced a corner entirely from sight. She lowered herself down into the dark carefully, using the gate for support. She drew up her legs and moved her weight back onto the bottom of her spine rather than the soft tissue before it. She could manage like this for a while. There were still occasional voices from the backstreets of Brighton. She was pretty sure she couldn't be seen. For a while she hoped, she might not even exist at all.

Her heart rate slowed and the breaths lengthened until they could accommodate a few thick sobs. She was choking them out. Her mind however, was turning more soberly. If nobody actually witnesses you crying, does it even count, she wondered? She was sick of crying. She'd cried more in the last four years of her life than in the rest of it put together. And what was the point of it, after all? It didn't change anything. It just made her feel more of a victim than she clearly already was. She was sick of being a victim, too. She was sick of everything. Perhaps it was time to examine the bigger questions. Perhaps it was time to face truths. Had she achieved anything at all – *really?* From the moment Dad had gone, had she made anything work, or had she just relocated her failures? On her own, she was nothing. And yet she had never been more alone. She closed her eyes. She was so tired of fighting – of being the only one to believe and yet she found herself completely unable to fathom a reason why anyone else should. She leaned back and felt the ornate framework of the Victorian railings at her back. The gaps between frames were great enough to slip through. She turned onto her side and crawled forward a little, her head and shoulders extended beyond the pier itself. She looked down into the rushing blackness below, calmed by the silkiness of white fringed, layered surf. She felt an urge to move further from the security of the floor. It took some careful manoeuvring, but she managed to creep out entirely to the outside of the balustrade. She stood holding on, with her arms stretched back behind her. She was still looking down. She felt as though she were almost airborne as she breathed in the salt spray, churned from seaweed and tide rush. An updraft blew her hair above her and she felt herself lift with it. She wanted to let go. She wanted to see what was out there.

"S'about forty foot, that" a reedy male voice said, matter-of-factly. "Prob'ly won't kill 'yer, if thas' what 'yer thinkin'". He added a second, "Prob'ly" to cover himself.

Lee turned her head to see who had destroyed this latest moment for her. She could make out a shadowy figure. Male, middle-aged, heavily bearded. He was carrying a large rucksack over one shoulder and holding a fishing rod with the other.

"Need to make 'yer mind up though" he explained. "Thas' my spot, thad is".

Lee took the front seat on the lower deck, the one to the left of the driver, where she could see what was coming. She usually preferred to head upstairs for the journey, but even by the early evening of the day after, she wasn't moving freely and found bending forward (a necessity if a person of her height were to negotiate the top deck), most uncomfortable. She'd had two baths today, one as soon as Dani, James and Luka had left the apartment and another in the afternoon, before anyone returned.

Brighton was already unreal. Only the physical evidence remained from her visit and fortunately, that had mattered least of all. She'd thought back over the hours between then and now; of leaving the pier and waiting at the station for the first northbound train; spending much of the journey to Victoria in the train's toilet, trying to make herself vaguely presentable for the underground leg of the journey back to Notting Hill. She'd looked pale and washed out when she'd emerged, not at all like someone who had spent a sunny day by the coast. She hadn't been able to sit at all for the journey home – though wouldn't really have known where to put herself anyway. The early morning commuters all looked so fresh and well turned out. She hadn't wanted to make any of them uncomfortable. She hadn't wanted to mark their pristine morning. While in the toilet, she had been able to check for blood. There was a stain on her jeans, but only about half of it really showed on the outside. She wished she'd been able to grab her t-shirt before leaving the hotel room – it could have covered her groin and backside. In the end, she'd had to stand with her back to the carriage walls on the tube. At least the bleeding itself had stopped. She must already have begun to heal. Perhaps Lancing had been right after all. Maybe she should've just 'loosened up' and not worried so much. Maybe after all the fuss and tears and melodramatics on a darkened pier, it really hadn't been a big deal at all.

Sleeping had if anything, made things more confusing. Nothing had felt normal that day. She'd still been getting used to having no day job. There was a sense that she should be somewhere else, doing something more. Yet, nothing more *was* to be done – until it would be time to head for *Oasis*. Lee's day had emptied, right at the moment she most craved the monotony of full working hours.

Now she sat looking out from her bus, onto the wet streets of Earls Court. She was at least glad to have left before anyone bar Luka, had returned to the apartment. She felt differently about Luka now, but they still didn't really speak much. She wondered how long she could avoid the others. They might ask questions about where she'd been. They would perhaps notice a change in her demeanour. Dani and James would probably think it was all about them. That had only been true before it became all about something so much worse. Could people tell when someone they knew had been changed?

She drew back her focus and watched raindrops head in opposite horizontal directions across the windscreen, split by contrasting influences of breeze and timing. She should see a doctor, maybe. But if she did, wouldn't they ask questions? Maybe the information would be written into a permanent record that would somehow count against her when the time for surgery approached. What if there *was* lasting damage inside of her? Would that need to be repaired before surgery? How would she find the money for that, on top of everything else? So many imponderables. She could really use someone to talk to. She didn't want to talk to anyone – except maybe Grant. No, talking to someone else would just make it more real. She needed it to be less real. She needed the memory of Brighton to stay away. She needed to keep running for the far horizon.

"Cheer up love, it might never 'appen". The bus conductor was standing over her. She showed her pass, offering a facial expression to match the blank visage in the ID picture. The conductor got the message, turned and sought sunshine elsewhere. She returned her vacant stare to the city beyond. It was late, it was raining, it was Tuesday night. 'Cheer up?' – *Jesus*!

Elvis was running the door that night. Tuesday nights had become inexplicably busy. Lee didn't get it at all. Why would normal people want to have a late night out drinking and dancing when they knew they were less than half way through a working week and would have to be up early the next day? Wednesday mornings couldn't be a good time to be waking up in a strange bed on the wrong side of town as some of tonight's punters no doubt would. She cringed inwardly at the idea of sleeping with strangers. Elvis nodded a greeting and held open the door for her. She smiled back at him. It was the only smile she'd managed that day.

She was one of the first to arrive. The cleaners were still finishing. Lynne was vacuuming – which meant someone hadn't
shown for their shift and she as usual, was taking up the slack. She
mouthed a 'hi' and Lee reciprocated.

Becky was in the locker room already. She was sitting on a
recently installed sofa, reading a copy of *The New Standard*. She
looked up as Lee entered, "Awright?"

"Hi". Single syllables might have to suffice for this evening.

"It's you an' me on the back bar, tonight."

"'kay."

"Yvonne's got the night off."

"Right."

"She's gone bowling with some bloke she met in Sainsbury's.
Mad cow."

"Uh-huh."

Becky clearly needed something more, "Well, you look like
shit."

The comment stopped Lee in her tracks. The mirror on the
inside of her locker door was facing her. Becky was right. She still
looked washed out, she hadn't bothered with any makeup and her
hair was flat and featureless. Still, Lee wasn't entirely sure that
it mattered – not tonight. If she could just get through the shift
and make it back home and under her duvet, this day might yet
be survivable.

"You all right, Babe? Is there anything you wanna talk about?"
Becky asked. Her tone was soft, genuinely concerned.

"I don't think so" Lee answered, still staring at her own
reflection.

"Right. Well let's at least get some slap on you and I'll try to
sort your hair out."

Lee had occasionally wondered at the description some women
gave of makeup as their 'face'. She hadn't thus far, used cosmetics
in that manner. But tonight her need had been less to put on a face,
than to entirely replace one. Becky's intervention at least enabled
Lee to look customers in the eye. The foundation was a little more
set than she was used to – though this should be okay in the dark

environs of the club. She liked the eyeliner, though. Becky had the hang of creating a flick out from the corner of the eye to create the illusion of a longer eyelid. Whenever Lee had tried that herself, the angle looked wrong and she'd either appear sleepy or as though she were the pantomime idea of a visitor from the Orient. The sides of her hair were tied to the back and the front teased up with rather a lot of hairspray. She looked kind of punky.

It really was a busy night. One of the famous Essex DJ's had been imported and he'd been followed by a couple of busloads of his adoring faithful. Added to the usual crowd, this made *Oasis* at least as jammed as a normal Friday. Lee moved through the orders swiftly, hearing everything, pirouetting around Becky and hitting all the right numbers on the cash register. She was perfect. All the more surprising since she'd declined Becky's earlier offer of a line of coke. She wanted to take it, she really did. But she knew that by the following morning, the high would have turned into a ticket to somewhere even worse than where she'd started. All the same problems – only with added dehydration and exhaustion. No, she'd see this through, raw.

Sometime around 11:30, three of the Essex crowd were hanging over the corner of the bar waving pint glasses. Lee hated that. She knew they were there and she knew who'd been waiting longer. She served a couple with a pair of rum and blacks. The Essex Boys upped their appeals. She continued to ignore them and turned to take the order of a girl in an interesting silver top. Suddenly a hand grabbed the shoulder of her t-shirt and pulled her to one side, "Oi, you dozy bitch!"

Lee was never quite sure how she'd managed the hand and eye co-ordination. She would reflect more than once in following years that if she'd missed, it could have all gone so very differently. But she was moving well. She was seeing everything and when she reached for the tie that she barely knew him to be wearing, she got it first time and with a single rotation locked it into a wrap around her hand. She pulled him to her and herself toward him. She was six inches from his right ear when she shouted. It was the perfect distance in a loud nightclub from which to be heard, but not overheard, "Listen, shit-for-brains. I was coming to you next – which would have been the *right* way, but being as you've jumped the queue, let me give you the *full* fucking picture. I've had a day you couldn't begin to cope with – and to be honest, I'm just about hanging on by my painted toenails. My Dad's dead, I lose best friends on an almost weekly basis so that now nobody really *gives* a flying fuck; I'm part-way through a full-blown identity crisis that would blow your tiny mind and last night I suffered the kind of assault that I can still physically feel through my skin. You think I'm even slightly intimidated by your pratting around? Why don't you just fuck off and try your charms somewhere nearer the rock you crawled out from!" Lee released the drunk, who appeared momentarily suspended between confusion and fury. The alcohol in his system had clearly stalled his thinking – and the pause mattered. By the time his right shoulder was drawing back to release some retribution a massive forearm had descended, barring any such chance. Lee watched her would-be assailant's wide eyes follow the exposed bicep up to Elvis' face. There wasn't enough alcohol in the entire club to stoke the courage he'd need to take on the monster bouncer. He satisfied himself with a glare back in Lee's direction and accepted the invitation to move away from the bar. His two companions looked bemused as they followed.

"You okay? What was that about?" Becky was at Lee's shoulder.

Lee was shaking from her scalp down. She put up a trembling hand, "I'm all right…I'm okay."

"No, you're not"

"No – I'm not. But I will be…"

february 1985
a wake in the life

I suppose it has kind of crept up on me, but it's got to the point that I think most of the time I'm now just assumed to be female. I don't <u>think</u> I'm kidding myself, I mean I know it helps that I'm mostly in public at night time and that most Londoners don't really look that closely anyway. I suppose things really changed when I wasn't thinking too much about them. I wasn't caring. Maybe people pick up on that. When I started this, I don't remember getting called 'love' or 'darlin' very much. Now it happens all the time. I can't remember the last time someone called me 'sir' – apart from sometimes on the phone (still need to work on that).

Carol's efforts and my agonies are beginning to show some results. I noticed it especially yesterday when I was looking around my face for some hairs to kill. I really don't have a lot of face fuzz left on the sides or the neck. Most of the time we're concentrating around the chin and up around the mouth. Thank God for cold soothing nights! It would be so great to get to the summer and not have to worry about enduring days with two shaves, more soreness and two lots of makeup. Electrolysis itself, doesn't get any easier though. I've been taking double dosages of Aspirins before going in to a session. I could probably do with a tranquiliser dart. (At least there would be a long list of volunteers to shoot one at me).

Things still aren't right. I know it and Dani + James know it. Maybe we'll never get back to the way we were with each other. I can't do anything more though to convince them that I've grown up. I've said it out loud to them and I've written it on an apology card. How many other ways can I show that I'm sorry? It does look as though it will work out for them though – and I am now honestly happy for that.

*My savings should cross £ 6,000 next week or the week after –
what with the proceeds from the car sale. I need to move up to 6 working nights a week. I'm really tired as it is and I know the hormones
are also working against me, but I need to make change happen faster.
I've come to a decision that I'd really like to have a first meeting with
a surgeon before the year is out. It'll be hard and apart from Sundays,
it really will mean working all the hours available to me. Luckily, I
don't have a life to give up.*

. . . .

Her curiosity about the letter had been driving her crazy for
the entire shift, ever since Rikki had mentioned it at *Crush*. She
stood now in the kitchen at half past three in the morning, staring
at it – the sound of the kettle's electric element heating up behind
her. She didn't recognise the writing. It was a London postmark,
so no clues there. She used a pair of scissors to slice her way in.
She recognised the magnolia-coloured stationery immediately. It
was from Dr Garner's office – though it wasn't from her psychiatrist. The author was Sue Millar, a counsellor attached to the centre. The letter was a reply to an enquiry made by Lee some weeks
earlier. Lee smiled and felt a butterfly somewhere inside of her
flap a weary few beats of excitement. Davey had agreed to meet.

It had been a tough week – and she wasn't done yet; she wasn't
done by a long way.

She had been up early on **Monday**. At that moment, the week's
first day still belonged to her and she would take every opportunity
to make practical use of it. Carol had offered her an early electrolysis
appointment. It had meant that Lee had been unable to shave over
the weekend in order to accrue enough stubble for the spiteful zap-
ping probe by Monday. Overall she'd coped, despite feeling pretty
self-conscious about what she perceived as a small shadow around the
line of her chin. At least her skin had been in pretty good shape by
the time she'd woken that morning. No weekend grazes to cover and
no stinging when she'd moisturised. Every day should start that way.

Carol had been really good. She'd given every single visible follicle a shot. Lee had been shattered from tightly gripping a new silver bangle from which she had quickly become inseparable – the tension had to go somewhere. She'd made her way home the short distance from Earl's Court, riding at the back of the top deck where hardly anyone would notice her. The conductor had looked a little freaked out, but hadn't stared too much. Her face must have looked as though it had been dragged along a gravel path backwards. She'd been given a real going over – and she was glad of it. More grief now – less grief later, she'd figured. She'd spent the rest of the day in splendid solitude. She'd taken a long bath, half-watched an old film on the living room TV and had then headed up to bed before the others began to arrive home.

Tuesday she'd been back at *Oasis*. Not quite such a busy night (the weather had been particularly cold). There were even moments when she'd been able to take a breath and chat with Becky or Yvonne. At one point, she'd taken to glass collecting just to keep herself up to speed. It was a gesture that had been noted by Lynne who had looked on appreciatively. Becky and Yvonne had later teased her about being a 'bosses pet'.

Wednesday she'd had some shopping to do and so had to be up and out before the afternoon drifted away entirely. It had been almost dark when she'd headed out. She'd needed a few groceries, but also had wanted to buy a bra, the purchase of which promised a new kind of terror. It wasn't even that she really needed one. Fully occupying an 'A' cup remained more an ambition than an honest experience. Still, her 'little buds' were these days showing through her tops like a pair of tiny tent poles. At least a bra might curve them into a softer line. She'd reflected that young girls at least had a peer group or a mother to see them through ordeals of such an intimate nature. Since the change in her relations with Dani, she didn't have anyone she could talk to at all.

She took shopping with her, the letter from The London Centre – the one that explained she was required to wear 'female attire' as part of her treatment. It wasn't enough to keep her company. Her courage deserted her before she'd even reached *Barkers* in High Street Kensington and she ended up browsing instead. She bought a top (far less challenging to her nerves). It was a dark blue – almost indigo – with long sleeves. It came down to her hips, comfortably covering her crotch area (as all of her tops must, these days). She'd also wandered into a book shop. She didn't read as much as she'd like to. She should try more, she felt. She liked biographies – especially those which told of unlikely success. Struggles with happy endings were ideal.

She'd started from the beginning, alphabetically. It wasn't long before she came across the story of Caroline Cossey. She knew the name of course – how could she not? Caroline was once Barry, but now she was a goddess. The boy who had yearned to be a girl had become a model. The kind of woman other women wanted to look like. Her story had been broken by the *News Of The World* in 1981, just after a fleeting appearance in a James Bond movie. Lee recalled at the time, buying every tabloid she could find for a whole week, in the hope of reading more about her new heroine. The newspaper reporting was of course sensationalist rubbish, but all Lee had wanted to do was see the pictures and dream in wonder. Of course, Caroline Cossey may just as well have lived on Venus itself for all that Lee Habens had in common with her – then and now. But here after all, was a book that would tell of the *real* story. It had been written by Caroline herself. These were footsteps to a future.

Lee had approached the bookstore cash register with a sense of pride and defiance. She was, in purchasing the book, registering her sororal solidarity and she was determined to look the shop assistant right in the eyes when paying. Said assistant hadn't in the event, displayed the slightest sign of interest. Still, who knew books could be more of a thrill to buy than bras?

She'd been up pretty late reading Caroline Cossey's story. She had picked it up again over her morning cup of tea on **Thursday** lunchtime. She would have even taken it into the bath if she hadn't been so worried about it being damaged. She actually couldn't *stop* reading it. Some pages had to be examined several times in order to ensure that she'd not just read, but imbibed it.

The experience was as double-edged as ever of course: For every picture page that fascinated, there was disappointment at how Lee herself compared. Caroline's face was a perfect portrait of female beauty. Her own was deeply flawed and on a bad day felt some way short of being reliably feminine at all. Caroline showed no signs of masculinity in any aspect of her appearance, while Lee remained engaged in a daily grapple with her hordes of boy-demons. Caroline's graceful curves compared uncomfortably with Lee's pale, skinny and featureless form – as another long session of reflective repugnance had confirmed.

She'd finally had to tear herself away from Ms Cossey in order to head for her scheduled meeting with Dr Garner. As ever, she had the day's last appointment which allowed her to head into town for a shift at *Crush* afterwards. She was dressed in black jeans with a neat pair of lace-up pointy boots. She was wearing another of her long silk shirts which she'd later exchange at the club for one of the staff regulation red 'T's. She had been pleased with her makeup that evening. Sometimes it would just work for her. Oddly, she tended to find that these were occasions she'd wear less of it. Her foundation would be less likely to show too many cracks and creases if it were kept lighter. That such occasions were even possible now, was testament to Carol's unyielding delivery of electricity to Lee's face.

There had been a newcomer to the waiting room. Probably in her late thirties. Tall – maybe a little too tall – and with long blonde hair (which certainly appeared to be real), she had presented an androgynous look. She'd seemed to know her makeup, but hadn't been overtly suggestive one way or the other with it. She had reasonable enough features, though tragically was likely to become even more familiar with electrolysis than had Lee. Newcomer's look was jeans under a long dark coat. Lee judged she'd probably make it.

The close inspection of random male strangers and their prospects of ever being able to pass as the opposite sex had become a favourite (if private) spectator sport for Lee. Mostly, she would practice this on the bus or tube – anywhere she could get a good long look at someone without them noticing. The game was simple: Firstly, she needed to hold a newspaper as cover. Then she would close her eyes at a tube or bus stop and listen as the seats around her filled. Next, she would imagine the following challenge being issued:

- You have four years
- You have a budget of £ 8,000
- You must successfully migrate from male to female
- Now, here is your body

Then she'd open her eyes and would have to assess the prospects of success with the first male she saw.

Sometimes of course, this would lead her to burst out laughing. Cue the newspaper as a handy defence mechanism, allowing her to appear amused by something she'd just read.

The point of the exercise was to help her own sense of perspective. So, she wasn't Caroline Cossey – but things could be worse. Many of the challenges she saw with the male faces and bodies around her, would not be hers to overcome. She wasn't overly large, she didn't have an 'adam's apple', she wasn't particularly hairy of limb and she hadn't lost any hair at all from her scalp. Facially, she didn't suffer with a strong brow ridge or heavy jawline and these fortunes had made life immeasurably easier. Most facial challenges could be solved with surgery, but not on her budget. She would have to learn to own the face she had and hope that chemistry would soften it sufficiently.

Lee had come to properly appreciate through her waiting room encounters, that transsexuality was a random curse. People didn't naturally 'look' transsexual. There were no signatures. Anyone could be suffering this turmoil within. Just because one patient was able to make the process work better than another, didn't make their case any more valid. There was no design. For every transitioning goddess, there may be a hundred large men in aquamarine frocks. All were equal, but because fortune favoured the already fortunate, some would find their equality easier to wear than others.

It had been her fifteenth visit to The London Centre. Familiarity had not dimmed her sense of excitement. To enter was to belong – with currency. What must be hidden beyond those walls, had a value through honesty, within them. She still didn't personally *know* anyone who had been through the process. She hadn't been able to relate to another who would understand and share experiences – even Dr Garner himself, couldn't help with that. Such wonderings had led her to thoughts of Davey – and further, to the idea of meeting him outside of The Centre. Their appointments hadn't coincided for at least a year now, but she could never forget him. His struggle would have been different in so many ways to her own, but she knew she wanted to learn about it. She somehow sensed it would help her – and perhaps she could even help him, too. She'd left a short note with Donna the receptionist who had said she would pass it to Davey's counsellor – but with no promises. Lee had learned from an earlier cursory enquiry that this sort of unstructured socialising wasn't generally encouraged. Lee had framed her letter very carefully. She had focused on the informative and supportive elements of such a meeting and had appealed to a perceived level of confidence in both her own and Davey's cases.

The waiting room hadn't detained her for long that day and she had soon settled into her favourite dark green leather, button-back chair. As always, Dr Garner had begun with the usual preliminaries and catching up with any updates to notes he had previously made. He asked about her hormone-taking, any illnesses, her sense of well-being; the usual. He asked whether she'd had any sexual relations since last they'd met. Lee had hated the question before – it just wasn't something she could ever comfortably discuss on a clinical level. But the asking now elicited strobed images of a night in a Brighton hotel room. "No, it's been a while now".

"Roughly how long?"

"It's pretty hard to say."

They'd moved on to how Lee's work life was going. She'd explained a little about the hours she was putting in and confirmed that her employer was now completely clear about her gender reassignment. Indeed looking the way she did prior to that night's shift, Lee hoped to clearly demonstrate her commitment to living the transition process outwardly.

She decided to further label the point, "This is as you know, how I go to work".

Dr Garner had nodded, "Yes, and how would you describe the way you look?"

"I don't know really. I'm not sure how to put it into words. Advanced androgyny, maybe?"

"How long would you say you have been presenting yourself at work 'androgynously'?"

Lee had thought back, "I guess I really moved things on a few months ago."

"And is there a point you have in mind at which you plan to present yourself in a committed female identity?"

It had always been somewhere off in the future, Lee had reflected. Dr Garner appeared to be implying that the future ought to be arriving rather sooner than later. Lee would have preferred some time to think through an answer and a strategy beyond it. She had about half a second. "I am ready. I'm ready now" she nodded with growing determination.

"Would it help you if I were to write to your employer?"

"I…suppose it couldn't hurt."

On any other day, a letter informing her employer that 'dressing in female attire would assist progress of her treatment in sex reassignment', would have been the single most important and exciting piece of paper in her possession – but now that title had been taken by the note confirming David ('Davey') Epstein's acceptance of her proposal to meet. There was a telephone number for her to call. She'd have called it there and then in the small hours of the morning, were it not to risk ending a friendship before it might begin.

A **Friday** night at *Oasis* meant lots of fun for the visitors. For Lee Habens it was usually about £45 closer to paying the bills and saving for major surgery. This night however, was not to be usual.

It had been six o' clock – much too early for her to be there at all. Even Elvis hadn't been attending the door when she'd arrived. As she'd sat watching Anita Macintyre complete her phone call, she'd mentally shuffled and reshuffled the words of the short statement she needed to make. She couldn't make it sound right.

"Lee. What can I do for you?" Madame had sighed, her patience clearly having been tested by the prior conversation.

Lee just let the words fall out of her. "Erm, as part of my treatment for...the thing I told you about."

"Yes..?" Madame urged warily.

"I have to...The thing is, my consultant who I have to see, he says..."

"Lee...?" she'd been smiling, but Lee had feared the tolerant expression to be dangerously temporary.

"I have a letter". She'd handed over the neat magnolia envelope and had watched as her employer – quite possibly the second most important person in her life apart from Dr Garner himself – pondered the text. There was a raised eyebrow. The letter was re-folded and replaced in its envelope. Anita Macintyre leaned back in her chair, "Not something I generally have to think about."

Lee felt rather apologetic, "No, I suppose not."

"Think you can carry it off?"

"I have done – on occasions."

Mrs Macintyre smiled back as she considered something. Then she shrugged, "It's just part of the process, right?"

"Right"

"You're at *Crush* on Wednesdays and Thursdays, aren't you?" Lee nodded.

"Then that's probably the best place to start. *Crush* will probably help you to feel confident about things before you're back here next Thursday. I'll brief Lynne and get the message through to *Crush*."

"Thank you" Lee said softly, adding "I really do appreciate everything you've done for me."

"You're good" Madame had replied. "You're an asset. You've never let me down or given me cause for concern. You get the support you deserve here."

Lee had stood and made to leave the office.

"If I might offer a little advice..."

"Uh, absolutely."

"Do your best at this. Do it right but be natural with it. You help the people around you to have confidence in you and they'll relax and go along with you. It's more than just swapping a wardrobe. I went through something comparable when I took on the business. It's about an attitude. You get it right and people won't even remember what changed when."

Lee was touched – and daunted. "I'll try not to let either of us down".

Minutes later she fell face first into the embrace of the staff room sofa. The sense of relief had been extraordinary – though she was already terrified about being back at the club next Thursday for what would, irrespective of how she wanted it to play, likely turn into a bit of a sideshow. She hoped everyone *would* be okay with it. Along with Lynne, Becky and Yvonne, she was now one of the longer-serving staffers and she was counting on familiarity to register in her favour. She would tell her two bar-mates herself – though not that night – she wasn't yet nearly calm enough for another uncomfortable conversation.

Saturday was still young when it met its destruction. Days don't matter when events take over. Rikki had woken Lee and everyone else around 9 o' clock and had asked them to come to the living room. Lee had only managed about four hours of sleep herself and imagined she wore a face to reflect it. She stood in her dressing gown, all of the seats having been taken. She looked around the room at Luka, Dani and James on the sofa and Rikki in the middle, perched on the coffee table looking ashen.

"I'm sorry to get you all down here so early. I can't sweeten the pill on this one I'm afraid – you'll just have to take it, bitter as it is." He was shaking a little, his heartbeat pulsing out to the corners of the single, stiffly held piece of paper he held in front of him. Lee noticed he also had a large opened padded envelope clamped under an arm. "A letter arrived yesterday and I read it last night

– this morning – you know what I mean. It's from Grant's brother, Brian. It's to let us all know that Grant passed away last week."

The only sound in the room was a slight gasp from Dani. Nobody else spoke. The dryness in Rikki's mouth made a kind of crackling noise as he went on, "I'm going to read a little of what Brian wrote:

'It is the saddest of news to have to convey and I'm sorry to have to send it. Grant was loved on both sides of the world and he knew it. We miss him here more than I can say and we know you all do, too. My brother anticipated that my words were never going to be adequate and so typically he wrote some of his own in private notes that I have enclosed. I know you'll see that they get to the people they concern. We're all so very thankful for the care and the love you showed our boy while he was with you. From the bottom of our hearts, thank you."

Rikki looked up from the page. "There were twenty-two separate small envelopes in the main package." He shook his head, sadly. "Bloody drama queen" he added, sweeping away a budding tear with the blade of his free hand.

Luka was staring into his lap. Lee noticed that Dani and James were holding hands. She herself, had only a tenuous grip on reality at this point. The shock to her was so great, it had annexed the moment from emotion entirely. She couldn't speak, couldn't think, couldn't do anything. She needed to sit.

"Luka, James, Lee, there's one for each of you." Rikki handed them out and Lee took hers in turn. She instinctively needed to be alone to read it and left the room without speaking.

Grant Jolley hadn't been a part of Lee's daily routine for one year and four weeks – yet his image and his voice remained within easy reach. She accepted that he didn't want the long goodbye with emotionally-soaked correspondence flying back and forth across continents. She could live with the separation, just so long as she knew he was out there, somewhere – a part of the same world. She even kept a hope in her heart that he just might, one day return. He would come back to her with his wisdom and wit and his confidence. She stared at the small envelope she'd propped up on a duvet ripple in the corner of her bed. "Had to have the last bloody word, didn't you?" After a wait of several minutes she braced, snatched up the note and slid to the floor, resting her back against the bed. She released the single page from its paper vessel.

'*Hey Chicken,*

Most folks have one life. You're creating a second, you lucky thing — we should all learn something from that! I'd like to take some of the credit for what you were able to achieve in the year and some that we knew each other. I'd like to claim that I took you from nothing to being the bright, shining star of a thing I know you must be now. But I can't do that. It would be pretty rude of me for a start, but it would also be untrue. You've done it yourself, with the likes of me watching on and cheering. I've cheered you 'til the last and I want you to carry on hearing me do that all the way to where you want to be.

I wrote this to kick your arse and to send you a message: Don't you slow down for one day. Not for one hour. Life doesn't last for any of us. While you have it, you owe everyone who's lost it the courtesy of giving your all to each moment you still have — I did and I wouldn't take any of them back.

So, don't you dare mope around, missing what's lost. The dead don't dance — except on Halloween. You've got a hell of a journey still left to make and that clock is still running. So turn your face forward and get on with it. I'll be watching!

With Love — and still a killer smile,

Grant — x

PS. My intern doctor is gay, but in complete denial!'

She read the note twice more before lifting herself back up onto the bed and rolling under her duvet. She'd been staring at the ceiling for at least half an hour when the knock came at her door. It was Rikki.

"Hey kidder. Can I come in?"

It immediately occurred to Lee that Rikki would have been hit harder than any of them. He'd known Grant longer and even now was having to act as his emissary. He was also several hours ahead of everyone else in processing the news and must she imagined, be feeling through the numbness by now. "Yes, of course"

Rikki didn't usually look humbled, but he did seem to have been physically diminished. He looked about a foot shorter standing in the corner by the door. Lee opened her arms to him and he moved to her bed so that they could hug. It was impossible to know who was consoling whom.

"How are you doing?" Rikki asked in a tight throated voice.

"I'm still too…shocked."

"Yeah."

Lee breathed in deeply, still resting her chin on Rikki's ample shoulder, "I always guessed he'd secretly kept in touch with you."

"There was stuff to be done" Rikki reasoned. "He addressed mail to *Crush*."

"Scheming bitch" Lee said quietly.

"Him or me?"

"Him" Lee half-grinned. "You've been a *conniving* bitch."

"Thanks kidder." Rikki broke the embrace and sat upright, looking Lee in the eye, "You read your note?"

Lee nodded, "You?"

"That's the thing – I got a note *and* a list."

"He sent you a list?"

"Oh yeah." Rikki held up a piece of the same cream stationary on which Lee's note had been written. Grant's familiar neat handwriting almost filled both sides. "Take a look at item 9"

Lee traced down the first page, '*9. Don't let Lee slack – not for a minute. No moping and no shirking work.*' She looked back up at Rikki.

"You gotta do your shift tonight, kidder."

"Oh, come on. How can I?" Lee was incredulous. "I mean I get the sentiment – it's what my note was all about. But *tonight*? That's just not reasonable." She began to shake a little. She began to slip.

Rikki reached across and took both of Lee's wrists, locking them and somehow infusing her with surety. He looked calmly at her. "You hang on. You hang on to me, to the others, to whatever the hell you can. You don't go down. You don't give up."

Rikki released Lee and stood, returning to his full height, "Tonight you're going to be at *Oasis*, pulling your shift and making the money you need to do him proud. I'm going to be at *Crush* playing a set list he would have danced his nuts off to." He paused for a moment. "We do what we have to do to make sense of what we have left. Tears don't bring anyone back – God knows, you've already learned that the hard way." He got up from the bed and looked back at Lee, "Nobody works tomorrow. By then I'll have had time to let others know what's happened. We'll all gather together tomorrow night at that shitty pub he liked, off the Kings Road. That's where we'll deal. Okay?"

Lee nodded slowly, her sinking feeling, sinking a little lower, "Okay."

Rikki looked back as he held open the bedroom door, "You hang on" he urged.

Lee made it through Saturday night. The first thing she'd needed to do was explain the morning's news to Lynne and ask her to hold off revealing her newly-public transsexual status until Tuesday. Her revised plans for the night left room only for the taking and processing of bar orders. She asked to take the solo bar in the restaurant area. Lynne said she thought Lee was incredibly brave – on both fronts. Lee didn't know how to explain that her dead friend wouldn't let her stay home that night, like she wanted to.

She explained directly to Becky and Yvonne. They hugged her together. It was a warm place to be, but really she told them, she needed to work through the night alone. They conceded space, but told her they'd be keeping an eye.

It rained on **Sunday** evening. Quite right too, Lee thought, listening to heavy drops popping against the bedroom window pane. London's sky *should* cry that night. Rikki had insisted that nobody dress down. Grant, he had pointed out, would be appalled if they did. Just before she began her own preparations, Lee made a decision to present herself as female. She had bought a purple dress in Kensington Church Street in a January sale, without ever knowing if she'd have the courage to wear it. Courage would not be required this night. She'd be numbed to street life anyway.

The dress was quite subtle, despite the rich colour. It was pretty straight in shape, made of a thin jersey, long sleeved and with a small 'V' neck. She emerged from her room at the same time as Dani from hers.

Dani smiled reassuringly, "You look really good in that" she said.

"Thanks" Lee replied, grateful for an ice-breaker. She took a step back and looked at Dani's black pencil skirt and red sweater. "You always get it right. Always."

There were more than twenty customers in the pub who Lee imagined to be likely invitees, by the time she arrived with the other flatmates. Several of the guest list had apparently been there all afternoon on an informal 'lock-in'. She recognised some faces from Grant's Christmas party. There was a clunking incongruity to the stoic expressions worn above some flamboyant outfits. A layer of sadness had been weaved into the cigarette smoke cloud hanging over the line of tables around which they were gathered. No matter how many hearts they squeezed into the little bar that night, everyone knew they'd still be one short.

Lee didn't want to press her way to the bar. She wasn't that badly in need of a drink – at least not the way some of the others clearly were. She stood back near the fireplace into which she'd once seen Grant toss Derek the Dog's tube pass.

Dani stood with her, "I feel a bit of a fraud being here. I barely had time to get to know him."

Lee smiled, "He liked you. He thought you were a class act. If he'd spent another few months with you, he'd have had you believing you were Audrey Hepburn."

Dani laughed at the idea, "So who did he have you believing you were?"

"Doris Day mostly. He really was such a queen."

They both laughed this time and one or two faces turned toward them. The expressions weren't disapproving. More, they were pleading – as if to be let into a joke at which they too, could find some release.

"How is James taking it?" Lee heard herself ask as she watched Dani's boyfriend at the bar being introduced to a tall, middle-aged man in white denim and bleached hair.

"It's hit him pretty hard. He felt he owed a lot to Grant. He says he had his eyes opened by him."

"Yeah" Lee nodded, agreeing deeply with the sentiment.

"Grant would have hated you and I falling out, wouldn't he?"

"Yes, he would. But he'd have enjoyed making himself busy putting us back together again."

Dani looked up at her friend again, craning slightly to cope with the six inches in height difference, "Did the note he wrote to you help?"

Lee smiled. She knew it off by heart by now. "He told me that those of us with lives to live had an obligation to those losing theirs. Basically, he told me to get the hell on with it."

Dani slipped a hand into Lee's, "I'm still here to help too" she said. "I hope we can go on helping each other – like we always have."

Lee smiled. She could still recall how upset she'd first been by Dani and James' liaison – she just couldn't imagine feeling it to be a problem anymore. "I do wish you both well – you know that, right?"

"You don't have to explain."

"Actually, I think I do. I'm not very proud of the way I reacted. There was absolutely no reason why something shouldn't happen between you. I was just jealous on about twenty levels – only four or five of which I vaguely understand, even now."

"It really doesn't matter anymore."

Lee almost left it. She shook her head, "No, I do want to explain. See, all my life I've felt like I'm standing outside the party, you know? That's how it seems. Everyone else pairs off and they get to experience the whole relationship thing. I never get to go into the party – do you see what I mean? I never get to be a part of what everyone else is enjoying. So now I'm here in London and I'm trying to make my own party by exploring new friendships and then somehow…I found myself standing outside of that party too."

"What happened wasn't meant to hurt you."

Lee squeezed Dani's hand. "No, I know that. I suppose it's was just hard to think that you can accidentally put two people together and then have them quickly not need you to be there at all."

Dani lit a cigarette, almost offering one to her friend, as had been the habit in a dozen other pubs down the years. She inhaled deeply and then breathed out a steady jet of thin blue smoke, "For what it's worth, James and I both knew the moment we saw each other."

Lee grinned, "That Christmas, when he came back from the country?"

Dani had a faraway look in her eye, though her direction of sight never moved from where James stood at the bar. "I spent weeks trying not to let anything happen. I didn't want to change the atmosphere around the apartment. I didn't want to be disruptive – to be the girl who comes along and 'breaks up the band'." Dani had used finger quotations marks to emphasise the phrase.

Lee nodded in appreciation, "No right, 'cos who would want to be *that* girl."

Dani grinned and let out another smoke stream through slanted lips. They fell silent, each for a moment considering whether to catch the odd word from neighbouring conversations. Then Dani added, "After you first found out about…things, I was really worried about you. You remember? You didn't come home one night and then you weren't really around very much for a while."

"Yeah."

"Did something happen back then?"

Lee kept staring straight ahead, beyond the walls and all the way to a faraway pier. "Something" she conceded.

Suddenly the entire room was sliced open by an ear-splitting shout. Dani physically jumped.

"Awright, that's fuckin' IT!!!" Rikki was standing on a chair. He looked furious, which wasn't easy considering he was wearing his

Carmen Miranda outfit. "We're supposed to be here to celebrate a *life*, not to swap stories of disease and misery." He scanned the room, locking everyone's attention – including one or two people in the opposite corner who weren't a part of the occasion at all. "Everybody dies, right? Fuckin'...*EVERYBODY!!!*" he shouted, his voice catching on the vowel. "But it's what you do while you're breathing that counts. That's what Grant *believed*. That's what he's always *preached*. He gave each and every one of us a ton of stories to laugh about. He gave us all joy and encouragement and a reason to be...Jolley." (The reference to Grant's surname struck a chord and a murmured laugh rose). "So, come on! You lot are supposed to be some of the least serious, least responsible, least uptight, party people in West London. Now, let's do our boy the honour of living down to the reputation he helped build for us. Let's have a night. Eh? I mean let's have a fuckin' *NIGHT!!!*"

The cheer was one of encouragement more than anything. A roomful of people wanting to help each other to rise above the shared gloom. To somehow find colour in the darkness. A wall of shouts followed, mostly friendly insults aimed toward the unofficial MC. Several small missiles flew past Rikki's shoulders, an empty packet of Rothman's lodging neatly between a plastic banana and orange in his elaborate headgear. The bar staff were encouraged (or perhaps intimidated) to increase the volume of the music. Tears For Fears filled the space above their heads, inspiring hips and feet below, to begin to move.

march 1985
two sides of the same impossibility

*W*hen Mrs Macintyre had said that nobody would notice me changing, I thought she was being a bit hopeful. Thing is, I think she might have been right. Sure, nobody cared very much at Crush (Miranda in the cloakroom even offered to sell me a pair of boots she said would go with the skirt I was wearing – As if I could fit into those!)

Maybe it's because I've been so preoccupied with thoughts about Grant, but I've not been anywhere near as nervous about it at Oasis as I thought I would be. I was changing at the club the first couple of times, but now I just get dressed normally at home and head out on the bus like everybody else (which actually is the only scary part). There's a certain amount of leeway you get working in a club where the lighting is low and there's a lot of booze around. People almost expect a bit of exotica after dark. In the harsh lighting of a London bus though, it's something else. You suddenly realise how close everybody is. Still, so far, so good – at least nobody shies away from sitting next to me or anything (not quite the bus nutter, yet!).

Amazing how quickly my body's movements have adapted to wearing clothing that is more restrictive. It does change you. Dani used to talk about how it would make me move differently when the time came. It's not just sitting or walking that changes, it's everything from the way you stretch to reach something to the way you stand. I hope I'm not looking ridiculous. How would I know? I can't keep asking people. That would just make them think more about it – and that's the last thing I want to do.

Becky and Yvonne have been really supportive all along of course (I still don't believe that they had guessed about me all along though, no matter what they say).

Do I feel different? Yes. Maybe not in the way I thought I might.
More than anything, I feel incomplete. It's like I'm lying a bit to
everyone around me. In a way, the more female I appear to be, the
more desperate I become to get rid of the part of me that is so offen-
sively male. It's as though I now need to live up to the way that people
are beginning to treat me.

I'm going to bring forward my first meeting with a surgeon. I want
to do it by the Autumn. I want to move on now. I have to!

. . . .

Lee had to make a Doctor's appointment. It would be tricky,
but a useful test. She had remained officially under the care of
Dr Jones for as long as she could, but the idea of living 70 miles
from her GP's practice was wearing thin on reason. In the early
days, she'd been able to make occasional, dedicated trips back for
blood tests and monitoring, but she was behind on these now and
needed make proper arrangements locally. She would make some
phone enquiries and would hope to have something in place that
afternoon. Rikki and Luka were registered at different places and
recommended both. That gave Lee at least two to try. The challenge would be to begin the relationship with a new practice using
her new identity. The GP would get the full story of course, but
even at the reception level, Lee was keen to start on the right foot.

The voice had always worried her. It was the great imponder-
able. She had read what she could find about vocal structure and
the differences between males and females. She feared her own
voice and its power to betray the rest of her. Dr Jones had said
that this shouldn't be too much of a problem for Lee as she had
a very soft voice. Lee didn't know how to interpret 'soft'. What
did 'soft' really mean – and how far would it take her? A soft
voice didn't make it female. She understood well that one of the
changes during male puberty was a relaxing of the vocal chords
causing them to vibrate slower and thereby produce lower tones.
The pure voice she'd had as a child would never come back. The
damage done during the androgenic assault in her teenage years,

couldn't be undone now. How can you un-break that which has been broken? She had heard about vocal coaching, but how could that really help?

Dani had remarked on the other hand – especially after Lee had left for London and they hadn't seen each other in some time – that her voice *had* changed and that it *was* more female. Lee could recall short conversations with strangers where her voice clearly hadn't been a problem. So, what *had* happened? It wasn't the hormones – there was no kind of effect they could have on a mature voicebox. Could it be that a simple unconscious liberation in the psyche, in the way she *felt* about herself, had made a difference? Was it possible that just *feeling* more female had caused her reflexively to match her vocal configuration, tightening the muscles around her vocal chords when she spoke?

Lee had seen Billy Connolly on TV recently, parodying a folk artist by singing with a finger closing one ear. Rikki had explained that this helped the singer to hear themselves more clearly and to monitor their own pitch. Lee had tried a test of her own in the bath earlier that day. By immersing her head until only her face was above the surface, she could judge her voice tones through reverberation from the tub's enamel walls. Through this technique, she discovered that she could in fact move her range quite substantially. She'd sourced her own naturally relaxed voice to a point somewhere between the top of her chest and the bottom of her throat. She guessed that if she could remove the lower tones and move the point of origin higher up along her throat, her vocal sound should improve. At an extreme, she tried to imagine that she didn't exist at all below the water line. She would be nothing more than a floating face among the bubbles – a bit like a bumpy water lily. Sure enough, the shallower source allowed her to radically alter her sound. It was still her voice, just without the bed of lower tones. This kind of control was exhausting though – requiring her to constantly stress the muscles around her vocal chords.

It was time to test her own theory – albeit without the aid of a safety net. She sat straight-backed on the coffee table in the living room and dialled the first of the two doctor's surgeries.

A receptionist answered on the third ring. Lee closed her eyes and tried to imagine that nothing behind her face existed, "Er, hello? Yes, I'm calling to see if I could register there as a patient?"

"Have you visited our practice before?"

"Um, no."

"And do you live in the area?"

"Yes." She needed to make herself say more, needed to find a groove but not force it, "One of my flatmates is registered there and recommended you." Modulation Lee recognised, was an issue. She needed to be more expressive and vary her range more than normal.

"Okay, we'd need to have you come down for a consultation" the receptionist said.

"Yes of course. Um, do you have a female doctor at the practice? I'd prefer to see a female doctor if I could" she winced a little at the thought that her request would sound very creepy to anyone who thought the caller might be male.

"I could book you in for Dr Casiris?"

"Oh good, that's great. What do I do now?"

"I'll need to take some basic details from you."

"Right."

"Your name?"

"Yes, it's Lee Habens"

"And is that Miss or Mrs?"

Lee's eyes opened wide.

Stargazer was a small and very neat place, nestled in a Noho backstreet. It wasn't the kind of place that needed to be found by accident. A dark and easy cocktail bar occupied the front half of a raised entrance. Wicker furniture over oak floors coddled those ordering early evening drinks and treats from a snacks menu. To the rear, a lemon walled, formal restaurant with no more than two dozen covers still awaited most of that evening's diners. The kitchen was in the basement, the dishes commuting via a dumb waiter.

It was quiet, being a Monday night and so finding Davey wasn't difficult. He smiled broadly on seeing her. She'd chosen to underplay things a little and had worn jeans but with a dressy black top and some long earrings. Davey stood to greet her. She saw that he was wearing a dark blue suit with narrow pinstripe and a yellow tie. She had to concentrate covering the last twenty feet between tables. On a smooth floor the narrow heels of her new court shoes could have her flat on her face like a floundering Bambi. Her heart pounded with anticipation.

"Lee, it's great to see you again" Davey's white teeth flashed out from his short dark beard.

"I'm really glad you agreed to it" Lee replied.

Davey offered his hand and when Lee took it he gently pulled her toward him and kissed her on the cheek. Not his first time, Lee guessed. She was about six inches taller than him. His soft beard bristled against her own smooth cheek.

"You look great" he said in the accent she'd found so charming on first hearing.

"Um thanks, so do you – and *really* um, professional"

Davey grinned and waved to the waiter, "Yeah, they kind of insist on it at work. Can I get you anything?"

The waiter arrived, "Yes sir?"

Davey looked to Lee for her order.

"I'll just have some Perrier for now, thanks" she decided, unable to come up with anything less compromising.

The waiter nodded and left. Lee's eyes briefly followed him before returning to Davey, "Can I ask, does that still give you a thrill?"

Davey looked puzzled for a moment, "You mean the 'Sir' thing? Oh yeah, that never gets old to me."

Lee smiled, "I'm kind of just getting to that point – at least sometimes – and I just feel so strongly that I don't ever want to go back, I don't ever want anyone to call me…well, *that* again."

"I don't think there's much risk of that. How long have you been in treatment now?"

Lee had to think for a moment, "I suppose about 3 years. I had a plan to make the change over 5, but some things have happened along the way and now I am where I am. I want to try for surgery by the end of this year if I can get approval." Lee hadn't come to talk about herself, "Forgive me, but this is just such a rare experience for me – y'know to talk to another (she whispered) '*TS*' person – and well, I may have quite a lot of questions."

Davey opened his arms widely, "Ask away. It's good to feel that I might be able to help – hell, I may even have a few questions myself."

Lee let out an anticipatory breath, "Okay, well I guess…I don't know, I want to know everything! I mean for a start, why here? Why are you not back in..?"

"Portland?"

"That's right, yes – there."

"A lot of things are easier and better here. There's more privacy – so my past has less of a chance of catching up with me. The access to the treatment was easier in every way – I mean I could get to doctors and surgeons right here in the city where I live and work – and there's more just over in Amsterdam. Back in the US, there are only a couple of places you can really go and the whole system is much more complex. I just think that the UK is just more patient-friendly."

Davey's voice wasn't deep, but it was authentically and effortlessly male. Lee knew that hormones would have sent Davey through almost the same route of puberty she herself had experienced – only much, much quicker and with very powerful results. She became aware that she was smiling the entire time the waiter poured her drink.

Davey advised that they'd need a few minutes before ordering. Then he looked back at Lee, noting her expression, "What?" he grinned back at her, "What is it?"

Lee shook her head, "I don't know. It's just so great to see… success. It's so natural for you, it's so right. I mean the voice and everything – it's amazing."

"Yeah well, it's a lot easier to break a voice than to…I don't know – fix it."

"How did it feel when it happened for you?" Lee asked.

"Oh, a little sore for a while – and kind of all over the place. But you know, it just happened. There was so much going on – and so fast" he shook his head in a way that suggested he wasn't used to telling his tale. "I guess the vocal episode must have been a less happy occasion for you growing up though."

Lee grimaced at the distant notion of her fourteen-year-old self, "I sort of blocked it out."

"Yeah, but your voice is fine now, how'd you do that? Did you get surgery?"

"No, I didn't even know there *was* surgery. Does it work?" Lee's interest perked to an even higher level.

"I've heard it's not great. Apparently you lose some of your control, you know. I guess you'd just end up sounding really... boring."

They both laughed.

"Boring's better than butch" Lee reflected, quickly adding "for some of us, I mean".

Davey nodded and grinned, "You may want to get that on a t-shirt."

"Not sure I know anyone who would buy one." Lee imagined Rikki in particular, objecting strongly. She snapped back to where she was, "So did the hormones take a lot of adapting to? They're really strong for you, aren't they?"

"I think the challenge is to maintain your character so that the personality doesn't change. I mean it's like suddenly being fuel-injected or something. I was energised – which was great – but I was also restless and impatient. I just wanted to get going – even when I had nowhere to go. I don't drive in the UK – and I think that was a blessing. I think I could have got myself into some serious trouble in traffic. How 'bout you?"

Lee recalled the first few months of oestrogens and anti-androgens. "Oh, the opposite. I didn't want to be seen, I cried myself stupid over nothing; I was listless all of the time."

"Yeah, some of that sounds familiar."

Lee was momentarily puzzled, "Oh, you mean from *your* past."

"Yeah. Like you said, I kinda blocked that out."

Lee sighed deeply, "Do you ever find yourself just sitting on the tube and wondering how on earth you made it so far?"

"All the time" Davey smiled, shaking his head in recognition of the sentiment.

They were encouraged to pay some more attention to their menus, but once they'd ordered, skated over a dozen mini-issues:

Names – Lee's was unchanged whereas Davey took his from a childhood best friend. His documents stated his name to be David – and that's how they knew him at work.

Work – Lee explained her nocturnal career and was then almost embarrassed to hear of Davey's achievements as a corporate lawyer, specialising in offshore tax rights. He'd freelanced through the first phases of transition. Nobody at his current office knew anything, outside of the information he'd been obliged to impart to the head of personnel.

Inverted Snobbery – Despite there being no actual 'community' of transsexuals, Davey had identified that there was certainly a hierarchy. 'Pre-ops' would always bow to 'post-ops' in recognition that the latter had transitioned through the process and had surgically, shed and/or gained the defining genitalia. 'Pre-ops' were essentially people on their way to that point and in some cases it was recognised, may never reach it – lacking in funds, fortune or commitment.

Loves – Davey had been part of a Lesbian community which had by and large, accepted him. His girlfriend of two years hadn't known him when his treatment had begun. She had previously only been into women, but had been drawn to Davey 'almost immediately' they'd met. (The description made Lee think again of Dani and James. She wondered what that must feel like.) For her own part, Lee indicated acceptance to be a major problem for her. Most straight men couldn't cope and those men who could, would often have a specific enthusiasm for transsexuality that frankly worried her. Again, no mention of Lancing.

Family and Friends – Lee described how only a single figure remained from her further past. Dani was the only person to have really known her before and still. Davey's family had almost without exception, rejected him. He indicated that their commitment to religion had proved a barrier too far – one that neither side had plans to breach. He'd had no contact with them whatsoever for almost five years.

The pair respectfully waited until their main course had been cleared before discussing surgeries. Davey had opted for a double mastectomy three years previously and a hysterectomy a year after that. Taking the private route, he had been able to find a good surgeon through his consultant psychiatrist.

"Did you ever have a doubt? I mean even for a minute?"

"Seriously?"

"Yes, I mean even a tiny one?" Lee's breath was bated.

"Not for one second."

Lee sat back in her seat and clapped her palms with pleasure, "Good. That's good – and I'm so…pleased for you!"

Davey laughed, amused at Lee's enthusiasm. "Yeah, I guess it is that moment of truth. I mean, you can take all the drugs and do all the right things, but if you back off of the treatment, your body can pretty much recover most of the ground – even if it wouldn't be pretty." He shook his head, clearly recalling a former state of mind, "But when the knife comes? *Man*, you have to be sure, 'cause there's no comin' back from that."

Lee sighed again and wondered when the beautiful shining blade would finally come for her.

Davey and Lee closed up *Stargazer* after a further two and a half bottles of wine. The owner was clearly on good terms with Davey and carried on catering to them as he was cleaning and tidying. They planned to meet again. Davey said he'd like to introduce Lee to his partner, April. Lee had beamed enthusiastically.

On a Covent Garden corner following a post-dinner stroll, Davey offered a parting thought, "Look you're finding this out for yourself anyway, but for what it's worth, I look at it like this: What we're doing is hard. It's hard for lots of reasons, but mostly because it's not supposed to be possible at all – and yet we somehow make it anyway. You and me may be headed in opposite directions, but we're really just two sides of the same impossibility."

Lee liked the summary, "We're *both* going to be all right, aren't we?"

Davey smiled back enigmatically, those white teeth flashing in the street neon.

Having a doctor wasn't just important for the usual reasons, Lee also needed one to help with her everyday treatment. The hormones she'd learned, could be sourced much more cheaply through a GP than with Dr Garner's private prescription. Once Dr Garner and her new GP Dr Casiris were connected, Lee looked forward to a small saving and a secure ring of health support. It was the one item of NHS assistance she would ask. She felt she'd earned it.

Dr Casiris was olive skinned and dark haired. She was in her fifties and probably of a heavier weight than she would like to see in her patients. Her English had a slight accent, which Lee found oddly reassuring – as if knowing that someone had taken the time to learn a language as well as the medical terminology somehow made their words all the more reliable. The doctor was pragmatic in approach, if not especially warm in manner. Lee imagined her round face to have a wonderful smile, even if she had little expectation of ever witnessing it. She had a feeling the GP didn't entirely approve of the process her new patient was undertaking.

A blood test would be scheduled for her straight away with the practice nurse. Lee had known this would be coming. She mustered all that she could to ask the question that had recently been keeping her awake through some of her darker nights, "Do the lab test for HIV?" she asked.

There was a sudden tension in the doctor's voice, though her demeanour was impeccable. "If I instruct them to, yes."

Lee nodded, "Then I think perhaps you should."

Dr Casiris' tone softened again to a more conversational level. She was probing for more information. "Do you have reason to be concerned?"

"There was an…incident. It was last year. There hasn't been anyone since, but I am a bit…It's in the back of my mind a lot of the time."

"We can have this checked. You know however that there may not be any sign for some time? You will require regular checks every six months anyway, because of the hormones. I will ensure that we also look for anything concerning."

"Thanks." Lee said, adding "I lost a friend a little while ago. We knew he was…It was still a shock, you know?"

october 1985
the last sunday night ever

· ·

*T*onight, we shopped 'til we dropped. They're opening late in High Street Ken and so I met up with Dani to make some important purchases.

I now own two bras — neither of which I need. They're just for my own sense of wellbeing really. (I imagine it must be pretty much the same for any woman who buys this size!)

I've also bought an electric typewriter! It has a little screen on it for word processing (Dani did explain that it means you can see what you're writing and correct it before the typewriter prints). Actually we've split the cost 70/30. She's put some money in as she says it'll be useful for her to have it around. I mainly want to learn how to type properly using 'qwerty' keys. If I can do that, I can maybe pick up some clerical temp work. I've bought a book to teach myself how to do it through exercises.

I need to try to plan ahead. I'm not going to be able to work in clubs for the rest of my life. I'm in my middle twenties now (!!!!).

· ·

There was no milk. Why did nobody else ever remember to buy extra milk? Lee let the fridge door swing solemnly closed. Sometimes it felt as though the dayshifters were the only ones who had any need to eat. They seemed to buy sufficient groceries for their own needs or use what had been bought by the nightshifters. And there was that emerging envy of the day people again. She'd try to work it out of her system over a black coffee.

It was nearly a quarter to three on Friday afternoon. Lee stood in the kitchen in her white knee length, cotton nightshirt and yellow dressing gown, mentally idling over the eternal bath versus shower debate, (bath feels warmer and more gentle; shower was quicker and would wake her up).

"Hey kidder, that you?"

Lee picked up her cup and wandered toward the living room, "No, it's just one of the help" she mumbled. Rikki was spruced. He was sitting on the sofa in the living room wearing a beige jacket and dark brown peg trousers. Lee was stunned and amused to see that he was also wearing a tie, "Whoa! – And I thought *my* change was radical."

"Oh…yeah" Rikki replied. He was working through some documents and tapping out some figures on a calculator he'd placed on the armrest. He wrote down the figure he needed and looked up at Lee, "Well aren't you pretty as a picture" he grinned. "Tell me, do I ever look that much of a shambles? Warning: If you say yes, I *will* shoot us both – though you first, obviously."

Lee managed a tired smile, placed her mug on a coaster and flopped down on the sofa beside her flatmate. She curled up and tried to snuggle under Rikki's arm, "I'm so tired" she yawned, "I just want to sleep 'til Sunday – and then lie in."

"Oh, you're so weak and lily-livered. Where's the backbone? Where's that stiff upper lip? Actually, there's a question: are you even able to get a stiff you-know-what anymore?"

Lee was used to Rikki's tangential asides and didn't even open her eyes when replying, "Not for fun, no." She drew in a sleepy breath through her nose, "Why are you awake? And why are you dressed so funny?"

"I swear I heard those very questions from my Mother late one night when I was a straying teenager."

Lee nudged her flatmate to answer properly.

"I had an interview."

That got Lee's attention, "For a job? What kind of a job?"

"Actually, it was more of a meeting – with Madame."

"You already work for her."

"Yeah, well not in New York I don't."

"New *where?* What on earth do you mean?"

"You can't tell anyone, it hasn't been announced yet. I asked her specifically if I could tell you and she said she trusted you to respect the confidentiality of it."

Lee was still wide eyed – and now struck dumb.

Rikki took a breath, "It's been in the planning for about a year. It's a joint project with a club owner out there. They've been working on the venue since June. For the most part, she'll be using local talent and staff, but she wants one or two people there she can trust – you know how she needs to trust people, right?"

Lee nodded twice.

"The Brits are invading New York, don't 'cha know. And now they're also sending their own Aussies."

"Right…"

Rikki took another breath – more a sigh this time, as he seemed to recognise the shock effect his news was having, "Okay, so I'm going to DJ and co-ordinate some of the themed nights. We agreed everything this morning."

"When?"

"We open on New Year's Eve."

Lee blanched slightly at the 'we' part of Rikki's answer. It made it sound as though he'd already moved on.

"Look, I'm…"

"Don't say anything" Lee interrupted. She stood up slowly, picking up her mug as she went. She walked over to the window and stared out for a moment, taking a sip of the still-too-hot coffee."

"All I'm…"

"Shhh!" Lee held up a hand, still with her back to her flatmate. She stared out to the street, seeing nothing. Inside, she was replaying visions of a cast of departed loved ones. Would she ever stop losing people? She turned and headed back to the sofa. Replacing her mug carefully, she looked a doubtful Rikki straight in the eye. Then she wrapped her arms around him and held him tightly, "Give 'em hell over there" she said quietly.

"Well, you know I will kidder."

"This is rather quicker than you had originally planned, as I recall." Dr Garner said, "You had imagined five years and this would make it what, just a little less than four by the time you would undergo Sex Reassignment Surgery?"

Lee was trying not to lean too far forward during her most important consultation to date. She wanted to control her body language, to relax into the green leather, button-backed chair the way she had on so many previous occasions. She had planned this conversation meticulously and had been completely focused all day in the build-up. It was hugely important she knew, to avoid signs of desperation. This didn't stop her of course, from feeling *desperately* desperate. She had fully expected Dr Garner's query – and she was ready for it. "The reality compared to the way I anticipated it to be, has been so much more positive. I have a great support network, I work hard and have been employed with a stable home life for several consecutive years. Now that my electrolysis is almost at an end, I do feel ready. In fact, delaying things any longer may I feel, begin to seriously affect my quality of life and chances of happiness." The last part was probably laying it on a bit. If Dr Garner held her up for another year, what would she really do? What *could* she do? This man alone had the power to decide if her life stayed on amber, or turned to green for 'go'.

"You *have* made very good progress" he accepted. "Ideally, I must say, I would prefer for you to extend your period of 'living in role'…"

Lee tried to dampen down her rising anxiety. She needed to be clear-headed and sound as reasonable as possible. "Yes, I appreciate that, but you do recognise that my circumstances were a little different to the norm. It's not entirely easy to say when my 'living in-role' period began. I haven't been overtly male in appearance or lifestyle for a very long time."

Dr Garner surprised Lee by nodding, "Yes, that's also a factor to be considered" he conceded. Then he added, "Look, I'm not going to make a decision on this today – and I'm sure you wouldn't expect me to, given I hadn't imagined we be discussing it at all."

"No, of course not – I do understand" Lee accepted, somewhat crushed inside, but grimly determined not to show it.

"I'm going to take this under consideration and I'll come back to you – shortly, I promise."

The journey into the West End was a reflective one for Lee. She'd done all that she could to make her case. She began to imagine the supportive remarks she would receive when sharing the news at home. It was now or later – that was the thing she should focus upon, they'd say. It wasn't as though she'd been refused treatment today. She would get there one way or another.

She had told one little white lie to Dr Garner: she *wasn't* entirely ready, financially. She knew that she may still need to borrow a small amount to supplement payment of the SRS fees – but that was only a guess. She wouldn't know for sure until she had a choice of surgeon and knew the final cost. Maybe for that reason, a delay wouldn't be the worst thing, she considered. It was a poor attempt at a consolation, but it was all she had.

She headed back above ground at Leicester Square and walked across Soho. She expected *Crush* to be busy that night. A good working pace would probably save her from thinking too much about the meeting. First though, she would need to stop at *Stargazer*. She wore a long black coat over her short black skirt and pastel-pink sweater. This had been an outfit designed to work a spell on Dr Garner. She'd attempted to create an image that would underpin her case for surgery. The gloves were off. When Dr Garner thought of her, she wanted him to see pastel, girly, sodding pink. She'd reasoned since of course, that the eminent specialist psychiatrist would have seen such a clumsy technique coming a mile off – and not just because of the colour.

She saw Davey almost immediately she was inside the door of the reassuringly busy cocktail bar. He was looking very professional again – this time in a dark grey suit and red tie. He was sitting on a high bar stool, leaning back against the bar and speaking with two men. Davey sat the way confident men do – legs apart, using the space. To his side also seated, was a very pretty woman with a short dark bob and deep red lips. She looked like a modern-day Louise Brooks.

Lee hadn't for some reason expected April to be so attractive. But then, she corrected herself, why should it be a surprise?

"Lee! Hey, great to see you."

Lee leaned in to the small gathering and exchanged cheek kisses with Davey. She liked kissing as a greeting. It was still pretty new to her but felt grown up and sexily continental. She enjoyed the occasional feeling of late-in-the-day stubble from men's faces, too. She was reminded each time of the contrast with her own skin – and didn't imagine she'd ever tire of it. "I'm not too late, I hope."

"Not at all, lemme introduce you to some good people" Davey offered. He turned to the young woman and held her hand. Her smile was as dazzling as his. Lee imagined that the pair probably managed to live at home without electric light.

"This is my best girl and most of my world – April"

"Hi, it's good to meet you. Davey's told me a lot about you" April opened.

"Oh wow – well, I'll try not to worry too much about that!"

These guys are my colleagues, this is Ed from our M&A team and Phillip who is our IT whiz."

"Okay." Lee shook hands with both of them, careful to narrow her hand and by moving her thumb across to bar her palm, offering them only her closed fingers to shake.

"Everybody, this is my good friend, Lee"

Lee smiled self-consciously, "So does anyone at your company have a job title without an acronym? she asked.

"There's a guy on the third floor who I've only ever heard referred to as an 'arsehole', will that do?" Ed suggested.

Lee thought 'arsehole' sounded funnier when spoken in a posh accent.

"What do you do, Lee?" asked Phillip in a rather dark, mellow voice.

"Um, I work in a club – where I mostly serve people like your man on the third floor." Lee earned some polite laughter and congratulated herself on not being entirely crap at conversation.

Phillip was definitely over six feet, she guessed. He was perhaps thirty years old. His black hair was short at the back and parted to the right in a way that suggested it had been styled rather than cut. He was wearing black trousers and a mint green shirt with cuffs rolled up. She was strangely mesmerised by his exposed wrists. He held a glass with what she suspected was gin and tonic in his right hand and a cigarette in his left. Her time serving drinkers had taught her that the cigarette hand was usually their bias. If she had been about to hand him change, she'd have offered it to his left. He would put the cigarette between his lips to take the money. It was a guess though. She hadn't served him before – she'd have remembered.

When arranging the evening, Davey had reminded Lee that none of his colleagues were aware of his transsexuality. Implicit in the instruction Lee felt, was a preference that she not reveal hers either, for fear of earning Davey a 'suspicious-by-association' tag. She was more than happy to keep both their secrets – and quite flattered that Davey had enough confidence in her to feel that his friends wouldn't guess. She wondered idly when she had last stood talking with this many straight people.

April, it turned out, was an illustrator. She worked for a number of magazines and also for a greetings card company. Lee liked her immediately and was impressed by her worldliness. She had come to London from Massachusetts nine years before. Most of her Mother's side of the family lived in the UK and she preferred she said, the more liberal and flexible society she had found when visiting. Certainly better she said, to "life under Reagan". She had dual passport status and very much enjoyed the privilege. Lee felt it important to spend the only hour she could spare, focusing on April. She wanted more than ever, to connect with women. She felt that she could be seen now. She could be related to.

April was another example of a human being clearly at home in herself. To Lee, she seemed so relaxed and accessible. She could instantly express feelings or thoughts about her work or the art for which she held such a passion. She didn't have to pause or stare off in a different direction while gathering and weighing thoughts; her opinions and beliefs were right at her surface. She was compelling company. Lee felt fortunate that she wasn't too tested on her own opinions – she could barely come up with any. Almost four years in the capital and she'd managed one visit to the National Portrait Gallery and another to the Hayward – the latter owing much to a search for shelter from the weather.

They were at least able to compare notes about London life – and how they as outsiders had adapted to it – unable now, to imagine being anywhere else.

Time ran out soon enough and Lee bade her farewells before heading on to work. She kissed April and Davey, and waved to Ed and Phillip, by whom she was still a little intimidated and hadn't yet felt she could be so familiar. Her thoughts never entirely arrived at *Crush* that night, some preferring to remain behind.

It was rare for them all to be home at the same time. Dani and James hadn't any visits out planned that weekend and had apparently been at the apartment the previous evening, too. Sunday had become a rather impromptu 'Movie Night'. Rikki was hosting and had rented, a copy of *Into The Night* – a film he'd described as 'a romance-caper-chase thing'. This was settled upon after a general thumbs down for his first suggestion of *Star Wars,* which he swore was the gayest movie ever set in space. *'C'mon, it's hilarious!'* he'd appealed. A bitter Rikki had nonetheless spent the last few minutes casting and thereafter referring to his co-residents, as *Star Wars* characters. There was some clear favouritism being shown in Lee's assignment as Princess Leia ('it's easy to work your name into it'), James and Dani were now being referred to C3PO and R2D2 respectively, with everybody's favourite MC as Darth Vader himself.

Luka had been sitting quietly in the corner, "You make me Wookie, I fucking kill you – is all I'm saying."

"You shall be young Skywalker" Rikki announced with some Vader-type heavy breathing for effect.

"Can I *not* be here for your light sabre fight?" James groaned.

"Oh, it's the best part. Mine's much longer of course and it has a throbbing…"

"Where's the popcorn?" James shouted out toward the kitchen.

"Coming!" Dani and Lee both called back in unison. Two huge bowls had been filled with hot salted popcorn according to Rikki's special recipe.

The bowls were set down on the coffee table, covered for the occasion by a white tablecloth.

"Where's the thing?" Rikki asked.

"What thing?" James responded.

"Oh, he means the zapper."

"The what?"

"The clicker thing" Luka proposed.

"Darling, there haven't been 'clickers' for years. C'mon who has it?"

"Oh, you mean the whatsit" James noted.

"'Whatsit'? That doesn't even *mean* anything!" Rikki exclaimed.

"Oh, and 'the thing' is perfectly clear?"

"You knew what I meant."

"Yeah, you meant the whatsit."

"Like I'd know" Dani chipped in, "I never get to hold the thing anyway"

A chorus of high-pitched "Ooo-ooo"'s came from the rest of the room.

"You mean the gadget?" Lee offered, holding up the remote control, which had been hidden between the popcorn bowls.

"YES!!!" everyone cried together.

Lee handed it over and looked around the faces in the room. Such disparate origins and characters. Soon she knew, this cast too, would begin to break up. She wondered if this might already be the last time they'd ever sit together.

The screen darkened and the opening music to *Star Wars* struck up.

"RIKKI!!!"

The host was Vader-breathing into cupped hands, "You cannot resist The Dark Side..."

The envelope arrived on the Saturday morning, suggesting that it hadn't needed too much consideration after all. What did its early arrival tell her though? If it was a 'yes', maybe she would have received the news over the phone. But then, apart from accepting her case in the first place, Lee had never had a telephone call from The London Centre and anyway, the decision – whatever it might be – would need to be documented. She'd been staring at the manila pouch on the sofa for about five minutes. She wanted to open it in the right room. Part of her even wanted to be dressed and looking her best. She couldn't put it off any longer – but she would need company. Ready or not, she was going to have to disturb Dani. She headed back upstairs clutching the envelope. She hesitated at Dani's door – now a barrier beyond which she couldn't venture uninvited. Only James bore that privilege now.

"Dani?" she whispered – rather pointlessly.

"Coming!" Dani's call was followed by the sound of giggling. The joke wasn't entirely lost on Lee.

Dani appeared in her dressing gown, holding the door to a six-inch gap. "Hi" she said breathlessly.

"Need a cigarette?" Lee ventured with a grin.

Dani grinned, "Not quite yet."

Lee held up the envelope.

Nonplussed for a moment, Dani took a sharp breath. "Is that..?"

"Almost certainly."

Dani turned back into the room. "Gimme a minute". She closed the door on the grumbling voice from within and followed Lee into her room next door.

"I'm so glad the walls in this place are thick" Lee said, nodding in the direction of Dani's room. She took a seat on the bed, looked up at her friend and held out the envelope, "Here, you read it."

"I can't!"

"No, *you* can – *I* can't" Lee pleaded.

Dani shook her head and reluctantly took possession of Lee's news. She opened the envelope. There were two pages. She scanned the first, ignoring what she knew to be Lee's expression of utter dread. She re-read the short statement on the magnolia coloured headed paper. Her eyebrows headed north. Without speaking she simply turned the paper and held it close to Lee's eyes:

Dear Miss Habens,

Further to our meeting and following due consideration, I am pleased to support your case for Sex Reassignment Surgery. My view will, as is the statutory requirement, require corroboration by a second psychiatrist.

In the meantime, The London Centre recommends several highly-experienced surgeons whose contact details can be found attached.

Please let me know your plans by the time of our next scheduled meeting.

Sincerely,

Dr A. Garner FRC Psych

don't take away the mu-sic

. . . .

'Can't sleep. Can't do much of anything. Why do so many things have to happen at the same time? Would it kill fate to get a Filofax and plan out the important stuff a bit more evenly?

It's just a few more hours until my consultation with Mr Hendry. It still seems odd to me that surgeons are called 'Mr', instead of 'Doctor' or something more medical-sounding. I need to sleep. I need to be sharp enough to convince him that it is perfectly okay to cut off bits of this body and to make them into other parts to put into it (gross, though that sounds!). I'm prepared to pay him a small fortune to do it for God's sake, so why shouldn't he just go ahead and book me in? Surely nobody gets this far without being right for surgery anyway.

I can't stop thinking about how he'll be. What does he look like? Will he be kind or is he perhaps contemptuous of people like me? Does he just do it for the money and think of his patients as deluded? How can he possibly understand how much his work can mean to someone who actually is TS?

Dani was so sweet tonight. She really would have taken the day off just to go with me to the surgeon's office tomorrow. I couldn't have let her do that though. And anyway, I should be able to do this kind of thing alone now.

Rikki took the time to call home too tonight. He told me to 'kick ass' tomorrow. I'm amazed he's got time to think about my issues, what with all that he has on his plate. One more week and he'll be gone. I can't bear it! I wish Grant were here. I wish I could talk to Dad.

Why don't the people I love just stay still?'

. . . .

She'd always liked the sound of the hissing steam machines in coffee bars. She listened to it now; a vaporous chord spilling out into the warm air from behind a Formica counter. She thought back idly to the afternoons she had wandered beyond the school gates, into Sittingbourne's town centre and *The Coffee Cup*, a terminally unexciting little place in the then fledgling shopping centre. Ten shops and a café hadn't exactly quickened the pulse, but it had been better than a corner table in the stuffy school library. Her last year of education had seen a schedule full of 'free' or 'study' periods – a time when she was left uninstructed and frankly uninspired. A cup of caffeine-driven milk accompanied by a newspaper always did pass the time more agreeably.

There was no newspaper today. No point – her mind hadn't room. Instead, she stared out through dark venetian blinds and across the street to a large black door under which glazed red tiles shimmered with recent rain. She'd be standing there soon, pushing on that large Edwardian doorbell. She was about to meet the latest, most important stranger to her life. This one wouldn't just get to know her, he would *physically* change her. This man she didn't yet know, who must right now be behind one of the deep, high-silled windows, would one day soon she hoped, cut deep into her body, releasing her from ugliness. She ached for the day to come. She, whose only previous brush with surgery had been the removal of tonsils aged five, was now embracing – indeed *craving* – a major abdominal invasion.

Surgery in general hadn't interested Lee very much before – apart from a brief time when it had been thought a possible route to recovery for Dad. She knew generally what lay ahead for her, but hadn't really cared to learn the detail. That her body should suffer was of little concern to Lee. That it should bleed, bruise or burn was nothing more to her than a clinical rite of passage – and now that she could sense her destination, she wished only to arrive.

Lee watched a young woman approach the surgeon's office. Pressing the large bell button, she put a hand to the door, awaiting the release of what must be an automatic lock. She was, even from this distance, stunningly beautiful. She had long dark hair and

Mediterranean skin. She wore black tights and long boots under a short thin coat, which wouldn't likely be keeping out any kind of weather. Whoever she was Lee mused, she was no Londoner – not dressed like that. The young woman pushed and disappeared inside. Lee opened her handbag and dug deep for Dad's wristwatch. She read the hour and took in a deep breath, releasing it audibly. Time.

Lee Habens' turn at the black door felt so much more real than the scene she had witnessed from across the street. A chill wind tugged at her hair, which she'd tied back to prevent tangling. An electronic buzz and accompanying clunk offered ingress. She underestimated the weight of the door, applying too little force to open it. The buzz had ceased and she rather embarrassingly had to press the bell a second time. Finally forcing her way past the black satin-painted portal, she was met by still and soundless calm in the form of a highly polished mahogany floor under a wrought iron chandelier. The walls of the wide hallway were painted in a muted olive shade. Her shoulders relaxed to the warmer tempera-ture. Her hearing began to adjust and she picked up sounds from along the corridor and to her right. Beyond a short series of heavy oak panelled apertures, she found one that was invitingly ajar. Inside, a middle-aged woman was seated at a computer and speak-ing into a phone. Lee placed herself just beyond the threshold of the doorway and waited for an invitation. The receptionist was small and delicate, with neatly coiffured Thatcherite hair, swept high off a still smooth forehead. She wore a short string of pearls and looked as if she had stepped out of a black and white movie. Lee wondered if she had been a classmate of Change Central's Cheryl at Receptionist School.

"Yes….Yes….No, that's fine. Yes, you just call if you have any other worries. Okay…thanks then." The woman made a notation on a pad with her left hand, before looking up toward Lee. Lee was suddenly conscious of her tied back hair – not her best look for a first impression. She quickly pulled out the hair band, feel-ing chilled locks fall free around her face. "Um, I'm…"

"Lee Habens?" the woman offered.

"Um, yes – is it that obvious?"

The woman smiled warmly, "Not expecting anyone else this afternoon – just an educated guess."

Lee took a couple of steps into the room. She began to unbutton her long cocoon of cashmere mix, "I'm seeing Mr Hendry."

"Yes, you are. Four o'clock. He's running a little late as it happens – we've had another patient turn up late for her appointment. I do hope you won't mind a short wait."

Lee smiled. "I've waited years to get this far, a few more minutes won't hurt."

The woman nodded in warm appreciation. "I'm Hayley. Can I get you anything?"

Lee couldn't think of anything at all – even to be polite.

Lee had already begun to wonder before she rounded the corner turn to the waiting room, but even when she saw the glamorous dark stranger sitting in the waiting room, leafing through a copy of *Cosmopolitan*, it still seemed improbable.

"Hi", Lee offered as she entered the small room. There were no more than ten chairs to choose from and she took care to select one neither too conspicuously close, nor obviously aloof from her fellow patient.

The young woman looked up through generously lashed green eyes, "Hello", she said. Her voice wasn't overly deep, but had a smoker's rasp to it. Lee observed her hands, which were thicker in the finger than they should be. She wore a long, dark blue sweater, with a deep 'v' revealing an enviable cleavage. The cues were mixed, but Lee had no doubt. As a woman, she was gorgeous; as a TS woman, she was mind-blowing. Lee would have to have been Caroline Cossey herself to have felt easy in such company. She felt an odd mix of fascination and bleak hopelessness. She could not dream to attain such a level of effortless outward femininity herself. She stared down at her skinny knees, clad in opaque tights. She instinctively pulled at the hem of her black skirt, as if her own aspirations toward womanhood now required extra modesty.

"You are for Mister Hendry?" the raspy voice enquired, revealing an accent to match the exotic skin tones.

Lee looked offered an almost apologetic smile, "I'm…yes, that's right."

The young woman nodded in understanding. "I am late. I hope I don't make you late, too."

"Oh" Lee shrugged. "Really, don't worry – I'm not important." The slip was most definitely Freudian. Something was curdling the milky coffee in Lee's stomach. Once upon a time, she had known the same feeling watching Dani get ready for one of their nights out. She recognised now as then, that the reflex was as pointless as it was unjust. Beauty was as much a lottery as her own gender issues. Dad had always taught her to run straight at the things she feared most. She reached past her own sense of intimidation, "Um, where are you from – if you don't mind me asking?"

"Oh, Italia – Italy. I am Mona" she smiled easily, offering her hand.

"I'm Lee from…here" she returned, receiving a surprisingly firm and full handshake.

"You are a patient?" Mona asked, "Like me?"

"Oh, I'm not quite like you – unfortunately" Lee laughed hoping that she'd successfully communicated her admiration.

Mona nodded and smiled broadly, revealing even, white teeth. "Ohhh, sure." She gestured toward Lee and added, "You look good."

Lee laughed at Mona's generosity, "Oh, I think I look barely acceptable – you look completely amazing."

Mona looked a little puzzled, "You have had no surgery?"

Lee shook her head, "Not yet."

Mona smiled again and raised her high-arched eyebrows, "Me, I have had…lots."

Lee had read of young Italian transsexuals who like their Brazilian counterparts, gained access to illegal feminising drugs early in life and were sometimes even able to avoid their natal puberty. "Can I ask at what age you started hormones?"

"How young?" Mona checked.

"Yes."

She raised her eyes to the ceiling in thought, "Fourteen" she announced "And you..?"

"Oh" Lee replied, pushing back down another swell of envy, "...later."

There was a silence between them for a moment or two before Mona volunteered, "Mister Hendry is very good."

Lee looked up from the magazine rack she had spied, "Yes, he was recommended to me through my..." Lee thought about saying psychiatrist but was unsure whether such a role was played by anyone treating Italians who had been taking birth control pills since their early teens. "...clinic".

"He made my operation last year."

"Oh, okay. And now you are back?" Lee asked, genuinely curious.

"My boyfriend at home? He does not know about...you know" Mona's eyes fell fleetingly to her lap, "We were still new to each other when I had operation. So, after operation, when I went home, we were more close and he wanted to have sex. Mister Hendry said no sex before six weeks of healing, but I could not explain and so we had sex."

"Ouch" Lee sympathised.

"Ouch" Mona confirmed, nodding. "And since then, more sex" she added. Now I need..." she hesitated over the English word, "help."

Lee wondered why Mona wouldn't have just left her boyfriend if he refused to wait longer. She was interested to complete other parts of the picture too, such as how Mona had funded the 'lots' of surgery – but there would be time for neither Q nor A.

"Mona?" Hayley was in the doorway – Lee wondered for how long.

Mona stood. She was about five feet seven Lee realised and able therefore, to wear serious heels.

"Bye" Mona smiled, collecting her coat, bag and glancing back over a slim shoulder.

"Good luck" Lee offered, doubting its need.

Lee spent at least half an hour in the company of the same edition of *Cosmo* that Mona had been reading. She wondered how the glossy ads and imagery of clothes and makeup played to the eyes of someone for whom they would all have an immediate relevance. Once more Lee had to snap herself out of the shallower obsession with aesthetics. It had been instinct that had driven her to this day – a desperate need for wholeness and to relate to the world around her, socially, romantically, philosophically – politically even. Beauty had never been the aim. Perhaps if it had, she'd first have invested in some very different types of surgery – maybe even some of the same procedures that Mona had undergone.

She slipped off her coat and took the opportunity of her solitude to visit the art deco mirror on the opposite wall. She fixed her hair, brushing out the confusion invested by damp windy London streets. Today was a good hair day, she reflected gratefully. She sat back down and pondered another visit to the magazine rack.

While Lee had looked away, Hayley had ghosted to the doorway again, "And finally, Lee?" she said, her head tilted in sympathy. "I'm so sorry about the time."

Lee stood slowly. Time no longer had any meaning for her. It didn't matter how long she had waited. Now was finally now.

Hayley ushered Lee back along the hallway. The receptionist knocked at one of the large oak doors and leaned in, "Lee Habens" she said softly. Lee moved into the room as a silver haired, slim man of around fifty, rose from a broad mahogany desk. He wore a charcoal suit and azure blue silk tie.

"Miss Habens, hello" he said reaching out a welcoming hand, "I'm Jonathan Hendry, please come in."

Lee hoped desperately that she didn't look as nervous as she felt. There wasn't a place on the planet she'd rather be at that moment and yet in another way, she couldn't wait to get the hell out of there.

Mr Hendry offered her a dark leather chair, "I must apologise for running late, the previous appointment was actually late *before* it began" he explained. Instead of returning to the seat behind his desk, he reached across, picked up a green folder and pen and took the other matching leather seat next to Lee.

The move slightly unnerved her and she tried to settle herself by making conversation, "Was it Mona – the late appointment, I mean?"

Mr Hendry smiled warmly and his eyebrows danced in a moment of amusement, "Ah. Yes."

"I met her in the waiting room. She was telling me her story. I can't believe she's…y'know, like me."

"Yes, she is very attractive – er, as…are you, I should say" Mr Hendry added quickly, covering any risk of offence. "I don't imagine you have too much trouble passing".

Lee considered her routine mix of bus and tube commutes, shopping expeditions and long nights of serving the drinkers and drunks of London's small hours, "I think I can mostly fit in – although I do wish I weren't so tall."

"Not something I can help with, I'm afraid." He pushed his silver-framed glasses a little higher along his nose as he read into Lee's case file. He was a handsome man, she decided. Not traditionally perhaps, but his poise and considered movements made observing him a pleasure.

Eventually, Mr Hendry looked up "So you have elected for sex reassignment surgery."

Lee nodded solemnly, "Yes – absolutely."

"And do you feel that this is the only option for you?"

"I do – I have. I *know* that this is what I need."

Mr Hendry took a short breath in through his mouth. Lee had heard that surgeons breathe more through their mouths than noses. Apparently performing deep surgery on people could mean an exposure to less than pleasant odours.

"Well Lee – can I call you Lee?"

Lee nodded.

"There are those who feel that such complex surgery isn't always the obvious end to their treatment. I know of cases where simple removal of the male genitalia is enough for them."

Lee must have looked a little surprised.

He went on, "I take it your intention is to fully function in the female role?"

"Um yes – absolutely." Lee responded, remembering what it was like to be suddenly discussing her most intimate thoughts and feelings with an erstwhile stranger, seconds into a first meeting – echoes indeed, of her initial encounters with Doctors' Jones, Garner and Casiris.

"And you are under the care of Dr Garner of The London Centre?"

"Yes, I've been seeing him for nearly four years in all" Lee replied, stretching the calendar as far as she dared.

"And you are presently taking a combination of prescribed oestrogens?

"Yes."

"You are also taking anti-androgens?"

"Yes."

"Any problems with those?"

Lee smiled, "Nothing more than you'd expect."

Mr Hendry smiled back and took in another short breath, "Well now, the options available to you are two-fold" he declared removing his glasses. The light in the room was soft, but still his eyes appeared a fairly pale blue. There was absolutely nothing soft or alluring about the pictures painted by his words. "Following removal of the core of the penis and the testicles, the skin of the scrotal sac is used to create the beginning of the vaginal canal and the labium. The urethra is relocated from its original penile placing to a recessed area toward the front of the vulva, while the penile skin – that which has qualities of elasticity, is used to create the inner walls of the vaginal canal itself." He paused, "But you probably know all of that already."

She did, pretty much – but still didn't care much to dwell.

"The element of choice concerns the creation of a clitoris which can be made from remaining highly sensitised penile tissue. You may want to consider this step however, as there are issues of over-sensitivity. Some patients find that even though a hooding for the clitoris is created, they are unable to control the level of sensitivity – unable as it were, to switch it off."

It was certainly a candidate for the most extraordinary offer Lee had ever been made. "I just want to be as normal as possible" she shrugged, "that's my motivation, really."

Mr Hendry nodded and smiled reassuringly. "You can give that aspect some thought." Suddenly the surgeon took to his feet, "Now then, if you wouldn't mind undressing your lower half completely and hopping up onto the examination table…" his arm gestured gracefully toward what Lee could make out as a hospital-type platform behind a green canvas screen. She hadn't been entirely sure that there would be an examination at the first consultation, but was glad that she had shaved her legs only a day before. She did exactly as she was asked, removing her skirt, tights and underwear, experiencing the bizarre sensation of feeling normal, but only from the waist up. In the meantime, Mr Hendry had placed a fresh section of paper sheeting over the table before washing his hands demonstrably at a Belfast sink in the corner of the room. Lee took her place. She hated being naked – perhaps more at that moment, than ever in her lifetime. She didn't know quite what to do with the limp and rather pathetic-looking organ that lay upon the testicles bunched in her lap. Her first thought had always been to hide the genitalia beneath either underwear or her legs. It was difficult to bare such ugliness – even in this place.

Mr Hendry returned to the table and asked Lee to lie back. She turned herself and raised her legs up onto the table. She noticed some support framing. She guessed their purpose—and was then invited to apply them to her pose.

"Now, if you'll just place your feet into the stirrups…" the surgeon requested gently.

As if it were indeed possible, Lee now felt even more exposed. Her knees were high and wide of her body, forcing her into an ungainly and alien pose. She let her head fall slowly back to the support of a strategically placed pillow and closed her eyes. 'Now if ever' she thought to herself, 'is the time for a forced, out of body experience'. She wondered if she could mentally send herself back over to the coffee shop for a second cappuccino.

"What I want to do now is to check the quality of the skin."

Lee still had her eyes tightly shut – though that didn't prevent her from feeling the sensations of the penis being held as the fore-skin was gently tugged in examination. This was followed by the scrotal area being similarly tested through stretching. She wanted to fall through the floor into an inky blackness. She tried to console herself with the thought that this man would at least be the last to touch these parts of her, just as he would also be the one to take them.

"Yes, you are fortunate." Lee heard the surgeon say.

Fortune was perhaps the last quality she had felt blessed with at that moment. "R-really" she replied, not actually wanting to hold a conversation of any kind while in her present position.

"Your skin is good. There is an excellent degree of elasticity and not too much in the way of hair."

"Hair matters?" Lee asked momentarily raising her head – before finding the view too awful to bear.

"Oh yes, we cannot invert an area of skin with excessive hair growth. It would be uncomfortable and would likely lead to infection."

"Yes" Lee reasoned, "I suppose so."

"Right, now I'd like you to look up for me." Mr Hendry encouraged Lee to bend forward while he raised the back of the treatment table to support her.

Returning to Lee's abdomen, Mr Hendry began to explain fur-ther, what lay ahead. He lifted the testicles, and pushed his closed fingers against the space beneath them, pushing against the area between genitalia and anus. "Here is where the vaginal opening will be created."

"Oh. Okay." Suddenly Lee was engaged. She held the bottom of her bunched sweater aside so that she could see what was going on. Now she had a graphic feeling for the destruction and disman-tling of the mess in her groin area. She almost wanted to sneer at the junk organs whose end was so openly being plotted.

"The cavity itself will have a depth that might be between four and six inches – depending upon how much skin we can use and its qualities of elasticity. It is very important therefore, that between now and surgery, you do all that you can to take care of the skin. You should try to moisturise and stretch the skin around the scrotal and penile areas." Mr Hendry stepped back, "Do you have any questions?"

Lee looked up and shook her head, "Not really – apart from, how soon?"

"Well Hayley will take care of that. You can get dressed now and then we'll talk through some other details."

"*March!*" Dani exclaimed, almost falling off the corner of Lee's bed, later that evening. "Bloody hell! That soon?"

Lee smiled self-consciously and stared into her mug of tea, "It doesn't feel that soon. I have to go back for another consultation just before, but yeah…March."

"Shit! I mean…*shit!* Are you really ready?" Dani asked, wide-eyed and stretching across to place a supportive hand on her friend's knee.

Lee shrugged and grinned. "Yeah, of course. It just feels a bit unreal – as if the date will never actually come."

"It'll come all right – and quicker than you expect."

"I suppose" Lee conceded, trying for some reason, to act cooler in manner than she felt.

"It'll be done at this brand new private hospital near The City."

"I can get there easily enough – I'll come to see you every day."

Lee smiled, but shook her head, "You know how I feel about that" she chided gently, "We can speak by phone."

Dani's shoulders fell in submission, "Just so long as you know I'm with you" she said softly, her compassionate expression then visibly morphing into one of mischief and dare, "*MARCH!*" she cried out again, grabbing Lee and almost soaking them both in a shower of hot tea.

Getting a Friday night off in December hadn't been easy. Perhaps Madame and Lynne had felt a special obligation, knowing how close Lee was to Rikki. The Drag Jockey's last gig in London was to be at *Crush* that night and Lee wasn't about to miss it. The club would be packed for the occasion and so Lee had advised Dani and James to be there early. Davey and April would be going along too and Lee was sorry that their first meeting with her showstopping flatmate, would likely be the last.

Rikki himself had been keen to urge Lee to treat the night as a celebration, rather than a farewell. "Look kidder" he'd said earlier that evening, already looking outlandish with half made-up eyes and hair slicked back pre-wig, "I'm going to New York, not the Underworld. Who knows, maybe it won't work out and I'll be back in a month or two with my tail between my legs." He hadn't been able to resist a purse of the lips at the mental picture. He saw that the image had been planted in Lee's thoughts too and they laughed a little relief.

"Do me proud and push the boat out, will you?" Rikki had requested. "Remember, there is no such thing as O.T.T."

Under Lee's coat was a dark red fitted dress. She wore lips to match and what were for her, rather high heels. It was absolutely not an outfit she felt confident of carrying off – but this was for Rikki, the man modesty had never known. Too late to go back now, she conceded, staring up at the neon sign outside *Stargazer*.

The bar was just about as busy as she'd expected. She went inside, her high heeled height at least allowing her a good view of all corners of the room. She saw James first and made her way in his direction. As she did so, she could feel the eyes of other patrons following her and she blushed in the dim light. She pulled the tie away from her folded ponytail, dropping curls down around her. The gesture probably got her added attention but at least now she could only see the stares coming from ahead. 'Walk like you belong...'

"Hey!" Dani called out.

"Whoah! Tall chick!"

"I feel like a lost giraffe." Lee complained.

Dani was black lace and exceptionally big hair. James wore a long white jacket with a white shirt. He had silver corners clipped to his collar. They glinted when caught by the light.

"Well, we've all given it our best" Lee observed. "Rikki will be pleased."

"What, dare I ask, will *he* be wearing?"

"Oh, he wouldn't tell – said it would be a surprise."

The trio exchanged alternate expressions of knowing, dread and excitement.

"Okay, well we have to find Davey and April". Lee turned back to the crowded saloon. One last thing occurred to her, "Just remember, even though I've told you about Davey's past, he doesn't like to talk about it with civilians."

"Ci-what?" James asked.

"Never mind!" Lee shushed.

She couldn't see them at all at first. Then she caught a glimpse of April who happened to be looking their way. She flashed a dazzling American smile of recognition. She was in fitted blue velvet and as the crowd made way, Lee also saw Davey himself. He was in a blue jacket two shades lighter than April's dress. The sleeves were turned up and he wore a white t-shirt underneath with white linen trousers. She couldn't see his feet, but she bet herself he wasn't wearing socks – despite the season.

Lee pulled Dani through the crowd behind her, with James following. She exchanged kissed greetings before introducing her flatmates, "Dani, James, this is Davey and April. Oh..." she paused, recognising another familiar face, "...And this is um...*Phillip.*"

"Yes, lovely to meet you – ah, but I'm just leaving" Philip chipped in.

"Something we should take personally?"

"Hardly. No, your evening sounds like great fun, but I've only just found out about it and you know – I'm not really geared up for a nightclub"

"I've told him he should come" April contributed.

"Yeah, absolutely" James joined in, perhaps looking for a kindred spirit in a sea of confusing sexual vessels.

"Really? In this?" Philip asked, looking down sceptically at his grey business suit.

"Oh sure, *Crush* is a pretty low-key kind of place, really", Lee assured.

Dani snorted. Lee found herself quite perked by the thought of Philip being around for the evening – though she took note that Davey wasn't offering guidance either way.

They were out of *Stargazer* and on their way within twenty minutes. *Crush* would welcome them in as friends of Rikki's and in Lee's case, an employee to boot of course, but Madame's clubs never flouted fire regulations and once the place was full, that would be it – no matter what their connection.

There was a substantial, slowly shuffling queue outside when they arrived. Lee went forward to speak with the door staff who, having assessed the numbers, advised Lee to take her group in through the service entrance, for fear of annoying those waiting their turn to pay. Once inside, Lee led them back up to the cloakroom. They passed some newly entered customers who eyed the group suspiciously, clearly recognising them from outside. Lee, Dani and April surrendered their coats to Miranda in the cloakroom.

Lee smoothed down her dress self-consciously, soothing her nerves with the thought that the place would be so busy that little of her would be visible anyway. She caught sight of Philip. He was ignoring whatever was being said to him by Davey and was instead staring warily back down the stairs. She smiled at his discomfort and placed a hand lightly to his back, "C'mon in Stranger – you ain't seen nothin' yet."

Dani and James knew exactly what lay at the bottom of the stairs, but for Davey, April and especially Philip, Lee knew the next few minutes might constitute something of a shock to the system.

No matter how many times Lee entered the main room at *Crush*, it always energised her. It wasn't just the ridiculously exotic clientele or the fact that she generally liked the playlist of 70's disco and 80's pop, it was the smile quotient around the place. She had never known an incidence of violence or boorish behaviour. There was almost an old-fashioned sense of bonhomie at *Crush*, as if everyone's evenings were connected. These revellers needed each other in order to achieve the night's potential.

Lee stepped to the edge of the sunken dance floor and breathed in the atmosphere of smoke, dope, alcohol and pheromones. She always saw Grant somewhere out there in the crowd. A part of him would always belong to this place. She looked to her side and noticed Davey's expression. He was beaming at the sight of an already bouncing dancefloor, twirling figures and the glimpses of angel wings, pirate hats and coloured wigs.

Lee was smiling herself, "Well..?" she shouted.

"Oh, this place is just fuckin' nuts!" Davey called back over some Shalamar.

"Yup. I know it's too much..."

"...But is it enough?" Davey completed.

Lee led them to one of the long bars and quickly attracted the attention of staffers with whom she'd shared shifts. As Lee relayed the drink orders she caught sight of a figure shadowed in a doorway at the back of the bar itself. She turned her attention to the confused looking debutant at her back, "You okay there Philip?" she asked.

He sidestepped a shirtless cowboy and grinned in a bemused way, "I was extending the network of our mainframe a couple of hours ago, and I'm not sure quite what happened after that."

Lee laughed, "Did you ever read *Alice In Wonderland?*"

Philip accepted the bottle of lager handed to him, "Fell down a hole into a weird underworld?"

"That's the one."

"Okay" he nodded, "I'll try that thought."

Dani slid a hand over Lee's shoulder and peered around, "What time is Rikki on?"

"I'm really not certain, but believe me – you'll know when he is." She looked over again at the figure behind the bar, "Will you excuse me for a minute?" Disappearing through a door to the side of the bar, Lee made her way along the back access corridor, emerging behind the serving area. Anita Macintyre was nursing what Lee guessed to be a white wine spritzer.

She turned, perhaps sensing Lee approach, "Well, look at you..." she smiled approvingly.

"Oh, it's just me not wearing black" Lee conceded, feeling conspicuously tall in the small space they shared. "We don't usually see you here on an evening."

"Oh, I had to come to see my boy off" she said, gesturing toward a stage that Rikki would soon occupy. "It's all my doing that he'll be lost here and gained there."

"Yes, of course" Lee acknowledged, knowing the depth of her employer and flatmate's relationship.

"Don't suppose you know what sort of outfit he has in store for us?"

The club boss smiled broadly, "Oh that I do, yes" she replied, staying steadfastly inscrutable.

Lee grinned along with her and then changed the subject entirely. "I just wanted to let you know that I have a date for my surgery."

"Oh, okay" Madame said softly.

"It's in late March."

"Wow. How do you feel about it?"

"I guess I…wish I could fast forward to then."

"Can't come soon enough, hey?"

Lee nodded. "Thing is, I'm afraid I'll be missing for about six weeks, but I'll get back as soon as I can – erm, assuming you can hold a spot open for me. It's just that I'll be a bit limited in what I can do physically for a while."

"We'll cope." Madame replied reassuringly. She thought for a moment and added, "Maybe there'll be some lighter duties you could help with while you're making your way back."

"Absolutely. I'd be happy to do whatever I can to help."

Madame consulted her wristwatch, "It's about time, I think. You'll want to get yourself a good view out there."

"Yeah – well, in these heels, pretty much anywhere's a good view"

It was good to see that Davey and April were chatting freely with Dani and James. Lee watched a still rather bemused Philip take delivery of another beer. She was impressed by his willingness to give the night's adventure a try. He may not quite fit the scene, but he wouldn't be meekly annexed. He had a pretty good attitude for a straight guy, she concluded. She moved to his shoulder. "You know, there aren't too many people I can see eye to eye with in these heels" she declared.

Philip took another deep breath of German ale, "Yes you really are *spectacularly* tall." He pondered aloud, "I'm 6'2", so what does that make you?"

"Taller than I need to be".

Philip thought for a moment, "You know apparently, we start shrinking beyond the age of about forty. By the time you're cashing your pension, you'll probably be pretty much normal-sized"

Lee tried not to laugh, but couldn't help responding to the tease, "You sir, need to take care of your friends in this place. I could just abandon you to the wild things" she threatened, gesturing toward a moustachioed figure in a tutu.

"Yes, of course. I will bear that in mind."

"Can I call you Phil?"

"You can, but then I'll pull your hair and call you Needle Nits"

"Well I'll bear that in mind too, then."

The lights dimmed as Duran Duran faded against the buzz of the live PA system.

"Laydeez, Gentlemen – *and* Others – welcome to a very special Friday night *Crush!*" Lee recognised the invisible announcer's tones as those of Rikki himself. "Tonight, it's Broad-way or *Her* way and *No* way are they r-r-ready for this! Hee-eeere's Rikki!"

The sound system exploded to some booming percussion that Lee instantly identified as the opening to Elbow Bones' *Night In New York*. She grinned at the selection and then, just as the horn section ramped up the anticipation, she gasped at the apparition that appeared stage front – to a cacophonic wall of cheers and whoops.

"Bloody hell!" she heard Philip exclaim.

"Oh my…" Dani never finished her reaction.

"Sweet Mother of God" Lee mumbled to herself.

Rikki stood in a long white gown with face and arms painted to match. He was wearing a white wig with a tiara and holding aloft a torch which appeared to be crudely fashioned from plaster of Paris.

"Is he actually trying to be the Statue of Liberty?" Davey called incredulously.

Lee nodded, unable to avert her gaze, "Really makes you wonder what the inside of his head is like, doesn't it?"

Rikki slowly lowered the 'torch'. It became apparent that there was a microphone inside of it. "For the very *last* time my friends, let me remind you that..." (much of the crowd joined in with his terminally clunky catchphrase), "...nobody said the 'D' in DJ had to stand for disc..."

Davey looked like he'd ingested the lime slice from his beer, "Oh God, that's bad!"

The fader went up right on cue to the vocal and the dance floor lights and coloured scanners whirled into motion.

Lee turned to the doorway behind the bar to catch Madame bathed in coloured rays, laughing like she had never seen.

Everyone had danced and everyone had drunk – a lot. Two and a half hours had passed of a night Lee didn't want to end. She watched Dani and James jammed into a booth, laughing heartily over something intimate. They really did belong together she reflected, cursing herself once more for ever having resisted the idea.

"You having a good time?" April called across the intro to Womack & Womack's *Love Wars*.

Lee smiled, "I am. How are you doing?"

April shook her glossy black bob to the baseline, "What a place! Thanks for inviting us."

Philip appeared, having finally parked his suit jacket with Miranda. His sleeves were rolled up, but he still wore his tie – albeit under an opened top button. "Oh, I like this one!". Before Lee knew it, her hand had been taken and the rest of her tugged with it onto the dancefloor. She'd not danced with Philip so far that night, but had noted that he moved well for a man of his height and alcohol content. Lip-reading him, she guessed that he knew about a quarter of the lyrics. The rest he seemed to be making up from random syllables as he swayed blissfully with eyes closed. Lee looked up to the rostrum and saw Rikki, headphones curved underneath his chin, so as not to disturb the wig and tiara. She caught his eye and the exotic DJ grinned, waving his plaster torch mic at her.

The Womacks fell into Jennifer Rush's *Power of Love*, marking what everyone understood to mean back-to-back ballads. The dancefloor shuffled some personnel while a few couples simply stayed where they were. Philip anchored them both and pulled Lee closer to him. She was caught out by the gesture – but hugely charmed, "You having a good time?"

"I'm having a *great* time" Philip declared, his hands slipping around Lee's waist. "Though it's not the kind of time I *imagined* I'd be having tonight when I left the office."

Lee leant back so that she could see her new friend's face "What *would* you have done tonight?"

"Take away curry, some Channel 4 and then bed, I suppose – you know, fairly rock n' roll."

"This is more fun, isn't it?"

"This is most excellent fun" Philip agreed heartily, slurring the word 'excellent'. "And what would you be doing?"

"Working behind a bar"

"Oh yes, of course."

"I wouldn't be here though, I'd be at the other club."

"Well I'm glad you're at this one."

"So am I" Lee agreed – though quietly, so she couldn't be heard.

Philip gently lifted Lee's chin so that they were eye to eye. He paused their slow shuffling, "You know something?"

"What?" Lee oozed, dreamily.

"You really are, almost certainly, one of the tallest women I've ever danced with."

Lee laughed, turning her head away. As she returned to face her partner, he added, "– Which does rather make you the most perfect fit." And then he kissed her, surprisingly tenderly and for some time.

All of the easy money had been on Sinatra's *New York, New York* for the last record of Rikki's *Crush* career. Instead, after a surprisingly brief speech, ("London, you're a dream! Over, and absolutely…out!"), he went Disco, spinning Tavares' *Don't Take Away The Music* before unplugging his torch, briefly resuming his statue pose as a final salute – and then falling stone-straight from the rostrum into the crowd. Wig askew, he cavorted with a number of his adoring worshippers before making his way into the heart of the Moray Crescent Caucus. There, he continued to groove and thrust inelegantly in a way his gown's designer could never have anticipated. Lee, Dani, James, Philip, April, Davey and even a late-arriving Luka made a circle around their hero as he spun and posed through the final ninety seconds of his tenure. When the last chorus had faded and the barely-noticed Mohawk had returned to play out the sated crowd with muted wallpaper music and half-raised house lights, Rikki fell into James' arms, coating him with dried flakes of white body paint. "Is it over? Have I given my public everything their buttery little hearts desired?"

"You have mate, yes"

"Then for Chrissake, somebody get a hardworking icon a triple Martini!"

Dani, James and Philip all left just after the main crowd. Lee walked them to the door and traded exhausted hugs and kisses with all three of them. She tried not to dwell in her farewell with Philip. A little sobriety was already creeping into her consciousness and she knew better than to meet his eyes so closely again. She didn't want to risk catching a glimpse of early regret in his expression. In the event, he actually did seem to linger in the embrace, his hand taking a little longer to leave her waist than it might.

Lee watched her friends round the corner back toward Golden Square. She smiled at the contribution they'd made to a wonderful night. Returning to the main room, she saw that Rikki was still hyped and holding court at the bar. The last stragglers of the well-wishing party were saying their piece and pledging future correspondence. By now, Dani had recovered their coats. Taking hers, Lee was surprised by how heavy it felt to lift. She really was tired.

"You okay?" Dani asked.

"I am" Lee admitted, finding herself suddenly short of conversation. There was something about a hushed club at the end of a busy night. It felt as though everyone's collective energies and emotions had faded with the music – regardless of Tavares' late pleadings. "How are *you* doing?"

"Oh, I just wish I could be beamed back into bed now" Dani yawned. "We're going to get a taxi rather than the night bus."

"Good decision" Lee agreed. "You go on though, I'm going to see Old Lady Liberty gets back safely."

"Well, I saw you, y'know" Rikki remarked dreamily as the *Hard Rock Café* flashed by the window on his side of their cab.

"Mmm?"

"Kissing that pinstriped city boy – I saw you"

Lee smiled in the dark beside the now clean-faced DJ.

"His name is Philip."

"Philip" Rikki mulled, lingering on the final 'p'. "Mmm. I see."

"Philip Easterhouse. He's in I.T."

"I.T. you say? And is that anywhere near *S.H.*I.T?"

"Shuddup!" Lee whined. "He's really nice – and normal."

Rikki threw an arm around Lee and pulled her to him. "I'm sure he is – and you kids sure looked groovy out there on my dancefloor together. You going to see him again?"

Lee let her head fall against Rikki's shoulder and they both said in unison, "Of course not."

Rikki let his smile fall first. "You know sooner or later, you will get a shot at being happy and *normal* – if that's what you want."

"Will I?"

"Seriously kidder – the day will come."

"Mmm. And soon you're going to be so far away."

Lee stared across at Ricki in profile as they emerged from under Hyde Park Corner into Knightsbridge. The store windows flashed behind her flatmate, outlining his pensive expression. "I'm pretty scared you know" he admitted. "I have no fuckin' idea what's ahead over there."

Lee kissed her friend gently on his freshly moisturised cheek. "You don't need to know what's there. As it comes, you'll take it. You're irresistible."

"Yeah, well I'm not so sure about that."

"Then I'll be sure for you" Lee hushed, taking hold of Rikki's hand. "After all, you've always believed in me."

Rikki kissed the top of Lee's head. "That I have."

"You do know that you're the just about the closest thing I have to family now – and I love you. Every mile away you go from me will hurt. Every day I don't see you will hurt. But at least I know you're there, safe and well and doing what you do. And I'll try to be there with you, every night you need me." Lee stalled the sorrow. Instead she sat up and took in a breath of smoke-stained cab air. "I'm so tired of sad goodbyes" she said. "Let's make sure this isn't really one of those."

Rikki smiled some ripples back into his features. "Tell you what, kidder. If you can handle whatever's at the other side of your big leap, I'll do the same – and we'll be there for each other."

Lee returned to Rikki's shoulder and watched the fairy lights of *Harrods* twinkle against the cold, hard darkness until they drifted away behind, like so many a Saturday night promise.

march 1986
a private rubicon

··

How do any of us know how we'll really feel when a dream arrives? I've run toward this with my head down for four years and now I feel as though I haven't really noticed just how big it was getting in front of me. I don't have any more days to wait. I don't have anything more to do.

Is this how it feels when a journey finally passes a point of no return and becomes destiny? I'm just a passenger riding on a fate of my own design now.

····················

Lee had wondered whether the luxury of a cab would have been more appropriate for such an occasion, but in a way, she was relishing a heightened sense of being part of the outside world for what would be the last time in a while. She had Dad's watch clasped in her hand so that she could mark the passing precious minutes. Soon she would be closeted away from noise and speed and snatches of overheard conversation. She wondered again what the hospital would be like. All she knew is that she'd have a private room. But there was no point in wondering about what was so soon to be revealed.

She shouldn't even have considered spending a cab fare to London Bridge. She need to save her precious pennies for the ride home when she'd certainly be more in need.

As expected, a small bank loan had been needed to bridge the gap between her savings and the £ 6,250 demanded in advance for the SRS procedure. Hayley at Mr Hendry's office had explained that much of the fee came from the cost of ten nights in the hospital, plus the anaesthetist and then the theatre itself. The surgery would take around six hours and would begin early the following morning. Lee's first afternoon at the hospital would be spent undergoing final precautionary tests in order to confirm her qualification for what was, she was left in no doubt, a major operation.

She closed her copy of *Today* and set it on her lap leaving just the legs and elegantly shod feet of the Princess Diana picture of the day. Lee studied the royal feet in isolation. They were a size 9, according to some reports. What with sharing the shoe size and height of the world's most photographed woman, Lee considered whether she might relax her republican viewpoint. She was fascinated by seriously tall women – particularly the way they managed their rarity and the space around them. She wondered if she'd feel better about being tall if she didn't owe her height to the legacy of a male skeleton.

She surprised herself with a small yawn. She eased back into the bench seat and looked around the carriage at her fellow Central Line passengers. She wondered what events and occasions they were all heading toward. She looked down at her little suitcase. It didn't contain much. She'd brought a nightdress (which she suspected she wouldn't need), underwear, toiletries, a make-up bag and a long loose black skirt to wear on the journey home, (she guessed it may be some time before she'd be ready for jeans again). She also had some items presented to her by Mr Hendry on their second meeting: Suppositories for use post-surgery, along with a strange blue plastic contraption that she would supposedly get to know intimately in months to come. It comprised a long, perforated tube with an attached chamber. The idea apparently was that the chamber should be filled with at first a special solution, but later just soapy water and the long tube should be inserted into the vagina. When the chamber was squeezed, jets of water would flush out the vaginal cavity – simple, but still weird for Lee to imagine. The procedure stood in for the more elegant, self-cleansing system nature had withheld from her. She was learning fast that dignity wasn't high on the list of the people who invented medical and hygiene treatments. Davey's words to the fore again, 'it's hard because it's not supposed to be possible'.

She made the change at Embankment for a southbound train, drawing deeply on the musty platform air. Every step she took in her comfortable flat-heeled courts felt charged with mission and meaning. She was alive with sensations. The alternately warm and cool airstreams circulating through the tunnel system lifted her hair from her face as she walked an easy but measured pace. It had been two weeks since she'd turned 26 and in all of those years, she'd never quite felt quite so certain of her path. She'd made it all happen. From Dr Jones, through Dr Garner, hours upon hours of electrolysis and hormone-induced sickness, working, saving and somehow keeping a coherent, functioning life on track. She'd already lost touch with so many memories. She could no longer return reliably to the fullest sense of fear, self-doubt and soul-sapping sadness that had cloaked those first months. The journey was ending; deliverance coming in the form of a grimy, clanking Northern Line train. Lee Habens, unremarkable in so many ways, had fired her own instinct with will enough to force her dream to be.

The last ten days or so had restored a level of clarity and balance. Her chemical state had calmed after what had at times, felt like a catastrophic reaction to the cessation of her hormone-taking. One of the effects of ingesting oestrogen Mr Hendry had explained, was a thinning of the blood – most undesirable in the face of serious surgery. She had been required to end the taking of her precious pills, six weeks prior to this day. She'd had no idea just how difficult an experience it would turn out to be. Her emotional frame had almost immediately disintegrated. She'd felt as if she had no governance at all over her feelings and at times was almost completely bereft of perspective. Within the first three days she had broken down hysterically over a broken egg cup at home and a difficult drink order at work. She was often nauseous and almost always unable to bear the sight of herself in the mirror. She knew she must have been hell to live and work with over the period. At home, she'd tried to stay away from company as much as possible and following advice from Dr Garner, she'd also taken care to explain to those around her that there was a strong likelihood of what she'd termed 'basket case episodes'. It took around four weeks in all, for her hormone cocktail to stabilise. These last few days, she'd begun to benefit from the return of some physical energy. She had been terrified that some of her facial and body hair could make a reappearance, but she'd been mostly lucky in this regard – although she was definitely spottier than usual. She would be able to make the re-acquaintance of her pharmaceutical lifeline a couple of weeks or so after leaving hospital. At least by then, she would have no need to combat male hormones with anti-androgen drugs – her body would have been finally stripped of the equipment to generate such horrors.

Arriving at her platform, she was careful not to stand close to the edge. She couldn't bear the thought of an anti-climactic accident now – not before she could at least draw a single breath of life without being attached to a penis. She stared at a poster advertising holiday breaks in the Caribbean. A happy couple were pictured walking hand in hand along a white sand beach. She looked closely at the two figures, trying to feel a sense of empathy with either of them. It didn't come. She didn't see the scene through the eyes of the male figure – and never would. She wanted to see it through the woman's eyes, but it wasn't happening either. Perhaps she would yet feel differently.

London Bridge station confused her. There was some construction work underway and a number of the foot routes had been diverted, making the original (and still visible) signs, redundant. Back above ground, she had to ask directions from a woman at a flower stall. The florist knew precisely where the new private hospital was. The new facility was after all, no doubt responsible for a fair boost to the stall's income. The entrance was tucked away around a corner, almost entirely out of sight from the station. Lee crossed the busy road and reached the paved access drive leading to the shelter of the hospital's entrance porch. She put down her suitcase and stood for a moment before recovering Dad's watch from her handbag. She was nearly fifteen minutes earlier than she needed to be. She wished she still smoked. A cigarette right now would be perfect. She looked up at the building in front of her. It looked no more significant that any of the other wharf side conversions along the Thames. It would in the past she imagined, have been a functional warehouse of some sort, but a coat of new brick had transformed it into something far more suitable for the 1980's. New life had been granted to a building within which others were reborn on a weekly basis.

The sky was jammed with white cloud, short on detail or beauty to savour. The roof over Lee's special day felt decidedly un-special. She looked back at the glass entrance door and crossed the final few feet of an outside world she would never walk again with her body intact.

It feels good to be writing. At least this is something I am used to. Writing is me making something happen, rather than just having something happen. I wonder how much of this I'm going to be able to do.

I have an Irish nurse who came out to meet me. She seems really kind and caring although I'm sure I'm really just another case to her. She must have seen the likes of me many times. Suddenly I wouldn't mind speaking to a few of her former patients – just to reassure myself by seeing how well they've no doubt done.

Nurse Irish gave me an idea of what is ahead today. I have to have various tests and then there is going to be some kind of bowel-cleaning session. Oh crap! – (literally!). This day is going to be a bit of a trial. I've already been given a strong laxative. Me and the loo will get to know each other pretty well, I think. I'm going to be drained of all sorts of things today apparently. I wonder what will be left for them to find when they come for me early tomorrow morning.

. . . .

The paperwork was unbelievable. Somehow, she'd imagined this sort of thing to be processed by an invisible army of clerical staff, based somewhere she didn't need to know about. The first forms had been presented to her as she sat with her suitcase in the plush hotel-like reception area. Once checked in she'd had blood taken and a test for pressure; she'd undergone a full chest x-ray and an ECG. She'd been given a small route map of the hospital which guided her around the building as she accrued a now substantial file of documents.

Finally, she was back in her room – No. 415. It really did resemble a luxury guest suite, complete with ensuite bathroom. When Mr Hendry had referred to the hospital as new, he hadn't been kidding. London Bridge had been opened just a matter of weeks previously. It felt good to be lucky for a change, Lee reflected. This was about as comfortable an environment as she could possibly have hoped for. The walls were painted in a soft pastel pink and were hung with occasional faux-impressionist prints. The bed was definitely of the medical persuasion, with controls for adjusting it to raised, lowered or tilted positions. The most immediately compelling feature of her home for the next ten days, was a huge multi paned window, perhaps six feet across at its base and arched to almost the same in height. Hayley had described the rooms to Lee beforehand and had advised that those on the inner corridor overlooked the centre atrium. Pleasant enough, what with the exotic potted trees and plants – but all efforts would be made to secure one of the outer rooms which offered the spectacular vista she now enjoyed. The River Thames stretched below, allowed a stunning view of the north bank and City district beyond. A large sill invited the viewer to sit. She was surprised at just how much river traffic there was – from larger passenger vessels and trailing barges to small private boats bobbing along on voyages of lesser purpose. What would an actual hotel room charge for a week or more of this view? Perhaps not six grand, she supposed. She could occasionally glimpse people moving between the buildings on the other side of the Thames and she felt a small stomach-punch of envy for their freedom. For some reason, Philip popped into Lee's thoughts. He must be over there, she imagined – somewhere in one of those glass and concrete towers. She hadn't seen him since the night of Rikki's farewell gig. She had spoken about him though. Davey had called on the Sunday afternoon. It hadn't been easy for him to do it she knew, but he'd asked her not to let things go any further between her and Philip. "I don't know how to better explain it" he'd said, "but I know you will understand that as you build a new life for yourself, the last thing you ever want is for something to drag you back to the old one. I just can't afford for my past to get out – it would undermine everything I've achieved. If Philip learns that you're transsexual and then comes to talk to me about it – and he would – it's going to place me in a difficult position. I would never deny what I am, but that doesn't mean I ever want to really discuss it with civilians."

And Lee did understand – already.

At times I really do wonder how on earth I came to make it this far. So much of what we do in life seems pre-ordained. We go to school, we defer to our parents, make our friends, fall in love and do the traditional things. We work and save and try to set in motion again, that same process through our children. Others define their lives through the loves they have and the circles of like-minds they find.

This now, is my definitive moment – my own private Rubicon. Dr Garner had referred to such a moment right at the beginning of this process and now I'm finally here. I feel as though this is what I've been directed toward, all my life – even before I properly understood it. I know that nobody else ever needed me to do this. They'd all be fine if I had never sought any kind of treatment in the first place – and why shouldn't they be?

So in the end, nobody can really hold my hand today.

Room 415 feels like a long way from anywhere – and yet where else can I be today?

. . . .

Lee crossed the room to the cupboard which held her bag. She dug out the cards she'd been given as tokens of support. One bore a romantic image of Edwardian women walking along a seashore under a lace parasol (from Dani), another handmade with pressed flower petals and lipstick kisses inside (Becky and Elaine) and then one of the Statue of Liberty with a long penis drawn on it. The card read 'At least some of us would never leave home without it!' (Rikki).

Rikki had called a couple of times this last month. He'd sent postcards too – often with just a random note on it ('I was walking down Broadway today and I thought of how far we'd both come'). Mrs Macintyre had said that the Manhattan club was going well. It was awfully early, but they were beginning to attract some celebrities and magazine attention. It looked as if it was all going to work out in the Big Apple. Rikki had kept his room for a while just in case, but eventually paying rent both sides of the Atlantic became too much and he had let it go. Lee and Dani had packed what was left of his things and taken them into *Crush*, from where they would be shipped. London was over for Rikki. While Lee was away, a new flatmate would be arriving – a Brazilian friend of Luka's called Gabriel. At least it would be company for him. Maybe he wouldn't be so grumpy in future – at least until the inevitable falling out.

Lee's thoughts were interrupted by a knock at the door. She thought about calling out 'Come in', but didn't have time to tighten and configure her vocal chords for the volume she'd need. The door opened anyway.

"Uh, Lee Habens?"

"Yes?"

An Asian man appearing to be no more than thirty years of age entered the room. He was slim – slight even, and had a nervous gait. He carried a clipboard and held out his free hand in greeting, "I'm Dr Choudrey."

Lee was meeting lots of doctors today – both white-coated and otherwise. This one was of the latter persuasion. She shook hands, noting that his effort was almost as poor as her own.

"I'm here to ask you some questions" he offered, with an upward lilt at the end of his sentence.

"Was that the first one?" Lee teased.

Dr Choudhury looked uncertain, but then smiled broadly. "Oh no, I'm just – I'm a psychiatrist and my role is to provide a second view of your candidature for surgery".

"I see." Lee replied taking a seat on the bed. "I've been expecting you" she tried in a Bond – villainous attempt at humour. Nothing.

"So" the doctor continued, "You regard yourself as transsexual?"

Lee was a little taken aback, "Well, yes – and somewhere in your notes should be evidence of others in agreement."

"Yes" the young doctor replied, making a notation of his own. "And you have felt this way for a long time?"

"I…" Lee really didn't know quite what to say or how to say it. "Um, look I'm hours away from major surgery after four years of treatment and you're asking me here to go back to the beginning?"

"No, no. These are just questions. Protocol – you know?"

Lee strained for some scraps of patience and rounded up enough to answer a further dozen or so inane questions with statements of the bleeding obvious. She signed two documents and bade farewell to Dr Choudrey who seemed satisfied, if increasingly nervous in Lee's company.

"A second opinion without a first clue" she muttered to the door through which the doctor had left. Then she grinned at her own shrink joke and lay back down on the bed.

Every so often she would flip on the TV in the hope that there might actually be something to watch – but the bright little box suspended from a corner wall mount, was never able to hold her attention for long. Her mind was unable to idle; to slip the bonds of anticipation. She realised that she was both willing the time to pass quicker and worried that she may not be celebrating these moments enough. She was a small child on Christmas Eve again. Tomorrow held all the promise – and oddly, she knew a part of her would miss the feeling, once it had gone.

There were more interruptions, too. She had been asked to change into a hospital gown and was fitted with a plastic bracelet that bore both her name and that of her surgeon, branding her officially as part of the hospital process. She was required to provide blood pressure readings at frequent intervals – and then of course there was the colonic 'clear out'. 'Funny the things you don't anticipate' she would later tell others, 'even though later you realise that of course they were going to happen'.

Two nurses arrived at about four 'o clock. They were armed with a collection of curiosities, including a long section of plastic corrugated hose. She did wonder for a moment if it was a scare tactic employed by the evil genius of Dr Choudrey, but it became apparent that there was a much less amusing prospect in order.

One of the nurses at least explained why the process was necessary. "There must be no bowel movement until some days after your surgery and in order to completely remove any such risk, the digestive system must be completely cleared." What followed was a clinically efficient insertion of tubes to Lee's rectum.

She couldn't actually see what was involved in the process and tried not to dwell too much on what was happening behind her, but just before the first 'flush', she voiced an honest thought; "Whatever they're paying you to do this, it isn't enough – and what's really galling is that they're short-changing you with my money." Lee felt slightly relaxed by the sound of laughter. And then the first of what would over the course of the session be sixty litres of water, entered her bowel. She was calmly instructed to clench and to hold the water in, before giving way to an almost diarrhoea-like sensation to let go. The sound of what flowed back out of her, caused an appalled Lee to close her eyes. She tried for much of the next half hour to wish herself away to anywhere else.

It's a kind of purgatory, being here just now. I've stopped being a real person. The staff address me in female terms, but what do they really see? I wear no make-up. My hair is tied back mercilessly, revealing me in all my 'un-glory'. I've paid my fee and set the process in motion. I've signed away the last of who I was supposed to be and I'm suspended now, somewhere between that place and where I've always needed to go. Now it's all about the skills and experience of the people around me. I just sit up, lie down, bend over and open any orifice I'm asked to. I guess that if I've been guilty of treating this body like nothing more than a shell, then it really shouldn't bother me that others are doing the same to it now.

There are apparently two other TS 'guests' here at the 'Exile Hotel'. Both are close to being discharged. Change places, anyone? One of the new 'post-ops' is Brazilian and one is Canadian. I am the

plucky Brit, doing my best to muddle through something I imagine
them to handle so much more serenely.

. . . .

Much of the afternoon was spent dozing. It wasn't proper sleep,
just a kind of stillness of being. She would lose half and quarter
hours in blinks, only occasionally rising from her bed to walk to
the window. She would stare out in each direction for a while, her
arms folded, tracing her ribs with her fingertips through the thin
cotton gown.

She heard the muffled sound of a PA system through the
thick glass of her window. Out on the river, a pleasure cruiser's
passengers were being informed about London's riverfront. She
imagined that the male announcer would not be including in his
commentary, any detail of the extraordinary happenings up there
on the fourth floor of London Bridge Hospital. She collected
a blanket, her journal and a pen and took a seat in the window,
gingerly leaning back against the cool of the wall, her body heat
slowly warming the painted white brick to a bearable temperature.
She looked down at a Thames Barge and made out the name *Lady
Daphne* on its flank, its red brown sails vibrant against leaden
waters. The heavy sky promised more rain.

When this is done, what will I feel? What will I know? How much of
myself should I really invest in this surgery? Does this single encounter
with sharp blades really define my gender? For society, it would seem
that it does. If you have one set of genitalia, then your life will take a
certain course; if you have the other set, your options are very different.

I haven't learned to live in this body yet. I've gambled in believing
that being liberated from parts of it will make what remains, bearable.

I keep wondering about those first moments when I wake. Will it be
revelation – like it was for George / Julia in the TV documentary? Or
will it just be relief, the way Caroline Cossey recalled it in her book? I
wonder if I'll still battle with the inadequacies that will remain. I'd like
to believe that I'll feel like more than just a fake female. I'd like to believe

that what will happen to me over the coming hours will unlock an inner confidence and perhaps give me a clearer understanding of my place.

I'm so tired of raging against myself. That kind of anger is an emotion born blind – a critique of what's wrong with me, rather than an honest understanding of what is or may one day, be right. That kind of energy did help to get me this far, but it has served its purpose now.

I remember reading somewhere that those who pass through this extraordinary portal, do find peace. That's what I want most of all. How wonderful it would be to stop searching for a beginning and to just simply begin.

. . . .

Very few days in Lee Haben's life had begun at 5:00 am – although plenty had ended at that hour. Lee sat at the end of her bed. She had showered and put on the long white itchy stockings given her by a softly spoken nightshift nurse. It seemed just now she felt, as though the quieter, smaller and more gentle a gesture, the more gravity it actually bore. From last evening's visit of Mr Hendry with his reassuring manner and easy smile, through the frosty whisper of an air-conditioned night, nothing had moved quickly or loudly. But the morning – if not the light – had duly arrived as scheduled. Around her, a calm sense of efficiency and order seemed to have persuaded her pulse to synchronise. She sat silently in a semi-meditative state, flushed inside and shaved below. There was simply nothing left to do but breathe.

Room 415 had a number of lighting options, each of which had separate dimmer controls. A low-light setting added to the other-worldliness of it all. Lee was momentarily reminded of her family home on the morning of their holiday to Spain. They had left for the airport at an ungodly hour of the morning. It had been as if they were the only ones awake in the world. Just a family of souls bound together in a pocket of light against the darkness. She had loved that feeling.

Nurse Nightshift wafted back into the room bearing a small tray upon which a plastic cup and a thimble-like vessel were borne. Little and large in matching white polypropylene. "This" she announced calmly, "is your pre-med. You're going to swallow this and then you're going to lie down on top of your bed."

Lee smiled and took in another breath of chilled air. She took the little cup and tipped the pill into her throat, following it quickly with a sip of water. She duly adopted the prescribed position and watched slightly amused as Nurse Nightshift raised the side bar of the bed. "I promise I won't make a run for it" she grinned.

Nurse Nightshift smiled back in the dim light, "You wouldn't get far" she replied. Lee couldn't be sure if there hadn't been just a hint of menace in the line. She stared up to the ceiling and sensed the gentlest first movement from within. She closed her eyes and felt a lightness of thought within her heavy head. Alone in the semi-light, she was warm and relaxed.

By the time Nurse Nightshift re-appeared however, Lee was also feeling something rather less welcome. "Oh dear, I'm terribly sorry" she began, "but I'm afraid I have to pee."

"What? Really?" Nurse Nightshift replied, for the first time revealing a tone other than soothing. "You're really not supposed to get out of bed now – not after a pre-med."

Lee smiled sheepishly, raising a woozy head, "I'm pretty sure I can make it."

"Oh, God. Okay – well look, let's be quick about it." She dropped the bed's side bars and Lee swung out her legs.

"Easy. You may not be very steady on your pins."

Lee felt her feet meet floor and she began to stand. Almost immediately, she had to return to a seated position. She'd not had enough momentum to stand and her muscles had been too slow to inject the energy needed to complete the move. "Wow" she sniggered, drunkenly amused at her own lack of control.

A second effort was more successful and she concentrated hard on the few steps to the bathroom.

"I'll wait just outside the door – don't lock it" Nurse Night instructed.

"Okay. I'll be just a mo'"

Lee found her way over to the toilet. The light in the small room had already been switched on, thankfully – she'd never have found the pull cord herself. Suddenly a thought dawned on Lee. This would be the last time she would pee through a penis. She grinned to herself in amusement as she raised her gown to reveal the sad looking organ nestling in her paper underwear. She let the thing fall loose, rolling back the foreskin a little so as to allow a clear stream. She'd done this with loathing so many times in her life. Now she did so as victor, allowing with grace a final relief to the vanquished. Shorn of pubic hair, the penis looked even more pathetic than usual. "That's right, you sorry prick. Just one last time and then we never see each other again." It took a moment before the urine came. Lee watched fascinated at the tinkling stream. She propped the penis from underneath on a single finger of her right hand. She could feel the urethral vibration of passing liquid. She'd always hated that sensation too, but it didn't matter now. "Bye-bye" she whispered as she adjusted her ludicrous knickers. She began to wash her hands, only for Nurse Nightshift to appear behind her.

"Really, you shouldn't worry. We just need to get you back onto the bed."

Lee knew of old that her fingers must be properly clean of any trace of the thing before she could relax. She completed soaping and scrubbing, while leaning on the sink. She was urged to begin walking before she had properly dried her hands. She was feeling extremely tired by now and the softness of the pillow beneath the back of her head came as a truly delicious sensation.

She closed her eyes against the room, opening them briefly to acknowledge the orderlies who had now come for her. There was a short flurry of clicking and clanking before she felt herself lighten and float magically to her left. She realised that she had been transferred to a trolley for the journey beyond. She was sorry to be leaving her bed behind. She caught a glimpse of her feet as they headed toward the door, guided by a man whose face she couldn't make out. They were smoothly out into the corridor in a moment. All of the lighting in the building seemed to be at the same level of reduced intensity. Lee stared up amused at some of the spots and strips as they sailed overhead in the shadowy ceiling sky. Lift doors closed softly somewhere behind her head and she felt herself fall through a world without floors. She danced inside and giggled sadly, along with the receding voices of children she knew, could now never be given life by her wretched body.

She had loved the pool and she was so glad to be there again, just drifting on her back, her head buoyed by sparkling water. She felt she could stare at the sky for hours as it turned blue to deepest red and back to blue again. She was weightless and free and she was safe. She could feel both of them watching her, the way they always did when she swam in the pool. Mum and Dad would always watch for danger so that she didn't have to. The water rocked her gently. A pattern began to repeat – lapping and hissing with just the occasional beep. The gentle sounds receded after a time and the sky became darker until only bronze stars remained. She blinked, hoping that when she opened her eyes again, the blue might return. But there were just the stars now. They were still and few – just four of them arranged in a perfect constellation. She was sad that they were plain and devoid of life – she usually enjoyed stars. The beeps were louder now and to her right. She turned her head a little in that direction and could see a pair of red coloured jewels in the semi-dark. A louder hiss broke the plane and she wondered if she should be fearful. She drew her senses in, pulling tighter on the lines connecting her to the world. A sound bed of steady whispering seeped through. Air-conditioning.

Lee tried to take a deeper breath to assist her rousing. The shock of pain from her abdomen instead robbed her of access to any air she held. Gradually, she relaxed. Something was helping her to relax. Now she felt as though she did not exist at all below her chest. She opened her eyes a little more. She recognised her ceiling. It felt as though it were night time. The curtains to her left were closed, just a high slice of city neon from beyond, lighting the top of the dark fabric wall.

More light – just briefly. And then a voice, "Hiya Lee. You're doing great. It's all over now, so all you have to do is rest", whispered Nurse Irish. "The morphine will make everything pretty woozy for a while. The monitor will slowly decrease the dosage automatically and then we'll get you onto the painkillers. You're doing just great."

Lee saw light and dark again before everything fell away once more.

Still not entirely sure of what I feel. Perhaps that's because no single mood seems to last for very long before I drift out of it. I don't have the strength to really explore my own thoughts and feelings. I'm as worn out inside, as I am out!

Don't know for how long I can hold book and pen. Doing this means using my top tummy muscles. Doing pretty much anything seems to mean using that part of me. I don't remember the middle section of me being so damned important before! This is really painful and would be completely impossible if I weren't held in tightly by the harness I woke up in. It is brown and made of a thick, stiff fabric that feels like leather. It starts around my waist and is tightly bound to me all the way down to my crotch. Underneath it is a layer of cotton wool, presumably to help make it more comfortable – that's like giving me an ice cube to hold while incinerating me with a flame thrower.

So much pain and aching. It's hard to describe. The painkillers that they give me just bring nausea and so once again I find that this experience is full of unpleasantness. I can't honestly say that I feel different as such. I'm just feeling really physically awful. I know something has happened down there, but I have no way of properly grasping it. I can't see anything and definitely can't feel anything. This would drive me even more crazy if I could stay awake long enough. I sleep every couple of hours – although only for another couple of hours. It's hard to keep a grasp of time at all really.

Mr Hendry was here a while ago. He said everything went very well and that my recovery should be very straightforward, providing I follow instructions and the schedule they have prescribed. He referred to my vagina – as did a couple of nurses when they were explaining things. It just seems crazy. Is there really one of those down there? Do they really mean me? Inside me apparently, is a 'pack', made of wadding. It's all that is keeping my stitches in place and my opening...open. They're going to remove it in a couple of days. They didn't mention how much it'll hurt, but it must do, mustn't it? I'm sure it will. Everything else hurts – why should that be any different?

. . . .

She was for the most part relieved and yet just a tiny bit disappointed that her ban on hospital visitors was being observed and respected. She had anticipated the bittersweet agony of seeing people come and go. Her heart would want desperately to follow them out the door and she knew the disappointment would only muddle her focus on recovery. Besides, she hadn't the energy to battle with her no-doubt awful appearance. What was required of her now was a sense of discipline and commitment. She must she believed, break down every day into small challenges – each of which must be overcome. She needed nothing less than a 100% success rate. No failures. She must be resolute – and absolute.

The first step required an increase in her intake of fluids. Her kidneys needed to function in balance, allowing her eventually to urinate through the urethra she knew to have been repositioned.

She would also need to learn about the different parts of a vagina that was still no more real to her than hearsay. She knew that the trauma to nerve endings meant that she would lack sensitivity for a while – indeed she may feel next to nothing in that area externally, but she would still need to find a way to come to terms with a new internal canal. The process of dilation lay ahead and Lee although determined, was dreading it.

So now I've seen it! And it looks...just like any other vagina – apart from being a bit red and swollen. There are some bruises too so I'm not terribly pretty down there, but it is really _real!_ I am definitely changed and I'm only just beginning to grasp that.

The harness was removed and then the inner pack. It hurt several times more than any other pain I've ever felt (with the possible exception of an extended electrolysis session).

Afterwards a nurse held a mirror for me so that I could see what I look like down there. (I mean _seriously_; they DO NOT pay these people enough!). Mr Hendry was back and he seemed quietly satisfied. I found myself wondering how many of these he'd seen – and how mine compared to others (already it begins!).

I took a bath – something I've dreamed of for five days. I still have to be attached to a cursed catheter tube. At the other end of it is a bag of pee that frankly so appals me, I have to keep it covered by a towel. The bath has bars along the side. Whenever I've seen those in the past, I've always been safe in the knowledge that they are not meant for the likes of able-bodied me. <u>Well they are now</u>! I need support to do anything – including stand. My chicken legs look completely wasted. I wonder how much I weigh.

. . . .

Bathing had been exhausting. Lee had originally planned to wash her hair, but she had neither the energy nor the upper body mobility. Instead, she managed to arrange her hair into a single loose plait and decided to forget about it for another day or so. She lay on the bed, feeling for something that might suggest a real recovery. She was spent from the shoulders down. The half dozen steps back from the bathroom had drained her of the brief rejuvenation leant by the warm waters. She let her head fall to her left, spying the room's rose coloured armchair. She yearned to sit in it like a normal person, but she was still some way from such a pose and knew that the boredom of lying on her back would have to continue for a time yet.

A few degrees further to Lee's left was the white water jug and a still half-full glass next to it. Her single most important responsibility right now was to drink water. Unfortunately, every sip tasted poisonous to her. There was a metallic awfulness to the taste. She imagined this to be a side-effect of her medication – and whatever else was going on inside of her. Still, it made even the thought of lifting the glass to her lips, hard to bear.

Lee's cloudy mood was shattered by the shrill interruption of the telephone just to the left of her shoulder. She grimaced as she drew her right arm across her left and twisted her torso to reach the receiver.

"Hello?"

"Lee? Is that you?" The uncertainty clearly belonged to Dani.

"No, this is Hell Reception Desk. Lee is presently off plumbing some new depths and won't be taking social calls for some years."

"Awwww" Dani soothed, "I'm so sorry. Is it really terrible?"

"Well yes – but hey, if it was easy, everyone would be doing it, wouldn't they?"

Dani laughed supportively, "But you must feel so proud."

"Not really. I just feel sort of on fire from the waist down."

"Come on, now."

Lee smiled. She had her eyes closed, imagining Dani the way she always spoke on the phone – one hand gripping the receiver and the other nursing a cigarette. The sound of exhaling through pursed lips confirmed her imaginings. "It's really hard to think about pride right now. Maybe in a couple of weeks when I'm able to be part of the outside world again."

"That'll come."

"I know" Lee replied, tiring already.

"Lee"

"Mmm?"

"*Please* can I…"

"No." Lee was determined not to be remembered this way – by anyone.

Mr Hendry visited late that afternoon. He was his usual calm and composed self, but it was apparent that he had a challenging schedule. Lee had brought with her, the prescribed set of dilators acquired from Mr Hendry's own office on her second consultation. Of course, the first night she'd taken them home, respectful pragmatism had quickly given way to raucous giggling between herself and Dani. There were a pair of them – shafts of solid and rather heavy white plastic around six inches in length. One had a diameter of around an inch, the other perhaps an inch and a half.

"You have to put these in how often?" Dani had asked, wide-eyed.

"Three sessions a day – about half an hour, each session" Lee had grimaced.

Later that night, long after the squeals and sniggers had passed and Lee had been left alone in her room, she had looked again at the dilators and had wondered at the prospect of their insertion. She couldn't believe it would ever be possible.

That had been then. Now they lay next to her thigh on the bed, along with a tube of lubricant.

Mr Hendry was standing over her and the twin tools of impending torture, "I will help you this first time and then the nurses may also assist for another couple of sessions, but it is essential that you take control of this part of your recovery as early as possible."

Lee nodded earnestly.

Mr Hendry picked up the first, narrower dilator and asked Lee to raise and part her knees. He expertly squeezed a blob of gel lubricant onto the tip of the dilator and smoothed it down along about half of the shaft. He showed it to Lee, "This is the depth we will aim for this first time."

"Okay" Lee agreed, trying not to sound as terrified as she felt.

There was no real sense of insertion as such. Instead, the overwhelming sensation was of being split in two. Lee may have had an opening down there somewhere, but it was swollen shut and its puffed walls of tissue were offering no available space. It quickly became clear just why a dilator was so uncompromisingly hard. Her immovable insides eventually yielded to the irresistible force of solid plastic, pressured by Mr Hendry's forearm. Lee bit down on her own arm at the wrist in a vain bid to distract her raging neuro network.

Mr Hendry's voice remained calm and encouraging. "Good girl. There we go" he assured. "Now, give me your hand."

Lee obliged and the surgeon guided her fingers to the far flat end of the dilator. She could feel that it was clearly embedded in her.

"I want you to press very gently."

Lee obliged again. It was like being told to stab herself, she reflected. After a few minutes, there was another shockwave of pain as the dilator was removed. She breathed out in relief as she sensed the shaft clear her. She opened her eyes and saw Mr Hendry preparing the larger one. Every sane cell of her being begged her to stop him, but she drew hard on the same reservoir of determination she had found to survive electrolysis. This, she reminded herself, was her price to pay for failing to be what she should have been to begin with; nobody's fault and nothing personal – just reparation. This time, Lee at least was able to grab her nearby copy of Caroline Cossey's book to bite down on. As her teeth sank into the paperback spine, she reflected that the author would at least understand – and most probably forgive.

I have to manage somehow, don't I? I don't really know quite how, but I have to keep dilating three times every day. The excruciating unpleasantness doesn't really seem to fade as such, (though there was just one time this morning where I can swear it wasn't entirely as agonising). There have been so many of these points along the way – times when I was sure I'd be stopped in my tracks. Each time I found a way through and I have to do the same with this. After all, it's not like I can go 'back' now, is it!

I could cheat – I know that I could. Now that I'm 'flying solo', there's nobody here to check whether I'm really dilating properly. But who would I be cheating?

I'm telling myself that each time that I push on one of these things and hurt myself, I'm actually doing good. Suffering is progress. Every push, every gain in depth is making my future better. One day, this won't hurt anymore.

Feels like I've been promising myself that for a lifetime.

I took a 'walk' this morning. My hair is washed now – Nurse Nightshift helped me with that. Amazing that such a silly thing can make a difference to a person's dignity. I put on my dressing gown and took a pathetically slow stroll to the fourth floor nurses station. It is a distance of about forty feet – though it felt like forty miles. I have to trundle a wheelie thing along which acts as a support to my body and something to hang my pee bag on. They say that if my pee gets to the right shade of yellow, they might take the tube out tomorrow. Tonight I'm going to offer a prayer to whoever for that. At the moment the bag looks like it's holding a quite expensive cognac. That's not a good sign. I have to drink more water – which would be easier if it didn't still taste like licking tin.

I saw into the room next door. Another TS patient. She was just back from surgery and not yet conscious. I wouldn't trade places for all the shoes in the shop.

I'll try to walk further tomorrow.

. . . .

The catheter was duly removed on the penultimate morning of Lee's stay. She had asked Mr Hendry beforehand whether withdrawal of the tube from her sore urethra would hurt. He advised that it probably would and she agreed with him in that case, the moments following should be regarded as a dignity-free period. She duly screamed into her pillow at full force for the three or four seconds it took to extricate the skinny plastic tube. Briefly, she attained a record new high in pain levels. The last of her stitches were also removed in an experience which by comparison, might have allowed her to read a magazine without blinking. Within two hours, the first big test of her new-found normalcy arrived. She needed a pee.

The sense of desire for urination was just the same as it had always been. She was afraid to leave it too long for fear of building up a wall of urine that might then press against her soreness. If she was going to have a problem, she needed some breathing space before things became critical.

Lee left her bed cautiously, but all the while relishing her new tubeless freedom. She was struck as she entered the bathroom that her first female pee would be into the same toilet as her last male visit. She turned and lowered herself gingerly into a seated position, careful not to overstress her stomach muscles. She sighed and waited. The wait became rather longer than she had anticipated. One of the nurses had mentioned that if a patient is unable to pee, a new catheter tube would have to be inserted. The mere thought of it stressed her insides and she had to count herself back down to a more relaxed plane. She would have to reason her way through this. She knew that she needed a pee. It was in there somewhere, ready. She mentally tried to fix the source of her need and found it, low down in her abdomen. She visualised a bladder and then mentally traced further fabricated images of her internal plumbing. She pictured beyond her closed eyes, a tube bearing a flow. She recalled the sensation nine days before, the underneath of the penis tingling as it lay across her finger. "Down you come" she whispered encouragingly.

She felt a new warmth under her and then heard a drop – and another. A tinkling sound below her delivered a sense of wonder and astonishment. She opened her eyes. She was doing it! Admittedly, she was peeing backwards, barely and rather haphazardly, but she was at least, actually *doing* it. She smiled at the trace of warm wetness against her skin "That's…really bad" she admitted to herself in a low tone. "But in a really good way."

april 1986
all the things she said

· ·

*F*reedom is a sweet thing. I don't ever want to be confined anywhere for this long again. Sure, my 'prison' has been very comfortable and my cause of the utmost importance – but seriously,
I'm not made for captivity. I've never been so glad of the prospect of
breathing crappy London fumes in my life.

· · · · · · · · · · · · · · · · ·

She caught a brief glimpse of herself in a tinted window pane
as she left the quiet protection of London Bridge Hospital's foyer.
She was bent at the midriff, the way some elderly people are. Her
coat was fastened only from the waist buttons up as she couldn't
reach the lower ones. She wore her Wayfarers – partly to cope
with the brightness outside, but also because in a way, the wearing
of sunglasses helped to make her feel less visible.
David J. Bailey would be her driver for the four-mile ride home.
She knew this from reading the ID card pinned to the barrel chest
of the t-shirted man leant against a blue Datsun Bluebird on the
hospital forecourt. He was aged about fifty, had a crescent of reddish hair curved around the back of an otherwise bald pate and
from the look of the fingers on his right hand, was a prodigious
smoker. David J. Bailey seemed completely unworried by Lee's
shambolic appearance. She shuffled pitifully slowly toward the
car, bearing a nervous smile the whole time. If walking was test-
ing all of her motor skills, the sheer sensation of being outside in
moving air was blowing her mind. The receptionist handed Lee's
bag to the cab driver who placed it into the car's boot. He had

time to move around and open the rear door of the blue-coloured saloon. He would have had time frankly, to change a wheel in the age it took Lee to reach the same spot. She stared in at the rear bench seat and wondered how best to fold herself to fit through the doorway. She wouldn't be able to sit and spin on her bottom as she suspected this might cause her to scream and pass out. She couldn't put one foot inside and follow it with the rest of her, as she imagined this may result in splitting her, right up the middle. She settled for an ungainly head first approach, half-crawling along the seat on all fours before ever so slowly turning and reversing onto her bottom. At least her stomach muscles weren't overly taxed. "I'm so sorry" she said to David J Bailey as he took his own seat, "That must have looked pretty bizarre."

"Don't you worry, love. I'm used to picking you lot up – I know it ain't easy for you. That's why the hospital always calls my firm when one of you needs taking home."

By 'you lot', Lee guessed he meant 'post-op' transsexuals of which she now was most certainly one. "Right yes, of course" she replied vacantly.

The driver turned and peered over at her. He smiled in what he must have intended as a calming gesture. It had the opposite effect. "You ready then?"

Lee had never been less ready for road trip in her life. "Absolutely" she smiled back.

"Yeah, right" the cabbie muttered.

The first fifty metres were a challenge in vibration. This took them off the paved forecourt and all the way to the main road – which was where the going got really tough. Lee suffered on two levels: Physically, areas of her abdomen were still bruised – and bouncing and shaking of any kind, delivered a bewildering rhythm of sharp pains and grinding aches. She thought about reaching into her handbag for some of the codeine pills she'd been given, but she didn't dare release her hold on the upper grab handle and centre seat support. To do this would risk a shift in weight and potentially a whole new dimension of problems. The other main issue concerned the ability of Lee's brain to cope with the motion of the car and the movement of people and vehicles outside. Ten days of single room stillness hadn't prepared her for the nauseous effects of what seemed like a city gone mad. She was short on conversation for the duration of the ride and was thankful not to be tested.

In all, it took around forty minutes to make their way across the metropolis. It felt to the mute passenger to be at least ten times that length. David J. Bailey helped extricate Lee from the Bluebird. She paid the fare and added a tip – as much in celebration of the end of their affair, as anything.

At home, James had taken the afternoon off, to be present for Lee's arrival. It was a generous gesture, recognised gratefully. She had negotiated three of the steps with her bag before her flatmate made it down and relieved her of the monumental strain of bearing half a dozen kilograms.

"You all right?" James said, taking Lee's arm.

"I feel about ninety years old" Lee replied.

"Yeah, we've all been there." They both smiled at the line "Well, in a manner of speaking" James added, sheepishly.

A short break was needed half way up, but they were eventually back in the home comfort of the soft, white living room. "Welcome…" James grunted, taking the strain as he helped lower Lee to the sofa, "…back."

Lee gingerly leaned to her side until she was lying down and let out a deep sigh. She could only detect two or three pains from this position. Downright comfy, she considered.

"Rosy lea?"

"Ta, luv" Lee replied in the customary manner.

James repaired to the kitchen, "Coming right up!"

Lee called after him, "What's been happening while I've been away?"

"Not much. Gabriel's in now. Seems all right. You'll meet him later, he's…" James stood in the doorway, neither requiring completion of tea-making nor his sentence. Lee Habens, still in her coat and sunglasses, and clutching her handbag to her side, was truly home…and fast asleep.

Her memory of making it up the final flight to her bedroom was somewhat sketchy. She'd been fully unconscious there for several hours before waking to the sight of a familiar shape draped sideways over the arms of Dad's chair.

Dani had been reading a magazine, but must have detected her friend's stirring and looked over with a beaming smile. "Hello you."

Lee tried smiling back, but a yawn intervened and she ended up offering an odd, gurning expression. "Hey-aay" she managed, eventually.

Dani left the chair and knelt down by Lee's bedside, propping her forearms on the bed. "How do you feel?"

Lee had no idea where to begin, but settled for "Um, kind of like when you laugh so much it hurts. You're happy, but really you just need to just calm the hell down."

Dani smiled "There's plenty of time to recover" she soothed.

"Yeah" Lee breathed sleepily. She reached out a hand, "Did you ever think this would really happen?" she asked croakily.

"You mean all those years ago, when we were secret sisters? You were always this person. The rest? All of this? This was just details."

The next few weeks saw a recovery of gathering speed. It seemed that each morning Lee woke, she had twice the mobility and energy of the day before, although endurance remained elusive. She set off a number of times for walks around Holland Park, only to find herself running out of steam before she could complete the return journey. She would have to search for a low wall or high kerb upon which to rest. This would attract contemptuous looks from passers-by who she knew, would have drawn their own conclusions as to why a person might be unable to stand up straight in the middle of a decent neighbourhood.

She had the consolation of wonderfully deep sleeps during the first week while the pain killers concluded their business. She embraced the return of her prescription hormones happily – albeit at a lowered dose.

The term of rest, reflection and solitude had been just what was needed. It might have felt like a holiday – were it not for the episodic torture of dilation. She had come to apply the euphemism, 'exercise' to these forty minute, fun-free periods in her day. If there was an easing of the discomfort involved, it was perhaps more through familiarity than anything else. She could now insert the first dilator in about three minutes without having to push too hard. The second and larger instrument would feel at first as though it simply would never enter her. She still had very little muscle control in her lower abdomen, though she had found that lying on the bed with a hot water bottle strategically placed for several minutes beforehand, could help with relaxation. Boredom during an exercise was becoming a major issue for her, too. She couldn't hold a book as she needed both hands to direct and push the dilators. What she needed instead she thought, was a TV – not that she could afford one. A TV on the ceiling would have been ideal. She did once try exercising in the living room while everyone was out, but she spent the entire time braced for a quick retreat should any of her flatmates return early on an unscheduled stop. She took to listening to entire albums on her headphones, quickly becoming acquainted with some of Rikki's left-behind vinyl library. She could play side one of an LP for the small dilator and side two for the larger one.

As sensation returned, Lee became able to differentiate between the textures of her underwear alone and the extra padding of a sanitary towel when pressed against her vaginal area. She was also adapting to the odd and permanent feeling of having been stretched and tucked into herself. She'd been well practised at pulling her male genitalia beneath herself, confining everything with tightly worn underwear or even strips of tape, but what she felt now was more intimate – and extended within her. There was no discomfort as such, but she suspected it would take time and plenty of stretching before the skin tension would fully ease.

Eventually, Lee was ready to journey further than the confines of residential Notting Hill. She would she decided one Monday, take a bus ride. It was also the first occasion she dared to wear anything other than a long, loose skirt. She chose her blue, high-waisted, and tapered jeans, which she teamed with her faithful ballet pumps and a leather bomber jacket. Assessing herself in the mirror, her gaze was immediately drawn to the crotch area – where gratifyingly, everything fitted the way it should. She handled the walk to the bus stop with relative ease, but still chose to ride on the lower deck rather than risk a slip walking up or down the staircase. Mr Hendry had been keen to explain the risk of muscle tears and even prolapse, which could be risked by over-stretching or straining during the first weeks. She had a choice of routes, but with nowhere special to go, she thought she might as well get the measure of the journey to *Oasis*.

The ride down Church Street introduced Lee to a new emotion – one of guiltlessness. This she realised, was the first time in her life that she had felt completely *entitled* to look the way she did. She had shed the inner urge to apologise out loud for her audacity to present a female identity. Now she felt a strengthening of her outer aura. Her vulnerabilities remained only on the inside now – where they should be.

Lee had expected only to make the ride along as far as *Oasis*. She'd been pretty sure she wouldn't actually go in.

Mrs Macintyre had been visible through the open doors to the office suite. She was staring intently at the screen of her computer when Lee tapped on the door frame.

Madame looked up, "Lee" she smiled patiently, "How are you?"

"I'm very well, thanks. I was just passing, you know…"

"Of course, well it's good to see you. Take a seat, why don't you?"

Lee lowered herself carefully onto one of the two blue sofas available to visitors.

"Not quite sitting entirely comfortably yet then" Madame observed wryly, leaning back from her desk and into a more relaxed pose herself.

Lee grinned, "Not just yet, no" before adding, "I'm getting there, though."

"So? How do you feel?"

It was the question everyone asked. It merited more thought than usual on this occasion.

"Gosh. Um – *better* certainly" Lee began, pausing for a moment before adding, "relieved, peaceful, sometimes elated, proud, independent" she looked up, "More balanced. More...*alive*, I guess."

"Wow. All of that sounds good."

"Yes, I suppose it does."

Mrs Macintyre clearly weighed her words, "So now, *do* you finally feel like a woman?"

Lee took the question in good heart. She liked it. It made her think. "I'm really not sure exactly – I mean, do you?"

Mrs Macintyre returned a smile – to Lee's relief. "You mean, how can anyone know, right?"

Lee nodded. "All I do know is that I feel more me – and that was always the point."

"Then you feel like a real *person*."

"That, I do"

"There's nothing like coming through the darkness."

Lee smiled and admired again, the woman she faced.

Madame's features softened to a lighter expression, "Well, you look great and it's good to see you back on your feet. Have you thoughts for when we'll see you back here?"

"Well, I'm making really good progress and feel so much better every day. I have to be assessed by my surgeon in a week or so and then I'll know for sure, but I think I'm on the same schedule he originally suggested."

"Excellent."

"I just have to be careful when lifting anything – and also I have some um, special exercises I need to do a couple of times each day so that means I can't be away from home for too long."

"Not the kind of exercises you could do in the workplace, then?" Madame asked.

"Um, no – not really." Lee momentarily imagined the horror of being disturbed in the staff room. "But I was thinking" she went on, "If you do have anything more...clerical perhaps, that I could do – for just a few hours a day?"

Madame's mind was visibly working through a series of options and Lee took the moment to add, "I've been learning to touch-type at home and I could help out with filing – that sort of thing. I'm just saying, I can do more for you than I've been able to."

"Well, with Rafal in New York as my eyes and ears" Madame supposed, confirming for Lee the reason for the weasely one's absence, "a little help in here would be welcome. I'm calling on temps at the moment until we're sure of when he'll return – he does rather seem to be enjoying the experience." She looked up, "I know he's not exactly Mr Popular around these parts, but I miss having him around to bounce ideas off."

"I think we've all wanted to bounce things off Rafal at one time or another" Lee risked.

"Yes – quite."

"Um, honestly though – what kind of things?"

"Excuse me?"

"What kind of things do you generally bounce?"

"Well, as I say, issues related to day to day operations, cost bases, likely reactions and outcomes, immediate development plans around the place – anything that benefits from a second perspective."

Lee nodded slowly and almost let it go at that. Her mouth how-ever, was acting independently when it volunteered, "It's just that, you know – I've worked both here and at *Crush* for some time. I've got to know them from the ground up. I might have some ideas too, from time to time – in a sort of 'shop floor' sort of way."

Madame smiled thoughtfully. "Yep, well these are the eighties – and I've managed without much of an academic grounding myself. I learned from much the same start as you. I like it when people care about the business. That doesn't just gain you experience – it gives you a sense of stake in things."

"Yes, it does" Lee agreed. Holding and expressing an interest in her job did appeal. Work had been nothing more than a means to an income for the past few years. "My Dad always said that what you know can't be taught; while what you don't know, can still be learned."

Madame nodded and paused again, before adding, "Okay, so you know about the bars and the way the customers use them. Just as an example: We have to make a decision about bottled mixers. Do we carry on ordering the same quantities or do we go over completely to the mixer hoses?"

Lee raised her eyebrows in thought. "God, I don't know – I mean we tend to reach for the hoses, but people don't like them as much. They don't trust that they're getting the right amount and they always think they can taste whatever you last sprayed. On the other hand, it is cheaper and there's no waste. Half the time when I'm collecting glasses, I'm coming across half-drunk bottles of orange juice or tonic."

"So?"

"I think we still need to offer both, but we could have signs behind the bar telling customers to state if they want a bottled mixer."

"The supplier is pushing us for orders – they're offering some interesting discounts if we commit to longer terms. I've usually left dealing with them to Rafal, but..."

"Are we on a sale or return plan?" Lee asked, conscious that it was perhaps the first time in her life she'd ever used the term aloud.

Madame seemed at least a little impressed, "Only on certain brands."

"Not the fruit juices, right?"

"Right."

So, okay. The suppliers know all about New York. They know we're growing and they'd probably imagine there are more plans for London. Couldn't we just call their bluff and only sign up on condition that they extend sale or return to all of their lines? We could always step back from our stance later if we had to. After all, what can they do? Refuse to sell to us?" Lee was using parts of her brain that had been dormant for years – and she was enjoying it.

Madame tucked a lock of her hair behind her left ear. "That's exactly what we decided to do two weeks ago."

Lee smiled and nodded. Any of the bar team with half a brain might have voiced the same opinion, but it still felt good to be right.

"You let me know when you're well enough to come back to work" Madame concluded, clearly preparing to move on with her day.

Lee was in good spirits by the time she reached home. She had spent the return journey thinking about more helpful suggestions she might make for improvements to practices at *Oasis*. Maybe she really could do more for Headrush than add up the cost of a six-drink round.

She climbed the stairs to be met by a glorious smell. Fish was being cooked. She could also pick up traces of onion and tomato. Whatever the bouquet was, it was certainly new to their home. This pleasingly had become one of the benefits of Gabriel's introduction to the apartment. He loved to cook – and he was really good at it. Sure enough, as she moved into the apartment, Lee caught sight of their newest flatmate busy in the kitchen. He was tall and dark – clearly losing his hair prematurely, but had cropped it very short to minimise its loss to his appearance. He was an athletic man who liked to show off his toned arms and shoulders by wearing a succession of pastel coloured vests. He worked as a waiter at one of the swishier restaurants in Covent Garden, though he aspired to create rather than serve. Suddenly everyone wanted to be more than they were.

Gabriel's English wasn't great and the conversation between them was pretty much limited to greetings and small talk.

"Hey" Lee offered.

"Hello" Gabriel smiled back, easily.

"Hello" Luka echoed, his smaller frame suddenly appearing from the far side of his compatriot. He was wearing an identical expression – and vest.

'Yup, they're sleeping together', Lee thought to herself. "That smells wonderful" she declared, taking off her jacket and approaching to see a little closer.

"Thank you" Gabriel replied, his renewed prodding producing a fizzing noise and glorious new wave of odours, "It is Moqueca. You would like some?"

"She'd clearly love to Gabriel…" Dani interrupted as she skipped down the stairs, coat in hand.

"I really would" Lee confirmed.

"But I'm afraid I have to take her away for a bit."

"I'm really pretty hungry…" Lee began to protest.

"And I'm really buying you pizza" Dani declared.

For Dani to insist on something like this wasn't usual, Lee knew. Something was up. She wriggled back into her jacket and took a last mournful sniff of kitchen smells. "Is that coconut?"

Gabriel smiled again.

"Lee!" called Dani.

Lee whimpered her regret to Gabriel before turning and heading for the stairs.

Dani dodged Lee's demands for a trailer to the main feature all the way down to High Street Ken. Even as she had whined for a hint, Lee knew that her friend would give up nothing. Dani always liked her scenes to be properly set.

The Holland Park pizza restaurant had changed names since they'd last been there together. It was now known as *Frank's*, but the staff, like the chequerboard floor, appeared unchanged. Unlike at home that evening, the menu was anything but exotic and didn't take long to negotiate.

Lee leaned across their chosen corner table, "Now, will you tell me what's going on?" she whispered.

Dani took a deep breath – and slowly held out her left hand for inspection.

"Oh, my God…" The ring was a single diamond on a white gold band. On Dani's delicate finger, it looked perfect – and oddly Lee noted, as if it had always been there.

"All the way down, you carried your coat – you..!"

"Well it was that or gloves"

Lee took Dani's right hand, enjoying the free view of the other. "When did this…I mean…"

"It was actually over the weekend while we were in Bath. I wanted to call you, but over the phone – it wouldn't have been right."

Lee smiled, still shaking her head with wonder.

"What's more, because I knew that you had to be the first person I told, I've not been able to tell anyone else!"

"Not even your parents?" Lee asked incredulously.

"I even took a day off work today so that nobody would see the ring."

Lee sat back slowly in her seat. "Tell me exactly how it happened – and remember, I *do* have all night."

"There's really not much to tell" Dani protested. "We were walking along, down by the river just talking about nothing really. He was being daft and making me laugh as usual and then we got to where there's this weir-thing. The water was just rushing and roaring and he was holding my hand and then he stopped and turned and kissed me – you know, really softly. He took my other hand and I could feel that he was also holding something. He just put it in my hand and told me he loved me and when I looked down it was this little box and well, y'know…"

Lee could picture it. It was just like James to let a gesture ask the big question, rather than speak the words.

"So..?" Lee asked "What else happened? What's the plan?"

"The plan…" Dani answered holding up the ring again, her train of thought seemingly halted by the sight of tiny crystalline flashes.

Lee laughed at her friend's distraction, "You are really bad at this" she said, "Don't you know that I require all details to be presented as early as possible so that I can feel smugly well-informed when we're around others. It's all about what you know, about *who* you know – y'know?" she assured, parroting Grant.

Dani giggled seeing the waitress approach, "There really is nothing much more to tell"

Their bottle of Frascati arrived and they paused solemnly as Dani approved its suitability. Once the waitress returned to the kitchen, Lee resumed her interrogation.

"Nothing to tell? Nothing to tell?"

"Cheers" Dani said casually, offering her glass up for the toast.

Lee obliged "Yes sure – absolutely cheers" and then the torrent continued, "So, did you know it was coming? Did you expect it? Had you talked about it before? Did you ever shop for a ring? And for pity's sake, do you actually have a date in mind? Come on woman – we've known each other all of our lives! This is just the biggest news you've ever brought me and I need to know all of it right now!"

Dani took a long white sip, "We had talked about it, yes. And we're thinking about next September – as in '87" she said. "I'm certainly not expecting my parents to pay for it so we're going to save up to do it ourselves – not that we're planning anything remotely extravagant – just something intimate."

Lee nodded in understanding. She thought about asking how Dani *would* actually tell her parents, but decided against inviting their phantom presence into the conversation. Instead she focused on Dani's features, "You never had the slightest moment of doubt about him, did you?"

Dani stared into her wine and shook her head slowly and surely, "Never."

Lee rose from her chair and moved to Dani's, at first confusing her friend – who a heartbeat later stood herself so that they could embrace.

"Well" Lee said to the back of Dani's shoulder, "It's just wonderful. *You're* wonderful – and you deserve to be this happy – both of you."

Dani pulled back gently and looked up, her expected expression of joy, clearly compromised. She took Lee's hand, "Of course, we've also given notice on our rooms yesterday. It's time for us to go."

It made perfect sense, Lee knew. Still, the thought landed with a dull thud in her stomach. She hoped she hadn't missed a beat when she returned, "I know. You should begin a whole new story now. Do you know where you're moving to yet?" she asked, re-taking her seat.

"We've found a small house in Ealing. It's only a little terraced place – a 12-month lease, but there's a chance that if we're comfortable there, we might even be allowed to buy it."

It was Lee's turn to take a stiff drink, "Wow! That's a bit bloody grown up!"

"Yeah, I know. Everything feels pretty grown up just now."

"It's good though" Lee said, offering her support, "You're great at being grown up – and I should know."

Dani beamed, "Yes, and speaking of you, don't be making any plans for September '87, you're going to have plenty on your plate."

"Of course. I'll be there to help every step of the way" Lee assured.

"Damn right you will, what else is a bridesmaid for?"

"Bridesmaid?" Lee coughed hard and tasted grape in her nose.

october 1986
the uncertainty principle

∙∙∙

*T*wo days of living alone and I'm feeling as though it's never been any other way. Closing the door tonight and shutting out the world just felt so normal. It's sinking in that this is the first time I've been by myself since Priest Close and yet the adjustment has been so natural. I just love this place! I loved waking up here this morning and I loved knowing all day that I'd be coming back here tonight.

I've also discovered that I like being able to walk around naked. It's funny how I realise I haven't ever really done that. I didn't do it growing up with Dad – mostly because even I didn't want to see my body then. I certainly couldn't have done it at Moray Crescent. But being here is like a fresh start for so many things. I get out of the bath in the mornings and I can wander around the place letting the moisturiser sink in before wrapping myself in a dressing gown. It's such a small thing, but it tells me so much. My body no longer shames me – and getting used to it and being naked is helping me distance myself from all those horrible old feelings. It's not perfect – of course it isn't. I still have all of the usual hang-ups that normal people have about themselves on a daily basis. But I can bear it now – and that's the big difference.

I'm not quite the finished article yet though, of course. I still have my one last card left to play. I guess it has been important to me to see it as a finishing touch rather than a defining feature. Maybe, given the timing, I can try to think of it as a Christmas gift to myself. Dani is still the only person I've told. I'm not sure she feels that I should do it, but she knows how long I've been thinking about it. I just want my body to balance. It's no longer male – I mean, I really don't believe that the brotherhood of men would any longer claim me as one of their

*own, but still I'd just like it to be a little more obviously female in
appearance.*

*I called Hayley at Mr Hendry's office yesterday and told her the
date I'd be going in for the op. (When she'd said they like to keep track
of patients, I believed her – and I still do). I sent a note to Dr Garner
too. I've done everything by the book, even down to waiting for the right
interval between anaesthetics. I think (I hope!) that's been appreciated.*

*I'm a bit nervous about subjecting myself to more surgery, but after
what I endured in April, I shouldn't really have anything left to fear.*

. . . .

She kept coming across it. It remained where she'd hastily
placed it at the beginning of what was still the ongoing process of
unpacking. The little tin box lived incongruously for the moment
on a kitchen worktop, next to a brand new electric kettle.

It was in the tin box now, she knew – that piece of paper. It was
in the little envelope, inserted into the pages of Dad's passport,
itself in another envelope – right there in the tin box. It would be
a lie to say that she'd thought much about it in the time it had been
out of sight. Her agenda had rather been dominated by other matters. But now, after following her to a third home, the box seemed
also to have found a permanent niche at the back of Lee's mind.
From there it could fire off occasional memories like postcards
from the far past. A flash of an image. A sound.

Lee sat down, gently – as had become her habit – on Dad's
chair. She crunched on a slice of breakfast toast. She was pretty
sure by now, that she would always have the chair somewhere in
her home, wherever that may be. Mrs Lewis, the flat's leaseholder
had offered to put in a sofa, but Lee had been keen to start at
least owning a few sticks of furniture she could call her own and
refusing to borrow would force her to start making acquisitions.
Besides, Mrs Macintyre had mentioned that they were changing
the sofas at the office and Lee had made an early enquiry about
one of them, (she'd have taken both had she the space). Provided
she could arrange transport, she could take delivery in about a

week. The sofa's shade of blue could have presented a problem – if Lee had owned anything with which it might clash, but the walls in the flat were plain magnolia and the carpet apparently 'a light biscuit', Neutrality in Lee's new home, had yet to face any material incursion of identity.

The decision to leave Moray Crescent hadn't in the end, been a difficult one. Once Dani and James had gone, taking with them the last sense of home, there really had been nothing to keep her there. Everything that had once represented safety and familiarity had been hollowed out. The walls had ceased to be and the outside world had just flowed in. New tenants (another of Luka's friends and a well-supported student from the Netherlands), had arrived with their own sounds and smells and routines and once more Lee sensed that she didn't really belong.

She had found the flat at Trinity House quickly through a local letting agency. It was in a three-storey modern block toward the top of the North End Road, close to the Olympia Exhibition Centre. She was on the second floor. It was to put it kindly, compact. The largest space was the living room – and that was no more than fourteen feet in length. There was a tiny galley kitchen to one end and across a short hallway facing out to the back of the building, a bedroom big enough for a queen-sized and a wardrobe. The bathroom did at least manage a proper bath. What the place lacked in size however, it at least made up for in convenience. It was warm, very secure and was well-insulated from the never-ending West London soundtrack. The two mornings she'd so far known had begun with nothing more imposing than birdsong, delicately chirruping in through her slightly opened bedroom window.

She was paying only a hundred pounds more in rent for a whole home than she had for a single room at Moray Crescent. The fee was manageable – especially on her new salary.

Lee returned to her miniature kitchen and picked up a mug of coffee, taking it with her to the bedroom. Despite – or perhaps because of the lack of room available, a proper routine would take time to forge. At the moment, she wasn't quite sure where to take breakfast. Neither so far, was there a place to put clothes for washing, or to keep a hair dryer without tripping over a cable. But Identity she knew, would come with familiarity.

She did very much enjoy being part of the day world again. She liked the speed of it and of course the glorious light. She loved the clothes she needed for her day job too – although she still had too few of them. She had bought three suits: black, grey and blue and she rotated them – sometimes also mixing the black and grey. The skirts were all pencil in shape and the jackets nipped at the waist. The structured nature of the clothes helped her a lot. She had a number of blouses to wear under the jackets too – several in white, a blue and a black. The outfits combined with black courts, made her feel professional and prepared in a way her male suits never had. The bus journey was for her now, a pleasure. She enjoyed being one of a number of similarly dressed women on their way to offices across the south-west of London – it encouraged her that she must be getting it right. She looked like them, she worked like them and she travelled like them. She was, was she not, simply one of them? Nothing more. Nothing less.

Working for Madame under the Headrush meritocracy had proved rewarding in every possible way. The first weeks of light duties, filing and typing, had been extremely convenient of course. She'd 'exercise' in the morning, go into the office for four hours and then head home for a second session.

An early ice-breaker in her new role, had been the gift to Lee from Elaine, of a rubber ring on which to sit. It had previously belonged to Elaine's sister and had apparently been very welcome during recovery from the birth of her first baby. It seemed for a few days, that every time Mrs Macintyre caught a glimpse of the thing on Lee's chair, she would laugh at the sorry sight of it.

Inevitable office conversation had led to an improved under-standing of Mrs Macintyre herself and a dawning realisation to Lee that Rafal hadn't quite been all that he might like to have appeared. Lee had picked up his duties one by one and quickly taken ownership. Her easy manner with suppliers and other staff seemed appreciated too – if only as a contrast to her predecessor.

She had become first a de facto, then acting, and finally official PA to Mrs Macintyre.

Lee took care always to be at *Oasis* earlier than required. Her aim was to arrive ahead of Mrs Macintyre as often as possible and to be at her desk working with the coffee pot hot and ready. Lee's commitment to the company may have been already recognised, but it was an impression she was determined to continually reinforce. Working for Headrush the company, was a very different experience to that of serving a single venue. The breadth of the overall operation still surprised Lee. The day ahead would see her not only handling telephone calls, correspondence and responding to Madame's agenda, but also liaising with local planners over the much hoped-for extension to the lower floor. (Intended to allow what at present was little more than a private bar with a swimming pool, to become a proper health club with spa treatments, masseurs and a small gym). There was the new computerised database system the company hoped to introduce for members; localised promotions to encourage – and always suppliers to either source, or fend off. Within the organisation itself, staff issues at all three UK venues required weekly attention. These were long established challenges compared to the New York partnership. The transatlantic dynamics were an interest of their own. Faxes would start to arrive in late morning as Manhattan was waking. There were now also early conversations taking place about the creation of a similar model on the Mediterranean island of Ibiza. Lee found everything about her work to be compelling and stimulating. She watched the clock only for her employer's sake, reminding her regularly of diary commitments, meeting and telephone-wise.

In the event, Madame hadn't been a presence in the office for long that day, needing instead to make it onto a hastily arranged Edinburgh shuttle out of Heathrow. Being alone in the office allowed Lee to become properly engrossed in her tasks and by the time she had covered off the last of the morning's fallout, she realised she'd be too late to take the fifteen-minute round trip to the nearest decent sandwich bar for lunch. She headed downstairs in the hope that there might be something decent on the limited bar menu. There were perhaps twenty-five visitors in seated groups around the yuccas and palm trees. Lee waited patiently at the small bar while a group of three in front of her deliberated over whether to order a sandwich or go for the chilli.

"There's not a lot of choice really is there?" the lone female member of the group remarked.

"It's more of a bar really, I think" explained the taller of the men.

"It feels a bit like being on holiday. I think I'd quite like to get pissed and lie by the pool for the afternoon" the shorter man contributed.

Lee looked across at the barman – a new starter known as 'Ralph', even though his real name was Gordon. He smiled at Lee patiently, though apologetically. The tall man tried to drive his partners toward a decision, "Well, I'm definitely going to try the chilli" he led.

The woman was not to be influenced, "Mmmmm" she pondered.

Lee sighed silently and studied the tall man for a moment. There was something about him. He was just about at her eyeline, she noted. The shape of his head, the curl in his hair at the nape of his neck, "Philip?" she blurted, immediately praying that she hadn't just made a mistake.

He turned. He smiled. He *was* Philip. Every inch of him. "Well, well" he said. "*Lee*, how are you?"

"I – I – I'm all right" she managed after a moment. "This isn't your part of town, what on earth brings you here at lunchtime? And won't it take you the rest of the day to get back to The City?"

"It probably would if I had any need to get there."

"Sorry?"

"Well…" he began, before seeming to remember his joint mission and turning back to the others, "I'm for the chilli, yes."

Lee noticed Ralph already making a note and she took the opportunity to wave silently in his direction and mouth the words, "Me too!"

Philip stepped away from the bar, inviting Lee to move with him. "I must say, you look…really, *really* well" he said in a way that suggested he was quite pleased about it. "I've never seen you in daylight. You're quite good at it."

"Erm thanks. You're, y'know – not bad at it yourself" she fumbled.

"I thought when you said you worked in a nightclub, that you actually worked, well – in a nightclub" Philip mimed what appeared to be the pulling of a pint of beer.

Lee forgave a gesture which leant itself rather more to a Victorian tavern, "I did that…thing, yes. Now I work in the office upstairs."

Philip closed his eyes as some pieces slotted together in his mind, "That explains it."

"Doesn't explain you though" Lee pointed out.

"Well the thing is, I work around these parts too, now."

"You do? No more City?"

"No more."

Lee thought for a moment, "What on earth do you do down here? This is Fulham and Chelsea – we don't do banking."

"*I* never did banking"

"Yes you did, you worked for a banky, law-type place thing – with Davey."

"I'm in IT" Philip reminded her.

"Right" Lee recalled. "That's…probably quite fascinating, isn't it?"

"I think so"

"Right"

"I sense that you're not convinced."

"I'm still not really sure what it is" Lee replied honestly, then immediately looking for some kind of supplementary positive, "It's increasingly important though, I know that. And as it happens, I work with a computer up there" she pointed back toward her office beyond the large glass panes a dozen feet above them.

"And what kind do you use?" Philip tested, slotting his hands in his pockets in a gesture that said, 'you don't know, do you?'

Lee grinned sheepishly, "Black one?" she tried.

"A black one?" Philip checked, stroking his chin, "You need to be careful with those" he said.

"Oh really"

"No absolutely, they have a built-in obsolescence chip."

"A what?"

"The button in corner marked 'C-t-r-l'? After you've hit that nine hundred and ninety-nine times, the whole thing just explodes. Terrible mess, coils and springs everywhere."

"I never press that button"

"Well how do you get it to switch on properly, then?"

"With the 'Power' button." Lee folded her arms.

"Yes, but that's only going to show you the right-hand screen. You have to use the Control button to see the left-hand screen."

Lee was remembering why she liked Philip. "Do you dress yourself in the morning or does the nurse sort all of that out for you?"

"Ah Nursey" Philip sighed, "she gives so much…"

Lee shook her head, "We are in a city of eight million people. I meet you in one part of it and now another. Don't you think that's a bit weird?"

Philip looked back in the direction of his lunch partners. They were taking a table over by the wall. He seemed to hesitate for a moment, "I've been working down here for six weeks. Every day I drive past this place with a big sign outside that says '*Oasis*'. And I remember that I once had this amazing night in a mad club with a girl who told me she worked at a place called '*Oasis*' somewhere around here. So, after work one day a week or so ago, I took a walk along here. There was a guy outside – huge guy…"

"Elvis" Lee imagined.

"Okay, well Elvis had most certainly left the building for a moment. So, I asked him if there was a tall girl inside called Lee. He asked me how tall and I sort of…showed him." Philip gestured as if indicating someone of about seven feet.

Lee gave him an annoyed grin, "Okay"

"So, he said I should come back during the day."

Lee was smiling curiously now.

"And I've been coming back. This is my third lunch here. I – I'm running out of people who will come out with me. They all think I'm on some kind of commission for this place."

"Seriously?" Lee asked. "You came here several times just to see me?"

"*Three* times", Philip corrected. "What can I tell you? It was one of my favourite nights. I couldn't forget you – even though Davey told me you were seeing someone."

"Uh-huh, he did?" In half a dozen heartbeats, Lee fought incredulity and a hint of irritation before settling for the same kind of understanding she'd always had.

Philip drew her back, "Oh look, really, I don't mean to be any trouble and I'm certainly no threat to whatever it is that you have going on. All it is, is that…well, I suppose I just wanted to see you again. I just wanted to check that you were…real."

"Real" Lee repeated. She looked into Philip's green eyes and then over to Ralph who had a couple of bowls of chilli and some rustic bread waiting for collection. "I have to go back to work" she said.

"Sure" Philip conceded.

Lee let another heartbeat pass. "Why don't you stop by here at about six and maybe we can go for a drink or something."

Philip smiled warmly, "You know, I *can* actually do that. Do I have to change my clothes?"

"No, of course not."

"Oh good. Nursey will be pleased."

The afternoon delivered plenty to keep Lee's mind occupied, though a corner of it stayed tuned to thoughts of Philip. It should she thought, be a simple equation: She liked Philip; Philip rather unaccountably seemed to think that she was worthwhile looking up – surely the rest would just flow naturally. And yet this wasn't going to be straightforward at all. Firstly, there was the issue of Davey. They still spoke at least once every two weeks and she was due to see him and April for dinner again soon – but by not mentioning Philip again, had Davey been sending the message that

Lee should still not entertain any thoughts of involvement? Would Philip even still know anyone Davey did? If not, how could the issue of transsexuality be of any threat?

Of course, even if the way *was* clear to seeing Philip, there would still be the big issue of explaining Lee's own past to him. Dr Garner had covered this over two sessions, citing examples of unnamed cases. The bottom line was that no outcome could be predicted. Lee imagined it would be a bit like the 'Russian Roulette' scene in *The Deer Hunter*. She would sit opposite her man, spin the barrel, pull the trigger and just expect everything to go black.

Sex reassignment was unlikely to prove any kind of asset in the search for love – an elusive enough prize to begin with. She'd never really spent time hoping for a real relationship. Even now when she would catch someone's eye or feel the first sensation of desire, she would dismiss the moment. She simply couldn't imagine a flirt ever growing into something more. It would never really happen. It *couldn't* happen – could it?

She wished her first real test wasn't Philip. If she could have had a couple of shallow affairs along the way beforehand, she would be better practised at talking to straight men. By now she'd have weathered her own shortcomings and might have been ready to face someone who mattered. Instead she was the failed game show contestant being offered a close-up of something she hadn't won.

Not of course, that she was planning to tell Philip anything that night – but she knew that by seeing him and by admitting that she was single, the prospect would exist of a real date. Once there was a first date, there could be others. If there *were* other dates – *good* ones – there would be eventually be sex. If there was sex she would have no choice but to tell Philip beforehand. She had to – didn't she? Mr Hendry assured her that a man would not be able to tell of her past through intercourse – and she did believe it – but any caring partner would still have to know the real her, she felt. She would have to feel free to talk to someone she loved about her childhood, her Dad, her home town and origins – all the things normal people would discuss as they got to know each other.

She couldn't live with the prospect of the truth one day spilling out all deep blue, across a pristine white lie of a relationship.

As six o clock approached, Lee propped up her compact mirror on top of a ring binder on her desk. She studied her face carefully. Her skin looked okay. She would like to have reapplied her makeup from scratch, but that wasn't going to happen – she didn't have everything she needed and wouldn't risk what wasn't entirely a bad face anyway. She settled for some fresh mascara and lipstick. She stalled part-way through brushing her hair, staring into the tiny reflection and losing her focal point somewhere beyond. Once more, Lee Habens found herself conflicted at living a stereotypical scene: the secretary fixing her face before meeting a man for a date. She was a little perplexed. Did these preparations really fit her or was she just mimicking a ritual she understood to be appropriate? And should she be worried at all anyway? Weren't other young women also living these moments? Just because an act was clichéd, didn't mean it lacked authenticity. She sighed her way back into the room and resumed brush strokes. Living as a woman through determination rather than birth, didn't mean she had to re-invent the paradigm. This was drinks in Fulham, not the meaning of life! The simplest truth was that she just liked what she was feeling at that moment. She was enjoying the thrill and anticipation of what was ahead. That was okay, wasn't it? Knowing that a man wanted to relate to the woman he saw in her was an understandably exciting thought. Wasn't this in so many ways, what the entire journey had been about?

The phone buzzed once, signalling that the call was internal. No more time to dwell.

Philip's smile mirrored Lee's on sight – as if they were sharing a private joke. Lee knew immediately that he was going to be very easy company. They walked to the nearest pub, followed all the way by a steady evening drizzle. They both crammed, giggling under Lee's umbrella which had a diameter entirely inadequate for two people. Lee's hair became damp on her right side, while Philip's left shoulder took on a coat of tiny watery beads. Arriving at the door, Philip held it open offering the entrance first to Lee.

She stepped through and wondered if she'd ever get used to that kind of courtesy.

The main bar appeared to have been recently refurbished. Brasses shone over an even dark wooden floor. Pictures and posters celebrating a London of a different age were retro-neat rather than original-worn. Solid wooden bar furniture awaited them under high ceilings, which helped to dissipate the high cloud of cigarette smoke. Lee identified a corner table with enough distance from others to allow them to speak easily.

Philip joined her from the bar, bearing a bottle of Pils and a glass of house white for Lee. He sat opposite her, looking a little unsettled.

"What?" Lee enquired.

"Mmm?"

"Your expression – what are you thinking."

"Well, I'm thinking that I'm wet – sort of, on one side. It feels weird – and not in a nice way."

Lee shook her head and scrunched some damp hair, "Yeah, I think I know what you mean."

Philip raised his bottle of beer in salute, "Well, cheers anyway."

"Cheers" Lee returned, savouring her first encounter with grape in a few days.

Philip smiled and seemed to study Lee for a moment. "I'm really glad you agreed to meet me."

"Well, it's very nice to be met – though I'm still trying to understand why you were so keen to find me."

Philip swept his fingers back through dark wet hair, leaving shiny new furrows. "I know, it must seem a bit odd, me coming along, out of the blue after such a while."

"Oh, I'm just curious – I mean do you do this kind of thing often?"

Philip laughed, "I'm not that tragic! I do this kind of thing, precisely never – that's how often."

Lee was warmed inside. Being an exception, felt pretty nice for a change. She softened her tone for her further enquiry, "What is it exactly that you're looking *for*?"

Philip shook his head and looked around the bar for a moment as he compiled the words, "Do you know, I'm honestly not sure exactly. I just…I just couldn't leave it alone. It was that and you know, being in the neighbourhood. It was like having an itch that I had to…I just had to see if I could find you again."

"Well" Lee conceded, "it's a nice surprise anyway". She offered her glass again in toast.

Philip's bottle made a flat clunk noise against Lee's vessel. "I'm not great at being impulsive, you know? I mean I usually need to properly know why I'm spending time doing something, but with this I just sort of went with the gut, you know?"

"Gut. Sure, yes" Lee grinned.

Philip acknowledged the tease with a matched expression. "No seriously" he steadied, "I've made some real life-changes recently. Changing my job, my lifestyle and just generally being a lot less… yuppiefied. It's all given me a chance to think more about life and what I really want to do."

"Life changes can do that to a person" Lee agreed, respecting the sentiment genuinely. "And so, what is it you've decided you want to do?"

Philip took another breath of Pils, "More of what feels good and less of what doesn't."

"That's very 'New Man'."

"I suppose it is – and I suppose I am."

"Good for you" Lee smiled, "Though repeated visits to a place you wouldn't normally go, just on the off-chance of bumping into someone, does seem like a bit of a long-winded way to make contact. I can't imagine that you usually need to go to such lengths." Lee felt that tacitly acknowledging Philip's attractiveness so early in conversation was a little risky, but hoped it would help with their balance.

The shy smile triggered by Lee's words was genuine, "I'm just not terribly good at this kind of thing" Philip admitted. "Pretty much the only women I ever meet are through being introduced by somebody else under circumstances that aren't particularly… loaded." Lee was momentarily back at *Stargazer* on a crowded night, silently thanking Davey again – and then whispering an apology for continuing to ignore his later request.

"There is definitely something that just sort of...draws me to you" Philip confessed through obvious nerves. "I don't know what it is exactly"

Lee laughed, expressing mock offence, "Oh thanks!"

"No, no" Philip scrambled, "You're lovely and so that's pretty simple, but there's something else that I just can't quite...process."

"Process?"

"Sorry – computer term" Philip acknowledged. "It's just that I've thought about you...a lot – ever since that night at *Crack*..."

"You mean *Crush*" Lee corrected, half-wondering if even Headrush could get away with a club called 'Crack'.

"Right. Well that night did leave me with...I don't know, a desire for more...of you – and I suppose, of me, too." Philip was visibly working hard at composing his sentences. "I'm not...not normally that guy – the guy I was, that night in the club. The surroundings, the people, the dancing – the *music* – I don't usually do any of that. But I loved it. I loved it and ever since, I've not been able to find a way back to feeling like that. I mean I knew that I could just look up nightclubs in *Time Out* and give some places a few tries – I could even go back to that same one. I could drink exactly the same amount of Dutch courage before heading out and try to match every other part of that night, but I knew it wouldn't be the same."

Lee was distantly aware of her own smile – and that she was sending it straight into Philip's gaze. "Well – um, wow! I'm really glad to have been a part of that experience. It was pretty special to me, too."

Philip pressed on, "Have you ever heard of quantum mechanics?"

"Erm, let me see...No." Lee giggled.

"There's a thing – they call it The Uncertainty Principle"

"Okay..." Lee murmured uselessly.

"I know, but bear with me – this is the kind of thing that I spend time thinking about." Philip physically re-set himself, took a breath and began to use his hands to help shape his words, "Some things – well, the more you work at trying to understand them, the more you unintentionally change them. If you just let them be, they are one thing – but if you look closer, try to really examine them and *understand* them, they can actually *become* something else. It's like…messing with the magic. Does that make sense?"

Lee wasn't used to feeling bewildered. She didn't like the thought that she might be missing out on a message. She strained to understand.

Philip shifted and tried another line, "My life…hasn't been that much fun, simply because it's been sort of over-planned and over-predicted. I've been doing all the things I was taught were right, but not necessarily for the right reasons. My personal life, my career, they've all made loads of sense on paper, but they didn't have the magic." Philip leaned closer, "For a while I suppose I settled for the thought that magic was something that just belonged in other people's lives, you know?"

"Oh yeah, I get that" Lee agreed, quite truthfully getting that.

"But then one night after work I end up in some mad club with bizarre people and I have this great time and it just sparked a thought in me: why *shouldn't* I have some magic? I mean, I'm not stupid and I'm not afraid. I should be able to make some magic of my own, *right?*"

"Absolutely" Lee cheered.

"So then, all I have to do is figure out what magic *is* – just without actually examining it too closely."

"Well, good luck" Lee smiled, clinking her half empty glass against Philip's now bone dry bottle.

Philip sat back and beamed across the table at Lee. "So, I kept coming back to one thought."

"You did?"

"What if it's you?"

Lee's heart rate disappeared and then returned more rapidly, trying to make up for the lost beats, "What if what's me?"

"What if the reason I can't get that night and that feeling out of my thoughts, is you?"

It was Lee's turn to pause and consider for a moment. She took another sip of her wine and felt the chill course around her tongue. She was sparkling inside even before the liquid left her throat. She offered a considered tone, "Well you know, it is possible to get hooked on change and adventure."

"You think so?"

"I think" she said steadily, "that I'd like to understand first, where you came from – and then hear some more about where you're headed."

Philip shrugged, "Okay. Where do you want to start?"

Lee's eyes narrowed. "Well" she began, "you used to work in the city among the rich and soulless..."

"I did."

"And now you work down here with the rich and pretentious..."

"I do."

"That still seems like a weird move."

"Okay..." Philip began, "Well, I live near Wimbledon..."

"That is near" Lee conceded.

"And I have a young daughter."

"That's...huge" Lee heard herself reply, with a softer tone.

"I wanted a shorter commute so that I could spend more time with Annie."

"and Annie is..."

"Yes, my daughter, Annie. Anne-Marie. You *are* with me on the whole father-daughter story?"

"Yes, yes of course, I get it. I just..." In truth, Lee hadn't seen it coming at all. Parenthood had so rarely featured in the lives of her recent peers. She reminded herself that she now lived in a world of primarily straight people where family and stability were realistic aspirations. Of course, Philip could be a dad. "I'm just a bit surprised because you hadn't mentioned it before, is all."

Philip shrugged "Well, our conversations have been a bit short of...context". He looked a little sensitive about the issue, as if concerned that the conversation might take a turn.

"Where is it?" Lee asked smiling and bouncing an eyebrow.

"What?"

"Lemme see" she urged.

"See what?"

"The picture. No, I mean pic-*tures*. You're Philip, so one won't be enough. You have several of them on your person, right now. Lemme see them."

Philip grinned sheepishly as he drew out his wallet from his inside jacket pocket and produced a small clutch of photos. They were clearly kept in a specific order, the top being the most recent. Philip offered them one by one from the bottom, beginning with a picture of his baby, then a blonde-haired toddler, followed by a smiling schoolgirl and finally one taken in a garden with Annie sitting across her father's lap.

"She's absolutely beautiful" Lee declared, especially touched by the last image. "How old is she."

"She's nine – and a half."

Lee attempted to negotiate the difficult but obvious questions, "And her mother?"

"Louise and I are on good terms. They live in Putney in our old house. I rent a flat in Southfields."

"That's...nice" Lee offered weakly.

"Well, it's all right *now*. We weren't always quite so grown up about it. I see Annie three nights a week now that I don't have my long commute. My days start and finish early. I get to pick her up from school sometimes and she even sleeps at my place on a Friday night. It works pretty well for us."

"Wow, that really *is* pretty grown-up" Lee observed, suddenly feeling the barbed absence of family from her own routine. All Lee had to worry about most of the time now, was Lee.

Philip went on to outline a story of two people who'd met very young – not long after they had arrived in London on separate adventures. They had found their way in city life together and set up home after about a year. Anne-Marie had followed not long after that, but there hadn't been enough between them to sustain the marriage for which they'd hoped. If Annie was the main reason for trying to keep a home together, she became in the end, the best reason to part. Too many rows were being played out in front of the one part of them they both loved – and two smart minds could find endless ways in which to express conflict. There was peace now between them and a mutual understanding that they hadn't failed together – they'd just not succeeded as much as they'd once hoped.

Philip was the party left with demonstrably less in his life than he'd had before. He said he didn't begrudge Louise her happiness with her new partner. She'd handled the changes well and had ensured that Annie was never confused about whom in her life, was who.

Philip's new employer was an international commercial property developer. They had interests in the Far East and Europe, including some involvement in the new Chelsea Harbour development where Philip himself, worked. He explained that his early mornings were spent liaising with Hong Kong and Singapore using something called 'E-mail', which he described as sending lots of digital post through the telephone networks. Lee feigned boredom as a tease. She was careful not to give too much away about her own life. She stuck to the safe items: new flat, new(ish) job; plans perhaps to take a trip away next year. She covered her family history by simply saying that she'd been brought up by her Dad who had passed away. She reciprocated Philip's picture show with a photo of the man who had constituted her own family. The failure to volunteer anything about her mother would usually she knew, bar further questions.

Eventually, she saw an opportunity to bring up their mutual friend. As Philip returned with their third or fourth round of drinks she asked, "So when did you last see Davey?"

"Honestly? My last day in The City."

"Why's that? I thought you two were good friends."

"Well, we were. We got on really well."

"So..?"

"Well, there really wasn't any point in staying in touch after I left."

"Really? Why?"

"Seriously, I mean when would we ever get around to seeing each other? I don't get over his way and he doesn't get south of the river so what would be the point? We were good mates there and now that time is…past."

Lee was genuinely surprised. "I still find it a bit…odd. Don't you miss him?"

Philip took another drink. Lee had noticed that their speed of alcohol consumption was increasing with each round.

"No, it's not like that. Haven't you ever just moved on from a situation you had in the past?"

"Um, well yes – but that was different"

"Maybe it's just a man thing. We don't tend to be quite so sentimental about friendships."

"Right" Lee accepted – not quite ready to venture into gender politics, what with her holding a hand full of jokers. "I think perhaps I still have a lot to learn about men."

"Really? Gosh, I'm not sure we're that complicated" Philip considered, placing his elbows on the little table between them.

Lee noticed that the closer he came, the greener his eyes seemed to turn. He was looming a little, in a way he perhaps wouldn't have, several drinks ago.

"I'm really not…treading on anyone's toes, am I?" he asked, his voice lowered. "Like I explained, I don't do this kind of thing generally and I think I'm pretty bad at it, but if you are seeing someone else I can…"

Lee smiled and shook her head, "I'm not seeing anyone."

Philip's eyes crinkled a little at the corners with a smile of his own, "Okay" he considered, clearly pleased with the news, "And so, is that a *conscious* decision – I mean, you not seeing anyone."

It was a tough one for Lee to answer. She settled for, "Well, I have a lot going on right now" – but then immediately fearing that Philip might take this as a hint to cool his interest, added "…So in the past few months, I've just not had time to even…see anyone." She hoped that would be enough.

Philip sat back once more and Lee worried a little about the body language. Still, he continued to scatter the occasional compliment as their conversation progressed. His eye contact with Lee remained unbroken when she was speaking. His smile might linger perhaps a little longer than might be expected whenever she tried to amuse – and his expressions seemed to reflect empathy, changing within heartbeats of her words. He *was* listening to her – and not just every so often.

Over the course of the next two hours, Philip gave a little more of himself. He had been born near Oxford and yet had graduated from Cambridge. His roots were solidly middle-class and he had been raised with expectation in mind. Nothing he had been told, was beyond him and so innocently, he had believed it. As a child, he had an aptitude for numbers and he had developed an appreciation for the beauty of logic. He had no interest in following his father's line into finance however, but instead found the field of computer science to be fascinating. He had studied the newer discipline along with more practical strands of applied mathematics. He tried to convince Lee that any human brain should be capable of most of what he'd learned, but she was retaining a healthy scepticism. To illustrate his point, he tried to explain transcendental equations, but was eventually stalled by Lee's fixed grin of bemusement.

Philip had worked very long hours during his time in the City. His job had been happy to drink every drop of commitment he'd had to offer. There certainly hadn't been much opportunity for dating. "You always think there's going to be time for it later" he said. "I've felt young all my life – never known anything else. But now I'm starting to realise that grey hair – or no hair – will come for me, too."

"There's a thought" teased Lee, looking a couple of inches above Philip's eyeline.

"Yes, well I've now decided to put *life* first" he reaffirmed, leaning forward again. His beer was cradled in both of his hands and his eyes stared off at something that wasn't in the room. "I want to do so much. I want to see things and try things. I want to go places and do something with the ideas I have. I want to show Annie how the world works – and watch her take it apart. I really understand now, that I need to *live* life and feel it and savour it – not just…turn up for it."

Lee wasn't sure she was going to kiss Philip until she felt her lips touching his. She was simply drawn in. It was only a moment, but it had the most extraordinary effect. "Wow, I'm sorry" she said, her hand raised to mouth. "I don't usually do that sort of thing in public", ('or anywhere else for that matter', she added in her thoughts).

Philip looked like a man who'd just found forgotten money in a pocket – pleased but a little baffled. "That's...really okay" he faltered, "think I've lost my train of thought though."

Lee sat back and as she did so, realised how many empty glasses and bottles they'd accrued. "Jesus – did we really drink that much?"

"That's all you, I think" Philip teased. "I don't remember more than two myself."

Lee laughed – perhaps over-compensating for her forward gesture, "I should probably go before I drink past the point of getting up tomorrow morning".

Gathering their coats, they headed for the door to the street. Philip opened it and stood back. They were faced by a sheet of rain.

"Well, that's not good" observed Lee, looking down at her too-small umbrella. "Did you want to even up the side of you that got damp earlier?" she asked.

He looked back at her and smiled mischievously, "Oh, to hell with it" he said, stepping out into the street and pulling Lee with him. She yelped with surprise and immediately realised how pointless her umbrella would be. She felt her hair flatten as streams threatened to breach the collar of her coat. The two of them ran hand in hand toward the New King's Road. Lee knew she was laughing out loud, but she couldn't hear herself above the torrent.

Philip stopped ahead of her as they reached the busy main road. He looked up and down the street for a cab. He turned back to Lee and smiled apologetically. He looked like he'd been swimming. There was a straight sheen across each of his shoulders under the amber street lighting. "You" he shouted above the hiss of a passing bus, "...look ridiculous!"

Lee imagined she must indeed look truly awful, but she could no more turn back the tide than protect herself from the one falling on top of them both. She ran a finger under each eye in a vain attempt to tidy up the imagined running eyeliner and mascara. "Yeah, you on the other hand, look your usual self!" she called back.

"Thanksh!" Philip replied goofily, water running off his grinning chin. He looked back out into the road and raised an arm, drawing a black cab to dock at the curb side. "This one's for you."

"You sure?"

"No okay – I'll take it and you can wait for the next one!"

"Okay – okay! I like your first idea better!"

Philip tucked a forefinger under Lee's chin, "I've really enjoyed tonight. I'm so glad I found you again."

"And I'm really glad to have been found" she returned, wishing she could think of something better to say. This time she felt his kiss come to her – and stay for a while. She had no idea how long, she lost track of space and time as silver rivulets trickled around their lips in search of a way to part them.

"Gotta rush you..." the cab driver called through his open window.

Philip ushered Lee into the back door and made a telephone gesture with his hand. Lee nodded happily, but then Philip knocked on the window. Cracking it open, Lee heard him shout "I don't have your number!"

"Oh no, I don't have anything to write on!"

"Just say it – I'm pretty good with numbers!"

Lee did as he asked and hoped that Philip Easterhouse really was as good as he claimed.

She saw it again shortly after squelching back into the flat, dropping her coat and collapsing onto Dad's chair. The watery light from passing headlights on the North End Road caught the metal corner of the tin box and oozed along its dented flank. It was in there now, she knew – the piece of paper. It was in a tiny envelope, inserted into the pages of Dad's passport and wrapped in a larger envelope. It was just there in the box. It would be a lie to say that she hadn't thought about it during the day. If not for Philip, perhaps she'd have thought about it more than anything else. She rose and felt the soft carpet on the soles of her feet and then the contrasting chill of linoleum floor as she crossed from living room to kitchen. She picked up the box, opened the bottom cupboard, reached to the far corner and set it down. Not now, she told it. Not this night.

november 1986
money for nothing

I'd *like to think that I know what I'm doing – but it's hard to be sure of very much right now. It's not that long ago that my life just crawled along. One day's tiny progress was stacked on top of another and none of it seemed to add up to very much. Now, I'm scrambling to keep up with events. It feels sometimes, like I'm running after a car I'm supposed to be driving!*

Every day at work I'm doing something new. So far everything I try is working, but how long before it doesn't? Madame must either think I'm an incredibly fast learner – or more likely, that <u>of course</u> I know this stuff! If she had any idea just how much I was winging it some days, I wonder if she'd keep me on at all.

The money is really helpful though. I couldn't go back to what I was earning. Still it isn't quite enough if I want to get things finished now – and I am desperate to do that – to be totally through this thing and to never have to think about any further treatment. I hate going to the bank, but if I don't, this will all drag out so much longer than it needs to.

Meeting Philip after work again tonight – and that's something else I'm not properly in control of! Hoping something might happen doesn't make sense and yet I look forward to seeing him more than anything. There's no room for this in my life and yet I cancel other arrangements to stay home in case he rings. Why can't I just be honest with him? I don't remember Mr Hendry taking out my backbone with all of those other pieces of junk!

. . . .

"Headrush?" he asked.

"Pardon me?"

"Your employer is called *Headrush*?"

"It is" Lee confirmed.

"Hairdressers, is it?" Lee returned her inquistor's smile and tried to keep calm, "International entertainment group. We have nightclubs in London, Edinburgh and New York and we're opening soon in Ibiza."

"I see. Well, leisure is something of a fast-growing industry, isn't it? And you're one of its young go-getters, are you?"

"You could say I'm something of a new woman, yes" Lee admitted.

Eric Meeker appeared to be around thirty years old, going on fifty. He had a soft looking belly and was rapidly growing through what was left of his dark brown curls. His irritating nasal voice wasn't one to which Lee planned to become any more accustomed than she absolutely had to – and yet he was the possessor of that damned job title. It was there, boldly emblazoned on his name badge 'Principal Loan Officer – Chelsea Branch'. Lee imagined that this was a man who lived through his corporate rank. Should he ever lose it she imagined, he would fall to earth like crap from a seagull. And yet right now, he mattered even more than he perhaps realised. She must be focused. She had worn the black suit to work that morning believing it to be her wardrobe's most professional vessel. Today she must appear attractive as an investment.

The charming Mr Meeker took a longer look through some of the pages in Lee's file. "So, you took a fairly small loan out in March and now you'd like to increase it?"

"Yes." Lee acknowledged. "There's just the one outstanding payment on the loan I have and I'd like to roll that into a new one"

"R-r-roll it into a new one" Meeker parroted.

Lee ignored the idiosyncrasy and asserted her case further, "My salary has increased significantly and I have made this breakdown of my outgoings." She handed to him the page of figures she'd printed off from the office computer. The document detailed rent payment, household bills, travel and other expenses.

"I see" Meeker remarked. He looked up at Lee again, "Very compelling" he conceded. "What may I ask, will the money be used for?"

"Well, nothing in particular" Lee began to lie.

"Oh, so it's…'*Money For Nothing*', as it were" Meeker offered. "Let's hope you don't fall into…*Dire Straits.*"

Lee managed a weak smile, "Very good" she declared and then before her tormentor could fill out the box on his form she added, "Mostly, I thought I'd get a car."

"So, what is it you really want the money for?"

"Don't ask"

Philip raised his eyebrows and then popped the lime slice out of the neck of his Sol. "I used to know people in banking."

Lee took a swig of her own beer and added, "Yes, and I used to know some of the people you used to know in banking."

"So you did" Philip concurred. "Where are they now, eh?"

"Rich and living north of the river."

"You live north of the river" Philip reminded Lee as she leaned back against his shoulder, pushing him into the corner of the booth they shared. "Not that you ever *invite* me to where you live" he added.

"You can come to my place when I can afford to buy some more furniture."

Philip chuckled throatily.

"What was that?"

"Bare scepticism"

"Why?"

"I think you're keeping me away from your place because there's something you don't want me to see"

"Oh, you do?"

"You're a woman with secrets and a dark past – that's what I think."

"You'd better believe it" Lee confirmed, settling again into the comfort zone between Philip's torso and arm.

What exactly was it she felt for this man? There was so much to be enjoyed about their being together. Such rewards could be found in regular friendships she knew, but there was another dimension to this entirely. Why did it feel so natural for them to be slumped together like this in the corner of a smoky pub on Putney's river bank? How could the few weeks they'd known each other feel like months of familiarity and shared experience? He was so easy for her to be with. He was interested in her, but not probing. He would volunteer plenty about his own life, thoughts and feelings – and yet he was sure enough about his plans and priorities to avoid giving the impression of neediness. He could so easily complain about his former marriage and not seeing his daughter as much as he'd like – but he did neither. He was by nature Lee was realising, an actual 'glass-half-full-type' – genuinely seeming to believe that today was merely the eve of better things to come. It was as infectious a quality, as it was attractive.

They could talk together about almost anything, sharing views on politics (his slightly to the right of hers), the arts (his slightly more to the mainstream than hers), London (he'd seen a lot more of it than her) – and then there were the issues upon which one *could* lecture the other: he had travelled quite widely abroad unlike Lee, but on the other hand she knew so much more about music and night culture. Both enjoyed delivering and hearing something new. She had wondered whether her feelings for Philip might fall short, turning to a comfortable platonic warmth. But she knew now that she wanted more. She loved being touched by him. He wasn't overly tactile, but every so often there would be a hand to her back or an arm around her waist as they'd laugh together and she would shimmer inside. She could feel his touch on her for an age after contact was lost. Occasionally as she spoke, he would lightly brush a hair from her face without seeming to realise he'd done so.

She wondered how long their kisses and gentle touches would be enough for him – and knowing that she *could* now make love to him as a heterosexual woman only added to the agony. The only bar to it happening was her sense of principle – the promise to herself that she would tell a partner the truth. Perhaps if he'd been a fling, she would have just taken a few more drinks and relented, but Philip wasn't anyone's one-night stand. She loved the idea of him being 'the first'. Something so important should happen with someone significant, she felt. Her desire for him physically was another new kind of feeling. She was drawn by the curiosity of exploring him and learning more about his shapes and textures. His arms and shoulders; face and hair, bore little resemblance to recollections of her own maleness. Perhaps it was as simple as these things just looking so much better on him, but she found herself in the odd position of enjoying in Philip, precisely the things that she had once loathed about herself.

She had an ache to be touched intimately. Was it the result of her recovered physiology – or more likely the chemistry building between her body and his?

She'd still only met Philip a handful of times, but they spoke on the phone almost every other night – and at extraordinary length. Still, she couldn't begin to sense the bottom of him. However much she learned, there was always so much more to know. She'd be talking to him about where he wanted his career to go and then he'd tell her of pioneering ideas he had about human neuro networks and how he felt there was so much more that computers could do to improve and enhance lives. He'd had a blameless childhood himself – and knowing it seemed to fire him with a sense of obligation to others. His outlook was peppered with beautiful quotes of Annie's, to which he would often return. He was loving learning about life through his own child's eyes.

Philip had very quickly grown into Lee's quiet life and now had a presence beyond all others. He was close and real – and becoming too precious to lose.

christmas 1986
cornflakes with all the trimmings

I wish I could get that blend of anaesthetic on a prescription. How wonderful it was to drift away to it again. Even four days later I swear I'm still enjoying it. I keep nodding off and having the most wonderful dreams. (In yesterday's I was in a tree, hiding from multi-coloured aliens! I have no idea why).

Without doubt, the weirdest Christmas I'll ever have. At least I hope it is!

Got home on Tuesday afternoon after another uncomfortable cab ride back from a hospital. I was actually having to hold my chest for the second half of the journey.

At least the recovery this time is easier. I'm perfectly able to walk around and have even been to the corner shop a couple of times. I still feel very heavy in the chest and the motion of going downstairs is not to be recommended. It's all bearable though. Amazing how an encounter with serious surgery gives you a whole new perspective on what you can cope with. The only thing that is driving me mad is this damned sports bra. I bought the right one, just as recommended. I handed it to the nurse before surgery as requested and of course woke up in it, just as they told me I would. After a few days in it though, this thing is really cutting into me. I swear once I can finally take it off, I am going to burn the bloody thing!

I haven't dared look under the pads yet to see the scarring. The surgeon was so definite about the scars fading that I'm really hopeful – but I guess I won't know for sure until I see for myself.

I wonder whether the bank would have loaned me the money if I'd told them what it was for. What would they do if I defaulted? Come and take my boobs back?

She tried again – as if the hours since her last attempt might have changed its location. With the bread knife held directly underneath the door, she could lever open the kitchen wall unit, taking care not to over exert the traumatised muscles and swollen breast tissue that lay over the gel implants. As the cupboard door opened, she could see it once more. She cursed again its position. Why did it have to be at the back – furthest of all the items from her? It mocked her, that damned chicken! Should her relationship with the iconic logo survive at all, she vowed never to forget this darkest of days. She tested the angle again, lifting her right arm slowly to around eighty degrees. She would need at least a hundred and twenty to get into that cupboard and not only pick up the box of cornflakes, but withdraw it.

"You hard-hearted bastard!" she heard herself mutter. "You...you fuck! You fuck-fucker!" she cursed, turning away from the cupboard in bitter disappointment. It was Christmas Day and all over the country, people were preparing to tuck in to the biggest meal most of them would eat all year. For Lee however, there was only one taste for which she inexplicably yearned: It had to be Kellogg's bloody cornflakes in a bowl of ice-cold milk. Nothing could take the place in her desires, of a great golden pile of flakes, drenched in a soothing pool of whiteness. If only she had foreseen this, she could have made it all possible – simply by placing the box with the evil chicken logo, where a post-operative patient could actually reach the damned thing.

She could have just bought a new box. It was after all, what she went to the corner shop specifically for, just the day before. But the little store was sold out and no amount of staring at Rice Crispies could make them as enticing. Snap, Crackle and Pop would never usurp The Chicken.

She would have even called someone to help – had there been anyone to call. Dani and James were at his parents for Christmas and she couldn't call anyone else without revealing the fact that she'd had a surgical procedure she'd rather not discuss. She had even knocked on her neighbour's door – which would have been a hell of an introduction, given that they'd not previously met – But they were out, anyway.

Lee sneered at the bread bin, with its shallow promise of yet more toast. She might have to go that way, she knew – but not just yet.

A rare sound rang out from the hallway. She shuffled out to the cream BT-issue telephone that was mounted on the wall, thankfully within reach.

She picked up on the fifth ring after a slow, careful stretch, "Hello" she heard herself say a little wearily.

"Oh sure – and Merry Christmas to you, too" Philip called in a mocking tone.

Lee was pricked into remembering that she didn't want to appear in the least bit grumpy. "Yes, all right Merry Christmas. I'm only irritable because I just burned a finger on the stove as I was checking on lunch."

"What are you having?"

"Ah – a chicken?"

"Are you sure?"

"Well, it's what I really, really want."

"Uh, okay."

"How's your day been?" she asked, spinning the conversation.

"Oh, lovely – if a bit weird"

"Yep, that's you all right"

"No, I mean I went over to Louise's this morning to give Anne-Marie her big present…"

"The little piano thing?"

"Keyboard, yes. Thing is, Louise's partner, Pete? He was still there – well he would be – and yet I was there too and you know, everything was really…okay. There was no tension, no problem – just a little girl enjoying Christmas and three grown-ups enjoying the whole experience."

"Philip, that's really good" Lee said softly.

"Yes, it is" he agreed, in evident good humour, "Just as I said, a bit weird".

"So, you're having Anne-Marie tomorrow?"

"Yup, all Boxing Day and overnight. We're going to have Dad-Christmas."

"Is that like normal Christmas, but with some burned food and extra farting?"

"I always knew that Scrooge was really a woman."

"Humbug, peasant" Lee replied, grinning audibly.

Philip let a moment pass, "I want to come over."

"Oh, Philip…"

"Okay, okay – stupid idea. Forget I mentioned it…How about you come over here?"

"You know the deal."

"Yeah, but it's a dodgy deal"

"I know it is, but it's *our* dodgy deal" Lee reasoned.

"More yours to be absolutely fair" Philip offered in gentle protest. "Remind me why I agreed again?"

Lee giggled, "Because you're so grown up and so mature and you *so* want to be sensitive to my feelings and not press me into something more than I can manage."

"Yeah, that was it. Christ, what was I thinking of when I signed up to that?"

Lee ran a mental rule over the lie she'd used to buy this latest parcel of time. She'd admitted a couple of weeks before, to the prospect of some non-essential surgery, while declining to offer any further detail. "It would be lovely to see you" she conceded now, "just not so nice to be seen."

"I wish you'd let me be the judge of that."

"Merry Christmas, Philip – to you and to Annie."

"Merry Christmas, Lee" Philip conceded reluctantly. "I'll call you in a couple of days."

"That'd be nice" Lee agreed, gently settling the receiver back into its cradle. She sighed deeply and leaned back against the hallway wall. Her cheek felt the brush of the sleeve from her hanging overcoat. She idly wondered whether space or time would run out first as she struggled to out-dance Philip's moves. All the time he continued trying to step closer to her, she could still dream the dreams of normal women. The moment she had 'the conversation' with him, it would be over. Surely it would.

The last few days before Christmas had promised snow. Sleet had excited the media and had encouraged plenty of speculation, but in the end, there was nothing festive about the London sky at all. December was as it so often seemed to be, a blanket of grey ambivalence. At least that meant the weather wasn't too cold to sit for a while in the lawned relief of Brook Green. It had taken about ten minutes of slow careful steps to make Lee's bench of choice, over by the children's play area. Her hands were thrust deep into her coat pockets. She had managed before leaving, through a bizarre arrangement of kneeling by her bed and using pillows as supports to her elbows, to reach back and create a pony tail of her hair. She was thankful now as the later removal of tangled knots would almost certainly have been beyond her means.

It didn't really feel like Christmas at all to Lee. Not like Christmases of old. It had been an awfully long time since the last happy noel back at Priest Close. Perhaps her memories were coloured with a convenient tint of rose, but she could recall only smiles, laughter and warmth in that house. Mostly it would be just the two of them, eating for England and cackling through Morecambe & Wise, but there were plenty of 'drop-ins' too. One or two of Dad's workmates would always appear – usually bearing beer. The neighbours either side would call to exchange gifts and of course by late afternoon on the 25th, there would be Dani.

Moray Crescent by contrast, had been insane in the build up to festivities and then thankfully silent for a couple of days, during.

This year however, Lee felt nothing. 1986 had been almost too big. There was no room in it for any further sense of occasion. She drew in some moist air and snuggled her chin down into the soft wool of her scarf. Within moments, she saw the first child on a new bike. He was aged about four she guessed, and was closely being followed on foot by his father. The bike's chrome spokes flashed against the day's dullness. The frame was electric blue with orange darts. Lee could almost feel the little boy's wary excitement as he struggled to own his gift.

The sliver of park was otherwise empty, apart from a tall black woman dressed in a long leather coat. She walked solemnly, head down along the footpath in Lee's direction. There was something about the hair. It shouldn't really have taken so long for Lee to figure it out, "Miriam?" she called out.

Miriam looked up. Her thoughts had clearly been far away. It took a moment and then another before she appeared to understand the picture drawing into focus, "Blimey, Lee Habens?"

Lee rose and waited to greet her old friend warmly. Realising in time, she held Miriam's shoulders to prevent contact with her own torso. She felt obliged to explain, "I'd love to hug, but I've had…something done…here" she indicated, pointed to her chest.

"Oh" Miriam remarked a little concerned, before adding a second more knowing, "Ohhhh. So…*really?*"

Lee shrugged a 'yeah, really'

"You're…"

"I'm Lee" Lee confirmed, swerving further discussion. "But, how are you? You look great – love that coat!"

"Christmas present" Miriam mumbled.

She had lost weight, Lee noted – but in a good way. Her hair was similar to before, but shorter and somehow more stylish. "Wow, how long has it been?"

"Well, I suppose it's nearly…two years, since Grant…"

"I guess."

Miriam took Lee's hand and looked directly into her eyes "What you did – bringing the letter in person. I've always really appreciated that."

The subject needed changing again. "What brings you over this way?" Lee asked.

Miriam looked down at the bench, weighing up whether it was clean enough to sit in a new leather coat. She lowered herself down and Lee gratefully followed.

"Lloyd's Mum and Dad live just down the road from here. As I speak at…" she consulted her wristwatch, "2:45 in the afternoon, I am the only member of that household actually awake."

Lee grinned, "Big lunch?"

"Huge."

"Yeah, I remember those."

"So how about you? This is a fair way from Notting Hill."

"Ah yes, but it is just yards from where I live now" Lee explained, adding "I have a tiny flat around the corner from here."

"Are you sharing with anyone?" It was the kind of question Lee reflected, that only a Londoner could ask without it referring in any way to a relationship status.

"No. That's why it's tiny – there's only me paying the rent."

Miriam took in the quiet emptiness of Brook Green. "It's exciting, isn't it? I've come out here so as not to be part of the sleeping collective and there's barely another soul to be seen anywhere."

Lee laughed and turned to a profile she had enjoyed so often during their days of sharing a South Kensington office. "Are you still at CC, by any chance?"

"No, I've been working in Hammersmith for over a year now. I'm at the head office of a company you've never heard of. We make things you never need to think about."

"Nice" Lee nodded.

"You?"

"I'm still with the nightclubs, only I'm now a sort of PA to the boss."

"Oh, well that's pretty cool. Well done, you."

"Yep, life is not too bad" Lee conceded.

"And so, were those a Christmas present, by any chance?" Miriam asked, nodding toward the chest under which Lee had her arms protectively folded.

Lee laughed at the idea, "I suppose in a way, perhaps they are" she reflected. "I really didn't have to do this – and I still feel a bit odd about it."

"Odd, how?"

"Well it's not like the serious surgery. This wasn't a procedure that was going to change my life or define me in any way. It doesn't make me feel like a woman, but it does make me feel a bit more woman-*ly*, I suppose. Does that make any sense?"

Miriam smiled. "Didn't Grant teach us that life is too short to be unhappy with it? If this works for you then you go with it."

"It works for me" Lee nodded.

They both watched the boy on the blue bike as he reached a point of exhaustion and had to be lifted into the arms of a father who would now in time-honoured tradition, have to carry both child and bike back home.

"Too much for a little white boy" Miriam observed, para-catchphrasing herself.

Lee laughed warmly.

"What's your excuse for being out here then?" Miriam asked.

"Oh, I just wanted some air. I've spent a lot of time confined this year and I feel the walls moving in sometimes. It helps to be outside".

"You're not running away from anyone?"

"Nope – this is a solo Christmas"

"What's that like?"

"Weird, but not bad. I need the rest, anyway."

"Isn't there anyone for you to visit?"

Lee looked Miriam in the eye and smiled reassuringly, "I promise – I'm okay."

"Yeah, but all the same – at this time of year? There's no friends?"

"Not really. They're being couple-y and together. Which I must add, is absolutely fine."

"Family?"

Lee thought again of the note in the envelope, in the pass-port, in another envelope and in the box now in the cupboard. "Nowhere near here."

Miriam looked along a side street at nothing in particular. "I used to tell people that was why I never managed to see Grant again after he left London. You know, 'Too far away', I used to say. And then finally he *was* too far away."

"He understood though – and he was with people who also loved him."

Miriam sighed. "Yeah, but it was just miles, you know? If you think about it in terms of time, it was just hours. So, because I didn't spend some hours getting to him, I never saw him again. These days I don't let spending a few hours cost me anything more valuable."

Lee reached across and covered Miriam's chilled hand with her own pocket-warmed palm, "He had no time for regret – and he was certainly right about that."

Miriam smiled broadly, though still with a trace of sadness, "Ah well…" she said standing, prompting Lee to carefully do the same, "I've got to get back – Lloyd's Dad has a tendency to set fire to the Christmas pudding. They lost a tablecloth last year."

"There you are, always making sense of things" Lee smiled.

It's really nice to see you, Lee. Merry Christmas to you." They kissed each other's cheek. There was fumbling for a pen and paper to exchange numbers. Neither had either. Miriam told Lee the name of her company and they both hoped she'd remember it. Lee thought for a moment of asking her old colleague to come home with her to help get something down from a high shelf. Instead, she finally let her Chicken dreams go. "Merry Christmas, Miriam."

Lee took a long and very bubbly bath that night – a reward for another session of bed-bound vaginal dilation. The process had become such a grind that Lee had taken to creating tiny self-rewards to incentivise her efforts. Tonight's bath was just such a treat. A quarter of an hour on her back, staring at the bedroom ceiling while she pushed unforgiving shafts into herself, would be countered by twice that time lying in a cloud of lavender bubbles, surrounded by half a dozen candles.

There was just one other promise to draw her bath-ward. Immersion in water was the only circumstance under which her surgeon had conceded brief removal of the hated sports bra. Lee had unhooked it gingerly, almost having to extract the straps from her flesh. She spied her second bra hanging from the bathroom doorknob, just waiting to begin its first shift of torture – but first some sweet, if brief ecstasy. She would like to have had a good look at her chest, but she was wise enough in matters of surgery to know that it wouldn't necessarily tell her much, so soon after a procedure. The bathroom mirror was too steamed to offer her an image, anyway. She was once more taken by the sheer weight of her new breasts. They weren't particularly large – she had been very clear about keeping her body in proportion – and yet, looking down on them from above, they did rather seem to stick out in a surprising way. They were held much higher than was natural. She recognised that their final shape was months away from being settled and that she was after all, comparing the sight of her chest now to a lifetime of featureless flatness.

She stepped into the bubbles, and sat cautiously, holding her breath. She lay back slowly, letting her skin adjust inch by inch to the just-slightly-too-warm water. She had pinned up her hair as best she could reach and had found just the right volume for Radio 1. Finally, she relaxed and let out an audible groan.

She was close to a decision on the tin box. Miriam had almost taken her there, but still she needed to speak with someone she could trust to be informed and yet completely objective. She needed the only other soul who had known both child and father. She needed Dani.

"Oh, my fucking God!"

"And a Happy New Year to you, too" Lee replied.

Dani's open-mouthed stare was still fixed to a point about eighteen inches south of Lee's eyes. "You really did do it, didn't you?"

"I really did, yes" Lee grinned, handing over her coat. She was wearing a dark purple silk blouse which hung loosely, over a pair of black jeans.

Dani squealed and made to hug her friend as would be their custom. Lee's arms reflexively moved to protect her chest.

"Ooh sorry! Of course" Dani shrank back with a grimace and instead offered a hand.

Lee took it and shook it formally, the two of them laughing at the ridiculous gesture, "You should have seen me on the way over here. I was edging along walls everywhere I went. You don't realise how often you bump into things – until you can't *afford* to bump into things."

Ealing still felt rather alien to Lee. It was like a separate town on its own with an old fashioned high street. Dani and James' Edwardian end terraced house certainly appeared more lived-in on this visit than on either of Lee previous trips. The walls all now wore paint and occasional lamps gave the small living room a warmth that spoke more of home and less of strained rent payments. Lee especially liked the bare floorboards which had been treated and stained. "This place looks so lovely now. You must be really happy with it?"

Dani looked up and around the room. "If the central heating will just see us through the winter without too much discomfort, we'll be fine" she nodded thoughtfully. "Come and join me in the kitchen – it's the warmest place, anyway."

Lee smiled to herself at how easily Dani moved around the first space to have been truly a home of her own. She recognised a familiar but unspoken delight.

Along the hallway, the extended kitchen was still in an earlier stage of development. Patches of test colours – mostly mints and off-whites – had been painted onto the walls. The cupboard units belonged to the 1960s and were Lee imagined, not likely to play a part in future plans.

Dani wanted to catch up on 'Boob News', while Lee was more inclined to learn about the house. They entertained each other for an hour over hisses of steam and occasional oven inspections. The first bottle of red brought by Lee, had easily been consumed by the time they sat down to dinner.

"What time will James be back?"

"Not sure" Dani placed a large salad bowl between her own place and that of her guest. "To be honest, I'm staggered he made it out at all. We didn't get home until three this morning."

"Where was it you went?"

"Well that was the official Rugby Club New Year's Eve thing last night and tonight it's just the players on their *unofficial* crawl around Ealing."

Lee had a mental image of twenty huge men completely dominating any room they entered. Exactly the type of crowd that used to terrify her and now would likely present nothing more than a nuisance.

"So, you didn't do anything for New Year's Eve?"

Lee swallowed her first forkful of mushroom risotto, "I didn't want to risk it. Big crowds, lots of hugging…"

"Right – I get it. Not a good idea."

"It'll be a better idea for new year 1987"

"– And before, I hope. Speaking of which, have you heard from Philip?" Dani enquired, fighting a sideways smile.

Lee grinned back. "We've spoken on the phone several times" she admitted. "It's a bloody nightmare trying to think of excuses *not* to see him."

"Do you *really* have to avoid him?" Dani reasoned.

"Well it's kind of the same problem – he's a tight-hug, kind of guy."

Dani shook her head. "How many times have you gone out with him now?"

Lee shrugged, "Four"

"And still nothing physical has happened?"

"*Dani!*" Lee pleaded, "I just can't."

"Er – I think you can!"

"Well, yes I could"

"You do really like him"

"I know"

"And he really likes you"

"I know that too"

"And it would be really good"

"I pigging *know*!" Lee grinned, with a cheek full of rice. She took another sip of red. "Look, it can't possibly work – I *know* it can't. He would never cope with the truth about me and God knows, he's too nice for me to wish it on him, anyway."

Dani tonged some rocket onto her plate, "What does *that* mean? After all you've been through, you can't possibly be ashamed of what you are. That can't be what all of this leads to. You deserve the same things as anyone else – and that includes being loved."

"*Because*, like I said, if I do tell him, I just know he won't be able to handle it."

"Well if you're going to go around making up people's minds for them…"

Lee smiled, popping a couple of folded leaves into her mouth, "Yes I am. I am going to do exactly that, thank you."

Dani shook her head in frustration bordering on amusement, "So if you're not going to have a thing with him and you won't let him sleep with you, what *are* you going to do with him?"

"Oh, I don't know. I just don't want the feelings I have for him to go away just yet. It's still so lovely and new. Maybe after a while, we'll just be…friends."

Dani choked on her wine and laughed loudly, "Oh *sure* you will! *That's* why he calls you every night and turns up where you work hoping to see you. He's just *desperate* to be friends!"

Lee was laughing too and then a sigh brought the amusement to a close. "I don't know. I do really like him. He's funny and he gets me and he loves his daughter and he's really…"

"What?"

"Tall" she sighed.

Dani sniggered again.

"What? It matters to me!" Lee protested through her own giggles.

This time Dani soothed them both back to sense, "You need to either be honest with him or just stop leading him on. If you're not going to let anything happen, you'll just end up hurting both of you."

"I know" Lee agreed. "I am going to talk to him – just not quite yet. I just want him in my life a little bit longer."

They finished dinner and carried the dishes out to the kitchen. Dani then showed off the work she and James had completed upstairs. The main bedroom had been decorated from a palette of creams with occasional deep, dark browns – including the colouring applied to the room's original Edwardian fireplace.

They passed Lee's bag on their return to the living room. The corner of a manila envelope offered itself. Lee gently lowered herself into an armchair while Dani took the opportunity to unveil James' pride and joy – a CD player. She put on some Simple Minds, grabbed a throw and curled herself onto the sofa.

"You two are so fabulously middle class" Lee observed, wryly.

Dani threw her head back and sighed, smiling at the idea, the way she often would after being generously wined. Miles were being mentally measured, all the way from Sittingbourne.

"Listen, I really wanted to get your opinion on something."

"Okay" Dani nodded, still smiling.

Lee opened the envelope and removed the contents.

"What's that?"

"This, is Dad's last passport. I've had his old tin box ever since Priest Close and there are all sorts of family documents in it, not least of which is my birth certificate – a piece of paper which now by the way, makes no sense at all."

Dani snorted and poured the last of bottle number two into their glasses.

"Thing is" Lee continued, I was looking through these just after I moved into Moray Crescent and this fell out."

Dani took the little envelope from Lee's hand and inspected the slip of paper within, "That looks Spanish" she declared.

"Mmm" Lee concurred, through a generous sip of wine.

"*Constantina – Sevilla*" she read in an exaggerated accent, "An address?"

"It's a small town – a village really."

"Okay" Dani said looking up with a quizzical expression.

"So, I need to know what this means" Lee stated, matter-of-factly.

"No idea..."

"I mean, I didn't even know Dad *had* a current passport. He hadn't been out of the country since our last family holiday"

"Shit! *You* all went to Spain, didn't you?"

Lee nodded.

"But you didn't go to Seville. You went to..."

"We were near Malaga – for the beaches. But Mum had friends out there. They came across to see us."

"You remember that?"

"Not exactly – I don't remember much of anything of that holiday – I think I just lived in a swimming pool. But there was a night a few years ago that Dad almost opened up. He was feeling pretty down and he'd had a drink"

"God – I don't remember your Dad ever having *too* much to drink."

"Exactly – he would only ever have more than one beer if it was a special occasion. Anyway, I remember it was years back and it's killing me that I can't put together what he was saying, but I know he talked about how if only 'they' hadn't come over from – and then I just can't remember where it was they actually *were* from."

Dani lit a JPS and exhaled a steady stream of mist to her side. She pointed her cigarette-bearing fingers toward Lee, "You think this is where your Mum is" she divined triumphantly.

Lee shrugged, as if to ask 'well don't you?'

Dani was looking again at the piece of paper, "It's a bit of a stretch, Lee."

"I know" Lee agreed. "So as the only other person in this world who really knew my Dad, I want you to come up with a theory – anything at all – to help me to figure out why else he would have this tucked away inside his passport, along with his most important papers." She placed the manila envelope with the passport on top, in front of Dani and waited for a response.

Dani looked at the ensemble. She was a while in looking up. When she did so, it was straight into Lee eyes. "You really *do* think this is where your Mum is."

Lee shrugged once more and this time shook her head for good measure, "Christ, I don't know. Maybe it's where she once was, but isn't now. Maybe it's just a trail. Maybe it's just an address. God Dani, I don't know what it is. But don't you think that for a man with no other earthly connection to that entire country, that it's just a little bit likely that this has something to do with the woman who led us there all those years ago and then disappeared from our lives not long after we returned?"

Dani was shaking her head, "Bloody hell, Lee…"

"I mean c'mon – Dad never even mentioned Spain by name in my presence!" Lee's voice was rising in tone and volume, "... and yet he has a *specific* address which he keeps in the safest most private place he has."

Dani gently returned everything to the larger envelope and handed it back to her friend. "One question"

"Just one?"

"Why didn't your Dad ever tell you about this himself?"

february 1987
eyes wide open and looking the other way

···

*I*bought 6 bras today. That's not a line I imagine I'll ever write again.

    It surprises me that I am still intimidated by shopping for underwear. I was thinking hard about it on the walk home and I think it's because my brain can still remember being effectively barred from those kinds of places. I grew up with a 'persona non-grata' status and wasn't even supposed to look into certain shop windows for fear of being thought weird. Now that I'm a welcome customer, I still can't quite shake the feeling of guilt. If I was still seeing Dr Garner, I'd be tempted to bring that up. Or maybe I wouldn't.

    I did finally get rid of the two sports bras. I tried burning them in the car park at the back of the flats. I couldn't get the first one to light properly at all – it just sort of singed and smoked for a while. I was also being stared at from a nearby window and so I gave up on the idea and just binned them instead. I'm just glad I'll never have to suffer that kind of misery again. The surgeon said he was very pleased with the results – and so of course, am I!

    I have found that I can't get comfortable sleeping on my front. That's the problem with breast implants – unlike natural tissue, they have nowhere to go when you 'squish' them. So I'll sleep on my side or back.

    But at least I now have a chest that doesn't look like a 12-year old's! I imagine at some point, I'll relax about having boobs and will feel okay about them in public. Right now, I actually just want to cover them up. I wonder if a part of me is still feeling a bit guilty about having them at all. Thankfully for me, the winter will last a while yet and so I still have time to figure that out.

. . . .

They were already calling it the coldest start to a year since 1963. Lee had to concur – even though she didn't actually remember much of anything about '63. The frozen Serpentine in front of them was proof enough of the extreme conditions. They stared out to where silver ice ended and inky water began. The ducks Annie had been anxious to see, paddled and flapped where they could still move freely. Getting close enough to feed them clearly wouldn't be possible.

"Sorry about that, Annie" Lee soothed, bending down to see the girl's expression.

Philip's daughter was looking concerned, "Are you sure they're all right?" she asked quietly from under a white woollen hat.

"All right?" Philip asked in exaggerated exasperation "*All right?* Listen, they love this kind of weather. The park people give them extra rations!"

"But don't they get cold?"

"Nope, they're absolutely fine. They don't feel the cold the way you do – that's why they don't have hats or coats"

"Da-ad" Annie complained, giving her father a shove.

"What? Seriously, nobody designs decent duck gear anymore."

Lee leant close to Philip's ear, "If you'd relied on that kind of humour when we met, I'd be somewhere warm right now."

Annie had asked to see ducks when they'd come out of the Natural History Museum – apparently, she'd always liked feeding them. Now that ducks and the outside in general were going to be of limited interest however, they'd have time for one more Saturday activity.

"Movies? I think there's a Disney film on at Marble Arch" Philip tried.

Annie looked unimpressed "I'm not a baby, Dad"

"Well we sort of need to do something that doesn't involve being out in sub-zero temperatures. Your Mum will kill me if you get a cold."

Lee thought she'd take a swing, "*Selfridges?*" she offered

"What?" Philip answered slightly incredulous.

"Mega!" Annie shouted.

"What?" Philip repeated, his pitch having been raised an octave or two.

Lee grinned and shrugged. "Bullseye" she muttered to herself.

They'd dropped Philip after about fifty feet of department store. He asked if he could wait for them in the restaurant. Lee had thought about saying 'no' just for the hell of it, but she was so flattered by Annie volunteering a chirpy 'sure – we can come and get you later', that she simply went with the moment.

As soon as Philip had disappeared from sight in search of a cup of tea, Lee crouched down to go eye-to-eye with her charge. "Okay Annie, here are the ground rules: you get to try on anything you like, but we don't buy it unless your Mum would approve. I'm new at this and I can't afford to be killed. Deal?"

Annie studied Lee's outstretched gloveless hand pensively for a moment – and then took it, "Deal!" she said, smiling widely.

Lee felt that Annie had been pretty easy on her, all things considered. She'd probably tried on less than a dozen outfits – Lee lost count. They spent another fifteen minutes looking at shoes. In the end, Annie admitted that she really would quite like the red boots she'd seen as soon as they'd entered the department. Lee agreed that they could be smuggled under the radar as a present from Dad and she'd be sure to get the money from him later.

At the store restaurant, they ordered milkshakes and released a grateful Philip to run for the bathroom, (theirs had been a two-cups-of-tea-absence).

Lee watched Annie as she focused on the straw that had drilled deep into the whipped cream floe of her strawberry special. She wondered again what the little girl's mother, looked like. The daughter Philip and Louise had created was certainly every bit as pretty as the pictures in Philip's wallet. She was bright and beautifully mannered, too. The break-up of her parents' marriage had clearly been managed with care. This was about as well-adjusted a nine-year old as Lee could hope to have met. A nerve-wracking prospect had become a very easy experience. Lee found it odd to realise that Annie was the only child she actually knew to speak to. None of her friends were yet parents – not even the straight ones. Today she'd had a day full of what her child-free world had been missing – and she suspected the feeling would sting later.

"I've really enjoyed meeting you today" said Lee. "You're a pleasure to know."

Annie reflected and then replied, "You're nice, too." Before adding, "You make my Dad laugh."

"I know – and I can even do that without meaning to."

"Are you going to be friends for a long time?"

"I really hope we are, yes" Lee answered easily. She very much liked thinking of herself and Philip as a 'we'.

Lee was dropped off first by the cab. Inside her front door, she cast aside the day's clothing, ran a bath and within fifteen minutes was once more offering up the trials of the day to candlelight and some overpriced bath cream that *Selfridges* had somehow made feel like a sensible investment.

Annie's presence as expected, could still be keenly felt. Lee thought again about children in general. She realised that she'd never really observed a parent and child relationship close-up. She had no experience of the closeness she'd witnessed first-hand between Philip and his daughter. There was rarely a moment when there hadn't been physical contact between them. Hand-holding, hugging, teasing – and it was all so very easy. So very natural. There were things father and daughter knew about each other instinctively – after all, they'd known each other for every moment of the little girl's life. They gave each other so much of their identity. *Of course*, Philip was a father – it made perfect sense now. He *should* be one. It fitted him perfectly. And of course, Annie had taken so much of her manner and outlook from the man who adored her. There was something utterly unbreakable and so beautifully reliable about the relationship she'd witnessed that day. She could draw on her own childhood perspective of course, but to get a glimpse of a parent's angle and to imagine how extraordinarily precious a child must feel, was overwhelming. She wondered at how parents managed to contain the kind of soul-filling love that their children brought and at how terrifying must be the risk of loss.

It suddenly struck Lee that she herself, was running the risk of becoming a child's disappearing adult. What if she did become a fixture in Annie's world only for the obvious to go wrong with Philip? After the awfulness of being a child deserted by a mother, could she really stand to be thought of as a small-time deserter herself?

It was almost a week before Lee saw Philip again. His company was opening new offices in Bristol and he'd been required to spend several days ensuring that the workforce and systems were properly served with computers and connected to the rest of the operation. They had spoken on the phone several times, Philip calling from his hotel. She missed thinking of him as being close by.

Mrs Macintyre had generously allowed her PA to head for Paddington in the middle of Friday afternoon, given that the office was comparatively quiet. The gesture was typical of the relationship they had developed. They both knew Lee would make up time the following week.

Dressing casually in the office that day had also been permitted. She wouldn't even have been allowed into the club looking the way she did, but she'd earned an appreciative smile from Mrs Macintyre when she'd arrived in a leather jacket with over-bleached blue jeans, neatly slit at the knees and held waist high with a wide black belt. 'Very Bananarama', she'd been told.

Lee's train pulled into Temple Meads Station just as the Bristol rush hour was heading out. She adjusted the headphones on her new Walkman and headed along the platform enjoying the sight of commuters unknowingly stepping and reaching to Steve Winwood's *Higher Love*. Philip had faxed a map of the hotel location and she chose to walk.

Being outside of London was still a very rare experience for Lee. Even another English city felt different to the place she'd made home. London made her feel closer to the cultural sun than anywhere else. Leaving it behind was to fear a chill. She'd heard good things about Bristol however – and anyway, it was Friday night. Time to be positive.

The hotel lobby was impressive enough to make Lee feel underdressed during the check-in. Philip had given her his room number so that she could call once settled in. "This all feels somehow…secretive" she confessed sitting on the side of a comfortable king size in her third-floor room.

Philip from 116 understood completely, "I know. Good, isn't it?"

"Is it childish to admit to feeling excited about being here?"

"Yes"

"Are you excited too?"

"Yes, but I got mistaken for a grown-up in reception so I can't show it."

Lee sighed and lay back across the scatter cushions at the pillow end "Thanks for suggesting this. I haven't done many things in life that feel decadent, but I'm pretty sure this qualifies."

"Well good for you. I'm really glad you came. Y'know I have to go and finish checking a couple of things before I quit work mode for this week. See you in reception at eight?"

"Absolutely." Lee heard the line click and closed her eyes. Once again, she sensed the acceleration of her own life. She wasn't sure that she was honouring these moments sufficiently. She turned her head to the side and sampled her surroundings. She had worried a little that echoes of another hotel room on a faraway coast might reach through time to sicken and distress her. But Jeremy Lancing wasn't in this room and she felt absolutely sure he never had been. This one felt fresh and clean and sophisticated. It had a subtle colour scheme of creams and purples. She liked it. She liked the bathroom too and she was keen to make the most of it. Lee guessed it couldn't be real marble, but it looked impressive enough. The bath and sink surrounds were in white, veined with dark green.

Her little bathroom at home would have fitted into this one twice. She had short of two hours to get ready – just about enough time. She showered in soft, white jets of warm water and felt refreshed and bright as she padded back into the bedroom, wrapped in a large bath sheet. She could of course, have spent her time resting and simply changed clothes for the evening. However, the sense of event would be lost if she weren't to begin her preparations from scratch. She moisturised and added foundation before mouss-ing and drying her hair (largely upside down and with the aid of her new best friend – a hair dryer diffuser). She used her fingers to 'scrunch' the root ends and by the time she straightened to a standing position and flicked her hair back, she was staring at the mirrored reflection of a huge lion-like mane. "Fu-uck!" she saw herself whisper. After a little comb-calming and some time for gravity to kick in, Lee's hair took on a more reasonable volume. She worked on her eyes next, including a smoky eyeliner effect that she'd learned from Rikki. She would leave her lips until it was time to head downstairs.

She went back to the bathroom where the longer length mirror had now cleared of steam. She stared at her glass sister and took in a deep breath, before commencing with the time-honoured prac-tice of critical judgement.

She started at the top, because she always had done – and because she could save the best until last. Her hair was longer than ever now. When she pushed it behind her, it reached past her shoulders and down to where her bra strap tended to be. Its condition was pretty good and Elaine had introduced some more highlights a week or so before. Her eyes – always in her own opinion, her best feature – now had a context in which to fea-ture. Under narrowed and styled brows, they now looked out *with* life instead of just at it. She still didn't love that bony nose – and never would, but at least some of her face was more comfortable to own. Her high cheekbones had indeed proved helpful. The more recent softness of the cheeks that overlaid them had created femi-nine flanks to her face when she spoke, curving to crescents either side of her mouth. Her jawline had softened too – just the way

Dr Garner always told her it would. Her face was long, yes – but somehow, not too long. Her eyes fell to her shoulders. They were still skinny and they still protruded somewhat, but on a rare day when she would have the confidence to wear something strappy, she had discovered that skinny shoulders were exactly what was needed. Her breasts were now the source of the longest stare and the closest inspection. Perhaps it was because they were still the newest part of her – or that the inner conflict over them would continue for a while yet. Aesthetically at least, she couldn't help but enjoy the sight of them. They were full and round and definitively female – at least in appearance, if not entirely in substance. They were still borne a little too high on her chest and they were slightly too far apart for her liking, exposing a wider sternum that she might have preferred. She understood that over time her skin and muscles would accept the presence of these new forms within her. A final shape was still being negotiated. The trace of scar around the bottom crescent of each areola was disappearing by the day. The darkened discs of skin themselves were now she estimated, four times the size they'd been on the male version of her chest. Across her torso there were other improvements too. Where previously there had been red patches, visible tendons and veins, there was now more consistency – a soft smoothness. Her ribs stuck out less than they once had. Her entire body it seemed, had accepted an additional layer of soft tissue. She knew herself to be about nine pounds in weight heavier than her lightest male form. Her bottom had changed shape somewhat and the contour of flesh continued around her hips and upper thighs. She could not by any means, be described as 'curvy' – but *curvier*? Sure. And then there was the place where the thing once lived. She couldn't see it now – either in her reflection or her memory. There were no traces, no suggestions and no need to ever fear or be disgusted by its presence again.

She drew back her focus and looked again at the entire picture. Was she a woman, in body? The image of her being would be for others to interpret. For her own part, she believed in the person she could see. Moreover, she *felt* like the person she could see – and to be one with the picture in front of her was at least to know a peace that had been worth pursuing. Lee Habens really was an awfully long way from where she'd started – and more than just the scenery had changed.

She'd found the black dress in a shop on Church Street, Ken. It was lycra, quite fitted, just below knee length and unusual because of its long sleeves. Lee had to remove the shoulder pads which were delivering a rather unfeasible upper proportion, but having made the adjustment, she really liked the line of it over her black tights and medium heel courts.

Returning once more to the bathroom mirror, she had one last check. She hadn't brought any other wardrobe options, so this was going to have to do, regardless. But she looked better she felt sure, than just passable. She checked the contents of her clutch bag for necessaries. She'd promised herself – and Dani of course – that she wouldn't allow her relationship with Philip to become sexual without telling him what she felt he needed to know. But she had no definite plans to tell him this night and yet still she would meet him carrying a bag in which she had secreted a condom and a small tube of lubricant. She was going into this evening with her eyes wide open – even if she might have to look the other way a little. She closed the bag, twisting the gold clasp shut. It would be academic anyway, she reminded herself. Nothing would happen.

Leaving her hotel room was a little unnerving. She shared the lift ride to the lobby with two young women dressed in outfits somewhat less conservative than her own. Again, she felt vulnerable to the attentions of non-Londoners. Standards once more felt so much more rigid to her. She could not afford to be unacceptable here. She exchanged small smiles with her fellow passengers, but still felt scrutinised to a level she wasn't sure she could stand. Perhaps it was just the close quarters of the lift, she thought upon landing. Perhaps every woman felt that way. She made a mental note to quiz Dani about it.

Lee took a seat in the lobby area. Standing alone in a public area is to be so much more conspicuous as a woman than as a man. Philip didn't keep her waiting for long. He appeared in black Armani, worn with a plain white shirt and a red silk tie. She noticed a white pinstriped lining as he raised an arm toward her in greeting.

"Wow!" Philip said as he covered the last yard between them.

"Well thank you, kind sir", Lee beamed. She shared a two-second kiss with her greeter, "I'll take that in the positive spirit you may or may not have meant – and may I add, you look very elegant."

"Yes, Nursey packed a bag for me."

Outside, Bristol's city centre was already thronged with early revellers. They made their way along a street flanked entirely it seemed, by restaurants, pubs and clubs. The unsociable certainly had no business there. There was more neon on show than felt decently English. Lee liked the pulse of it though. It was more compressed than London and therefore more co-ordinated. The people who headed to the centre of the city all had the singular aim of celebrating the beginning of a weekend. This she felt, did not have the appearance of a place one should pass through on the way to somewhere else.

"So how has your week here been?" Lee managed while concentrating hard on matching Philip's long-legged stride and keeping her narrow heels out of the paving cracks.

"It's been pretty good really. I quite like it here."

"You do?"

"Maybe it's just change being as good as a rest. I just found myself thinking that there we are in London believing it's the centre of the universe and we don't really think about what might be beyond. Here, they've got access to so much. You can be in Cornwall in a couple of hours – or Wales. You know, in the not so distant future, *where* you are won't really matter for most businesses. We'll be able to live where we want and still have the jobs we want. Remind me to bore you sometime about Information Superhighways"

"Okay. And how bad will I have to have been to deserve that kind of punishment?" Lee asked, biting her bottom lip and focusing once more on her footfalls.

"Yeah, actually, you *would* have to be pretty bad" he conceded, taking a right along a pedestrianised street and heading for a dark glass-fronted venue. It had a French name that Lee didn't have time enough to study.

Philip held open the door "I'm not up with French socio-politics, would the term Mademoiselle still be okay to use?"

"For me?"

"Yeah."

"Probably only the once."

They ate lightly – but sank rather a lot of white wine. Philip elaborated on his week, telling of places he'd visited – including an evening in Bath, a place Lee had already connected to Dani. After an hour, Lee checked to find that the tip of her nose had begun to develop a familiar numbness. She knew well that the sensation heralded a significantly more relaxed state. She would find it easier to speak now.

"So, listen" she began, taking a deep breath, "I'm going to tell you a really short version of a story about a woman I've never really known and a time I don't properly remember. At the end of it I'm going to ask your advice about whether I should do something I've already made up my mind to do."

"Okay" Philip acknowledged with a furrowed brow, "But just remember, I have the Information Superhighways thing still in my back pocket"

Lee laughed, "All right – I will try not to deserve that."

She had to be selective of course. Philip still hadn't heard very much about Dad and nothing at all about her mother. She edited huge gaping holes from her own story. It wasn't too difficult for Lee to avoid being gender-specific about her past. She had after all, always referred to her young self as 'child' rather than anything more incriminating.

"So, you have a piece of paper with an address in Spanish?"

"Right."

"You once went to Spain as a family?"

"We did."

"Long time ago."

"It was."

"So now you're going to get on a plane and turn up at the address on the piece of paper?"

"I am."

"This makes some kind of sense to you?"

Lee shrugged an expression of helplessness, "I don't know. I just have to do it."

Philip was thoughtful for a moment. "What do you honestly expect to find there?"

Lee took a long kiss of Chardonnay, "Your parents still live where you grew up, don't they?"

"Yeah, I think they probably always will."

"So, when you think of them and their house, you have a real sense of where you came from, where home really is."

Philip nodded.

"Well I don't really have that anymore. Since I left Sittingbourne, I have no real feeling for places I should centre myself or to where I should feel a sense of...connection."

"You know that you could get there and find that there's nothing – just an empty space."

"It's a risk."

"Or maybe there is still a place there – at which are some confused Spanish people, unrelated to you in any way."

"That" Lee accepted, "is precisely what I'm expecting."

Philip leaned an elbow on the crisp, white tablecloth between them, "Do you think you'd even know her if you saw her?"

Lee smiled, "I'd know her" she assured him, "but I'm pretty sure she wouldn't know me."

The familiar bass boom as they entered the club, relaxed Lee's shoulders. She was in a world she understood – that is, apart from the entrance protocol. Philip was charged a fee while Lee was ushered past the pay desk for free. It was she realised, another of so many 'firsts' – and she wasn't entirely comfortable with the idea. Was it really a compliment – a genuine appreciation of femininity? Or did it mean that she just didn't weigh-in as much as a 'proper' customer? Philip had insisted on paying for dinner and so Lee had countered by claiming the right to foot all expenses in the club. This included covering Philip's entry fee and so normality was at least informally, restored.

Inside, the club was lighter than *Oasis*. The walls had been painted in bright pastels and white scanners permanently patrolled the dancefloor borders. Lee took an early interest in the bars and the expressions of the staff. She wondered if she'd looked that poker-faced when on duty. She ordered a Sol for Philip while she continued to walk the dry white line. They were still relatively early and so managed to find a booth near the main floor area.

Philip sidled over to Lee, if only to ensure that they could hear each other, "What do you think?"

Lee smiled, "I think I'm getting old" she called back, "It's the music – it's changing – getting more frenetic and...computerised" She thought for a moment before adding "No offence."

"Taken – and you *do* sound disapproving"

She shrugged. "It's just change. You can't stop it. I can see how people love it and respond to it, but personally, it's not my thing"

"Why's that? Too loud for you? Can't hear the words?" Philip grinned, raising an eyebrow.

Lee brightened, "Oh, I'm just impressed that you're still getting out and about at all, at your age" she countered.

"I'll have you know I'm quite the mover!" Philip protested.

Lee smiled sceptically as synth drums heralded Madonna's *Open Your Heart*. Video screens in darkened corners began to show the promo film in sync with the music – another development of which Lee had her doubts. Nonetheless, she pointed to the dancefloor and raised an eyebrow of her own.

Facades loosened by wine and with no-one to impress but each other, they moved with freedom and pure enjoyment – especially Philip who took to occasional echoes of Madonna's own televised moves.

Being away from London was liberating Lee from herself. Or was Philip doing that?

Dances and drinks alternated. As the temperature rose, Philip's jacket stopped visiting the dancefloor and Lee was left to rue her own choice of long sleeves. They fell into each other's arms just before 2:00am, just as Phyllis Nelson implored them to *Move Closer*. They obliged in a dance that felt more intimate than anything they'd ever done before. Lee realised that since they'd been spending time together, a great many of their previous hugs had been from inside separate overcoats. There certainly hadn't previously been the same heat and intensity, the same undercurrent of sexual possibilities.

"I always have a great time when I'm with you" Philip said, leaning back a little so that he could speak to Lee's face.

"Really? How do you manage that?"

"Well cocaine mostly, of course."

A smiling kiss brought their slow dance to a full stop.

She'd imagined that she'd feel a little more sober once outside the club and exposed to the cool night air. Both of them however, had weaved arm in arm, the entire way back to the hotel.

As they arrived at the foyer lift doors, Philip took Lee's hand, "Can I see you back to your room, Madam?"

Lee looked him in the eye, "Do you know, I think you'd better. I can't actually remember where it is."

Philip frowned.

"What? I've only been there once" Lee protested.

"You have a key?"

Lee foraged in her clutch bag for the grey plastic tag she'd been handed at reception. Her fingers were still numb from cold and alcohol, "You mean this thing?" she said, holding up a neatly wrapped condom.

"Um, no" Philip checked, straining to focus in the subdued lobby lighting, "That opens something else – at least on occasion."

Lee groaned as she realised her mistake. "Oh dear. Can you pretend that didn't happen?"

"Oh, I'm brilliant at pretending things haven't happened. I'm the bloody world champion of *that*" he slurred slightly, grinning to himself.

The third floor was quiet and the couple made their way along the corridor in silence – until they got to Lee's door. Somehow the sight of each other trying so hard to concentrate, made them splutter into snigger fits. Lee tried anxiously to get her key tag to work. It steadfastly refused. Philip took it in a let-the-professional-take-charge manner – and summarily failed himself, inspiring strangled squeals and giggles. Somehow, the warmth of the corridor seemed to be giving the alcohol in their systems a second kick. Lee recovered the tag and tapped it on the door frame before finally triggering a mechanical whir and click.

Lee had left on the bathroom light. Had she not done so, it's unlikely they would have made it to the bed on their first attempt. As it was, they both fell onto the mattress at the same time.

Lee's hair, so carefully arranged just hours ago, tumbled across her face. "And now, I am blind…" she mumbled.

"Oh, bad luck" Philip breathed, turning onto his back. He laughed hoarsely, "Christ, I'm fucked."

"Yup" Lee agreed, weaving her way closer to Philip, "It's all the fuck they put in those drinks." She sighed deeply, brushed away her tresses and stared up at the ceiling, "God, I hope this really *is* my room."

Both of them were laughing lustily at the idea – until they were kissing. And then nothing mattered, but kissing.

For Lee, the world was in freefall – and right through her. She had been so terribly confused before about which way to take things with Philip. She still hadn't answered any of her own questions – but her body was taking charge in a way she'd never known. Her priorities were suddenly primal. She couldn't even hear her own conscience anymore.

There was an urgency about the way they kissed each other, as if trying to repay the debts of missed moments. She was suddenly desperate for closeness; to feel nothing between them but their own skins. She could hear them both breathing hard and yet couldn't be sure which gasps were her own. His hands coursed down along her hip as she sent her own fingers up over his back and shoulder.

Suddenly a moment of reason invaded, "Wait, wait" Lee breathed. She needed a moment. She needed to figure out which way was up. Her eyes adjusted to the gloom. She rolled herself upright and headed toward the bathroom. Closing the door quietly behind her she quickly undressed, flinging clothes up over the shower rail.

"If you've left the building, I will...feel very silly" came Philip's uncertain call from the bed.

Lee heard her own laugh bouncing back at her from the bathroom tiles. "Give a girl a minute, will you!" she called back. She found her tube of lubricant and gently slid some of the cold gel into herself. She straightened and saw again her naked figure in the mirror. She picked up a fresh white towel and wrapped herself in it before turning back once more to her image. "Do you really know what you're doing?" whispered the woman in the glass. Lee turned out the light, vanishing her sister from view with a defiant click.

Philip was sitting up on the bed, his own composure somewhat restored, "Well, I won't lie – I would have had no idea how to get that dress off you"

Lee smiled, standing just a yard away from him, "There are at least a dozen cheap answers to that, but I'm not supposed to know any of them." Her expression straightened and then moved to one of uncertainty. "Honestly, I suppose I hoped we'd get here and yet I didn't know how I would deal with it."

Philip shook his head a little and started to say something without seeming to know quite what.

Lee continued instead, "I haven't been with anyone in a long time – and I know that you don't take these things lightly either. I suppose I just want to know that you're sure – because if you're not..."

Philip stood and moved to Lee. He brushed her hair back behind her shoulders and kissed her softly, just for a moment. "Well *I've* wanted to be here since I first met you – and for what it's worth, I'm not even sure where exactly we are."

Lee grinned, "Just shut up". She felt Philip press against her. They both sank again to the bed, Lee's towel falling away behind her. As they lay side by side, Lee watched Philip's eyes through the half-darkness. She searched for any hesitation, any sign of doubt.

She had time later to think about her body and the way it had reacted to something she'd craved for longer than she'd known. She had burned inside to join with Philip; to complete a journey that might lead them to another. They had collided with equal intensity and hunger. When he'd found his way into her there was pain, but she knew it would fade. He'd pushed deeper into her than she had expected, but as she'd relaxed she had found it easier to feel him. It became more natural than any sexual experience she had known; more shared than anything she had imagined and in the end, she knew it would stay with her like no other.

Lee woke first and blinked into focus the profile of Philip's shoulder. She followed the contour down to his face, speckled with the first stubble of a new day. Wherever he had sailed away to, she hoped it would keep him for just another few minutes. Slipping out from under the sheets she picked up her towel and headed off to the bathroom. The mirror had its revenge. Her hair looked like the bush other girls dragged their hair through. Her make-up had managed to smear both left and right. She looked like a blurred freeze frame of *Cyndi Lauper.* "Oh crap" the glass sister observed.

Fifteen minutes or so later, Lee gingerly returned to her place at Philip's side, carefully arranging her pose. Hearing a soft stir from Philip, she closed her lightly mascaraed eyes. Philip slowly rolled to his back, the depth of his breathing increasing.

"Oh, give me a break" Lee murmured, taking a peek and noticing the smile spreading across Philip's face.

He opened one eye, "Wow, Lee – you look just beautiful first thing in the morning. How *do* you do it?"

"I *could* kill you with a pillow, you know."

The wind in the Avon Gorge seemed to defy normal rules by rising from the ground-up as they walked out onto Clifton Suspension Bridge. Lee's hair was blown back from her face and she struggled to tame it into a hasty ponytail. It was a bright morning and both Lee and Philip wore sunglasses.

"Not something you see every day" Lee declared, peering over the top of her Wayfarers.

"Not from West London, no" agreed Philip looking down along the Avon from the narrow pedestrian way.

"I think I like Bristol"

"Yeah. Some good things happen here."

Lee felt Philip's hands slip around her waist from behind. "I feel I should point out that I don't have life insurance – I am absolutely worthless in death."

"Oh really? I heard you owned a sofa now." His lips were close to her ear and the breath of his voice warmed the wind rush. "When are you going to Spain?"

"A few weeks I guess. I'll need to do it over a weekend with maybe a Monday off, so I'll need to talk to my boss." She could almost feel him calculating.

"I just can't imagine how you are going to manage this alone – whichever way it turns out"

"I can't either" she admitted. "I don't have all the answers – I'm not sure I have any, actually. But now that I've had time to really imagine it being possible, I have to see it through. I have to just…try."

Philip nodded thoughtfully. "You know, I don't speak Spanish and I'm horribly embarrassed by any sort of confrontation" he smiled broadly, "I think I should definitely go with you."

march 1987
interloper

....

I really ought to be calm enough about it. Nothing is honestly likely to happen there anyway. All I'm doing is spending some money I don't have, on a trip I shouldn't be taking, for something I don't know I even want. And now I'm making Philip do it, too!

I caught an edge again in Dani's voice tonight. She called to wish me well but she can't hide how cross she is with me about Philip. I know that she thinks I'm going to regret not telling him now, but the opportunity has passed. There is a window for these things, a chance when talking can help. That's gone now. All there is left is what we feel for each other – the way we are together. Nothing can be more honest than that, can it? It feels much too right to be wrong. I may not have loved too often, but I know this is special and I won't risk it just because of something from a past I've already sacrificed so much, to overcome. The past is past for a reason.

I may not have always been the woman he knows. I am now!

I'm ready for tomorrow – for whatever is out there. After years of hardly thinking about her at all, suddenly she's in my mind every day. I close my eyes and try to feel if she exists out there, somewhere. Do we still share the same earth? After all the loss, do I really still have family?

I can't feel her at all. I wonder if she feels me.

. . . .

Lee put down her journal on the sofa and picked up her passport again, flicking to the photo page. It wasn't a terrible picture, but she wished she could have had a few more tries at the shop to get it right. All that really mattered of course, was that this passport showed the Lee Habens she was now. This one officially described her as female. She'd needed letters from Dr Garner and from Mr Hendry (who in his, included a graphic description of the SRS he'd carried out on her body, as contextual justification for the granting of a letter 'F', under the heading of 'Sex'). The precious little document had arrived two weeks before and she must have opened it up twenty times since. She was looking forward to handing it to the first airport security guard.

The doorbell rang and the letter flap knocked a moment after: Philip, covering all the bases.

They embraced and kissed at the door. Lee stepped back and looked doubtfully at her visitor's compact overnight bag. "Really? You can get three days and nights of your life in a bag that small?"

He held it up and grinned, "Toothbrush, second pair of jeans, one shirt, two t-shirts and the very best that the Jockey Short Company of Wherever can provide. And you?"

"Oh, I may need to make some tough choices."

Philip groaned. "Why can't women just go places without trying to take entire *other* places with them?"

"Because you just never know what you're going to need. What if the weather changes?"

"It's Seville. They're forecasting a flat seventy degrees all week. It probably won't rain there until October" Philip implored, following Lee into the little bathroom.

"Really?" Lee looked perplexed, "Oh crap!"

"Okay, well I'll leave you to do what you gotta do."

"No, I mean crap I forgot something!"

"What? Tickets? What?"

"Moisturiser!"

"Moisturiser?" Philip sighed.

"Yes, it's my brand, it's special and I meant to get some at lunchtime from the place in the Fulham Road, but I worked through so that I could leave early and now I don't have enough."

"It's moisturiser – they'll sell it at the airport, they'll sell it in Spain, there are in fact, almost limitless opportunities to buy moisturiser between here and where we're going."

"Not my brand."

Philip was continuing with his own reasoning, "I may even buy moisturiser myself – just to see what all the fuss is about. It has to be important otherwise my girlfriend wouldn't be freaking out about it."

Lee loved it when he called her his girlfriend. "I'm not freaking out" she said, pulling him to her by his lapels and kissing him softly.

"Well good then" Philip managed, between returned kisses.

"I'm not freaking out" she said triumphantly, "because there's a late-night chemist just around on the Hammersmith Road and I can get there and back in ten minutes."

"Want me to come with you?"

"Nope" Lee said, grabbing her coat. "I want you to study this pizza menu and choose something without anchovies." She handed him a leaflet, picked up her purse and headed for the door.

She decided to jog her way to the chemist. It paid to keep moving after dark in London – even on a busy thoroughfare like the Hammersmith Road. Lee bounced lightly in her Pumas and was reassured by the beacon that was her local chemist. Her moisturiser mattered because it was formulaically balanced and didn't irritate her skin – no small feat considering the two and a half years of electrified assault she'd suffered. The soothing cream contained in a tub and tube (she bought one of each), could be relied upon to last throughout a day and that she felt, might be important in hot weather.

It had rained that afternoon and there were still puddles in the street. As she headed back toward home with her prize, Lee found herself looking forward to some unseasonal warmth. She hadn't really thought of this trip in terms of a break – but if it did turn out to be the expected wild goose chase, at least she and Philip would have some time to kill in the sunshine. Maybe she should take a swimsuit she wondered, trying to think of where she'd put the only one she had. It had to be in the bedroom somewhere, she imagined.

A nagging feeling grew in her stomach. It headed north and sent a chill to her scalp. Her gentle jog quickened and then broke into a full stretch run as she tried to outpace her own panic. Rounding the corner to the rear entrance of her building she took the chance to save a few seconds and bolted through the pitch-dark car park. She took the two flights of steps in half a dozen paces and had her key in the lock before her feet were at the door. She looked along the corridor breathing hard and went straight toward the bedroom. She had left it in the bedroom, hadn't she? It didn't usually matter of course – it's not like she generally had visitors. She didn't see it – she didn't see Philip. She turned to the living room and found him. It was okay. He was looking out of the window onto the North End Road. She slowed her breathing – and then felt it stop entirely as she saw the open pages of her journal spread like white wings against the blue sofa.

She felt the door frame press against her shoulder as her legs weakened. Her heavy breath returned, and she heard it rushing through her head. Philip still hadn't turned.

"How much did you read?" she asked quietly, holding back her chest's demand for more air.

There was a pause before he answered with a measured calm, "Enough".

Lee hoped for something else, a line to reach for; an opportunity to make her case. But the air in the room was dead. "It's over, isn't it?" she conceded.

Philip already had his jacket in one hand. Now he picked up his bag and made for the doorway, "You know" he said as he reached her, "the toughest thing for me now is to find a way to forget that anything ever happened. I mean, I'll give that my all, but frankly I'm so…disgusted with both of us that I don't know how long it's going to take for me to feel clean again." He raised his hand to move Lee aside, but seemed to withdraw it for fear of touching her. "I need to leave now" he muttered impatiently, avoiding eye contact.

Lee took a step back out into the hallway, allowing Philip to pass. "I'm not dirty" she whispered.

Philip found her response provocative enough to turn back "Excuse me?"

Lee was staring at the floor "I'm just – I'm not...dirty" she repeated.

"Do you really want to have a discussion about the things you're not?" he asked, the tone of his voice beginning to rise. "How about whether you're a woman – shall we start there?"

"I don't know. I'm just me" Lee replied hopelessly, knowing the answer would do nothing to help either of them.

"And what the hell does that mean?" Philip was clearly infuriated. The narrow passage seemed barely able to contain his shoulders. "What do I even *do* with that? Jesus! You know, you can be as fucked up in your own head as you like, but you cannot – you *cannot*, just go out into the world and freely start messing around with other people's lives."

"I wasn't messing with you or anyone else. This isn't some kind of a game."

"Oh, don't I know that!" Philip shot back. "*My* life isn't some kind of...crazy fantasy!" he strained, his voice breaking a little. "I have a daughter. I have real responsibilities."

"What you have" Lee began – just barely sure that she should, "is the luxury of being yourself"

"What the fuck are you talking about now?"

Lee looked Philip in the eye for the first time. "You wake up every day and you know what you are, you know what you're here to do and what's expected of you. The moment your foot hits the floor for the first time, you know that you're in step with the rest of the world around you. All I ever wanted was to get to that same place, to have the same chance. And I *did* my part; I worked hard to get where I should have been all along. I've *always* been the person I am, the rest is just... pictures."

Philip nodded as if he'd heard enough. "I was about to fly to another country to help you find someone who probably isn't there anyway. And you know, the irony is that the whole time, the woman who really doesn't exist – is actually you."

"Please don't leave" Lee whispered, taking a half step but also fighting the urge to reach out to him. She could think of nothing more to say. No more ways to appeal. She could feel him being ripped out of her, along with the dreams she'd so foolishly dared to hold. Her eyes began to brim even as she watched the sight of Philip's back disappearing down the hallway. "Please don't leave" she whispered again. She heard the door open, but it didn't close. Instead a cold, damp breeze entered through shadows, breathing echoes of all the other departed ghosts.

If the world falls apart and nobody notices, has it really even happened?

. . . .

"Your sunglasses, please?" asked the uniform behind the departure gate desk.

Lee removed her dark lenses. She blinked and squinted her sore, red eyes under yellowing neon. She'd been seated in the waiting area along with her fellow passengers for around an hour. This had followed a further twenty minutes queuing through security – which itself had tailed a first hour spent shuffling along a line at Iberia check-in. Oh, the glamour of international travel, she reflected.

She had wanted to call Dani from the main terminal, but it was still early and besides, what on earth could she possibly say?

Lee looked at the woman who now held her passport. This wasn't quite the triumphal debut for which she had hoped. "I usually look less horrible" she explained croakily.

The uniform smiled politely, "Have a good flight" she said, handing the passport back, together with a boarding stub.

Lee took her seat on board at the window of row 22 and stared out onto Gatwick's concrete glare. The Wayfarers were quickly restored. She wondered if she could sleep once they were in the air. It wasn't that she had spent the entire night crying – she hadn't. There had been great gaps when she'd done nothing but stare silently at the dark.

She'd surprised herself by fulfilling the booking at all. Perhaps it had been bare instinct to take literal flight out of London and leave everything she knew behind. She'd had a stark choice between escape to Seville or lying under her duvet, trying to be nowhere. She looked now at the empty seat next to her and imagined Philip in it. He'd be saying something irritatingly clever – or perhaps just irritating. She wanted a cigarette. She looked up at the no-smoking and seatbelt illuminations and knew that she'd want one even more once those went out.

It occurred to Lee that for her even to have met Philip, a huge number of factors were required to align. Working backwards, she had to have had lunch in the office that day he came to *Oasis*. His lifestyle had to be able to make sense of moving to a job in south-west London. She had to have once mentioned in conversation where she worked – and he had to remember it. Davey had to introduce them and she had to come across Davey which would never have happened were she not undergoing treatment for gender reassignment at The London Centre with their precise appointment dates. In short, if she weren't who she was and Philip weren't who he was, they never would have encountered each other at all. She wished she'd thought of that to say, the night before. She could perhaps have gone on to explain how serendipity demonstrated the beauty of an unstructured life. She might have been able to start him thinking about how new opportunities embrace open minds. But what could have been, was of no value to her now. After all, it wasn't as if she felt Philip to be wrong. Even if he hadn't exactly been lied to, Lee had identified early on, a truth that she should have – and *could* have – shared with him. In the end, she'd simply been afraid once more of not belonging, of not being able to fit her profile into the perfect picture of a relationship.

Lee realised now that she had a complete set of failures in love. There were her early dalliances with girls, probably exemplified by an enormous crush on Dani. She'd not managed to find any depth in a gay relationship with an older man. She'd resisted structured, straight matchmaking. Then, although she'd been instantly accepted by a generous gay community, she had been unable to identify as one of their own. Her old self had suffered these failures patiently. But now she had failed reborn, in a straight world. Still in her twenties, she had almost entirely run out of ways to either love or be loved.

The flight wasn't long – especially as she'd lost about an hour of it over France. The expression on the man's face two seats to her right, suggested she may have snored in her sleep. Philip's absence at least allowed her to stretch her legs diagonally so that she didn't lose feeling entirely from the hips down. She simply couldn't remember aeroplanes being so cramped inside.

Passport control at San Pablo Airport took very little interest in Lee or her documents. Perhaps she should have taken it as a compliment, were compliments only for the taking. Collecting her suitcase, Lee followed the signs to where the buses picked up. She had booked her trip using the same travel agent with whom she would arrange Mrs Macintyre's movements. The familiarity with their service allowed her an extra degree of confidence in a journey that might otherwise feel fraught with risk. The folded itinerary she kept in the back pocket of her jeans told her that she needed a shuttle bus to get to Plaza de Armas Bus Station and then she'd get a second bus out to Constantina – a trip that would take the best part of three hours, in all.

She followed fellow passengers, moving in her own emotional fog. The physical distance between her present and the awfulness of the night before, was helping – but mostly because much of the last 24 hours felt so unreal anyway.

Seville itself seemed hot, especially for so early in the year. She'd needed a drink badly at the bus station and to pass the time before departure, she'd found a bar from which she could order a coke. If she'd thought it was tough to walk into an English pub as a woman alone, then she quickly learned that this part of Spain was in another league entirely. Not a word had been said to her throughout the nine minutes or so of her visit – and yet she'd felt every one of a dozen pairs of eyes on her, the entire time. She wondered if she'd unintentionally broken a taboo.

The ride out to Constantina was surprising. She'd expected an arid, empty landscape but instead found cultivated fields and a commercial farming industry in full flourish. Shades of green were more in evidence that she had imagined. This finally began to lessen as they pushed further north. Shrubs and bushes with needle leaves began to outnumber trees and the crops receded from the roadside. She thought it looked like cowboy country, the kind of place Clint Eastwood ought to be roaming. Dad would probably have liked it.

Constantina itself appeared rather unceremoniously. After an hour of dusty highway, the bus was slowed by whitewashed houses and narrow streets. The afternoon was predictably quiet. It may have been a while since Lee had been in Spanish territory, but she was familiar enough with the concept of 'siesta'.

Lee was relieved that she'd slimmed down her suitcase. Not having Philip with her meant a stone-like drop in her vanity. Now she was the one with a couple of pairs of jeans and some t-shirts.

She had a walk of several hundred yards to her small hotel – one of only two in the little town. Check-in couldn't have been more different to her last paid accommodation, in Bristol. The front desk staff were endearingly polite and struggled to say as much as they could for her in English. Her room was white painted, tile floored and quite sparse, but very clean. She didn't unpack, but instead lay down on top of the bed and slept the previous night's sleep.

She woke just after 11:00pm. She was suddenly hungry – and grateful that she'd bought a sandwich at Gatwick before going off the idea. She sat on the edge of the bed and ate cheese and pickle while watching an episode of *Cagney & Lacey* dubbed into Spanish on a black and white portable TV. It would be all about tomorrow now. Within an hour, she was back on the bed – this time under the covers, but wide awake.

Lee surrendered further efforts at rest to the bright advances of a very early morning. She dressed in her blue jeans with a wide belt and white blousy cotton top, throwing everything she would need into the soft black leather handbag she'd deemed most appropriate for a long day on foot. A light continental breakfast was on offer in the dining room. Lee gratefully took coffee, juice and two bread rolls, consuming them while facing the wall at a corner table so as not to make eye contact with anyone.

Hotel reception provided a folded, two-page elementary guide to the town. It had a map which detailed Constantina to be essentially a one street town with the main thoroughfare running north to south. Lee had shown the receptionist the address she was looking for. Looking puzzled, the young woman had disappeared into the kitchen reappearing with a large moustachioed man who indicated with a red pen, where on the map Lee should look.

It was almost 10:30 when Lee eventually left the hotel. She found a shop where she could buy bottled water. She carried the litre bottle around with her, taking frequent gulps until the weight became irritating and she drained it. This she knew, meant that she'd soon need a bathroom visit – once again, a much easier thought to manage as a male when alone and far from home.

It would have been easy to think of the pristine, white painted houses with their clustered terracotta rooftops, as being of design for the sake of tourists. But tourists didn't generally come to places like Constantina, Lee realised. This was a working town. Still, it really was picturesque, especially under a light blue sky. Lee headed north toward the centre. Casa del Peso's buildings seemed to become older, the further along it she progressed. Early on, she could see a tower which dominated the townscape. She'd been hearing bells every quarter hour for a while and she soon realised the tall tiered building to be the source. She found a square nearby and sat for a while, watching the bustle and strangely enjoying the almost constant insect buzz of mopeds echoing through the streets as young men rushed recklessly to nowhere in particular.

Lee was further from home than she'd ever been. She had run to Spain, as perhaps her mother before her had done. Only Lee hadn't left a ruined heart behind. It was with her now, in this faraway place. And yet her alien soul might not be alone, after all. She was close now. She stood and hoisted her bag once more onto her shoulder. She turned right and away from the main street, almost instantly exchanging tiled plaza for worn cobbles. The street names were set in blue over white wall tiles. She matched Calle Nueva to the words on her piece of paper and started up the inclined pavement. The houses were without exception, two storied and almost all featured tiny wrought iron balconies. Pavement only served one side of the street and number 223 was opposite. Intense anticipation began to spark against the stone sadness inside her. She suddenly felt as though she should not be in this place. She should not know this street and this house.

She stood motionless for a moment, facing double doors of Spanish oak, iron hinged and foreboding. She looked again at the piece of paper. She shuddered out a sigh, "Why *did* you have this, Dad?". The day's heat began to warm her back. Not for the first time, her future was barred by a door. There were answers on the other side. Perhaps a new direction. She crossed the street and was still pondering the timing of her next move when she saw an index finger press the electric doorbell in front of her. The finger was wearing her nail colour.

The door was opened within seconds by a stout woman, Lee guessed her to be in her late sixties. Her hair was steel grey and tied back severely. She peered out at Lee suspiciously.

"Hola" Lee offered with a smile, exhausting her Spanish language skills in her two opening syllables. "Speak English, by any chance?" she tried.

The blank expression suggested that conversation would be animated, but sparse.

"Um…" Lee tried "Looking for Sophia?" She emphasised the name again, trying not to raise her voice "Sophia? You know Sophia?"

The door was closed – though not completely. Lee heard the woman's shuffled footsteps and then voices – two of them, both female. More shuffling. The grey lady reappeared. She shook her head and added a 'No', for good measure before closing the door on a thousand-mile journey.

Lee continued to stand on the same spot for several minutes. Her frustration at not being able to make herself understood was difficult to bear. Clearly the woman who answered the door wasn't Sophia – she was older than Lee's mother would have been – and surely about two feet too short. Had Sophia ever lived here?

Lee headed back down to her hotel, somewhat stunned and with more questions than she'd carried northbound. All of that wondering, for a couple of words on a doorstep? It didn't seem right – and yet what more could she do?

Lee bought a chocolate bar from a café on the return journey – if only so that she could use their bathroom. She picked up some more water, too – though this time saved it until she was back in her room. Once there, she kicked off her shoes, luxuriating in the cold tiles against her soles. Fresh sheets and towels had been introduced. She opened the shutters to her window, revealing a view of the street and the hills to the west of town. As Constantina began to take up a Londoner's strain, she realised that she needed a siesta of her own – and she needed it to begin early.

The sky was bluer under closed eyes, she found. Perhaps it was just being a child that made the world a more beautiful place. The wind purging the warmth of the car's interior was silent. Dark tresses flexed and flew like night flames against the white beyond. The woman turned from the seat in front. Darkened lenses were removed to reveal happiness and hope in the fullness of a mother's smile.

Lee took a deep breath as a prelude to rising from the firm mattress. She was beginning to wonder if she would ever recover a normal sleep pattern. Her conscious hours – the ones relied upon for stability and perspective – were drifting back to the margins. She was sleeping when others lived and addressing her life as they slept. It was almost 7:00 pm when she felt the floor beneath her again. Standing up from the bed she mused groggily, that she still had a little time left. Too much longer and the opportunity would pass.

It wasn't just the anti-climax that she was finding so hard to manage. The grinding irritation that had waited for her to wake was the question of why it had taken a discussion inside the house, to arrive at that flat 'No'.

She weaved to the little bathroom and groaned at the reflection the mirror had waiting. The lighting was less than subtle. She kidded herself that she probably didn't look quite as bad as her insecurities might suggest. She tied back her hair and washed. She tried to put back a little life into her skin and eyes with some light make-up. Ten minutes later she was making her way toward the town centre again – this time by early streetlight. The main street was still reasonably populated and she moved easily. She wondered if she'd be the only outsider walking to town that night. Certainly, she'd be pretty hard to take for a Spaniard. She felt even more conscious of her height than usual. She had yet to notice a single person of either gender to be taller than her since arriving in Spain. Being far from home made such things matter less. After all, she'd be running *herself* out of town tomorrow.

The street lighting was much less in evidence away from the centre and she was glad not to venture too far into the semi-darkness before again finding No 223. There was no hesitation this time – her expectations having been reduced to dust by the earlier disappointment. If this attempt was on a nothing-to-lose basis, she ought to at least ensure that she'd enquire a little more firmly. She would engage someone in some kind of conversation and then finally put the escapade behind her. The door buzz seemed to spark a little consternation from within. She felt as though she'd just disturbed a tree of roosting birds. She could pick out at least three voices. One of them – male – approached and a moment later, the door cracked open. Golden light sliced out into the dark blue and grey of the street.

Lee was looking at a young man – perhaps four or five years' junior to herself. His dark features were of grown up proportions, but the eyes were unlined. She imagined he wouldn't previously have met a Londoner; but then, Sittingbourne hadn't delivered many foreigners to her youth either. "Buenas tardes" she tried ambitiously, having heard it from the receptionist back at the hotel.

The young man nodded and looked her up and down warily.

English would have to do, she knew. "I'm from London – England" she ventured.

"Yes" the young man said softly.

Lee smiled with relief, "Oh, you speak English?"

"Little" he shrugged.

"Okay. Um, okay. My name is Lee Habens" She spoke slowly, but reminded herself not to mistake volume for clarity. "I am looking for a woman. Her name is Sophia."

The young man considered Lee's explanation but then began to shake his head, smiling shyly. "Nah" he said simply.

"There is no Sophia here?"

"Nah" he repeated.

"Not ever?"

"Nah"

"How about the name, 'Habens'? Have you heard of anyone called Habens?'

The head shaking was quite adamant.

Lee wasn't as disappointed as she thought she might be. If anything, she was relieved that she had at least finally closed the possibility. What was at this address, she would probably never know – but at least she could be sure it wasn't Sophia Habens. She took from her pocket a small piece of paper. It had the name and number of her hotel printed on it. She had earlier added with a ball point, her own name, room number and a time. She pointed in explanation, "I am staying at this hotel until tomorrow at twelve o' clock. If anyone in your house knows of Sophia or Habens, you can reach me there."

The young man took the piece of paper and smiled generously. Lee instinctively liked his smile – it made her return the compliment.

The walk back to the hotel was almost over too quickly. She wished she had something more to do. She was hungry but couldn't see anywhere to buy food. She thought of trying a bar – and then remembered yesterday's experience. Darkness was descending fully and she knew she no longer had a place on the street.

I keep telling myself that this hasn't been for nothing. I had to find out, didn't I?

What I couldn't have anticipated of course, was how much I would need to get away. Being here even for a day has helped – at least a little.

I realised today that in a way, I've been a foreigner all my life. I suppose I always will be. I can learn the language and try to look like the people I live around, but deep down, I just don't feel that I come from the same place.

Maybe I should try to meet up with all the other foreigners and start a new country.

. . . .

Unsurprisingly, there was no queue for checkout. The humble little hotel gave up its English guest in little more than the time it took to sign over a couple of traveller's cheques. Lee had filled her stomach with bread rolls and apricot jam and now looked forward to returning to a place where she understood how to access food at will. The bus stop was two hundred yards back down the main street. It was already pretty warm and she changed carrying hands several times as she covered the distance. There were two local people already at the stop by the time Lee arrived. She lay her case down on the pavement and used it as a seat. The purest sunlight from a cloudless Andalusian sky fell around her shadeless spot. She was grateful at least, for the lack of humidity.

Staring back across the street, she watched a figure emerge from a small Seat car. The woman was immediately notable for two reasons. Firstly, that after emerging from the little white vehicle, she simply stood, leaning back against it, her arms folded. Rather more significantly however, it was immediately apparent that the woman was Lee's mother.

It was impossible for Lee to reason how she could recognise a person she hadn't seen since she was a small child over twenty years before. It wasn't the hair – that was tied back, something she never remembered her mother doing. The figure was dressed simply but elegantly in a grey, knee length skirt and white short sleeved blouse. Around her neck was what appeared to be a silk scarf, coloured white with a green print. Her eyes were protected behind dark glasses. She looked as if she were on her way to a job in an office and had perhaps just stopped to pick up some dry cleaning. It was the shape of her that triggered the instinct deep within Lee. There was something in her form and stance – her very poise, that spoke so surely.

She was surprised at her own calmness. Not for a moment was she shocked or wrong footed. She stood slowly and slid her hands into the back pockets of her jeans, staring back through her own smoked lenses. Lee had through her pose, acknowledged the presence of the woman who had given her life – and in so doing she had invited the next steps of their dance. The person who once had been Sophia Habens responded, crossing the road in a straight, measured stride. She moved gracefully in low courts, the slightest breeze rippling her crisp blouse. She removed her glasses as she walked, revealing a direct gaze that finally did steal the breath from her child. Lee suddenly felt unaccountably guilty of something, though she knew not what.

They stood, perhaps eighteen inches apart, yet closer than they had been for more than two decades. Lee suddenly remembered to remove her own glasses. She saw that the woman who faced her was much less confident in close-up. She still looked less than her age. She had remained slim and supple of limb, but there were crinkles at the corners of her deep brown eyes and along the sides of her mouth. Traces of a thousand moments that had flown through her, etching the story of a second life. She was perhaps four inches shorter than Lee and seemed in her momentary confusion to be diminishing further.

"*You* are Lee" Sophia stated with incredulity.

"Yes."

"You look…"

Lee nodded and felt herself smile, settling her a little, "I know. I kind of…grew up in ways you probably wouldn't have expected."

"You…you're a woman?"

A thoughtful pause, "I'm...Lee" she replied softly.

Her mother's hands reached for Lee's face, tracing her profile down past her temples and falling lightly to her shoulders. The touch felt light to Lee. But the fingertips truly belonged on her skin. Time and deeds melted away in the bare heat of truth. All that was left was the honesty of two people connected in unbreakable ways beyond even their understanding. Lee had forgotten the primal power of that touch. Now inside of her, a child finally felt company again – and yet ached at a loss she hadn't truly before admitted. Sophia gently pulled her child's hands around to the front where she held them tightly in her own. Lee could see that her mother was beginning to tremble with confusion and shock and the weight of a present erupting around them. Lee began to shake too. It was all just instinct now. There were no more thoughts, no more words. The plane between them was broken and they fell into each other. Lee wrapped the woman to her and was washed by waves of compassion and relief and desperation. She was twenty-seven years old and as far as she could recall, she was holding her mother for the very first time. For a moment, she was struck that in such an embrace, the child would normally be the smaller, the one more in need of comfort. And yet she could feel a distinct desperation though her mother's fingers as they pressed into her back. They seemed to grip her almost as in fear of further loss. Lee's unbound joy brought her to laugh and cry in time to her mother's own sobs. Neither spoke for a while. They were each locked into the embrace of the stranger they had always known. And they were whole again.

Lee noticed as she drew back and tried to snatch a few breaths, that the other two bus passengers-to-be were watching and smiling openly, silently enjoying the moment in their own ways.

Sophia stroked Lee's cheek, separating a lock of hair from the trail of a cried-out tear.

Lee held her mother by the slim shoulders she'd never before been able to reach. "Is there a place we can talk?" she asked.

From the outside, it had looked like more of a bar than a café – and a closed one, at that. Lee would never have had the confidence to cross its threshold on her own, but her mother had on entry, exchanged pleasantries with the man behind the counter in flawless Spanish and they had taken a corner booth as the only customers of the moment. Lee noted that her mother had been addressed as 'Maria'. They ordered cokes and held themselves from further exchange until the iconic little bottles had been delivered. Then neither could let go of the other's hands to drink.

Unsure of where to start, Lee simply asked about the most immediate new thing she had learned, "You changed your name?"

"I became Maria soon after moving here. I needed to fit in, to make a life. I didn't ever want to forget, but it hurt so much to remember and I knew that I could never go back." The accent was still English, but slightly halting as if from a lack of practice.

Lee scrutinised her mother's face, her mind turning over questions and trying desperately to form an order of learning. "Back there on the street, you knew who I was. That *was* your house I came to yesterday, wasn't it?"

"Yes. This morning I came and waited at your hotel. I watched for you to leave."

"The others who live there at the house – your family?"

"My mother in law and my son"

Lee smiled and nodded, "I knew there was something about him"

"Miguel. His father says he has my eyes."

"I have a half-brother" Lee said incredulously, shaking her head.

Her mother smiled back, perhaps a little more guardedly. "I can't believe you are here – and that I am with you. I never thought…I would ever know you."

Lee squeezed her mother's hands gently, "I really didn't know that I'd make it here. I didn't think I would get this far."

The woman Lee now knew as Maria hesitated, "I want to understand how you became…like this". She held her child's arms apart as if to see her better.

"I was always like this" Lee began, "It just took a while for me to…mature."

"And now? Are you happy with your life?"

Lee tried to compose ways explanations of the last few days. "I'm happy enough" she conceded.

Maria took her child's hands to her lips and kissed them softly before pressing them to her cheek. "Tell me" she asked thoughtfully, "What made you come here?"

Lee saw that the question was meant without malice. She shook her head "I'm not totally sure. I guess I needed to see you, needed to touch you, to make sure you were...real. I have memories of you, but I was so young and they're kind of misty. Over the years, I had almost completely lost you. And then I came across your address in Dad's things."

More hesitation, "Your father is..?"

"1981 – January" Lee said quietly, her eyes trying to blink away the soreness. She brought him to their table for a moment and imagined how wonderful togetherness might have been.

"He wrote to me a few months before that time – when he knew what was ahead."

"Was he in touch with you the entire time – I mean after you left?"

"No. I wrote to him a couple of years after I had gone. I wanted to reach back, to make sure you were okay. We worked out our divorce and then I heard nothing until..." she hesitated, "What happened back then, it broke both of us in different ways, but what hurt most was knowing that you could never understand."

"Dad and I were okay. If there could be a right age for that kind of experience, I suppose it was mine. I was loved and safe growing up. I know now that I've missed you, but back then..." Lee thought for the words, "I suppose Dad and I just found ways to not speak of you. I knew he was so hurt, but there was nothing I could do but love him back and help him know that I'd always be there."

"I'm so glad he wasn't alone."

Lee smiled broadly at a picture of Robert Habens again, "He was never alone. He was my Dad" she recalled. "He was the biggest man in the world". A tear fell fast past her cheek, landing on her bare forearm. She brushed it away instinctively as another was born. She reached for a tissue and for a distraction to help hold back the tide.

"He was a *good* man. And he did nothing wrong to deserve the pain I caused him and I have wished every day since that there could have been another way."

"Wasn't there?" Lee asked, dabbing at her eye, "– Another way, I mean?"

"We were so young. We were so reckless. We loved, but weren't in love. In truth, I only found this out when…"

"Your friend who met us on our holiday?"

Maria nee Sophia, looked surprised at the recollection. "Uh, they introduced me to a man – my husband Franco. And that's when I knew. My world just came apart. I suppose depression had always been with me, but that was when it all just spilled over the edge. I couldn't face my own life any longer. I felt as though I just didn't belong in it"

Lee nodded, a faraway click of understanding locking perfectly into place.

"What was worse, was knowing where I should be, where I *needed* to be". She shrugged as the years fell away, "I would have been wrong to stay – and I was certainly wrong to leave, too. Neither you or your father could have hated me as much as I hated myself."

Lee watched Maria who had married Franco and had led a long family life of which Lee herself had never been a part. She watched the features she'd held in memory, move in ways she couldn't quite recall, speaking of things she'd never imagined.

"Dad didn't hate you" Lee responded. "He never said a single word against you. He just chose never to discuss it and I chose to respect him and his wishes."

Maria paused and composed her words with caution, "Did he know…about you?"

Lee smiled and stroked a trail through the condensation along the contoured neck of her Coke bottle, "I'll never know what he suspected" she answered. "I waited until a year had passed before

I began my treatment. I don't know if he could have handled it. I don't know if he'd have been disappointed in me. There was never time."

"He would be proud, I'm sure – just as I am"

Lee grinned with a little mischief, "Oh *sure*, come and tell me that when my half-brother goes the same way."

Maria gave a wide, white smile of her own at the notion – clearly from a very secure perspective. They smiled on at each other, enjoying the intimacy of a shared family reference.

Lee took her mother's hand again. She frowned as a thought crystallised in her mind, "You know, I keep a journal. I don't write every single day, but I just jot down notes about things that I feel or experiences I have". To illustrate the point, Lee retrieved the battered fawn-coloured notebook from her bag and placed it on the table between them. Loose leaves were bound in by nothing more than a wraparound elastic band. "That book" Lee continued, "has even got me into trouble recently and then I've ended up writing about the problems caused by the book in which I write about my problems". She grinned, ruefully, "I take this stupid thing with me everywhere. I wrote in it last night. I wondered if I actually belonged anywhere. And you know, I don't think I do." Lee smiled as she shook her head, "And that might be a problem, if it hadn't just dawned on me for the very first time in my life that I don't *need* to belong – not to anywhere or to anyone. That's not what life is about really, is it? When it's all over and we're gone, there are others left behind and they manage somehow. Christ, I've been losing people all my life…" Maria started to say something, but Lee went on, keen to finish her point, "No, it's okay. See, life just goes on – it has to. So, we don't really *belong*, do we? The places we've known – they're still there and their routines still go on too. The buses on our routes still run and all the shops and all the bars and the clubs still open their doors, even though we're no longer there to use them. The problem is that none of it means anything unless we really know how to just…be. All my life I've felt like some kind of interloper, just finding myself in places and situations where I don't belong. What I didn't understand until now is that, that's okay."

Maria shook her head in uncertain appreciation of her child's reasoning.

Lee's free-flowing truth, continued to become words, "I think life is about finding a sense of peace. It's all just one great search for a sense of calm. The life that I remember seemed to have started with confusion – almost a panic. I always *knew* something wasn't right – I just didn't know what it was. As I grew up I could feel that other things were wrong too, but I couldn't fix any of it so I just got used to…living wrong."

"I am so sorry for my part in that."

"No, no – that's the thing – it really wasn't your fault. It wasn't *anybody's* fault – it never has been."

"Now though, now you're living – right?" Maria ventured, trying to follow the trail.

Lee smiled. "Only because I did what you did all those years ago. I stopped trying to find the answers in people and places. I followed the voice inside and it led to where I should have been all along – just like it did with you."

Maria took Lee's hands again. "You've found your own peace."

"Oh, I'm still a pretty long way from true peace – but if I squint, I think I might be able to see it from here."

"Business or pleasure?"

Neither of the options really applied, Lee considered. Certainly not the first – and the second only really became the case, late on. She'd headed for Spain in search of truth and escape and had unexpectedly discovered hope. She decided to gamble with an answer that might end further enquiry, "I went to find my mother" she explained quietly.

The representative of Her Majesty's Customs & Excise raised an eyebrow and then closed Lee's bag. He picked up her passport again and gave another cursory look at the photo page, "You'll do" he ruled, passing the little blue book back to its owner.

Lee followed the narrow corridor back into the main flow of passengers exiting Gatwick baggage collection. The bright neon of the arrivals lounge forced her to retreat once more behind her sunglasses. They had been either perched on her nose or atop her forehead ever since the car ride back to San Pablo Airport. Her mother had driven her south, refusing to hear of any other such plan. Maria had indeed, been due at her workplace – the 7-day week offices of one of the largest olive farms in the region. Her boss she said, had been understanding when told that a family matter of a most urgent nature had arisen. The drive had been full of chatter – mostly from Lee, who had recounted sanitised versions of various London adventures and sketches of the people she'd known and cared for. Oddly, she felt coy about explaining any of her treatment. Her mother had not known a grown son in Lee and didn't seem to mourn his absence. The relief and joy of knowing a new daughter seemed too perfect an idea to blemish with the ugliness of an origin through surgery and chemistry.

Maria Salgado would visit London soon and a fledgling relationship would be rejoined on English soil, where it had begun. The thought brought a smile to Lee's lips as she strolled past the massed ranks of other families, awaiting glimpses of those to whom they were tethered in love and succession. Perhaps, not that long before, Lee Habens would have felt overtly self-conscious, knowing that her emergence from the airside double doors meant scrutiny by hundreds of eyes, anxious to identify every arrival. But London was welcoming back a person of greater confidence now. She had substance. She had family.

Toward the end of the walkway were the drivers. Professional greeters who stood solemnly holding aloft cards bearing the names of people they'd never met. Lee read some of the signs as she approached. There was 'Hadlow', 'Givens', 'Hussein' and one hastily scrawled on a piece of paper that simply said, 'Sorry'. The man standing below the torn page of A4 was tall and slim and was undeniably Philip Easterhouse.

Lee put down her bag and pushed her sunglasses back up, sweeping back her hair to reveal clear blue eyes. She shook her head, "Oh, you have got to be kidding."

"Airports, eh? You never know who you'll run in to." Philip had a weekend full of stubble and looked as if he'd not slept. "I went out for a drive last night – or the one before. And then y'know, kind of ended up here."

"You're a plane spotter – that fits with being a nerd, doesn't it?" Lee teased, with more than just an edge of tone.

"I just come here for the drama, really." Philip sighed. "Also, over there in that café place, they give you coffee that could keep up the dead."

Lee nodded at the now lowered piece of paper, "Is that for me?"

"No, I'm standing here to apologise to the whole world as it passes through Gatwick. I've met a lot of people from a lot of places. I must owe some of them" he reasoned, before shrugging off the veneer of levity, "Exactly how angry *are* you at me?"

Lee pushed her hands into her jacket pockets, "How can I be angry? I was never angry" she considered. "I was…diminished, humiliated and generally devastated, but I couldn't be angry at you."

"Okay. Well that's a relief, I suppose" Philip winced, lowering his gaze.

Lee let go a breath and took a step closer, "It wasn't your fault" she said. "Really, I understood that pretty quickly. The fault *was* mine – for thinking that there could be a chance; for thinking that my past didn't matter. I started thinking I was…a real girlfriend. I started expecting what a girlfriend does – and I had no right. I really didn't."

Philip shook his head, "It's not like that."

"Sure, it is" Lee continued. "If I start expecting things from people, I'll just end up relying on them. And people *leave*. It's what they do. Most of the time they don't even mean to, but they always leave in the end – one way or another. Look at you – you've left my life twice already."

Philip's brow wrinkled as he worked back, "Wasn't one of those a bit your fault?"

Lee's head tilted with slight bewilderment.

"Anyway" Philip continued, "It didn't feel like I'd left you. I felt like I hadn't actually *known* you to begin with. As if what I'd believed in, hadn't really happened." Philip was struggling for the words. The muscles at the corners of his jawline pulsed a little. "But I look back at our time and I'm really not quite sure when you *could* have told me about…" He took a breath, "I mean when in our relationship, did the point come that it was my business to know? When we were just friends talking in a pub? When we were dancing? When we were in public?"

"Maybe before we shagged ourselves senseless in a Bristol hotel room?" Lee suggested.

Philip let the breath go again, "Okay yes, that might have been sensible. But we were both way past sensible by the time we set foot in that room. We both knew what was going to happen there, didn't we?"

"I *would* have explained it all to you – sometime. But that night was so…"

"Right?"

"Right" Lee confirmed. She thought for a moment and then looked Philip in the eye. "What do you suppose would have happened when I finally *had* told you?"

Philip grinned, seemingly playing the plot through for a moment, "I honestly don't know. I keep trying to imagine – and honestly? I just don't know."

"I think I do. I think it would have been more or less the way it was."

Philip conceded a sober nod of probable agreement.

Lee took her sunglasses from her head and ran a hand through her hair as she searched for her next words. "Earlier today I was asked why I'd made a journey" she said. "So now I'm asking you: Why have *you* come here?"

"Because apart from when I'm with my daughter, I don't know how to be anywhere else, anymore."

Lee smiled and nodded, thinking of Annie's infectious grin. "You'll figure that out" she said softly, picking up her bag.

"Wait – wait a minute!" Philip was incredulous, "So you won't even give it a try?"

"No" Lee answered calmly, shaking her head.

"No? That's it? Just *no*?" Philip's frustration was prompting him to become rather more animated than Lee had seen him previously. An airport arrivals area is a big space and perhaps the sweeping of hands along temples and the leaning back in hope of divine inspiration filled what must otherwise have felt to Philip like a lot of dumb, useless air. "Okay then" he reasoned, "Spell it out for me – your reason."

"My *reason*?"

"That's all I need to hear – just one good one" he said.

Now Lee looked perplexed, "This is ridiculous – there are plenty of *reasons*" she said.

"All I need is one. But it has to be a good one; one I can't shoot down" he demanded, finger wagging as he spoke.

Lee looked away and then back again. She tried to keep her voice down, conscious that they didn't look anything like most couples who might venture into the hallowed zone of the reunited. "Okay" she said, returning her bag to the floor once more, "Think about this: One day there will be a disagreement – maybe over something stupid. I'll make you cross and you'll say something like 'that's not the way real women react'".

Philip looked amused and incredulous, his arms flung wide in open innocence, "I would never say something like that."

"Oh, trust me, you *will* say something like that. You won't mean to hurt me, but in a heartbeat I'm back – back at the bottom of a climb I just can't keep making."

"That's it? That's the best you have?"

"That's it! I can't help it if you don't understand." Lee reached once more for her bag and this time took a step past Philip.

"*Understand*?" Philip laughed, "Well that's just tragic" he pronounced. "That's pathetic. That's just about the worst..."

"Don't you think I know that?" Lee whirled around and hissed in a loud, failed-whisper.

Philip was grinning in a self-satisfied way that oddly suggested he felt more confident of his own case. Indeed, his voice in contrast, was noticeably more controlled. He jabbed an accusatory finger at her, "*You're* scared."

Lee's eyes narrowed. She felt her scalp tingle as the blood vessels received a more ready-supply than a normal demeanour might require. "Not...really" she stumbled, "It's just the *unnecessary* risks that scare me."

"No, sure, that is reasonable, of course" Philip grinned smugly, hands apart in understanding. "I get it completely. You've come all the way along your journey to this point...and now you've just plain run out of courage. You made yourself a nice perfect so-far-so-good picture and now you're too *scared* to actually do anything with it."

"It's not like that at all" Lee muttered indignantly.

"Oh, but it *is* like that" Philip announced cheerfully. "*I*, am willing to give this a try. Ergo: *I*, am braver than *you*."

"Oh, that's really stupid! How can you compare..? You're just..." Lee couldn't complete a thought, never mind a sentence. "It's not a bloody competition!"

Philip was performing a small dance, hopping from one foot to the other around her a little like a jester in a medieval court, "Braver than you, taller than you, smarter than you, a better arguer than you..."

"I really don't think there is such a word as 'arguer'"

Philip loomed in close to Lee's face, "I don't care. My prize is the knowledge that I am indeed, as I pointed out, *braver*...than... *you*." He pecked a cheeky kiss on Lee's pursed lips.

Lee fought the grin that was trying to break out, to Philip's all too obvious delight. Her voice was low and even through a clenched jaw, "It just can't work".

"Then we'll ride it straight down to the bottom – together" Philip's teasing smile was gone, replaced by an absolute determination in his tone and in his eyes.

"You *really* think you could handle this? You *really* think that you're not going to look at me one day and realise that I just don't fit with the rest of your life?"

Philip took Lee's hand and breathed away the rest of his exuberance, "Honestly? I don't know" he admitted. "I don't *know* anything anymore – partly because I'm suffering from acute sleep deprivation and partly because I've never been here before. Can you imagine that? Being in a whole new situation you've never known?"

Lee blinked the heat out of her instant reaction.

Philip continued before Lee could compose anything, "Of course you can imagine it – you're the bloody *Queen* of it. Well then, I want *you* to tell *me* what that's like." Philip continued, reaching over and stroking Lee's cheek. "You tell me how someone faces something new and yet deals with it because even though they don't understand it, it just...*feels* right." Philip shook his head and looked first away and then back at her. "Look, all I know is that I'm standing here in the middle of a bloody airport on my own free time because right now, I just want to be wherever you are. If I'm anywhere else, I'm just wondering where you are anyway and wanting to be a part of whatever you're doing, so..." Philip was holding both of Lee's hands now, "Look, don't get me wrong, I have...absolutely no idea how this might work. I mean, every time I go over it, all I can see are the same problems, the same reasons as you can, for why we won't make it. But then I see you come through those doors and I remember how much more I prefer *having* those problems to not having you at all."

Lee finally smiled – if only at the closeness of Philip's face to hers. She was having trouble concentrating and making sure to say just what needed saying. She winced a little as she weighed her options before settling for, "You're an idiot, Mr Easterhouse – and you have absolutely no idea what you're getting yourself into." She kissed him softly and gently on the lips, hers tingling at the brush of his stubble.

Philip nodded, leaving his head bowed as he looked back at her, "Sure, I'm an idiot. But then, I know that you can't be too fussy, so..."

Lee smiled. She moved her lips to his ear and whispered, "You'll be sorry."

"Yeah. I was already sorry." He slipped his hands inside her open coat and around her waist.

Lee felt his closeness again and arched her back a little to match his forward curve.

They kissed softly again, just for a second, maybe a minute. She tasted coffee and a bare, heated honesty.

Lee leaned back and looked deep into Philip Easterhouse, past green flecked irises and a lifetime of reasoning, "Right now" she said sternly, "you make me one promise".

"One promise, sure" he grinned back in agreement.

"You ready?" she checked.

"I'm ready."

She nodded and leaned her head against his so that their eyes could see nothing but each other's, "No promises."

About the Author

Kim Erin Cowley

I was born on the Kent coast in 1963, in the midst of a winter that famously froze the sea. Everything was fine until I realised what I was - and wasn't.

As for so many young people raised in the orbit of London, the pull of the capital proved overwhelming and I eventually left for the big city at the age of 19. I spent the next few years trying to ignore and then placate my own instincts. I began to realise that my future might ask rather more of me than I might have to give.

I began a media career in the 1980's, dealing with promoters and record companies on behalf of various music magazines including Sounds and Kerrang!. By the beginning of the 90's I'd found my way to the film business - initially in the shape of trade titles, Variety and Screen International and for an extended period, at the British Film Institute. I've since spent almost two decades providing support services to producers, distributors and broadcasters.

In addition to earning a crust and negotiating all of the usual trials of love and life, I needed to resolve the conflict at the heart of my very existence. Changing sex has been an experience more challenging and amazing than I could ever have imagined. It has been in turns, harrowing, terrifying, infuriating and soul-crushingly lonely, but following raw instinct and a drive beyond reason brings a special sense of liberation - and ultimately, a kind of peace.

What I lived through all those years ago, naturally informed the writing of *Interloper* - and I hope it will continue to help me to interpret and create in the future. Writing the book has in itself been another attempt to make happen, the unlikely. There have been a few special people who have also believed in the plan to breathe life into this story and its characters. That the book exists at all is due in no small part, to that encouragement and support.

Who I am has ultimately proved to be more important than what I am - but harmonising both has given me the chance to love the life I am now so fortunate to live.

For more information, go to www.kimerincowley.com

Your opinion is welcomed. Feel free to leave a review at your point of purchase.

Lightning Source UK Ltd.
Milton Keynes UK
UKHW01f1820140518
322593UK00002B/352/P